AIR AND DARKNESS

TOR BOOKS BY DAVID DRAKE

Air and Darkness
Birds of Prey
Bridgehead
Cross the Stars
The Dragon Lord
The Forlorn Hope
Fortress
The Fortress of Glass
From the Heart of Darkness
Goddess of the Ice Realm
The Gods Return
The Jungle
Killer (with Karl Edward Wagner)
The Legions of Fire
Lord of the Isles
Master of the Cauldron
The Mirror of Worlds
Mistress of the Catacombs
Monsters of the Earth
Out of the Waters
Patriots
Queen of Demons
Servant of the Dragon
Skyripper
Tyrannosaur
The Voyage

AIR AND DARKNESS

DAVID DRAKE

A TOM DOHERTY ASSOCIATES BOOK

NEW YORK

This is a work of fiction. All of the characters, organizations, and events portrayed in this novel are either products of the author's imagination or are used fictitiously.

AIR AND DARKNESS

A Tor Book
Published by Tom Doherty Associates, LLC
175 Fifth Avenue
New York, NY 10010

www.tor-forge.com

Tor® is a registered trademark of Tom Doherty Associates, LLC.

Library of Congress Cataloging-in-Publication Data

Drake, David, 1945–
    Air and darkness / by David Drake.—First edition.
        p. cm.—(Book of the Elements ; [Book 4])
    ISBN 978-0-7653-2081-0 (hardcover)
    ISBN 978-1-4299-5172-2 (e-book)
    1. Magicians—Fiction.   2. Monsters—Fiction.   3. Romans—Fiction.   4. End of the world—Fiction.   5. Europe—Fiction.   I. Title.
    PS3554.R196A73 2015
    813'.54—dc23

                                                                    2015023073

Our books may be purchased in bulk for promotional, educational, or business use. Please contact your local bookseller or the Macmillan Corporate and Premium Sales Department at (800) 221-7945, extension 5442, or by e-mail at MacmillanSpecialMarkets@macmillan.com.

First Edition: November 2015

Printed in the United States of America

0 9 8 7 6 5 4 3 2 1

To Bobette Eckland,
*who did not run me down in her Oldsmobile station wagon
the day we met in 1973*

ACKNOWLEDGMENTS

Dan Breen continues as my first reader. Occasionally I get queries from people who want to join my editorial board, so to speak. No: Dan catches things that are wrong. He does not try to improve my writing; he improves my typing and grammar.

There are people who could improve my line-by-line prose; Harriet Mc-Dougal is one of them. There aren't many, however, and Harriet was unique in my experience in making the lines better without trying to make them hers.

Writing is not a group activity in my mind. Dan doesn't imagine that it is, or that he can change me.

My webmaster, Karen Zimmerman, and Dorothy Day are my continuity checkers and, with Dan, store my texts against the possibility of disaster here in central North Carolina. I tend to think in terms of small, carefully aimed meteors.

A more likely problem, however, is a computer catastrophe. Boy, I had a few of these during the course of this book. I only lost (and replaced) one actual computer (the older notebook), but there were repeated software glitches. I tend to blame myself when things go wrong in my electronic world, but this time (these times) I don't think I was the cause. (The prize was when I got an apology from Oracle for sending horrible things that I hadn't accepted instead of the ordinary Java update that I should have gotten.)

In all these cases, my son, Jonathan, fixed matters, twice by shifting everything to an earlier state and reloading the necessary software. In one case, the computer had completely locked up; *I'm damned* if I know how he simply got it off Top Dead Center (to use a phrase from technology I'm more familiar with).

I'm very fortunate in my friends and family. They make my life better and my work possible.

Which is a good place to mention my wife, Jo. She keeps the house running and feeds me delicious, healthy meals. I'm in good shape for my age. This is partly exercise, but in no small measure it's due to meals cooked from scratch instead of being heated with all the additives put in packaged food.

My thanks to those who help me.

The setting of this novel and the series The Books of the Elements is the city of Carce (pronounced KAR-see, as in *The Worm Ouroboros*) and the empire that Carce rules. These are extremely similar in history and culture to Rome of A.D. 30.

Carce is *not* Rome, however. This was implicit in the earlier Books of the Elements, though the fact seems to have passed over the heads of some commentators. The difference becomes explicit in the conclusion of *Air and Darkness*, but it's been there all along.

The society of Carce, like that of Classical Rome, is built on slavery. In The Books of the Elements I generally use the term "servant," but this almost always means "slave." The horrors of slavery are not my subject—I tell stories; I don't send messages—but I'm well aware of those horrors.

War, like slavery, is an awful business. When I began writing military SF in the early '70s, I described war as I had experienced it in Vietnam and Cambodia: my viewpoint characters, my *heroes*, saw and did terrible things, as I had seen and done terrible things. At the time, quite a number of commentators believed that I must be advocating the things that I described.

I was not advocating war then, and I'm not advocating slavery now; but my heroes are slave owners and not particularly enlightened about it. To describe them otherwise would be to give a false picture of their society and the society of Classical Rome on which theirs is modeled.

I don't apologize for this, any more than I apologize for giving civilians a glimpse of the reality of war in *Hammer's Slammers*. Many pundits of the '70s and '80s were horrified by that reality and angry at me for describing it. If what I imply about slavery angers people who romanticize the civilizations of the Classical World or the Antebellum South, so much the better.

As in previous Books of the Elements (and in my fiction generally), I use real places and events whenever possible, and I often work literature and folktales into my fiction. The tags from the *Sibylline Books* are real, and classicists may recognize (loud) echoes of the *Dionysiaca* of Nonnos in *Air and Darkness*.

I suspect even most classicists are unlikely to recall the City of Magicians, which Philostratus describes as being located between the Ganges and Indus river basins in northern India; and I have taken the haunted city buried in the Indian jungle from *Adventures of a Younger Son* by Edward John Trelawny. I don't vouch for the historical accuracy of either Philostratus or Trelawny, but *I* didn't invent the stories.

I've taken a number of the incidents and themes from Indian folktales. One of them put me in mind of *Apollonius, King of Tyre*, which made me wonder how many Greek prose romances may have been drawn from Indian originals (or the reverse, of course).

There's an enormous non-literary influence on *Air and Darkness:* my trip to Italy while I was planning it. This comes through in matters as minor as the carpet of acanthus beneath the Tarpeian Rock, to my description of Bomarzo: ancient Polymartium.

Bomarzo, carved into the Park of the Monsters in the 16th Century A.D., has an amazing spiritual aura, which I hope pervades *Air and Darkness*. I expect the experience to be part of everything I write for the rest of my life.

And that's not a bad thought with which to end this introduction and The Books of the Elements themselves: there is a truly wonderful world out there. Open yourself to it; become a part of it. There are Bomarzos around the corner for every one of us, if we're just willing to accept them.

DAVE DRAKE
www.david-drake.com

AIR AND DARKNESS

"Help us, Mother Matuta," chanted Hedia as she danced sunwise in a circle with eleven women of the district. The priest Doclianus stood beside the altar in the center. It was of black local stones, crudely squared and laid without mortar—what you'd expect, forty miles from Carce and in the middle of nowhere.

"Help us, bringer of brightness! Help us, bringer of warmth!"

Hedia sniffed. Though the pre-dawn sky was light, it certainly hadn't brought warmth.

The dance required that she turn around as she circled. Her long tunic was cinched up to free her legs, and she was barefoot.

She felt like a complete and utter fool. The way the woman immediately following in the circle—the wife of an estate manager—kept stepping on her with feet as horny as horse hooves tipped Hedia's embarrassment very close to fury.

"Let no harm or danger, Mother, menace our people!"

The things I do to be a good mother, Hedia thought. Not that she'd had any children herself—she had much better uses for her body than to ruin it with childbirth!—but her current husband, Gaius Alphenus Saxa, had a seventeen-year-old son, Gaius Alphenus Varus, and a daughter, Alphena, a year younger.

A daughter that age would have been a trial for any mother, let alone a stepmother of twenty-three like Hedia. Alphena was a tomboy who had been allowed to dictate to the rest of the household until Saxa married his young third wife.

Nobody dictated to Hedia, and certainly not a slip of a girl who liked to dress up in gladiator's armor and whack at a post with a weighted sword. There had been some heated exchanges between mother and daughter before Alphena learned that she wasn't going to win by screaming threats anymore. Hedia was just as willing as her daughter to have a scene, and she'd been threatened too often by furious male lovers to worry about a girl with a taste for drama.

"*Be satisfied with us, Mother of Brightness!*" Hedia chanted, and the stupid *cow* stepped on her foot again.

A sudden memory flashed before Hedia and dissolved her anger so thoroughly that she would have burst out laughing if she hadn't caught herself. Laughter would have disrupted the ceremony as badly as if she had turned and slapped her clumsy neighbor.

I've been in similar circumstances while wearing a lot less, Hedia thought. *But I'd been drinking and the men were drunk, so until the next morning none of us really noticed how many bruises we were accumulating.*

Hedia wasn't sure that she'd do it all again; the three years since that party hadn't turned her into a Vestal Virgin, but she'd learned discrimination. Still, she was very glad for the memory on this chill June morning.

"*Help us, Mother Matuta! Help us! Help us!*"

After the third "Help us," Hedia faced the altar and jumped in the air as the priest had told her to do. The other dancers carried out some variation of that. Some jumped sooner, some leaped forward instead of remaining in place as they were supposed to, and the estate manager's wife outdid herself by tripping and pitching headfirst toward the altar.

It would serve her right if she knocked her few brains out! Hedia thought; but that wasn't true. Being clumsy and stupid wasn't really worthy of execution. Not *quite*.

The flutist who had been blowing time for the dance on a double pipe halted. He bowed to the crowd as though he were performing in the theater, as he generally did. Normally the timekeeper would have been a rustic clapping sticks together or perhaps blowing a panpipe. Hedia had hired Daphnis, the current toast of Carce, for the task.

Daphnis had agreed to perform because Hedia was the wife of a senator and the current Governor of Lusitania—where his duties were being carried out by a competent administrator who needed the money and didn't mind traveling to the Atlantic edge of Iberia. Saxa, though one of the richest men in the Republic, was completely disinterested in the power his wealth might have given him. His wife, however, had a reputation for expecting people to do as she asked and for punishing those who chose to do otherwise.

The priest Doclianus, a former slave, dropped a pinch of frankincense into the fire on the altar. "Accept this gift from Lady Hedia and your other worshipers, Mother Matuta," he said, speaking clearly but with a Celtic accent. "Bless us and our crops for the coming year."

"Bless us, Mother!" the crowd mumbled, closing the ceremony.

Hedia let out her breath. Syra, her chief maid, ran to her ahead of a pair of male servants holding their mistress' shoes. "Lean on me, Your Ladyship!" Syra said, stepping close. Hedia put an arm around her shoulders and lifted one foot at a time.

The men wiped Hedia's feet with silken cloths before slipping the shoes on expertly. They were body servants brought to Polymartium for this purpose, not the sturdier men who escorted Lady Hedia through the streets of Carce as well as outside the city, lest any common person touch her.

The whole purpose of Hedia's present visit to the country was to demonstrate that she was part of the ancient rustic religion of Carce. *The things I do as a mother's duty!* she repeated silently.

Varus joined her, slipping his bronze stylus away into its loop on the notebook of waxed boards on which he had been jotting notes. He seemed an ordinary young man, handsome enough—Hedia always noticed a man's looks—not an athlete, but not soft, either. A glance didn't suggest how extremely learned Varus was despite his youth, nor that he was extremely intelligent.

"The reference to me," Hedia said, "wasn't part of the ceremony as Doclianus had explained it. I suppose he added it on the spur of the moment."

"I've already made a note of the usage," Varus said, tapping his notebook in acknowledgment. "From my reading, it appears that a blood sacrifice—a pigeon or a kid—would have been made in former times, but of course imported incense would have been impossibly expensive for rural districts like this. I don't think the form of the offering matters in a rite of this sort, do you? As it might if the ceremony was for Mars as god of war."

"I'll bow to your expertise," Hedia said drily. There were scholars who were qualified to discuss questions of that sort with Varus—his teacher, Pandareus of Athens, and his friend, Publius Corylus, among them; but as best Hedia could see, even they seemed to defer to her son when he spoke on a subject he had studied.

When she married Saxa, Hedia had expected trouble with the daughter. It was a surprise that both the children's mother and Saxa's second wife, the mother's sister, had ignored their responsibilities so completely—letting a noblewoman play at being a gladiator!—but it was nothing Hedia couldn't handle.

Varus, however, had been completely outside Hedia's experience. The boy wasn't a drunk, a rake, or a mincing aesthete as so many of his age and station were. Hedia's first husband, Gaius Calpurnius Latus, had been all three of those things and a nasty piece of work besides.

Whereas Varus was a philosopher, a pleasant enough fellow who preferred books to people. That was almost as unseemly for the son of a wealthy senator as Alphena's sword fighting was. Philosophy tended to make people question the legitimacy of the government. The Emperor, who *was* that government, had every intention of dying in bed, because all those who had questioned his right to rule had been executed in prison.

Even worse, Varus had set his heart on becoming a great poet. Hedia was no judge of poetry—Homer and Vergil were simply names to her—but Varus himself was a very good judge, and he had embarrassed himself horribly with the disaster of his own public reading. Indeed, Hedia would have been worried that embarrassment might have led to suicide—Varus was a *very* serious youth—had not a magic disrupted the reading and the world itself.

In the aftermath, Varus had given up composing poetry and was instead compiling information on the ancient religion of Carce, an equally pointless exercise, in Hedia's mind, but one he appeared to have a talent for. This shrine was on the land from which the Hedia family had sprung, and they had been the ceremony's patron for centuries. Her only personal acquaintance with the rite had come when an aunt had brought her here as an eight-year-old.

Hedia had volunteered to bring Varus to the ceremony from a sense of duty. His enthusiastic thanks had shown her that she had done the right thing. Doing your duty was *always* the right thing.

"Oh, Your Ladyship!" cried a stocky woman rushing toward them. Minimus, a big Galatian in Hedia's escort, moved to block her, but the woman evaded him by throwing herself prostrate at Hedia's feet. "It was such an honor to dance with you. You dance like a butterfly, like gossamer in the sunshine!"

Light dawned: the estate manager's wife. The heavy-footed cow.

"Arise, my good woman," Hedia said, sounding as though she meant it.

She had learned sincerity by telling men what wonderful lovers they were. "It was a pleasure for me to join my sisters here in Polymartium in greeting the goddess on her feast day."

The matron rose, red faced and puffing with emotion. She moved with a sort of animal grace that no one would have guessed she had from her awkward trampling as she danced in the company of a noblewoman.

"Thank you, Your Ladyship," she wheezed. "I could die now, I'm so happy!"

Hedia nodded graciously and turned to Varus, putting her back to the local woman without being directly insulting. Minimus ushered the local out of the way with at least an attempt to be polite.

"Did you get what you needed, my son?" Hedia asked. *If he hasn't, I've bruised my feet for nothing*, she thought bitterly. *Heels and insteps both, thanks to the matron.*

"This was wonderful, Mother!" Varus said with the sort of enthusiasm he'd never directed toward her in the past. She'd seen him transfigured like this in the past, but that was when he was discussing some oddity of literature or history with his teacher or Corylus. "Do you know anything about the group on the other side of the altar? They're from India, I believe, or some of them are. Are they part of the ceremony usually?"

How on earth would I know? Hedia thought, but aloud she said, "Not that I remember from when I was eight, dear boy, but I'll ask."

She turned to the understeward who was in charge of her personal servants—as opposed to the toughs of her escort. "Manetho," she said. "A word, please. Who are the people at the lower end of the swale from us? Some of them look foreign."

"Those are a delegation from Govinda, a king in India," said Manetho. "They're accompanied by members of the household of Senator Sentius, who is a guest-friend of their master. The senator has interests in fabrics shipped from Barygaza."

Manetho was Egyptian by birth and familiar with the Indian cargoes that came up the Red Sea and down the Nile to be shipped to Carce. A less sophisticated servant might have called Govinda "the King of India," which was one of the reasons Hedia generally chose Manetho to manage her entourage when she went outside the city.

She cared nothing about politics or power for their own sakes, but the wife of a wealthy senator had to be familiar with the political currents running beneath the surface of the Republic. That was particularly true of the wife of the unworldly Gaius Alphenus Saxa, who was so innocent that he might easily do or say something that an ordinary citizen would see as rankest treason.

The Emperor was notoriously more suspicious than an ordinary citizen.

"What are they doing here, Manetho?" Varus said. He added in a hopeful tone, "Are they scholars studying our religion? I know very little about Indian religion, and I'd be delighted to trade information with them."

Manetho cleared his throat. "I believe they're priests, Your Lordship," he said. "The old one and the woman, that is; the others are officials. They're here to plant a vine."

Hedia followed the understeward's eyes. Two dark-skinned men with bronze spades had begun digging a hole near the base of an ilex oak; in a basket beside them waited a vine shoot that was already beginning to leaf out. The men wore cotton tunics, but their red silk sashes marked them as something more than mere menials.

Hedia thought of Corylus, who had considerable skill in gardening. He was the son of Publius Cispius, a soldier who served twenty-five years on the Rhine and Danube. That service had gained Cispius a knighthood and enough wealth to buy a perfume factory on the Bay of Puteoli on retirement.

Nothing in that background suggested that his son would be anything more than a knuckle-dragging brute who drank, knocked around prostitutes, and gravitated to a junior command on the frontiers similar to that of his father. In fact, Corylus—Publius Cispius Corylus, in full—was scholar enough to gain Varus' respect and was handsome enough to attract the attention of any woman.

Furthermore, Corylus demonstrated good judgment. One way in which he had shown that good judgment was—Hedia smiled ruefully—by politely ignoring the pointed invitations to make much closer acquaintance of his friend's attractive stepmother.

"Do you suppose they'd mind if I talked to them?" Varus said, his eyes on the Indian delegation. The priests—the old man and the woman—oversaw the work, while the remaining Indians remained at a distance, looking uneasy.

The woman's tunic was brilliantly white with no adornment. Hedia wondered about the fabric. It didn't have the sheen of silk and, though opaque, it moved as freely as gossamer.

"If them barbs bloody mind," said Minimus, "I guess there's a few of us here who'll sort them out about how to be polite to a noble of Carce."

"I scarcely think that will be necessary, Minimus," Hedia said, trying to hide her smile. "A courteous question should bring a courteous response."

Minimus had been brought to Carce as a slave five years ago. His Latin was bad and even his Greek had a thick Asian accent. For all that, he thought of himself as a member of Senator Saxa's household and therefore the superior of anybody who was not a member. Freeborn citizens of Carce were included in Minimus' list of inferiors, though he understood his duty well enough to conceal his feelings from Saxa's friends and hangers-on.

Varus wandered away, also smiling. He was an easygoing young man, quite different from his sister in that respect. When Hedia arrived in the household, it had seemed to her that Varus' servants were taking advantage of his good nature. Before she decided to take a hand in the business, Varus had solved the problem in his own way: by suggesting that particularly lax or insolent members of his staff might do better in Alphena's section of the household.

Doclianus had waited until Hedia had finished talking with her son, but he came over now and bowed deeply. For a moment she even wondered if the priest was going to abase himself as the heavy-footed matron had done, but he straightened again. The bow was apparently what a Gaul from the Po Valley thought was the respect due to his noble patron.

"Allow me to thank you on behalf of the goddess, Your Ladyship," Doclianus said. "I hope everything met with your approval?"

There were a number of possible responses to that, but Hedia had come to please her son and Varus was clearly pleased. "Yes, my good man," Hedia said. "You can expect a suitable recognition when my gracious husband distributes gifts to his clients during the Saturnalia festival."

The priest didn't look quite as pleased as he might have done; he had probably been hoping for a tip sooner than the end of the year. Hedia was confident that her earlier grant of expenses for this year's festival had more than defrayed the special preparations, including the cost of frankincense. Hedia wasn't cheap, and her husband could easily have afforded to keep an army in the field; but neither was she willing to be taken for a fool.

"Who are the Indians?" Hedia said, changing the subject. She was willing to be as direct as necessary if the priest insisted on discussing fees, but she preferred to avoid unpleasantness. Hedia was not cruel, though she knew that those who observed her ruthlessness often mistook it for cruelty.

"Oh, I hope that's not a problem, Your Ladyship," said Doclianus, following her eyes. "Senator Sentius requested that a delegation from the King of India—"

Hedia's lips quirked.

"—be permitted to offer to Mother Matuta a shoot of the grapevine which sprang up where the god Bacchus first set foot on Indian soil during his conquest of the region."

He cleared his throat and added, "Perhaps your husband knows Sentius?"

"Perhaps he does," Hedia said, her tone too neutral to be taken for agreement. "I don't see why the Mother should be particularly connected with grapes, though."

In fact, Hedia recalled that Sentius had visited Saxa recently to look over his collections. That was the sort of thing that took place frequently and gave her husband a great deal of harmless pleasure.

With the best will in the world, Hedia herself had to fight to keep from yawning when Saxa showed her the latest treasure that some charlatan had convinced him to buy. He owned the Sword of Agamemnon, the cup from which Camillus drank before he went to greet the senators announcing his appointment as dictator, and Hedia couldn't remember what other trash.

That was unfair. Some of the objects were probably real, though that didn't make them any more interesting to her.

"That puzzled me also," Doclianus said. "The man in blue, Arpat—"

A man of forty or so. Arpat wore a curved sword, but its jeweled sheath and hilt looked more for show than for use.

"—told me that according to their priests, these woods have great spiritual power, and Mother Matuta, as goddess of the dawn, links them with the East."

Hedia nodded. For the first time Doclianus spoke in a natural tone without the archness that had made his voice so irritating. The priest had obviously been trying to seem cultured to his noble patron, but he didn't know what culture meant in Hedia's terms.

"I see," she said. "Well, I'll wait here and meditate until my son returns from his discussions."

Varus was having an animated conversation with the priest in the ragged tunic. Hedia wondered what language they were speaking in. It wouldn't have amazed her if Varus spoke Indian—his erudition was remarkable—but it seemed more likely that the Indians knew Greek.

Doclianus accepted his dismissal without showing disappointment. Hedia watched him returning to the cluster of women who had taken part in the ceremony. There were a hundred or so local spectators besides. Hedia wondered if they had come to see the nobles from Carce.

She considered the ceremony. Though Hedia observed the customary forms, she didn't believe—and never had believed—in gods. On the other hand, she hadn't believed in demons or magic, either, but she had recently seen ample proof that both were real. And beyond that—

Varus and the Indian priest were examining the successfully planted vine.

My son is a great scholar, Hedia mused. *I've never had much to do with scholars.*

But Varus had shown himself to be a great magician also, and that was even more surprising.

"Good health to you, Master Corylus!" called the woman at the counter of the bronze goods shop. "When you have a moment, I'd like to show you a drinking horn that we got in trade."

"Not today, Blaesa," Corylus said, forcing a smile for her. He was tense, but not too tense for courtesy. "I'll try to drop by soon, though."

The smith himself in the back of the shop was Syrian, but Blaesa, his wife, was an Allobrogian Gaul from close to where Corylus had been born. She liked to chatter with him in her birth tongue, and an occasional reminder of childhood was a pleasure to Corylus also.

He and Marcus Pulto, his servant, had come down this narrow street scores of times to visit the Saxa town house. They were as much part of the neighborhood as the merchants who rented space on the ground floor of the wealthy residences.

Pulto exchanged nods with the retired gladiator who was working as doorman of the jewelry shop across the way. Although the mutual acknowledgment was friendly enough, Corylus knew that at the back of his mind each man was considering how to take the other if push came to shove. That didn't mean there was going to be a problem: it was just the way men of a certain type related to each other.

Corylus' father was the third son of a farmer. He had joined the army and had risen through a combination of skill, courage, and intelligence to become the leading centurion of a legion on the Rhine: the 5th Alaudae. After twenty years' service, Cispius was promoted again, becoming tribune in command of a squadron of Batavian cavalry on the Danube; he was made a Knight of Carce when he retired.

The other factor in Cispius' success in the army was luck: all the intelligence and skill in the world couldn't always keep a soldier alive, and courage was a negative survival factor. Choosing Pulto as his servant and bodyguard might have been the luckiest choice Cispius had made in his military career.

Cispius had led his troops from the front. Pulto was always there, anticipating dangers and putting himself between them and the Old Man. On one memorable afternoon Pulto had thrown himself over his master, unconscious on the frozen Danube, while Sarmatians thrust lances at him.

When Corylus went to Carce to finish his education with the finest rhetoric teachers in the empire, Cispius had sent Pulto with him. The dangers of a large city are less predictable than those of the frontier, and in many ways they are greater for a young man who has grown up in the structure of military service. Pulto would look out for the Young Master, just as he had for the father.

Corylus hadn't thought he needed a minder, and perhaps he hadn't: he was an active young man who avoided giving offense but who could take care of himself if he had to. In the army, though, you were never really alone, even when you were—unofficially—on the east side of the Danube with the Batavian Scouts.

Early in his classes with Pandareus of Athens, Corylus had intervened when Piso, a senator's son, and several cronies had started bullying a youth who was both smaller and obviously smarter. Corylus could have handled Piso and his friends easily enough, but he hadn't thought about the retinue of servants accompanying the bullies.

The servants hadn't gotten involved, because Pulto stood between them and the trouble with his hand lifted just enough to show the hilt of the sword he wore under his tunic. The weapon was completely illegal within the boundaries of Carce, but nobody made a fuss about it, since the youth being bullied was the son of Senator Gaius Alphenus Saxa. Saxa's influence couldn't have saved his son from a beating, but it had been more than sufficient to prevent retribution on those who had stopped the beating.

Varus had been appreciative. He had as few friends in Carce as Corylus did, though in Varus' case that was because he didn't have any use for hangers-on or any interest in the drunken parties that were the usual pastime for youths of his class. Corylus was scholar enough to discuss the literature and history that mattered to Varus; and because Varus gave his new friend use of the gymnasium that was part of the Alphenus town house, Varus started exercising also.

The sauce on the mullet was that the household's private trainer, a veteran named Marcus Lenatus, was a friend of Pulto from when they both served with the Alaudae. Quite apart from the good that exercise did Varus, Pulto had had a word with his army buddy. Varus never again left the house without an escort who were willing to mix it with three times their number of thugs, if that was what it took to keep their master from a beating. The youth himself was probably oblivious of the difference.

"I should have worn a toga," Pulto muttered harshly. "I don't care what you say, I should've worn one!"

"Absolutely not," Corylus said firmly. "The senator won't set eyes on you, and you're not here to impress the staff by wearing a tent. Besides, they *know* who you are."

In Corylus' heart he wondered if Pulto might not be right, though. It was too late to change now.

The toga had been normal wear in ancient Carce, but now the heavy square of wool was worn only on formal occasions. Corylus wore a toga in class, because Pandareus was teaching them to speak in court, where it was the uniform of the day. Even when Corylus came straight from class to the town house, he doffed the toga inside before he went back to the gymnasium or upstairs with Varus to his suite of rooms.

Today Varus was with his mother forty miles north in Polymartium; Corylus had been summoned to the town house by Saxa himself. There were any number of reasons the senator might have sent for him, but none of them seemed probable and some of the possibilities were very bad indeed.

He can't possibly think that I've been trifling with his daughter. Can he?

Realistically, Saxa wouldn't be talking with Corylus about his dealings with Alphena. Saxa's wife would have taken care of that.

Corylus thought Hedia liked and respected him; they'd been through hard places together and with Alphena as well. But if Hedia thought Corylus was jeopardizing Alphena's chances of a proper—virgin—marriage with another noble, she would have him killed without hesitation. Once Alphena was married, she became the responsibility of her husband. Until then her purity was the duty of her parents, and Hedia took family duties very seriously.

But if not Alphena, why?

Saxa's doorman saw them approaching and bellowed, "The honorable Publius Cispius Corylus and Marcus Pulto!"

The blond doorman still had a Suebian accent, but it wasn't nearly as pronounced as it had been the first time he had been on duty when Corylus arrived at the town house. Besides taking elocution lessons, the doorman had learned manners and no longer treated free citizens of Carce as trash trying to blow into Saxa's house from the street. That was particularly important when dealing with a veteran like Pulto or with the frontier-raised son of an officer.

Corylus nodded in acknowledgment, as he had seen his father do a thousand times to the guards when he entered headquarters. Nobody saluted on active service, but courtesy was proper anywhere—and courtesy toward the men you expected to follow you into battle was also plain good sense.

In the past when Corylus visited the Alphenus residence, the entrance hall had usually been crowded with Saxa's clients and with people simply trying to cadge a favor or a handout. Today the staff had crowded the visitors into the side rooms where ordinarily servants slept. Three understewards—the fourth must be with Hedia and Varus—in embroidered tunics stood to the left of the pool that fed rainwater from the roof into cisterns. Agrippinus, the majordomo, waited at the back of the hall at the entrance to Saxa's office.

"Welcome, Publius Corylus!" Agrippinus said. Nothing in his accent suggested that twenty years before he had come to Carce as a slave from Central Spain. "I greet you in the name of Gaius Alphenus Saxa, Governor of Lusitania, former consul, and senator of the Republic of Carce!"

Saxa came out of the office, beaming and holding out his hands. "Thank you so much for coming, Publius Corylus," he said. "Come into the office, if you will. I have a business on which I hope you can help me."

Varus' father was a pudgy man of fifty who was starting to go bald at the top of his head. He sometimes looked kindly, as he did now, or worried, or startled, and often completely dumbfounded. Saxa had never displayed harshness or anger that Corylus knew of.

"Guess we were wrong to worry," Pulto murmured in a voice as low as he would have used at night on the east side—the German side—of the Rhine. "I'll look Lenatus up in the gym."

"I was honored by your summons, Your Lordship," Corylus said, walking forward with his own hands out. "I will of course do anything I can to aid Your Lordship."

This was even more surprising than it would have been to find the public executioner waiting for him. Better, of course, but still not a comfortable experience. Corylus had grown up in the Zone of the Frontier, where "unexpected" was too often a synonym for "fatal."

Corylus touched Saxa's hands, but he was too unsure of himself to grip them as he would have done with Varus under the same circumstances. *What is going on?*

"Well, I certainly hope so, my boy," said Saxa, drawing Corylus into the office. Agrippinus closed the door behind them.

ALPHENA BACKED AND SIDESTEPPED LEFT as the trainer came on at a rush. Marcus Lenatus was using his weight. He kept his infantry shield advanced, a battering ram that would have knocked her over if she had waited to meet it.

Lenatus turned to keep facing her, but the weight of his heavy shield slowed him. Alphena thrust for his right wrist. Lenatus got his sword up in time. The wooden blades clacked together nastily, but it had been close.

If Alphena had been an instant quicker, her lead-cored practice sword would have numbed the trainer's arm and caused him to drop his weapon. If they had been using steel swords, her thrust would have severed his hand.

She sidestepped left again. Lenatus would tire, and when he did her thrust would get home.

The door to the gymnasium opened. "Stop!" Alphena said. She hadn't given specific orders that she wasn't to be disturbed while she was fencing with Lenatus, but she was going to make sure that whichever servant had opened the door wouldn't do so again.

Alphena turned, wheezing as she gulped in air. Instead of being a servant, the intruder was Marcus Pulto, Corylus' man.

Corylus is here!

"Your Ladyship," Pulto said with a nod as he closed the door behind him. "I can leave if you'd rather. I'm just here to chat with Marcus Lenatus while my master's in with the senator."

While the door was open, Alphena had seen at least a dozen servants crowding the hallway beyond. Saxa had more than two hundred servants in this town house. Many of them had nothing to do most of the time and some never had anything to do, so anything unusual drew a crowd.

In this case they were probably hoping to hear Lady Alphena screaming abuse at the fellow who had interrupted her sword training. Not long ago they would have gotten their wish, but Alphena had recently begun to moderate her temper. The change surprised her even more than it did those around her.

Alphena had grown up angry and frustrated because she wasn't allowed to do certain things: she was a girl in a world ruled by men. Her brother could learn literature and public speaking in classes, then prosecute or defend others in court, or he could enter the army as a general's aide and proceed to command legions and even armies.

In fact, Varus had no interest in either of those careers. Instead he wanted to read books and discuss their ridiculous contents with scholars as addled as he was, an activity open to the poorest freedman in the Republic.

Alphena declared that she wanted to become a gladiator. Not even Saxa was so easygoing that he would permit his daughter to debase herself in a profession filled by slaves and criminals, but Alphena proceeded stubbornly to practice swordsmanship in the private gymnasium, wearing the full armor of a soldier of Carce.

Even so, she wasn't allowed to spar with a human opponent. Instead she hammered a stake with her weighted practice sword. Lenatus critiqued her form and demonstrated technique, but Saxa had warned him that he would be executed if he allowed Alphena to bully him into engaging her directly.

The trainer was a free citizen of Carce; no one had the right to execute him without trial. That said, neither Lenatus nor Alphena herself had any doubt that Saxa would do exactly what he threatened, nor that the wealthy senator would escape any retribution for his action. The authority of a father over his offspring was one of the most revered customs of ancient Carce.

The rule against Alphena sparring had been loosened recently. Alphena and her sword had stood between the world and monsters that would have destroyed the world, and Hedia had watched.

"Didn't know you were supposed to be doing that," Pulto said mildly, making a brief gesture with his left hand that might have been meant to indicate the gear in which his friend was sparring.

"Oh, it's all right, Pulto," Alphena said. "For Lenatus to fence with me, I mean."

"*I* never had a problem with it, Your Ladyship," Pulto said in the same falsely calm voice. He looked back to Lenatus and said, "You remember Tiburinus? Had the Third Century back when the Old Man had the Fourth?"

Alphena frowned. The change of subject made as little sense to her as one of her brother's declamations would have. She set her practice sword in the rack, wondering if she should unstrap her shield as well.

"Yeah," said Lenatus. "We're none of us going to forget that soon, are we?"

"We all thought Tiburinus was screwing the maid of the Legate's wife, Your Ladyship," Pulto said, turning to Alphena again. "Pardon the language."

"Go ahead," Alphena said. She had started to understand where this was going.

"Thing is, it wasn't the maid but her mistress that he was seeing," Pulto said. "Which the Legate figured out too. I was on headquarters guard that night, but I guess you could hear the shouting in the cantonment outside the walls. After that, Tiburinus manned a one-man listening post on the other side of the river until he deserted."

"Tiburinus stuck it out a month," Lenatus said, shaking his head with a rueful smile. "I guess he hoped the Legate would calm down eventually."

Pulto smiled at the recollection. He said, "He hopped it when he heard there was going to be a sweep into Free Germany. He knew when that happened he was going to be sleeping outside the palisades of the marching camps."

"But this"—Lenatus tapped his shield boss with the flat of his sword, making a clack instead of the clang of steel—"is straight. The senator called me into his office and told me he was letting Lady Alphena"—he nodded toward her—"spar now. Only not with Corylus, that's the only off-limits. It nigh knocked me on my ass to hear him say that."

"My mother thought there should be a change," Alphena said, speaking precisely and a little louder than she would have needed to. She could feel herself blushing, but part of her hoped that if she pretended that it wasn't happening neither of the men would notice. "She talked to Father, and he agreed."

Pulto chuckled. "I don't guess there's many people who don't agree with Lady Hedia when she makes up her mind to do something. Men, anyhow."

"I don't have much luck arguing with her, either," Alphena said. She suddenly smiled.

"Partly," she blurted, "because I see that she's right when I really listen and think about it."

Alphena was treating these two commoners as equals. That would horrify and amaze virtually any noble or member of a noble household; Agrippinus would be furious if he heard the discussion.

But another way of looking at it was that these two veterans were treating a sixteen-year-old girl as an equal. Alphena had earned their respect because of what they had observed and because people whom they respected, Hedia and Corylus, respected her.

"Say, you couldn't promote a jar of wine, could you?" Pulto said, speaking to his friend but looking sidelong at Alphena.

"Well, we just got started here . . . ?" Lenatus said, also eying Alphena.

She took the hint, but as she opened her mouth to end the session Pulto said, "Say, go ahead. Now that I think about it, I'd like to see this for myself. If that's all right?"

Instead of speaking, Alphena picked up her sword and faced the trainer again. She was breathing normally again after the break.

Lenatus cinched the strap of his shield tighter to the stud over his left shoulder; he'd loosened it to rest the bottom of the shield on the ground while they talked. Without warning he thrust for Alphena's right shoulder.

She circled back and left as usual, letting the blade barely tick the top of her body armor. Lenatus followed her, one step and then two. His shield lagged a hair farther out of position at each step.

Alphena retreated a fourth step and then, as Lenatus advanced, thrust for the point of his right hip. Lenatus jumped away, but he stumbled and dropped to his knee to keep from sprawling on his back.

"Buggering Venus!" the trainer shouted.

Alphena backed away. She bent forward so that she could fill her lungs more easily. She had gotten solidly home that time. *And he didn't touch me!* she thought.

"That the best you can do, Marcus?" Pulto said, leaning against the gymnasium's shaded wall.

"You think you can do better?" Lenatus said. He straightened carefully, rubbing his hip with the pommel of his sword. "She's bloody good, I tell you."

"That suit you, Your Ladyship?" Pulto said over his shoulder as he walked to the racks of equipment.

"Yes," Alphena said, trying not to snarl. She had almost objected that she was winded from the bout with Lenatus, but Pulto was an old man and clearly out of shape. Besides, that would have been whining.

Pulto took down the wooden equivalent of a long cavalryman's sword and small buckler whose twin handles he gripped together in his left hand. He turned to face Alphena.

"I'll wait for you to get the rest of your armor on," she said, puzzled.

"I got the web of this helmet adjusted for me," said Lenatus, holding it out to his friend. "It oughta fit you unless yours has been swelling since you left the Alaudae."

"I'm all right," Pulto said, smiling toward Lenatus. "We'll pretend I'm a German, though their crappy shields are generally bigger'n this."

He grinned broadly at Alphena. "I'm ready, girlie."

It was the tone more than the words that drove Alphena to a sudden rush behind her upraised shield. Even as she started to move, she realized that Pulto hadn't been carelessly relaxed the way she had thought.

He took the shock of her heavy shield on his buckler without any more give than a fortress wall. An instant later, something banged into the back of Alphena's head, knocking her helmet off and spilling her sideways in the sawdust.

Alphena rose to her knees with difficulty, tangled with her equipment. Besides the shoulder strap, her left forearm was through the double staples on the back of the shield, a part cylinder of laminated birch two inches thick. It was heavy and awkward when she was in the best of shape; now she was sick to her stomach and her eyes weren't right.

Her helmet had bounced off the wall and now rocked beside her. The bronze had a deep dimple just behind the left earpiece.

Her fury scoured away the dizziness. Alphena jumped to her feet and shouted, "Lenatus, you hit me from behind! I'll have you *crucified* for this!"

"Peace, Your Ladyship!" the trainer said in surprise. He had been bending toward her but jerked upright.

"He did not," said Pulto, stepping between Lenatus and his furious mistress. "I don't need help to larrup a recruit who leaves herself as open as you did. Watch!"

"I wasn't open!" Alphena said, but in a calmer voice. "I was behind my shield!"

"Watch!" Pulto repeated. He turned to the heavy post that Alphena had dented with over a year of blows with a practice sword. Pulto's arm swung wide as he leaned forward. The tip of his long blade moved sideways and cracked the top of the post from behind.

Pulto straightened and looked at her. "You *were* behind your shield," he said. "So you weren't watching me. Got it?"

"Yes," said Alphena. She had dropped her sword when she went down, so her right hand was free to unbuckle her shield strap. "Master Lenatus, I apologize. I'm a fool."

She wiped her eyes with the back of her hand, hoping that she wasn't crying or that, anyway, the tears would be mistaken for sweat. Her whole body was trembling. As soon as she had shrugged her arm out of the shield loops, she sat heavily on the bench built into the back wall.

"Don't move," Pulto said. Alphena felt his fingers probing her hair. He was extremely gentle, so she wasn't expecting the sudden jolt of pain when his finger moved slightly. She gasped and jerked her head forward.

Lenatus rose from the cabinet he had opened, holding two faience mugs and a pear-shaped glass jug. He unstoppered the wine and poured some into the mug that he offered to Alphena.

"She's all right," Pulto said as he stepped away. He was speaking to Lenatus. "Look, Your Ladyship, I'm sorry I caught you so hard, but I figured you had to learn."

"I don't feel all right," Alphena muttered. She drank, spluttering as some of the wine went down the wrong throat.

"You want some water with that?" Lenatus said. "I didn't think . . ."

Then he said, "Your Ladyship, it's my fault. You're not a recruit, and we shouldn't have treated you like one."

"If anybody's going to the cross for this one, it's me!" Pulto growled. "I did it and I'll take the punishment."

"Stop it, both of you!" Alphena said. "Nobody did wrong except me. I thought I was good and I wasn't. If anybody asks, I slipped when I was practicing on the post—"

She gestured.

"—and hit my head on this bench."

She took a deep breath, then finished the wine. "And the wine's fine, I don't need to water it," she said. "I just drank the wrong way."

"Thank you, Your Ladyship," Lenatus said. He looked the other way.

"Yeah, from me too," Pulto said.

"Lady, you really are good," he went on. He squatted instead of sitting beside her on the bench. "You're as quick as I've seen in a while, and you've got a lot of strength for a girl."

"Bloody Death, she's strong enough for anybody!" Lenatus said, rubbing his hip gingerly.

"What you don't have yet is thirty years' practice killing people," Pulto said. "One of these days you're going to meet somebody who does and who isn't using a wood sword. From what I'm told, you're likely to be closing the left side of my boy Corylus when that happens. So I don't want it to happen."

Lenatus poured her more wine. Alphena looked at him and said, "Lenatus, have you been going easy with me?"

She spoke calmly, but the implications were threatening even if the tone wasn't. Pulto stepped verbally between his friend and the noblewoman, saying, "Naw, he wasn't coddling you. I watched, remember? But you're used to him, and you're not used to me."

He grinned and stretched out his right arm. "I got more reach than Marcus, here, and besides—"

Lenatus was grinning also, expecting what was coming.

"—I figured you wouldn't be playing your top game against a fat old man. And I was right."

Alphena burst out laughing. "Yes, you were right," she said. "I won't make that mistake again."

She sobered and looked squarely at Pulto. "But I'll make others, which I hope you'll help train me out of, Master Pulto. If Publius Corylus permits it, that is."

"Well, you see how your mother feels about that and I'll talk to Master Corylus," Pulto said, sounding ill at ease. He was still thinking about what his training exercise—his little joke, really—might have led to.

Alphena felt a pang. It would have been unjust for her to punish the two veterans for doing what she had dared them to do, but the person she had been six months ago might have done so in a blind rage.

Hedia wasn't interested in making Alphena "nice," but she did want her to be effective. The older woman had repeatedly demonstrated that out-of-control people weren't effective, and her contempt for failure was more cutting than anger could have been.

"Say, what are you doing here today?" Lenatus said, offering Pulto the other mug. "Lord Varus is off to some shrine in the north with Her Ladyship, isn't he?"

Pulto tossed off the wine and handed back the mug. "Wouldn't mind another," he said. "I didn't *half* get a dry throat there."

"Sorry," Alphena said into her mug.

"I'm just here with Master Corylus," Pulto said without seeming to notice the apology. "He come to see the senator."

"He's looking for a posting to a governor's staff?" Lenatus said. "Say, will you be going off with him?"

"No, it's the senator wants to see *him*," Pulto said. "Don't ask me why, because the boy didn't have any notion himself. It must've been good from the way the senator led him into the office, which was a load off my mind and no mistake."

The gymnasium door opened again. Pulto turned his head and said, "Come on in, young master. And if you don't mind sharing a mug with me, Lenatus here has some bloody good wine to drink!"

WHEN VARUS STARTED toward the Indian delegation, Minimus began to swagger along with him. "Stop," Varus said, halting. "Minimus, go back to Lady Hedia and remain with her until she orders you to move."

The big slave blinked as though he didn't understand the simple Greek. Varus realized that was possible, but it was more likely that Minimus didn't understand the concept of a chief wanting to meet strangers without a threatening entourage at his back. Furthermore, Varus hadn't shouted at him the way a chief was expected to do when he corrected a warrior.

"Go back to Lady Hedia," Varus repeated, still without raising his voice. It was very hard to keep one's philosophical calm when people listened to a speaker's tone and volume instead of the words he was speaking.

Minimus blinked again. "Yes, Lord Varus," he said reluctantly as he turned away.

To make sure that his would-be protector hadn't changed his mind, Varus watched for a moment then resumed walking toward the Indians. The gardeners were backfilling around the vine they had planted. To Varus' surprise, the old man stepped away from the delegation and came toward him.

"Good day, revered sir," the old man said in good Greek. "I am Bhiku, in the service of the Rajah Raguram and his master, King Govinda. May I ask what brings a magician of your eminence to this place?"

"I beg your pardon?" Varus said, startled into saying the first words that came to his mind. "I am Gaius Alphenus Varus. Who told you I was a magician?"

Close-up the Indian was even older than he had seemed at a distance. He was barefoot, and his only garment was a thin cotton singlet that had been washed so often that it was almost translucent now. Varus could see Bhiku's ribs through the fabric.

The old man glanced down and chuckled. "I look like a victim after the sacrifice, don't I?" he said, plucking the singlet out from his scrawny chest. "Nothing left of me but the tongue and the guts. But as for you being a magician, Gaius Varus—"

Bhiku looked Varus in the face. His own brown eyes were bright and alert.

"—I am in a small way a magician also, a very small way compared to you. But I see you for what you are, as surely as I could see a burning village if I were standing beside it."

"I, ah . . . ," Varus said. Memories stirred in his mind, demons and monsters and perhaps gods whom *someone* had seen and things that *someone* had done. The person seeing had been Gaius Alphenus Varus, and the person working the terrible magic had been that Gaius Varus also . . . but—

"That wasn't me!" Varus said, snarling at himself rather than at the little man before him. Bhiku gave no sign of having heard, save by an almost invisible twitch of his right eye.

"I'm sorry, Master Bhiku," Varus said. "I think of myself as a scholar, a philosopher if you will. Things have happened in my presence that I could not explain better than as manifestations of magic, but I have no conscious power over such things. I don't, I certainly do not, hold myself out as a magician."

For the most part, the members of the Indian delegation were ignoring Bhiku and Varus. The three richly dressed Indians looked profoundly bored. They stood apart from their own subordinates as well as from the half-dozen members of Sentius' household under the direction of an understeward.

The exception was the woman, who watched Varus intently. Her skin was as dark as aged oak and contrasted sharply with her white garment. She had no wrinkles or visible blemishes.

Varus started to break eye contact with the strange woman, but he caught himself before his muscles obeyed the thought. *I am a citizen of Carce,* he thought. *Why should I allow myself to be cowed by a stranger while standing in the ancient lands of my people?*

"Who is the woman, Master Bhiku?" he asked without turning his head. After a moment she walked toward the pair of gardeners, putting her back to Varus.

"Our lords' lord, Govinda," said Bhiku, "is not a trustful man. He is a great magician as well as the greatest of kings, but his duties prevent him from making the long sea voyage that was required to come here for the first time. Rather than send a magician to carry out the rites he wishes, he sent two of us."

Varus felt his face stiffen. "What rites would those be, Master Bhiku?" he said.

"Govinda wishes the god Bacchus to be summoned to this place," the old man said agreeably. "You might think that priests rather than magicians would be the proper parties to carry out the rites, but this is not the judgment of my master's master."

Varus grimaced. "I see," he said. "I don't set much store by religious rites myself."

"In that," Bhiku said, "you and I are of the same opinion as Govinda."

The old man coughed, then continued, "He sent myself and Rupa, whom you asked about, to carry out the rite and to open a passage through the Otherworld by which we and our colleagues will return. Rupa is a member of the household of Ramsa Lal, a rajah subject to Govinda, but Ramsa Lal and Raguram, my master, are on terms just short of war. If indeed war has not broken out in the months since we sailed."

The old man smiled. Varus found Bhiku's personality engaging, though their contact had been too short for him to be able to support his reaction with logic.

"Govinda thinks that because our masters are rivals," Bhiku said. "Rupa and I will make sure that the rites are carried out as he wishes."

The gardeners were watering the vine from a brass barrel. The container was certainly from India. Varus wondered if the water had been transported also, in furtherance of the "rites" to which Bhiku had referred.

"You told me what Govinda thinks, Master Bhiku," Varus said. "What is *your* opinion?"

Bhiku laughed, a cackle that could have been threatening had it not been for the old man's cheerful expression. He said, "People rarely ask me what I think. They want to know what I can do for them, only that. But what I think, Gaius Varus, is that I do not need to be threatened to carry out the duties I agreed to do in exchange for my keep."

He plucked the thin fabric away from his ribs and grinned like a frog. "Very modest keep," he said wryly. "And as for Rupa . . ."

His eyes followed the woman. She appeared to be examining an outcrop on the slope above the altar.

"Govinda is a very great magician, beyond any question," Bhiku said musingly. "But I would not care to guess how powerful Rupa is, or what her real purposes might be. I have heard it said that she is ancient. I am an old man, but it is said that she is older than I am by hundreds of years. To the eye she does not appear old."

"She looks," said Varus, "as though she were made of polished chert. Smooth and so hard that steel could strike sparks from her skin."

"Yes," said Bhiku. They were speaking with lowered voices, though there was no one near them, nor, in all likelihood, anyone who would have cared about what they were saying if they had been shouting. "It may be that her soul is that hard also."

Then, in a still softer voice, Bhiku said, "I think that Rupa may be searching for a word that will split this world the way a knife cuts a pat of butter . . . and that if Rupa should find that word, she will speak it."

The gardeners stepped away from the vine shoot. One spoke to the officials. The bearded man in blue made a peremptory gesture toward Bhiku, who bowed in obedience and started toward his fellows.

He turned as he walked away and said over his shoulder, "It has been a pleasure to meet you, Gaius Varus. I hope that we may meet again."

CHAPTER II

"Please sit down, Master Corylus," said Saxa, gesturing him to one of the two backless folding chairs in the office. The curving legs had been carved from burl elm and polished to bring out all the rich figuration. Saxa's seat was ivory, the curule chair on which he sat in the Senate and at other public events.

"Thank you," Corylus said quietly as he seated himself. Death masks of Saxa's more illustrious ancestors formed a frieze around the top of the walls. In many cases the wax had blackened with age. Against one sidewall stood a cabinet with drawers in the lower portion; above were display shelves protected by a bronze grating.

Bronze busts of Homer, Vergil, and Horace stood on top of the cabinet. Vergil's head was wreathed in laurel. *Today is Vergil's birthday*, Corylus realized.

He had met a man—a sort of man—who might have been the living remains of Vergil, the greatest of poets and according to rumor the greatest of magicians as well. That incident seemed now to have been a dream, like so many other incidents of Corylus' recent life. They had been real at the time, though, real enough to have meant his death and the death of the very world. . . .

"I'm in a difficult position, Master Corylus," Saxa said, clasping his hands in his lap and then changing the grip as he clasped them again. "I suppose you know that I have the honor to be the Republic's Governor of Lusitania? Yes, of course you know that."

Corylus lifted his chin in silent acknowledgment. He had rarely spoken with Varus' father. It had been a disconcerting experience every previous time, and the present occurrence was that and worse.

On the one hand, Saxa was wealthy even by the standards of the Senate. He had the power of life and death by virtue of his position, and his enormous wealth could gain him almost anything available within the empire over which the Republic ruled.

On the other hand, Saxa was a little man who dithered and babbled and whose great store of knowledge was as disorderly as a squirrel's nest of sticks. Saxa's worst punishment was that he had enough intelligence to understand how completely he lacked wisdom.

The latter Saxa was the man talking to Corylus at present, but the wealthy senator stood behind the speaker. Corylus was naturally courteous, but he had to remain aware that discourtesy, real or misconstrued, to this man might literally be fatal.

"I am carrying out my duties in the province through the agency of a vicar, Quinctius Rufus," Saxa said, staring at his hands. "Rufus is a Knight of Carce with a great deal of experience in administration. He has commanded a legion on the Libyan frontier, so he's used to difficult conditions of the sort that service in Lusitania entails."

"A wise choice," Corylus said mildly. That was true in two fashions: Lucius Quinctius Rufus was well suited to govern a mountainous province on the Atlantic coast, and Saxa himself had no business trying to govern anything, not even a two-man board game like Bandits.

"Yes, yes, I thought so," Saxa said, looking confused and increasingly agitated. "But I've been hearing rumors that Rufus is behaving badly, very badly indeed. That he's looting temples, stealing the wives and daughters of citizens of Carce, and doing all manner of awful things."

"I don't . . . ," Corylus said, then paused to rephrase his words. "That is, I don't know Quinctius Rufus personally, but his reputation is that of a sober and trustworthy man. And besides, you have other agents in the province, surely?"

Corylus had checked with his father when he heard of Saxa's arrangements for the practical aspects of his duties—as opposed to ceremonial matters carried out in Carce. It wasn't something anyone had asked Corylus to do; nor did he mention what he was doing even to Varus. It had just seemed like the sort of precaution that you took when you were in dangerous country. Politics had as many potential ambushes as there were on the east bank of the Danube.

Publius Cispius had never served under Rufus, but his contacts in the army included many old soldiers who had. Rufus hadn't been enthusiastically liked—one veteran had said that the windblown desert sand had more personality than the commander did—but nobody complained about his honesty or competence.

"Well, that's *it*," said Saxa miserably. "There are reports from Upper Spain that say Rufus has bribed all the officials in his province, even the Agents for Affairs who report directly to the Emperor. And if it's true, well, it would be very bad for me."

Corylus lifted his chin in agreement. "Yes, I can see that," he said. He still didn't know why the senator was talking to him, but he certainly understood the cause of the older man's agitation. "Everyone will assume that Rufus is funneling much of the money to you, and—"

"Oh!" said Saxa, sitting bolt upright in shock. "Oh, surely they wouldn't think that! *Me* steal *money?*"

His amazed innocence was quite real, but most people didn't know Saxa as well as Corylus had come to do through the friendship of Varus over the past few months. Saxa had as little concern for money as Pandareus of Athens, Corylus' teacher, did.

Saxa had more wealth than a team of accountants could figure in six months of working, while Pandareus owned little but the clothes he stood up in and a modest number of books. Despite what an outsider would have considered to be huge differences between the men, neither one thought in terms of money.

"There are evil-minded people in this world, Lord Saxa," Corylus said. "Even, I'm afraid, in the Senate."

"Oh, that's *so* true," said the senator. "Atilius Priscus, a truly great scholar whom I'm proud to call a friend—"

Priscus was indeed a great scholar. His acquaintance with Saxa had come through his scholarly friendship with Pandareus and the respect the teacher had for Gaius Varus. Unlike his father with his magpie mind, Varus combined memory and organization with a wisdom that came from personality rather than age. For the son's sake, Priscus socialized with the father.

Saxa had seen his son save the world. To Saxa, however, the fact that Varus had gained him the friendship of truly learned men was a greater blessing still.

"Priscus, as I say, warned me that the stories originate with Lucius Sentius. The Governor of Upper Spain, Romanus Pulcher, is a colleague of

Sentius in the Indian Ocean trade, and Sentius himself has been bribing people to spread rumors about what's going on in Lusitania."

"Why in the name of Pluto would Sentius do that?" Corylus said. Other than the fact that he was a senator and therefore wealthy, Sentius had little public profile. The only reason that Corylus had even heard of him was because the man had recently dedicated an altar to Eastern Fortune in the harbor of Ostia. Pandareus had taken his whole class to the ceremony to critique the speech delivered by Formianus, a rival teacher.

"Yes," said Saxa. "I wondered about that."

He stared at the wall painting above the closed door to the entrance hall. It showed Ariadne, abandoned on the shore of Naxos, waving to Theseus' ship as it disappeared over the horizon. Poking through the right edge of the painted frame were the heads of two harnessed leopards, implying that the god Bacchus was about to rescue the girl to become his queen.

"I hadn't had much contact with Sentius in the past," Saxa continued, still looking toward the painting. Corylus doubted there was an answer there. "Just last month, though, he visited and asked to see my collection of historical treasures. I'm always pleased to show other scholars the fruits of my research, you know?"

"Indeed, Your Lordship," Corylus said. Saxa's spirits had risen as soon as he started talking about his collections. He was a remarkably good-natured man. That was reason enough for Corylus to want to help him, quite apart from Corylus' friendship with Saxa's son.

"Sentius was particularly interested in the objects which had originally been collected by Marcus Herennius," Saxa said. "The one he kept asking about was the Ear of the Satyr, though, and I've never heard of it. Well, hadn't till then, I mean."

"An ear broken off a statue?" Corylus said, frowning.

"I really don't know," said Saxa. He had stopped wringing his hands. Intellectual puzzles intrigued rather than worried him. "The collection . . . well, it wasn't an estate sale, exactly. Herennius was proscribed during the Second Triumvirate. The man—his nephew, I believe—who was responsible for his arrest was granted a third portion of the estate. I suppose the nephew might have taken the ear, whatever it is. But that was two generations ago, and I don't know where the broker who sold the collection to me had acquired it."

"Was it a collection of artwork, then?" Corylus said while he tried make sense out of what Saxa was saying. Marble statues were merely cheap copies of bronze originals, and it wasn't likely that a bronze ear would be broken off . . . or that it would be of any importance if it was.

"Well, no . . . ," said Saxa, suddenly embarrassed. "Not exactly. That is—"

He grimaced and met Corylus' eyes. "In fact, Master Corylus," he said, "it was a collection of magical paraphernalia. At one time I was, well, interested in, ah, hidden knowledge."

Corylus showed no expression. If his host wanted to believe that the spells he had worked with the wizard Nemastes six months ago were a secret to those close to him, Corylus wasn't going to disabuse him.

"I haven't involved myself in such matters in some time—"

Not since Nemastes had destroyed himself and nearly destroyed the world.

"—but I still have some of the books and objects which I acquired while I was studying them."

"Did Sentius' visit to you occur before these rumors began?" Corylus said. His throat was dry, but he didn't want to break the mood by asking for a carafe of wine while Saxa was talking in a lucid fashion.

"Why, yes, I suppose he did," Saxa said, raising his eyes to the ceiling while he tried to tried to organize events in serial order. "At least *I* hadn't heard the rumors before. I wouldn't have accepted Sentius' request to visit if I had, would I?"

"Do you think . . . ," Corylus said. This was much like getting information of military importance from a civilian who didn't care what weapons a group of strangers had carried and who couldn't count above five.

"That is," he continued after a moment's pause, "do you suppose Sentius thought you were lying about not having the Ear of the Satyr? Perhaps he was either punishing you or he hoped to acquire the object if you were condemned for malfeasance in office. Your estate would be condemned, then."

"But why would he think that?" Saxa said. "If I had this ear, I'd have shown it to him. I'd *give* it to him if that would make this business go away. This is a terrible situation!"

"Yes, I see that," Corylus agreed. The Emperor was a suspicious man. If he believed that his own secret service, the Agents for Affairs, had been subverted, his reaction would be more enthusiastic than reasoned. "Ah, I'm not sure why you're telling me this, Your Lordship?"

Saxa flashed him a sad smile. He said, "I suppose you think I'm a woolly old fool, Master Corylus. And perhaps I am."

Corylus said nothing. Saxa was probably speaking rhetorically; and regardless, Corylus saw no benefit in answering the implied question.

"You're a friend of my son," Saxa continued. "I trust his judgment, and I trust my own, though perhaps I shouldn't. I believe you would carry out a mission faithfully, no matter what bribes or threats were used against you."

He paused. Corylus swallowed, then said, "I hope you are correct, Your Lordship. I think you are correct."

"Furthermore, you are levelheaded," Saxa said. "More so than one would expect of a boy so young. And your age is an advantage also, since no one would expect me to be sending a youth to Lusitania as my personal agent, my spy if you will. You will appear to be a young man going off as an aide to the vicar. A very junior aide."

Saxa cleared his throat and added, "If the rumors are true, I will go to the Emperor and throw myself on his mercy. If they are false, I will lodge a formal complaint against Sentius."

"Ah . . . ," said Corylus in the silence that followed. Not long ago Corylus had considered using his friendship with Varus to gain a position on the governor's staff. Corylus was suited by background and education to act as the vicar's messenger and observer in a province with rugged terrain and no little banditry . . . work very similar to what Saxa was asking him to perform, in fact.

Corylus hadn't executed that plan, however, in part because a series of magical events had left him too stunned to consider his future. The other part was the fact that he, Publius Cispius Corylus, had been a significant factor in preventing those events from overwhelming the world and humankind.

He grinned tightly. *My major contribution was in helping keep my friend Varus alive . . . but that was real.*

Either Varus was a magician or the magical onslaughts that Corylus remembered so vividly were the hallucinations that he had initially tried to convince himself they were. If they were real, it had been a good thing for the world that Corylus had not been in Lusitania when Varus needed his sword in Carce.

On the other hand, if Saxa and his son were executed out of hand for treason, Corylus' presence in Carce would be of little benefit against a squadron of the Emperor's German Bodyguard.

"Your Lordship . . . ," Corylus said. He licked his dry lips. "I am honored by your request, but before I accept it, I need to consult with others whose opinion I trust."

"Yes, of course," Saxa said, lifting his chin. "Your father, Publius Cispius. A very responsible man and an honor to the Republic."

"Yes, my father," Corylus said. *And your son and your wife. And your daughter, Alphena, as well, because she too has been part of this, whatever this is, which involved demons climbing from the depths of the Earth and things even more amazing than that.*

Saxa rose with Corylus. "I trust your judgment, boy," the older man said. "And there are few enough things that I can trust in this matter."

Corylus opened the side door of the office. There was a scurry of half-seen motion, servants scattering like mice on the floor of a granary when a watchman enters with a lantern.

First to the gymnasium to find Pulto, Corylus thought. *After that . . . well, I hope then I'll figure out what to do after that.*

ALPHENA SCRAMBLED TO HER FEET. Dizziness made her knees buckle, but Pulto must have expected that; his hands gripped her shoulders and held her upright until the spell had passed. She wanted to throw up, but that was momentary also.

"You all right now?" Pulto said, staring into her eyes.

Offended by the stare, Alphena jerked her head back. "Yes, I'm all right!" she said.

"He's checking to see that your pupils are the same size," said Corylus, closing the door behind him. "Did you take a knock on the head, Your Ladyship?"

"You might say that," said Lenatus. He'd picked up Alphena's helmet; now he turned it so that the dent was toward Corylus. Corylus whistled.

"I slipped and fell!" Alphena said. "I'm fine now."

Her skin felt prickly, but that was more or less true. At least her stomach had settled down and her eyes were focusing normally.

"Naw, I caught her a whack on the back of the head," Pulto said harshly. "Same as I did you, lad, when you got too big for your britches the once."

Corylus suddenly hardened, but after a moment he relaxed. "We'll let it pass," he said. "If you'd tried to do it in front of me, I'd have stopped it."

"Yes, master," Pulto said.

"He wanted you to be able to trust me," Alphena said. The words came out as she formed them in her mind. "He said if I was closing your left side, I needed to be better. I'm glad of the lesson, and I won't forget it."

Pulto stiffened. *To attention*, Alphena realized, and she realized also that it was a compliment to her.

"I'm sure you won't, Your Ladyship," Corylus said with a broad grin. He touched his head behind his left ear. "I certainly haven't forgotten the time he taught me the same lesson."

Alphena started unlatching her body armor. It was of silvered bronze, molded with a triton battling a snake-legged giant on the front panel: officers' armor, not the mail or articulated iron bands that a common soldier would wear. She'd cramped something in her left hand during the bout and it didn't want to bend up to get the catches.

"Just lift your arm, missy," Pulto said, guiding her arm out of his way. With the ease of long practice his other hand turned the catches where the front and back joined. "Your Ladyship, I mean."

"Were you hoping to find my brother, Master Corylus?" Alphena said.

She winced as she heard the words come out of her mouth. *I should have either shut up or just asked him directly. Mother can be arch and sound charming, but it's just stupid from me!*

"Ah, no," Corylus said, becoming ill at ease. "Ah, Lord Saxa requested that I visit him."

Corylus paused; the three others in the room were looking at him. "He, ah, has offered me a position. I . . . well, there are a number of things to consider. Do you know when Varus and, ah, Lady Hedia are to return from Polymartium?"

Alphena felt Pulto lift away the armor. She spread her right arm to make it easier for him, but she didn't take her eyes off Corylus. "I believe Mother was planning to come back today," Alphena said. "I suppose Varus will come with her since they left together, but I don't know that."

She cleared her throat and went on, "What position would that be?"

"I'm sure your father would tell you, Your Ladyship," Corylus said. "But I think it would be better if you asked him, especially since I'm not sure of my own plans until I've had time to discuss them."

With Hedia and my brother. Or maybe just with Hedia!

"Pulto," Corylus said, "I want to get back to the apartment. I have some thinking to do, and I'm scheduled tomorrow morning to deliver a set argument in class."

"Thanks for the wine, buddy," said Pulto, nodding to the trainer. He opened the door as servants vanished from the corridor into the house. He and Corylus walked toward the front and the street beyond.

Florina, Alphena's chief maid, had stayed in the corridor because she had a reason to be there. She squeezed against the wall to be out of the guests' way, then bowed toward Alphena. She didn't speak or enter the gymnasium.

"I think," Alphena said aloud, "that I'll bathe here in the house. Is the bath ready, Florina?"

"Yes, Your Ladyship," Florina said. "I saw to it myself!"

The furnace in the bathing annex was always kept burning. Saxa's wealth made this practical, but most people, even the very wealthy, preferred to walk a few blocks to the public bath where there was more space and the surroundings were more impressive.

The original builder of this house had included a gymnasium and private bath. They hadn't gotten much use until Alphena decided to train to become a gladiator. They were used even more often since Varus and Corylus had become friends. That also meant that Varus was getting more physical exercise than he otherwise would.

Varus wasn't a social youth, but he valued Corylus as a friend—probably his only friend. Though Corylus didn't actively encourage Varus to train, his friend's presence and example caused Varus to show interest in things he had never before considered.

Florina called a sharp order down the hall. Two junior maids scurried into the gym and unlaced Alphena's heavy sandals. When Alphena lifted each foot, they slipped on wooden bath clogs.

Florina's giving herself airs with the other staff. . . . But that was what people did. You could punish them for it, but why? It would be like punishing the sky for raining.

"Your Ladyship?" said Lenatus with a worried expression. "Is something wrong?"

"No, not at all, Master Lenatus," Alphena said as she walked from the gymnasium. "I was just realizing that because of the time I've spent talking to my brother and his teacher, I've begun to think about things that I didn't used to."

Talking to Varus and Pandareus, and also to Corylus.

Alphena took off her tunic in the steam room and sat on the stone bench while the two attendants dropped furnace-heated blocks of pumice into a bronze basin of water. Steam billowed through the room. The basin's handles were cast in the form of the heads of broad-mouthed catfish. The head nearer the bench appeared and vanished again in the steam like glimpses of a monster.

What will it mean to have Corylus in Father's entourage? He'd be here every morning. Will he join Father for dinner?

Alphena didn't ordinarily dine with the family, but she had done so and could do so again if she wanted to. There wasn't anything wrong with it, though women weren't usually part of the sort of decorous dinners that Saxa gave.

"Are you ready for your rubdown, Your Ladyship?" Florina asked. Though the bath had full sets of male and female servants, she had entered the steam room with Alphena.

How long have I been sitting here? Alphena thought. Sitting and thinking about things she shouldn't have been thinking about.

"Yes, all right," she said, getting up and walking to the massage bench. *Florina isn't showing her power,* Alphena saw in a flash of clarity. *She's afraid that if she isn't with me all the time, other servants will arrange that she be demoted back to kitchen staff, where she'd been before she was assigned to Lady Alphena as punishment.*

Alphena had been angry at everything, all the time. She screamed abuse at her father and brother, and she struck servants—even the free ones—with whatever was in her hand.

And then Saxa remarried.

Hedia had never threatened her stepdaughter, but Alphena had spent a great deal of time observing gladiators and the scarcely less brutal sport of chariot racing. The first time Alphena threw a tantrum at her new stepmother, she saw Hedia's face change. The utter ruthlessness in Hedia's expression had shocked Alphena to silence.

The two women hadn't become friends immediately. Alphena would have hated any stepmother, even if Saxa had married a former Vestal Virgin for his third wife. Hedia's reputation had been about as far the other way as a woman could go, and for once rumor had understated the truth.

The angry truce between mother and daughter didn't change until Saxa fell under the spell of a wizard who wasn't a charlatan. Magical disaster had boiled under Carce and the world. Alphena had seen her stepmother react to bad situations and to worse ones.

Hedia remained poised, cool, and just as ruthless as Alphena had realized the first time she saw the older woman angry. Hedia would do her duty or die; it was much more likely that the person or thing trying to prevent her would die instead.

Alphena's respect had deepened into something more, but respect was enough. It was one of Alphena's greatest sources of pride that she believed Hedia respected her as well.

The olive oil that an attendant poured from a cruet was cool on Alphena's skin. The masseuse began working it in with her palms more than her fingers. As she moved down Alphena's body, another servant used a curved ivory scraper to remove the oil along with the dirt and sweat that it had floated from the girl's steam-opened pores.

Alphena felt herself relaxing. The bump on her head had stopped throbbing also.

"Isn't it thrilling that the master is sending Publius Corylus off on a secret mission, Your Ladyship?" Florina said in a delighted whisper. "And how awful it would be if he failed!"

Alphena jerked her torso off the bench to look at Florina.

The masseuse yelped and skipped back. "Oh, Your Ladyship!" she squeaked with an African accent. "Did I pinch you? Oh, please, don't beat me!"

"Be silent!" Alphena snapped. She was angry, but not at the masseuse— or even at Florina, if it came to that.

The servant's terror had given Alphena a chance to collect her thoughts. She had nearly blurted, *What?* which would have made her look like a fool.

Of course the servants knew everything that was discussed in Saxa's office. There were probably keen-eared servants posted at every partition to pass anything interesting on to the whole staff.

A house in which over two hundred people lived had no privacy for any occupant. The owners and their social acquaintances were the focus of the attention of everyone, from Agrippinus, to whom all the other servants reported, to the junior potboy who came from somewhere east of the Tigris River and didn't speak a language that anyone else understood.

Alphena relaxed again. *I should feel flattered that Florina thinks I know as much as she does.* Aloud Alphena said, "I'm sure Master Corylus will be able to handle whatever task my father sets him, Florina."

"Oh, he's a very fine young man, certainly," Florina said, but her tone was doubtful. "Why, do you know where Lusitania is, Your Ladyship? It must be ever so far away."

Alphena jumped again, though not as badly. *Corylus is going to Lusitania?*

She coughed and said, "I believe it's close to Britain." She hadn't been interested in the province when her father became its governor, but she would learn shortly.

"Well, he didn't say he was going, did he?" said another voice. The speaker was another attendant—not the masseuse—but Alphena couldn't tell which one without turning her head.

The servants weren't supposed to be talking in front of her. The Alphena of six months ago would have had them all beaten. . . .

The Alphena of six months ago, however, might have had them beaten because she'd bruised her hand while fencing at the stake. It could be that the servants were becoming too familiar in their behavior with her . . . but Alphena was learning a great deal that she wouldn't otherwise have known.

For example, she had learned about the task her father had set for Corylus.

"Oh, Master Corylus isn't going to turn down a chance to get in close with His Lordship the Senator," Florina said. "He's just pretending in order to make the senator offer more for his help."

Her tone of flat certainty sounded convincing even to Alphena, who knew more about the background than her servant did but had no idea what Corylus would decide.

"Well, maybe getting close is *just* what the senator is worried about," said the attendant scraping Alphena's right leg; a separate servant worked on the left leg. "This Corylus won't be seeing much of the senator's pretty young wife if he's off in the back of beyond, will he?"

"Shut up, you fool!" Florina hissed.

"But—" said the previous speaker. She spoke Greek with a Gaullic accent and was probably one of the group from Provence that had arrived just the day before. Alphena had happened to be leaving the gymnasium when they arrived at the alley entrance.

"*Shut up!*" Florina repeated, followed by a loud slap and the attendant's yelp. "Felix!" The bath master. "Get her out of here!"

Alphena chose not to open her eyes so that she could pretend to be unaware of what had happened. A different—and more skilled—hand finished scraping her left leg. The masseuse herself had taken the scraper when the attendant was summarily ejected.

"Is Your Ladyship ready to turn over?" Florina said.

Instead of answering, Alphena rolled onto her back. She kept her eyes closed. The masseuse resumed rubbing the oil into her skin.

"Marta really isn't a bad girl, Your Ladyship," Florina said softly. "She hasn't been here long, is all. She has to learn our ways."

"Um," Alphena said in the darkness of her closed eyelids. "I'm sure there's no need for me to take any action."

She was surprised and pleased to hear Florina try to protect a fellow servant—a servant who wasn't, judging from the recent incident, a particular friend of hers. Perhaps Lady Alphena's effort to moderate her behavior had rubbed off on her immediate staff.

I've seen too much random cruelty recently—whole villages wiped out by monsters and worse things still—*to want to commit more of it myself.*

The skill of gladiators fighting one another still fascinated her, but there was no skill involved in watching prisoners mauled to death by big cats, and there was nothing for Alphena any longer in seeing animals feathered with arrows and javelins shot from behind grills.

Mankind had real enemies. Chasing animals in circles till they coughed their blood out from punctured lungs wasn't the way to fight those enemies.

The attendants were scraping again. There would be soft towels to rub her down and then clean clothes to wear when she went out to the Coelian Gardens this afternoon. She wanted to think.

Father knows that Hedia has lovers. I don't understand, but he knows and he doesn't care.

Or perhaps Alphena *did* understand. Hedia wasn't a wife for ancient Carce, wearing woolens that she had spun and woven herself. And yet she was just as incorruptible as those ancient heroines, and Hedia was far better suited to guide her dreamy husband through the dangers of modern Carce under a suspicious, ill-tempered emperor.

Saxa wouldn't send Corylus away to prevent his wife from having a discreet fling with him . . . but he *would* care if he thought there was a risk to his virgin daughter.

Alphena felt her body tingle. *Perhaps Corylus really does notice me!*

VARUS MOVED TO AN OUTCROP from which he could watch the Indian delegation gathering on the slope below. The three officials in colorful silks were giving Bhiku their full attention, and the dozen or so members of Sentius' household stood respectfully behind the Indians.

Bhiku raised his arms toward the rising sun and began to chant. From where Varus stood, the words were only a rhythm.

I could go closer, Varus thought. But the chant wouldn't be in any Western language, and all Varus knew about the languages spoken in India was that there were many of them. He had picked up some Pahlavi while studying the sources of Herodotus, but he was sure even from this distance that Bhiku's chant wasn't Persian.

The sun was above the horizon from this vantage point, but the air around Varus began to darken; he was slipping into a familiar trance. A slope led upward. He began to climb without consciously doing so.

Sometimes shapes moved in the darkness, but he ignored them. The darkness was of his mind. He had come to understand that the shapes were no more real than the surface of the hillside or the skin of the hands with which he imagined he touched the gritty stone.

He reached the top of the ridge. Above Varus was a bright sky with neither sun nor clouds. He knew from experience that if he looked back the way he had come there would be only roiling gray chaos, as featureless as the depths of the sea.

The old woman turned toward him. Her face under the cowl of her blue cape was so wrinkled that her smile was barely visible.

"Greetings, Lord Magician," she said.

"Greetings, Sibyl," Varus replied. "Why have you called me here this time?"

The Sibyl laughed like hens cackling. "I exist only in your mind, Varus," she said. "How could I summon you?"

She turned toward the scene on the other side of the seeming ridge that Varus had climbed. He walked to her side so that he could look also.

She can't be me. She's told me things that I didn't know until she spoke. But Varus knew nothing certain about the Sibyl except that when he left her seeming presence he had the power to work what seemed to be magic.

Varus was a scholar and philosopher. He would prefer any explanation other than magic to account for some of the things he had done, but his rigidly logical mind could not find one. He would keep looking; perhaps a natural explanation would yet appear.

On a plain below the ridge wheeled an ivy-crowned figure in a chariot pulled by a pair of leopards. He held a torch. Following him were hundreds of men and women, half-dressed or dressed in animal skins. They waved thyrsi, pinecones stuck on fennel stalks, and shouted exuberantly.

Those are horsemen, Varus thought, noticing torsos rising above the milling crowd. At closer look he saw that they were centaurs.

"This is the Otherworld," Varus said to the Sibyl. "You're showing me the god Bacchus in the Otherworld."

"It is the Otherworld for now," the Sibyl said with another crinkly smile. "This is not Bacchus, however, but rather his companion Ampelos leading a small part of Bacchus' train into the Waking World."

"But why?" said Varus.

The Sibyl didn't respond immediately. A lens of reddish light glowed in the air before Ampelos' chariot, then swelled to twenty feet in diameter. Vaguely through it Varus saw the rocks and slopes of Polymartium where his physical body remained.

Ampelos shouted and lashed the air with his thyrsus. The leopards sprang forward, dragging the chariot into the lens. The hundreds of cheering celebrants, male and female and unhuman, surged through behind their leader.

"But what are they doing?" Varus said, amplifying his unanswered previous question.

"Watch," said the Sibyl, and the scene below them changed.

A battalion of troops, Praetorian Guards according to their standards, advanced in close order across broken terrain of glade and outcrops. Varus saw the altar around which Hedia had been dancing; this was the countryside near Polymartium, but the Sibyl was showing it under bright moonlight. The ceremony to Mother Matuta had followed the night of the new moon.

Figures swept through the woods surrounding the Praetorians, swinging their thyrsi and raising their faces to the sky. Their mouths opened in silent whoops. Ampelos led the band Varus had seen in the Otherworld, disciples of Bacchus dressed in ivy and hides of dappled fawns, but there were others as well, hundreds and perhaps thousands of men and women capering in the moonlight.

Some were peasants and many were slaves, but Varus saw also the garish finery of farm managers. There was even a woman in pastel silks riding on the back of a centaur and followed by a group of well-dressed servants—a great lady of Carce with her personal entourage. His breath caught, but she was not Hedia.

They swept over the Praetorians like surf reaching ramparts of sand. Vine lassoes wrapped soldiers and dragged them from their ranks; pinecones struck like thunderbolts, shattering shields and breastplates. Soldiers hurled away their weapons and fled while others joined their attackers. The Bacchic throng danced and laughed and drank from wineskins that they brandished like military standards.

The Sibyl made a small gesture with her hand. In place of the routed Praetorians, Varus saw the outcrops where his physical body gazed down on the Indian delegation and the other spectators.

The Indian woman, Rupa, remained apart from her fellows. Turning, she looked at Varus—at his spiritual form on the ridge with the Sibyl. Rupa's eyes were as bright and as cold as the stars. For a moment Varus felt pressure, but it was so slight that after it vanished he thought he might have imagined it.

Rupa turned and walked in the direction of the road to Viterbum. The vehicles had been parked beside the road, so as not to pollute the rites with animal dung and because the track to the ceremonial grounds was at best doubtful.

The lens of faint light had appeared here in the Waking World as well as in the Sibyl's vision of the Otherworld. The male Indians strode toward it. Bhiku brought up the rear. The spectators including the members of Sentius' household gaped at the lens and chattered among themselves.

The Indians stepped one by one into the lens and vanished from the Waking World. The Sibyl said, "They are returning to King Govinda through the passage they have opened. Their work here is finished."

"Sibyl," said Varus, hearing a hint of desperation in his voice. "What am I to do?"

"I cannot advise so great a wizard as yourself, Lord Varus," the Sibyl said. Her voice sounded like the rasp of a locust's legs on its wing cases. "But if Govinda's plans go ahead, riot and madness will rule your world."

I am a citizen of Carce. The authority of those words came with responsibilities for every citizen.

"Then I had best see this King Govinda," Varus said. His spiritual form walked forward. In the vision of the Waking World before him, his body was stepping toward the disk of rosy light.

VARUS IS IN A TRANCE, Hedia thought as she watched her son tramp toward the lens. He moved with the rigid calm of a priest leading the procession of Isis. Hedia was too far away to reach him unless she ran, which would require her to either hike up her dress again or simply strip it off.

It probably wasn't necessary to do either of those things. In the past Varus had stumbled when he came out of a trance, but that would be at worst an embarrassment. All other things being equal, Hedia preferred that she avoid the loss of her own dignity above protecting her son from losing his.

"Lady, what's that light in the air?" Minimus shouted. He grabbed Hedia's shoulder and pointed with his other hand, as though he imagined she wouldn't have noticed it on her own.

He must be very frightened to treat me *that way,* Hedia thought. To her surprise, her flash of anger—*I'll have him crucified!*—replaced her own fear and settled her.

She prodded the Galatian's hand away with two fingers. "Remember who you're speaking to, Minimus," she said calmly. "And as for the light, it's harmless. It appeared because of our prayer to Mother Matuta."

That was nonsense or at least probably nonsense, but it was as likely as any other cause Hedia could think of at the moment. It served to calm Minimus, which was the important thing.

At least it calmed the big slave until he realized what he'd just done. He grabbed his right hand—the one that had touched his mistress—with his left and jerked it to his side as though he were trying to crush it. He cringed away from Hedia, his eyes staring at her in horror.

Hedia smiled faintly. She was no longer angry, but it was just as well that Minimus would be careful not to repeat *that* panicked mistake.

Varus had reached the lens. Hedia watched without concern, expecting her son to stop and chant a phrase from the *Sibylline Books* as she had seen him do before. Varus remained the quiet, bookish youth whom Hedia had met when she married his father; that he was a powerful wizard as well seemed to surprise him as much as it did her.

Varus stepped forward again. "Varus!" Hedia shouted, grabbing her tunic with both hands and running toward him.

Too late! Varus vanished into the lens while Hedia was still fifty feet away. For an instant he remained as a shadow against the faint light; then that too was gone. She continued to run.

The morning sky was cloudless, but an east wind had begun to blow. Hedia lowered her head slightly against it and slitted her eyelids.

A capering army flooded through the lens. With them like the perfume of a spring garden came an indescribable onrush of emotion, lust and joy in a mixture beyond human imagining.

Hedia shouted in delight. The chariot that swept past was drawn by great

spotted cats, larger than the leopards she had seen in the arena. The charioteer was lithely muscular, with flowing hair bound by a chaplet of vine leaves.
His only garment was a dappled fawn skin fluttering about his waist.

The charioteer's expression was as haughty as a god's, and he himself was
as handsome as a statue of Adonis. He glanced at Hedia as he passed; a rush
of desire filled her, heated her. Then he was gone, but hundreds of revelers
followed him, male Bassoi and female Maenads, dancing and whirling.

A young man as shaggy as a faun caught Hedia's arms and tried to pull
her away. She kissed him, feeling the tickle of his beard, but she used his momentary relaxation to swing out of his grip. He made a moue of disappointment, but he was gone into the rout in an instant.

A few of those who had attended the ceremony to Mother Matuta were
turning to flee. Most, however, stood transfixed for a moment before joining
the riot that flowed about them. It was like watching wax figures melt in an
oven.

Around the altar to Mother Matuta danced a pair of men in fawn skins,
six local men, a goat-footed satyr, the priest Doclianus, and the matron who
had been treading on Hedia's heels throughout the ceremony. Skins of wine
were passing around the circle as they danced.

The manager's wife drank deeply, handed the skin to the satyr behind
her, and began to twirl out of her clothing. She kept time perfectly, in contrast to her performance earlier in the morning. The satyr, his member suddenly erect, mounted her like a cockerel treading a hen. The matron began
to laugh raucously.

Hedia felt a surge of lust, but orgies were familiar ground to her. *Though
never so many participants at the same time,* she qualified. She had learned to
keep control, to keep a sliver of reason that was always aware of what everyone about her was doing. Hedia took risks, but she took them after judging
those risks against the urges of her body.

Other women—and most men, judging from her experience—acted in
response to the fire in their veins. Hedia had made cold choices. More recently
she had killed men after giving the situation the same icy consideration.

The chariot made wide circles. Vines grew in its wake, winding about tree
trunks and draping themselves from branches. They moved with the speed
of snakes in the summer's heat, leafing out and setting fruit more quickly than
water could drop from an upturned bucket.

Revelers snatched grapes into their mouths and spun onward, laughing and shouting, "Io Bacchus!" and throwing themselves into one another's arms. The delicately aesthetic understeward who led the contingent from Sentius' household was locked in an embrace with a farm laborer, probably a slave.

He'll hate himself in the morning, Hedia thought. *Perhaps they both will. But at this moment there's no tomorrow, only lust.*

She looked for members of her own entourage. The only one she saw was Minimus with a thyrsus-wielding Bacchante on his shoulders and a woman hugged close to either side. On his right was another Bacchante, but the woman to his left was local and was at least sixty. She looked eighty, but Hedia knew that rural women aged quickly from a combination of work and the harsh weather.

"Io Bacchus!" someone shouted from behind. Hedia turned. A handsome youth and a girl rode toward her on the back of a visibly male centaur who whirled a vine lasso; leaves and bunches of grapes dangled from the loop. The centaur's ruggedly handsome human face was transfigured by lust.

Why not? Hedia thought with a flush of excitement.

The answer was as sudden and shocking. *Because my son may need my help and the world certainly needs his help.*

Hedia turned and stepped through the glowing portal to the Otherworld.

CHAPTER III

"Have my usual breakfast brought to the summer dining room," Alphena said as she started up the stairs to the roof alcove. She'd eaten a scrap of bread in wine lees when she got up, but she preferred to wait till after her workout for anything more substantial.

And a good thing I waited yesterday, she thought, *or I'd have sprayed the meal all over the gym when Pulto clocked me behind the ear.*

Florina loudly—and needlessly—relayed her orders. The food had probably started for the roof as soon as Alphena stepped out of the bathing annex. It was likely enough that the same meal would be waiting in the inside dining room, just in case Her Ladyship chose to eat there instead.

Alphena reached the top of the stairs. This was a normal business day, so Saxa, surrounded by a cloud of servants and clients—hangers-on—would have gone off to a session of the Senate. Pandareus and other teachers would be holding classes in the Forum; Corylus had said that he was preparing an oration to deliver this morning.

"Did my mother and Varus return from Polymartium yesterday?" Alphena said as she reclined on the masonry bench prepared for her with pillows. By mid-morning the air was warm enough for anybody, and she wanted the fresh air of the rooftop after exercise and a bath. "I didn't hear them come in."

"No, Your Ladyship!" Florina said. "Do you suppose there's something wrong?"

"No," Alphena said, "I don't. I think my brother found some grandmother with stories about the way the ceremonies used to be held and Mother stayed to help him."

Or Hedia might have stayed because she had met a man she wanted to get to know better. Alphena tried not to think about that, but sex was as surely part of Hedia's character as the disdainful sneer with which she had faced demons. The complexity of her character was beyond Alphena's ability to fathom; but Saxa accepted the mixture, and his daughter owed her life to it.

A servant set a footed bowl before Alphena. It was filled with milk and raw egg whipped with spices. Another servant offered a tray of bread cut in varied shapes. Alphena took a thickish crust and used it to scoop a mouthful of milk and egg.

Other servants waited with covered trays holding fruit and whatever else the chef thought Her Ladyship might call for. An underchef waited to rush down to the kitchen with any unexpected requirement.

This is silly, Alphena thought. *I always eat the same thing for breakfast.*

Neither Saxa nor Hedia set much store by fancy meals, either. As for Alphena's brother, Varus would be perfectly happy with a plowman's diet, sour wine included. He didn't seem to notice food. But for the kitchen staff to accept that would mean that their very existence was pointless, so they continued to try.

And what's the point of my own existence?

Alphena laughed, almost snorting milk gruel out of her nostrils. Servants froze, afraid that they had done something or should have done something.

Alphena swallowed and wiped her lips with a napkin. "I should get more exercise," she said mildly. "I found myself worrying about philosophy, which is my brother's business."

From the open doorway of the stair cupola, someone—Alphena thought it was Charias, a recently promoted understeward—said on a rising note, "You shouldn't be here! If Her Ladyship wishes to go out, she will call you!"

"If you don't get outa the way . . . ," snarled either Rago or Drago—the Illyrian cousins spoke Greek with indistinguishably bad accents—"you're going down the stairs headfirst."

Alphena jumped to her feet. "It's all right, Charias!" she called. "Send them up!"

"It's two of the outside escorts, Your Ladyship!" the understeward called back, which Alphena could see for herself now. At least Charias had shown the sense to jump out of the way. That pair of Illyrians didn't joke about mayhem.

Rago was leading. They were comparably but not identically scarred, and Drago's missing left ear set him apart from his cousin.

"Your Ladyship," Rago muttered, grimacing. The bravado that had carried him through the house, ignoring rules and propriety, had deserted him in Alphena's presence.

Drago stepped forward. "Lady," he grunted. "Minimus and mosta the others just come back. It all went to shit somehow up there with the mistress and your brother, only nobody's got the balls to come tell you. So we come."

"Who is Minimus?" Alphena said, as much to give herself time to recover from shock as because she really cared. She felt her knees wobble, but staggering to a seat would give the wrong impression at this moment.

"He's honcho on the mistress' guard," Rago said. "They went up to some bloody place two days back."

"The big Galatian," Alphena said, placing the man. Hedia chose good-looking men for her escort. Minimus was unscarred, but he had been trained as a gladiator and would give a good account of himself if anyone attacked Hedia.

"I kilt plenty men as big as that 'un," Drago said with satisfaction. *"Plenty."*

That was likely enough. Rago and Drago were former sailors—and doubtless pirates—who'd been bought to work one of Saxa's farms in leg irons. Before they were transported, Agrippinus had diverted them to string awnings over the central garden when Hedia decided to give a summer fete for other senatorial wives. The pair had remained at the town house as much as anything because nobody had bothered to send them away.

"A whole mob come out of the air, Minimus says," Drago said. "Whoop! Right outa the air. And when things settled down, they, whoever *they* was, went back where they'd come, but the mistress and your brother was gone."

"Out of the air . . . ?" Alphena repeated.

She saw Charias standing at the stairhead, quivering with interest and concern. "You!" she said. "Get all the secretaries in the household to write down what the servants who've returned from Polymartium are saying. Everyone who can take dictation, I don't care whose suite they belong to."

The understeward's lips pursed in hesitation. *"Now,"* Alphena said. "If anyone makes a problem, tell him I'll come down and deal with him at once."

"Hey, send *us*, lady," Rago said. He smiled so broadly that Alphena could see that half his teeth were missing. "You told him nice, so give us a turn."

"I doubt I'll need to do that," she said. "But a crowd of people out of the air? You mean magic?"

"Dunno," said Drago. "Sure sounds like it, don't it?"

"Are we going up there to sort it out, lady?" his cousin asked.

"The first thing I plan to do," said Alphena, "is to discuss the business with Master Corylus and Master Pandareus. Once we know what the business is, as best Mother's escort can describe it."

She looked at the cousins. Both wore clean blue tunics, but apart from that they appeared to be dangerous roughs—which of course they were.

Hedia had chosen the members of her escort. The servants who accompanied Varus when he went out had been picked for him, probably by the majordomo. They would be eminently suitable for the task of maintaining not only Varus' physical safety—rarely a real concern in Carce, where he spent most of his time—but also his status as a member of the nobility.

Alphena hadn't chosen her escort: they had chosen her. On a night when Lady Hedia had vanished in the hands of demons and the household was in uproar, Alphena had held herself in the icy calm that she had learned from her stepmother.

A few servants had grouped themselves around Alphena, simply because the young lady hadn't lost her head. They were odds and ends, supernumeraries and outcasts. Most spoke bad Latin or none at all, and the Illyrian cousins weren't alone in having shaky Greek. There was a potboy, a gardener's assistant, and a spare litter bearer.

What they all had in common was the willingness to face *any* bloody thing, so long as they had a leader who would tell them what to do. For these men, uncertainty was a worse enemy than demons. They were willing to follow, and they had decided that Alphena was able to lead.

Which I was, Alphena thought. *Which I am.*

"I'll wait for the information that my colleagues will want," she said calmly. "It will take some time to get the reports together, even with everyone available to write them down. We'll leave in an hour, though, if we can't leave sooner. I don't want to risk class breaking up and Corylus and his teacher being gone."

She took a breath and added, "You can alert your colleagues now, but there'll be a delay."

"Right," said Drago as the cousins turned toward the stairway. "We'll make sure everybody's dressed for business."

"No!" Alphena said. "No, no weapons for now. We're just making a visit to scholars in the Forum in broad daylight."

"Aw . . . ," Rago said in disappointment. Being caught wearing a sword within the religious boundary of Carce meant a death sentence even for a freeborn citizen; the slaves of Alphena's escort could expect even less consideration. And what good would swords do against magic?

"Wait," Alphena said to the cousins' backs. "Come back for a moment. We have time."

Rago and Drago came up from the stairs. They watched her uneasily, afraid they'd done wrong but not sure how.

Florina and the breakfast servants stood in a silent row. They were thrilled to watch others deal with a crisis but terrified that they would be dragged into it as well.

"Aren't you afraid of magic?" Alphena said to the Illyrians.

Everyone was afraid of magic. Corylus' servant Pulto was as brave a man as ever faced a German ambush or a charge of Sarmatian cavalry, but he trembled to admit that his wife, Anna, was a witch from the Marsian region.

"I guess," Rago said. "I'm scared of lots of things."

"Being crucified," said his cousin, nodding in agreement. "Bloody near happened too. Near happened twice."

"Thing is," Rago said, "Drago and me likes fronting for you, lady. I guess that's the same with the rest of your outside crew, right?"

"Yeah," said Drago. "You tell us where to go, lady, and we'll go there ahead of you."

Alphena swallowed. "All right," she said. "For the present, that's to the Forum. I don't think we're in any danger except for the chance that we'll be bored to death by speeches. You may go."

Grinning, the cousins trotted down the stairs. Alphena took a deep breath as she watched them go. *How can they trust me?*

"I'll dress to go out now," she said to Florina. "With traveling shoes but not army sandals."

Pandareus will know what to do. And Corylus. Corylus will take charge.

"THIS WOMAN COMMITTED ADULTERY, you say!" Corylus thundered from the north end of the Rostra. "The sacred laws of our forefathers, the founders of Carce, demand that she be punished!"

Pandareus and his class, save the absent Varus, watched below the steps. A pupil of Fulvius Glabrio was declaiming to his immediate left. Corylus had been taught to project his voice by centurions on the frontier where lives depended on their troops hearing orders in the crash of battle. The Forum, though crowded, wasn't much of a test for him now.

"Well and good!" Corylus said. "Her punishment is to be flung from the Tarpeian Rock, that awful crag!"

He pointed his whole arm in a broad, dramatic gesture. He would have used a motion as quick as a spear thrust if he were informing a legion's commander—or directing the troops he was about to lead in an assault.

A noble entourage was pressing through the crowd, past the ancient altar to Vulcan. Corylus recognized the leaders as the Illyrian members of Alphena's suite. No other noble would be seen in daylight guarded by such men, so even before the girl's head became visible beyond the taller escorts he was certain that it was her.

"And so she was punished!" Corylus said. A successful orator couldn't allow himself to be distracted by what was happening in the audience or beyond it. "But since the immortal gods preserved her unharmed by the fall, what business is it of mere men like ourselves to object to their august decision? The laws of our forefathers have been carried out, and the mercy of the gods has been displayed. Release her now!"

He swept his pointing arm across the arc of his fellow students. Piso was ostentatiously chatting with his toady Beccaristo, but the others listened intently. Two were even jotting notes.

"Release her," Corylus repeated. "Or set yourself against the will of our ancestors and the judgment of the immortals!"

He lowered his arm. Pandareus nodded approval, and a pair of strangers—Corylus didn't know their names, at least—stamped their feet in applause. There were always loungers in the Forum; some of them had become good judges of a speaker's ability.

I'd like to think these were two of the more knowledgeable ones, Corylus thought. He smiled at himself.

Pulto stood at the back of the class with the servants of the other students. Alphena spoke with him and he—not Alphena's own escorts—led her through the chattering students to the teacher's side. Pandareus bent his ear to her words, then mounted the first step of the Rostra.

"Young gentlemen," he said, "we will delay our discussion of Master Corylus' presentation to the morrow. Other business calls us now, and possibly pleasures call some of you."

Laughter rippled. The class broke up with the suddenness of a bird's egg falling to the pavement.

"Your Ladyship," said Pandareus, stepping down from the Rostra to meet Alphena. Julius Caesar had rebuilt in marble the curving steps decorated with the bronze rams, the Rostra, of Carthaginian warships captured centuries before. The Rostra was the Senate's original meeting place, but today and most days the senators were under the cover of the Basilica Julia on the southern edge of the Forum.

Alphena's escort had moved up. They pressed closer to their mistress than better-trained guards would have done. Pulto stood back, watching with a friendly smile. Corylus hadn't been sure how the old soldier would get on with Alphena's toughs, but there hadn't been any trouble. The parties respected one another, and nobody felt he had anything to prove.

Corylus joined them on the Forum pavement. Alphena backed to give him room, bumped one of her Illyrians, and snapped, "Drago! All of you! Get back three steps or I'll leave you back at the house the next time!"

That struck Corylus as an odd threat, but the escorts retreated obediently—not three paces, but enough to provide elbow room. Alphena made a grimace of apology to Corylus and said, "They have something to learn about deportment, but they're very, well, loyal."

Corylus lifted his chin in agreement. "They can learn deportment," he said. "I noticed you asked Pulto to lead you through the crowd, though."

"I thought that was better than explaining to Father that my guards had broken the ribs of some of his colleagues' sons," Alphena said with another grimace.

"I applaud your restraint, Your Ladyship," said Pandareus. "I have enough difficulty collecting my teaching fees as it is. But I presume you had a reason for visiting this morning? Besides the excellent presentation by Master Corylus, that is."

"What under Heaven was that about, anyway?" Alphena asked.

"An adulteress was thrown from the Tarpeian Rock but survived," Corylus said, embarrassed to hear himself explaining a rhetorical conceit to a layman. Laywoman. "I was defending her against the opinion that she should be thrown down again to complete her execution."

Alphena frowned and looked up the rugged side of the Capitolium. The roof of the Temple of Juno—the Mint—was barely visible from this angle.

Acanthus plants grew over the rocks at the bottom, but their tender leaves would not cushion a hundred-foot fall.

"But nobody could survive that," Alphena said.

"The purpose of the rhetorical exercises is to teach students how to reason and to argue," Pandareus said mildly. "The stated facts are merely to provide an occasion for learning."

He coughed and added with what Corylus thought was a smile, "I could explain this at any length that Your Ladyship might wish, if that is really the purpose of your visit?"

Alphena looked startled, then realized that Pandareus was making a joke. Her expression went in an eyeblink from anger—the old Alphena, being mocked by a wretched little Greek—to ruddy embarrassment.

Corylus frowned. The new Alphena who didn't rant and raise her voice if balked had been a pleasant metamorphosis. He wasn't sure how he felt about an Alphena who blushed, however.

"Varus and my mother disappeared yesterday," Alphena said. "In Polymartium. I just learned about it."

Then she said, "I'm sorry. I'm afraid. I was jabbering because I was afraid to face what happened. Whatever it was."

"The Temple of Saturn is empty at this time," Pandareus said, nodding toward the ancient building behind him. "There's a useful library in the attached treasury"—a pair of matching outbuildings on the opposite side of the altar platform from the main temple—"so I've gotten to know the priests and staff. They won't make a problem."

One of Alphena's guards said something Corylus didn't catch, but a scarred Illyrian growled, "Let 'em try," in bad Greek.

"Yes," Corylus said in Greek in a carrying tone. "Pulto, only the three of us will enter the building. You and the other servants will remain outside."

"Huh?" said Pulto. "Sure, it's just an empty temple, right?"

"Thank you, Corylus," Alphena said quietly. "Stylo"—a servant, one of Saxa's librarians—"give your case of notes to Master Corylus. All of you wait for us out here."

Pulto might not understand that his master had just avoided an embarrassing scene, but she did. While Alphena might not have her brother's intelligence—Corylus wasn't sure he knew anyone else who did—she was a great deal smarter than he had given her credit for being when he first met her.

Corylus took a basket of pierced wood inlaid with ivory and burl. There were over a dozen slim rolls of papyrus inside and a number of wax tablets besides. It was an ordinary book storage container, pressed into service for transport.

Pandareus beckoned from the temple entrance, where he was discussing matters with the doorman. Corylus palmed a silver piece from his purse as he followed Alphena, slipping it to the servant discreetly. It was an excessive tip for the purpose, but Publius Cispius was well-to-do by any standard but that of a senator.

Alphena's father was wealthy, of course, but the girl didn't carry cash. Besides the guards, her entourage was limited to her maid and the librarian. Alphena must have rushed off without the understeward who would ordinarily have accompanied her with a purse—which underscored the degree to which this wasn't an ordinary affair.

Even with the main doors open, the interior of the temple was dim to eyes that had been in the sunlight of the Forum. Tablets of thanks hung along the walls. Some were shaped to suggest the help the god had provided the dedicator: a ship saved from wrecking, a leg that had healed.

The limestone statue at the end of the room was of Saturn seated with a real sickle inset into his right hand. It was very old and had not been replaced by bronze or marble in the rebuilding that both Caesar and his adopted son, Augustus, had carried out in central Carce.

Corylus set the basket on the floor. He and Pandareus each pulled a scroll out to read as their eyes adapted.

"They all say about the same thing," Alphena said. "A circle of light appeared near the altar where the rite had taken place. An uncertain number of men and women came out of the light wearing skin garments or no clothing at all. There were horsemen or perhaps centaurs with them, and there was a chariot."

She took a deep breath. "There was confusion for many hours," she continued. "Then the intruders went back through the light, and the light vanished. Afterward the servants couldn't find Hedia or Varus. Most didn't remember seeing them after Mother had finished dancing the rite."

Pandareus finished reading the report he had taken at random. He waggled it and said, "This one is from Abinneus, a clerk with Manetho who was in charge of the entourage. He says there was a group of Indians in company with members of Senator Sentius' household and he thinks they caused the red light to appear. Then he became unconscious."

Corylus started to repress his chuckle, then realized there was no need to. "This," he said, tapping the report he'd been reading, "is from Minimus, one of Hedia's guards."

Corylus remembered the big Galatian as an individual. The fellow's deposition read oddly because the scribe who'd taken it down had put it into grammatical Greek—the Greek of ancient Athens, in fact. It was disconcerting to visualize the words coming from Minimus' lips. Corylus didn't doubt that account was accurate, though.

"What Minimus says is that Bacchus led a procession out of the rosy light and that there was an orgy like nothing he'd ever dreamed of," Corylus said. "Minimus is clearly worried that Her Ladyship disappeared—and worried that he'll be punished for letting her get out of his sight—but he's not embarrassed about the orgy. Rather proud of how well he acquitted himself, in fact."

Alphena's face had frozen. Pandareus gave a tiny smile and said, "It may be that Abinneus was not unconscious as he claims to have been, but for the moment I would accept his claim that he remembers nothing useful about later events."

He coughed into his hand and added, "When I was younger, that might even have been true of me under similar circumstances. Not that I was ever fortunate enough to find myself in similar circumstances."

"Mother may . . . ," Alphena said. She swallowed and went on, "It may be that Lady Hedia is quite all right and is simply taking advantage of opportunities."

"A Bacchic procession bursting out of thin air means that something potentially dangerous is happening," Corylus said. "Lady Hedia would regard it as her duty to report this. To us, because of what's happened in the past. Your mother would never shirk her duty."

"Quite right," said Pandareus, lifting his chin in approval. "And even granting that your brother is a young man, I do not believe that anything but knowledge would entrance him for more than perhaps a few hours."

The two men smiled. Alphena swallowed and bobbed her head in agreement.

"There's something else there . . . ," Corylus said. He realized that he was hesitating to discuss Gaius Saxa's problems publically. These were two of the people Corylus had intended to discuss his *own* plans with after Saxa had offered him the job, however, and it was the same information.

"That is," Corylus said, "you mentioned Lucius Sentius. Sentius apparently believes that Senator Saxa owns a magical object which Sentius wants. If Sentius' household was involved, is it possible that they kidnapped Varus and Lady Hedia to force Saxa to give up the object, the Ear of the Satyr? Saxa says he doesn't have the ear."

Corylus had been speaking to his teacher. He realized the implications of what he was saying and turned to Alphena. "I believe Lord Saxa," he said. "But Sentius apparently doesn't believe him."

"Lucius Sentius has the reputation of being interested in occult matters," Pandareus said. "A number of nobles do, of course."

"You mean my father," Alphena said sharply. "You don't have to hide his name."

Pandareus looked at the girl and smiled faintly. "I was thinking of the Emperor," he said in a mild tone. "In this company, I don't have to hide his name, either. Besides which, I am an old man and childless, so even imperial anger is not much of a threat to me."

"I'm sorry," Alphena said. She was expressionless, but her cheeks looked hot again. "I don't know what to do. There must be *something* to do. Should we take armed men to Polymartium?"

"I don't see what they could do, Your Ladyship," the teacher said. "I'm more interested in the fact that Sentius was looking for the Ear of the Satyr."

Pandareus looked at Corylus and raised his eyebrows in question. Corylus nodded and said, "That's correct. Lord Saxa is very precise about minutiae of this sort. Have you heard of it, the ear?"

Corylus and Pandareus were being very careful to avoid offending Alphena. Despite her recent campaign to control her behavior, the girl was used to giving free rein to her spiky emotions. In her present state she might react very badly to a perceived insult to a member of her family.

"Heard of it, yes, but only as a myth," the teacher said. "Atilius Priscus and I were discussing the relationship of music to speech. He said that in his grandfather's day a Marcus Herennius had claimed to have an iron locket which he called the Ear of the Satyr. With the ear he could hear birdsong as speech. Herennius was proscribed by the Second Triumvirate, and no one had heard of the ear since."

"Is that possible?" Alphena said. "Listening to birds speaking?"

"Judging from bird behavior," Pandareus said, "they are very stupid. I suspect one would have a more interesting time arguing philosophy with a group of gladiators. It seemed to me that the object was a myth which Herennius invented to raise his reputation. In certain circles."

"I remember Father talking about buying a collection that had belonged to someone named Herennius," Alphena said. She had recovered her composure. "He wouldn't tell me what the collection was, though. He gets, well, he *got* very 'I've got a secret' sometimes, and it was always something silly. It made me really mad."

"Pandareus?" Corylus said. "Do you know where Herennius was arrested?"

"He was at his country estate near Aricia," Pandareus said carefully, obviously wondering what Corylus meant by the line of questioning. "He'd rushed there from the city, hoping to go abroad. He grabbed up a saddlebag of gold and ordered his servants to hide the rest of the valuables, which included his collection. A pair of centurions caught him a few miles from the estate and cut his head off."

The old man smiled at the memory. "The reason I know that," he explained, "is because the servants threw the collection in the well. Priscus had acquired a parchment that was supposed to be the words and musical annotation that priests of Isis used in raising the dead. It was in a beautiful golden box decorated with jewels and enamel . . . but the manuscript itself had been completely destroyed by soaking. The box could be duplicated for a few thousand coppers, but the manuscript was irreplaceable."

Corylus laughed in sudden excitement. "A manuscript wouldn't have meant anything to common soldiers," he said. "Soldiers wouldn't have paid any attention to an iron locket, either. Which means if the Ear of the Satyr really did exist, I think I know where to find it."

"Let me talk to Father," Alphena said. "If we have to buy the whole estate, we can. I'm sure he'll be willing to trade this locket to get Mother and Varus back."

"That is a way to proceed," Pandareus said, starting for the outside door. "But I have my doubts about Sentius having kidnapped the pair by magic. Your brother has demonstrated magical power which I would rather not admit to believing."

"And Lady Hedia," Corylus said as they walked out of the temple together, "has proved considerably more dangerous than any magician she's faced."

. . .

HEDIA STEPPED THROUGH THE LENS of rosy light and found herself in what appeared to be a well-kept park. The lens had vanished.

She had expected to be in India. She had *feared* that she would be somewhere in the Otherworld facing a screaming mob of demons, monsters, and Who-Knew-What-All, like the band that had charged into Polymartium, only worse.

Hedia looked about her. She was certainly in the Otherworld. She had no real idea what India was like—she didn't know what Lusitania was like, except that she didn't want to go there any more than her husband did—but she was confident that in India a tiny human face wouldn't peek from beneath dock leaves. As she watched, the creature flew away on butterfly wings.

On the other hand, she wasn't in the midst of demons or even a Bacchic revel. The low brick wall in front of her seemed to have been the foundation of a building, but apart from the single wall there was nothing left, not even rubble. A line of junipers on the other side might have been planted, but the trees could as easily have grown from seeds dropped by birds sitting on the wall when it was higher.

Hedia turned to her right and began walking parallel to the wall. She saw no sign of a road or path, though there may have been one when the bricks were part of a building.

After fifty feet or so she came to a face of rock layered like a fancy dessert, purple-red and pale beige stone separated by thin bands of dark brown. Water bubbled from it. The flow seeped between the layers, she supposed, because there was no visible opening.

Hedia paused, then turned left to follow the course of the rivulet instead of continuing in the direction she had been going. She would have liked a guide—

Venus! I'd simply like someone to talk with!

—but that wasn't available. Hedia would walk as long as she could, and now at least she had water when she became thirsty. She looked at the stream, wondering what the best way of drinking would be. Probably from her cupped palms, but she supposed there was no reason not to bend over and suck water in directly. It would be undignified, but there was no one here to laugh at her for sticking her buttocks in the air.

The surface of the small creek eddied. One of the eddies looked like an ear, while the other could almost be a pair of lips. . . .

"Well, you could talk to me, Hedia," the lips said.

Hedia missed a step. The eddies hung in place while she hesitated, then moved downstream beside her as she walked on.

"Where are you going, anyway?" the lips said. "There's nothing *you* want in this direction."

Rather than answering, Hedia snapped, "How do you know my name?"

The stream laughed. "Oh, I know much more than that, Hedia," the lips said. "I know that there's a fellow named Boest on the other side of the ridge beyond me—to your right, as you're walking now."

Hedia looked in the direction indicated. The slope didn't look impossibly steep. The terrain was similar to that outside Polymartium where she had danced to Mother Matuta; Hedia wondered if she was in the same place—but in the Otherworld.

"Why should I care about this Boest, Stream?" she said, continuing to walk.

"Why indeed?" chuckled the stream. It was less than two feet wide and shallow; she could step across it easily. "Perhaps because Boest knows where the Spring of True Answers is. Aren't you looking for true answers, Hedia?"

Hedia raised her left arm to sweep aside the fronds of a weeping willow that hung across the path. Before she touched them, the branches support- ing the tendrils swept upward and cleared her path.

"Do you know where this spring is, then?" Hedia said, looking down into the clear stream.

"You should ask Boest," the lips said, wobbling as they spoke. "He's a water spirit. He'll know."

"All right," Hedia said, stepping over the water as easily as she had ex- pected. "I will. Good day to you, Stream."

Because of the outdoor ceremony, she had worn sturdier sandals than she might otherwise have done. The circle around the altar had been raked clean of pebbles—almost clean—so the soles of her feet hadn't been badly bruised even during the barefoot dance. Hedia had no immediate problems.

As for Boest . . .

Hedia smiled. Spirit or not, he seemed to be male. She'd generally gotten along well enough with males.

VARUS STAGGERED AS HE ALWAYS DID when he returned to the Waking World after visiting with the Sibyl. Unfortunately—

He looked around to be sure, but there could be no question.

—he wasn't in the Waking World this time. He stood on a pond covered with water lilies. The three women watching him flicked their fish tails as they dived.

Varus waggled his toes; the water didn't ripple. He was standing in the air *over* a pond. The shore was a hundred feet away at the nearest and much farther in all other directions. He must have followed the Indian delegation into the Otherworld as he remembered telling the Sibyl he would, but the Indians were nowhere to be seen.

A few clumps of large shrubs grew on land near the shore, but their crooked trunks shouldn't have been able to conceal the bright clothing of the Indian officials. Other than the shrubs, the land seemed to be arid scrub with more bare dirt than vegetation.

A chicken-sized bird sat on a shallow nest of reeds. She was almost close enough for Varus to have stretched out his leg and tickled her with his sandal.

Even when he glanced that way, he might not have noticed the bird if she hadn't said peevishly, "Look, you don't belong here. Just get on back to land and leave us alone."

"Good morning"—*is it morning?*—"Bird," Varus said. "I'm looking for a party of seven men, some of them wearing bright clothing. They may have passed by here—"

Or simply appeared out of the air, as he probably had.

"—about ten minutes ago."

The bird's back and breast were brown, but there was a bright golden patch on the back of her neck. Varus couldn't imagine why he hadn't seen the creature immediately.

"I don't know anything!" she shrilled. "Get out of here, why don't you?"

Varus pursed his lips. He didn't lash out the way his sister did—or anyway, as she used to do—nor could he make anybody believe the sort of cold threats that Hedia used when she thought they were necessary, but he had learned ways of coping with unreasonable and unpleasant people.

"I'm sorry to hear that, Bird," he said. "Perhaps I should ask your eggs what they may have seen."

There were three eggs in the nest, their shells the same glossy brown as the bird's feathers. They were so large that Varus could see them even with the bird brooding. When he spoke, it—she?—leaped to her feet. Her claws were very long. She shrilled, "What are you talking about! Can't you just leave us alone?"

Then, in the calmer tone that Varus had hoped to hear in the first place, the bird said, "There may have been some people that way—"

She extended a brown-and-white wing toward the near shore.

"—but it was way off on the horizon, and I didn't pay much attention. They weren't bothering me, so why would I bother them?"

"Thank you, Mistress Bird," Varus said. He bowed slightly and started toward the shore.

"Say . . . ?" the bird called after him. "Human?"

He looked back over his shoulder. She was still standing above her eggs.

"Yes, Mistress Bird?" he said.

"How is it you're able to walk on water?" she said. "You're not running across the lily pads like I do."

Varus weighed the response in his mind. With a smile of self-mockery he said, "It may be because I'm a great magician, Mistress Bird."

The bird bobbed her head quickly. "Thought so," she said. "Thought so. Well, you go find your friends or whatever they are. I don't guess there'll be any reason for you to come back this way, right?"

"I do not think so," Varus said. *I have absolutely no idea what I'll be doing in the future. For the moment, I'm walking in the direction you pointed.* "Farewell, Mistress Bird."

When Varus walked beyond the surface of the pond, his feet squelched in the marshy ground. It was firm a few steps farther on, but his sandals and toes were muddy.

Perhaps the Sibylline Books *contain a spell to clean the feet of magicians,* Varus thought. He couldn't accept intellectually the idea that he had magical powers. He didn't *really* believe that anyone had magical powers, yet here he was in a realm of magic.

A lizard raised its head from the slanting trunk of one of the shrubs. "If magic isn't real," the lizard said, "then you must have gone mad. Have you?"

The lizard was nearly as long as Varus was tall, but he hadn't noticed the creature before it moved. *I'm not very observant of the world around me.* Its forked black tongue flicked the air when it spoke.

"I don't think I would accept myself as a reliable witness to that question," Varus said politely. He walked on.

The Sibyl claimed she was part of his own imagination. If that was true, then his imagination could have invented the bird and lizard also. *And per-*

haps I am mad, but then are my friends who see the same things mad also? Or are they as imaginary as the bird and lizard?

Varus looked back the way he had come. The pond, which from this higher ground seemed to be a swelling in a shallow river, was at the edge of his vision. That meant the people the bird saw must have appeared near where he stood now.

He couldn't see the bird. *I didn't see her when she was in arm's length,* he thought wryly.

Slightly to the right in the direction Varus had been walking was what he had thought was a gray stump. Now that he was closer, he saw that it was a waist-high stone cone on a square base. The sides of the base were carved in high relief with figures whose supple limbs intertwined. The curves put Varus in mind of Scythian broaches, but Scythian work was stylized while these in stone were intended for real humans and animals.

"It's a spiritual focus," said a rasping voice behind him. "A group of humans from the Waking World used it to enter here not long ago."

Varus turned, pleased with himself not to have jumped. A lion peered from a clump of dry grass that Varus had walked past a moment before. The lion's mane was short and almost as pale as the cat's tawny hide, but he seemed a very healthy animal.

"Three of those humans had swords," the lion said musingly. He stretched out his right foreleg and spread the claws. Varus had never looked so closely at a lion's paw. It was much wider than he would have imagined. "And at least one was a magician as well, or they wouldn't have been able to appear the way they did."

"That's the party I'm looking for," Varus said. His voice did not waver. "Can you tell me in which direction they went, Master Lion?"

"Well," said the lion, rolling up onto all fours, "I'm not sure that the question really matters to you. You don't have a sword, do you?"

When the lion spoke, his breath stank of rotting flesh. His great teeth were mostly yellow but black at the gum line.

"I am a citizen of Carce!" Varus said. His voice was firm. Perhaps even a philosopher could be granted a final grain of pride in the last moment before he was devoured.

The lion gave a thunderous laugh. "No doubt, no doubt," he said, "but again it seems a distinction without a difference to either of us."

He hunched, his hind legs drawn up as tight as the arms of a cocked catapult.

In the back of Varus' mind, an ancient woman cackled, *You will be utterly devoured by fire!*

The words didn't reach Varus' lips, but the lion snarled and sprang sideways, hitting on his shoulder in his haste to escape. He rolled to his feet and disappeared into the brush in a flat fifty-foot leap. His voice quavered back, "How was I to know!"

Varus blinked. Dust was settling where the lion's feet had kicked it from the ground. Other than that—and a remaining hint of rotting meat—the beast might never have existed.

I suppose that was a line from the Sibylline Books, Varus thought. Which he would not be permitted to see unless and until he became a senator and was appointed to the Commission for Sacred Rites. *I wonder whether my being told the contents by the prophetess herself is a violation of religious law?*

That was the sort of whimsy Varus used to discuss with Pandareus and Corylus. Good training for the mind, he supposed, like the formal subjects set for declamations.

He felt a stab of nostalgia for that time a few months past when he dreaded having to make presentations before the class. *I was more afraid of my classmates in the Forum than I was to face demons not so very much later.*

Varus continued walking in the direction he had followed from the pond. *A pity that the lion didn't take my question seriously, but on balance I can't complain about the way matters had worked out. It might have been a great deal worse.*

He reached better-watered country with frequent palm trees and stands of supple-limbed bushes. Ivy covered the soil between the larger vegetation.

The palms swayed as Varus approached. *Breezes?* he thought, though the air at ground level was still. When he came close to a palm, he saw that it was crawling away on tiny roots. They wriggled like handfuls of worms at the base of its trunk.

It's afraid of me! he realized, suddenly furious at the injustice. He wouldn't hurt trees; he *couldn't* hurt them!

I will burn up mountains and rivers! chirped a tiny voice in Varus' mind. *I will dry up springs with my fire!*

He thought that the Sibyl's voice sounded coldly amused, but he might have been reading too much into what was barely a whisper. *I've been ignored for most of my life, even by servants,* Varus thought. *Now I'm a monster.*

And he thought, *I'd rather be ignored.*

The brush ahead swished as Bhiku pushed through it.

The old man smiled to see Varus, then bowed deeply with his palms pressed together in front of him. "Lord Varus!" he said. "I hadn't realized you wished to come with us. I'm delighted to see you again, delighted!"

"I . . . ," Varus said. "To be honest, I didn't make up my mind until you and your party had already gone through the portal. Ah—will I be welcome with your companions?"

Bhiku laughed cheerfully. "I left them in a safe place, an outcrop surrounded by a flowing stream," he said. "They're terrified of being without me in the Otherworld, even Lord Arpat. They'll fall all over themselves when I tell them that you are a magician of such power that we have nothing further to fear in this place."

"I would be pleased to accompany you," Varus said. He thought of adding that he didn't claim to be a magician, but he had already told Bhiku that back in Polymartium. It irritated him to be told the same thing repeatedly by someone, since it implied that he was too stupid to have understood it the first time.

Besides, given the way the lion—let alone the palm tree!—had reacted, it seemed that Varus *was* a magician in this place. Suggesting a lie was the same thing as lying, which he would do only if it was necessary.

As the old man led them through the shrubbery, Varus said, "How did you find me, Master Bhiku? I was at a loss as to where you had gone."

Bhiku chuckled, sounding disturbingly like the Sibyl. "I suppose that to a magician of your power, other students of the art are invisible in your own glare," he said. "For me to notice you, however, is like seeing that the sun has risen. Even with my eyes closed, your presence is unmistakable."

"I see," said Varus. He didn't, of course, but it was the polite thing to say.

Bhiku pushed through the last fronds of brush and onto a slope of ivy leading to a stream. Varus thought he saw human faces looking up from the vines, but the figures could only have been a finger's length tall if they really were people.

The rest of the Indian delegation crowded together on a barren rock. The two gardeners and the general servant were at the narrow tip, while the silk-clad nobles shared the remaining two-thirds of the space. All six looked unhappy.

The blue-clad leader snarled something in an unfamiliar language. There wouldn't have been much doubt about his meaning, even if he hadn't rested his hand on the pommel of his curved sword.

"It was time well spent, Lord Arpat," Bhiku said in Greek. "This is the great wizard from Carce, who can protect us as only Lord Govinda himself could. We will be perfectly safe under his escort."

"Can we get off this rock now?" said another of the nobles.

"Indeed you can, Lord Yama," the old man said. "We will go immediately to our entrance to the Waking World and to the enlightenment of Lord Govinda."

The Indians hopped to the shore. Arpat's right sandal landed short, wetting the silk. A trio of frogs raised their heads from the stream and began laughing, only to duck underwater again when Varus glanced toward them.

"I'm looking forward to discussions with you when we've reached home, Lord Varus," Bhiku said brightly as he set off at a brisk pace. "To be honest, I'm not comfortable here in the Otherworld myself. A magician of your power probably can't imagine that."

"Oh," said Varus. "I think I can."

And I'm not very comfortable about what I'll find in India, either. But I'll deal with that when I come to it.

CHAPTER IV

Varus walked directly behind Bhiku along the path worn through the forest. *Worn by what?* He wondered if the trees would be any more familiar to Corylus, who had a real knack for the subject.

"Is this vegetation the same as that from where you come?" he asked Bhiku. "The same as India's?"

The sage paused beside a palm tree. A vine curled up the trunk and dangled scores of brilliantly white flowers from the crest.

"I can't really say," Bhiku admitted, walking on again. "I'm afraid I never studied plants, interesting though I'm sure they are. We could ask the gardeners if you like."

"Of course they're the same!" called a voice from above.

Varus and Bhiku stopped again and looked up. The three noblemen had held their swords in their hands ever since the path had led them into the jungle, but they jumped into a posture of defense. Yama even slashed his curved blade twice through the empty air.

"*We're* not the same, though," said one of the white flowers, its petals forming lips as it spoke. "You've never seen a datura vine as handsome as we are."

Bhiku looked at Varus and raised an eyebrow. Varus shrugged and said, "He's probably right. Or she is, of course. But I'm not sure I'd ever seen a datura vine before."

He shook his head and added, as much to himself as to his companion, "There are so many things I ought to know about."

Bhiku cackled laughter.

"Shouldn't we get to the portal soon, servant?" Lord Arpat said. Snarled, rather.

Varus looked back at the husky Indian noble, his face still. *I'm not a noble-man here*, he remembered before he spoke. *I'm a foreigner with no friends except for an old man of no status.*

"We have arrived, Your Lordship," said Bhiku, bowing low. He straightened and gestured ahead with his left arm. Varus could see a pile of reddish rock through scattered gaps in the vegetation.

Varus walked past the rock alongside Bhiku. *It's a pillar rather than an outcrop*, he thought. Then on the other side he saw the rock was carved with the huge beaming head of a man wearing a high headdress. The pillar faced a twenty-foot area in which the vegetation was stunted to ankle height or less.

"This stupa is our focus here in the Otherworld," Bhiku explained. "We will return—arrive, that is, in your case—at a temple in the territory of Ramsa Lal, a dependent of Lord Govinda."

Bhiku drew Varus to the side so as not to be in the way of the noblemen, who had broken into a trot at the sage's words. The three commoners lurched after them as quickly as they could without treading too closely on the heels of the men with swords in their hands.

The Indians—except Bhiku—were badly afraid, Varus realized. Thinking of Lord Arpat as a man lashing out in terror made him a less unpleasant figure that he had been as a surly brute.

Not that I would ever find Arpat a congenial companion.

Bhiku knelt in front of the stone face. "Would you help me prepare the ground, Lord Varus?" he said. He looked over his shoulder and added, "You're welcome to join us, Lord Arpat. There's no danger at this stage. Well, almost no danger."

The three nobles rushed back to the edge of the clearing. The gardeners and the general servant would not have understood the Greek, but they reacted to the nobles' panic with similar haste.

Varus knelt and copied Bhiku in pulling little plants out of the dry soil. The vegetation close to the pillar was even more stunted than what grew farther back where the other Indians cowered.

"Danger?" Varus said quietly.

The sage smiled. "There is always the chance of danger, is there not?" he said. "But not as great a danger here as our companions seem to believe."

He coughed. "I noticed your smile as you turned away from Lord Arpat," Bhiku went on. "Were you amused by his belief that a wizard of your power could be threatened by a mere sword?"

Varus smiled again. "No," he said. "I'm not sure that's true, and it *certainly* isn't the way I think. I was remembering that the soldiers who guard the frontiers of our Republic undergo terrible hardships and risks. Certainly worse hardships than anything we've undergone in reaching this place—"

He gestured to the stupa.

"—and probably worse dangers also, at least when the tribes are restless. But for the past century they've been volunteers, so they don't have reason to complain. From what my friend Corylus tells me, they *don't* seriously complain, though all soldiers gripe at all times."

Varus smiled more broadly. "I came with you by my own choice," he said. "I volunteered. I have met many men like Arpat in Carce. They treat me with deference because of who I am and who my father is. But I *chose* not to stay in Carce."

Bhiku smoothed the dust with the edge of his palm. He looked at Varus and said, "It is a pleasure to meet a man with so similar a viewpoint. Though in my case, the humility came with my birth."

Bhiku wore a satchel of coarse cloth over one shoulder. He hitched it around in front of him and took out a square of singed linen with a steel fire starter and a lump of pyrite. He dipped into the pouch a second time and brought out a bundle of barley straw—tied with a longer strand—and small roll of bark.

"Get on with it, servant!" Lord Yama called.

"Yes, Your Lordship," Bhiku said without looking up from his work on the fire set. He hefted the bark and added quietly to Varus, "This is cinnamon."

Holding the fire starter next to the linen, he scraped the pyrites down the ridged steel. Sparks sprayed out with a whiff of brimstone. The cloth smoldered, then flamed as Bhiku breathed on it and began feeding bits of straw.

When most of the bundle was alight, he set the cinnamon on the flames and stood up. Varus rose also and moved back a little distance.

Bhiku raised his arms at an angle before him and began chanting in a language that Varus didn't know. Varus frowned, because he didn't think—he couldn't be sure, of course—that the incantation was in the same language in which the sage spoke to his fellow Indians.

The smoke rose, thicker than Varus would have expected from dry straw and a thin scrap of bark. Bhiku stopped chanting.

For a moment Varus saw flames; then a pink blur replaced the fire set and began to expand. Though it was small at the moment, the disk was much like the one Varus had seen in Polymartium this morning. Bhiku backed away and joined him.

"There will be soldiers from Ramsa Lal at the other focus," Bhiku said softly. "They will escort Arpat and his fellows to Lord Govinda, but I will take you to the palace of my own master, Raguram."

"Will I be welcome?" Varus said.

Bhiku laughed. "No one will notice you," he said. "No one notices me unless they have a need for magic. I hope you have a taste for lentils and barley, because in that case you'll have plenty to eat."

Arpat shouted to Bhiku. The sage bowed and in Greek replied, "You may enter the portal now, Lord Arpat."

The nobles rushed forward. Yama had sheathed his curved sword, but the other two still held theirs. Arpat was the first through the shimmering lens, and his fellows jostled to follow him. The servants ran through a step and a half step after them.

Instead of running to the lens at once, Bhiku said musingly, "I am a very slight magician, Lord Varus, but I like to think that I have gathered a good deal of wisdom in the course of a long life. Yet almost no one is interested in what I think is wisdom."

"I haven't noticed . . . ," Varus said in answer to the implied question, "that the priorities are any different in Carce."

Laughing, the two philosophers stepped into the portal.

HEDIA LOOKED AT THE SLOPE before her and pressed her lips into a moue. Her sandals were well enough suited for the hike—better than her thigh muscles were, she suspected.

Her long silk tunic, however, had been chosen to swirl attractively during the dance. It was not ideal for walking through brush. She'd had to gather it up as soon as she realized that the manager's wife would otherwise be walking on it and rip it off.

Hedia sighed and drew up the tunic again, tucking the excess fabric under her sash. That meant her shins would be scratched, but it was better than being constantly tangled *and* still scratched, for the thin silk would be very little protection.

"I was thinking, Your Ladyship . . . ," said a piping voice.

Hedia whirled around. The eddies had vanished from the water, and the voice didn't sound as the stream's had anyway.

"I'm down at your feet, Your Ladyship," the voice said, sounding mildly exasperated. "As I said, I was thinking that you might—"

She looked down. "You're a toad!" she said.

"Yes, named Paddock if you care to know," said the toad. He was about the size of her clenched fist and a rusty red color. "Now that we've taken care of formalities, I was thinking that you might carry me with you when you visit Boest."

"Why did you think that?" Hedia said coldly. "Why in the name of *Venus* did you think that?"

"Perhaps because your aura shows that you are kindly person, always looking out for the downtrodden?" said the toad.

"You are either very stupid . . . ," Hedia said as she finished tucking up her skirt, "or you are mad."

She strode off. The toad hopped clumsily along beside her. "Not stupid," he said. "No no no, not that. And not mad, either, though I do have a very dry sense of humor. And I don't weigh very much."

Hedia paused and looked down again. The toad looked up expectantly at her.

"Will you give me warts?" she asked.

"I will not," said Paddock. "If you're worried, though, just squat and make a sling of a fold of your skirt. I'll get into it myself."

Hedia tugged a pocket into the extra fabric. "I'm not concerned," she said. She bent down and lifted the toad to the pocket. His skin felt rough but dry against her palm.

Instead of hopping from her hand, Paddock clambered into the sling. He really did seem clumsy.

"Why do you want to climb the hill?" Hedia said, pushing into the waist-high grass. There wasn't a path. The grass made her lower legs and bare arms itch, but it was more of an irritation than a serious hindrance. Higher up the slope, heather and a few palmettos replaced the grass. Farther down she could avoid the clumps of heather.

"Oh, I used to know Boest," the toad said. "I haven't seen him in a long time, and since you were going that way I thought I would accompany you. With your permission, of course."

Hedia paused. "Do you know where the Spring of True Answers is, Paddock?" she said.

"I never traveled much," the toad said. "I was content with what I had.

But when Boest moved to where he is now, I had to leave. It isn't a good place for a toad, you see."

The heather bushes didn't grow as closely together as Hedia had thought when she was standing beside the spring. She found herself cupping her hand to prevent branches from slapping the toad, but it really wasn't a problem. A few prickles pulled tufts in her skirt, but that was of no consequence.

"What do you mean?" Hedia said. "Toads live anywhere, don't you?"

She had never really thought about the question. Varus probably had, though; the boy seemed to think about everything. And Publius Corylus was much the same. Toads were simply something you saw in the garden in the evening. They ate slugs, a gardener had told her, presumably imagining that she cared about toads, or slugs, or much of anything in a garden.

"Not really," Paddock said. "We're almost to the valley where Boest lives, so you'll see."

Hedia was winded from the climb, but she was forcing herself to breathe only through her nose. Gulping mouthfuls of air would be undignified. Though the only person present to observe her was a talking toad, the principle was a good one.

Her legs, however—her hamstrings—burned fiercely. She stopped for a moment just below the crest of the ridge, wondering if she was going to be able to climb the last twenty feet or if she would have to crawl on all fours.

"The dancing you did earlier strained your muscles," Paddock said. "It isn't serious."

Hedia looked down at him. "I didn't think it was," she said sharply.

She strode to the top with no difficulty; the brief pause had been enough to relax the muscles. Then she said, "I suppose I was worried. I shouldn't have snapped at you."

"I am just a toad," said the toad.

Hedia looked down with a smile that would have soured wine. "What you are is of no consequence," she said. "But I was lying to myself also, which is an offense for which I would flay anyone else."

Paddock nodded. "Of course, Your Ladyship," he said. She could not detect mockery in his voice, but she suspected it was there anyway. She continued to smile.

The valley into which they had crossed was beige, not green as the one behind them had been. For a moment Hedia didn't think that there was any vegetation. There was, but the heather bushes were widely scattered and nearly leafless. What foliage there was seemed almost as pale as the dry soil.

"Not a good place for a toad," Paddock repeated sadly.

"I see," said Hedia.

This was a horrible place. What little breeze there was picked up wisps of dust and curled them along. The dust was the only thing moving. *Venus! What a horrible place.*

As Hedia looked longer at the scene, her eyes began to discriminate within the initial sameness. There were goats among the heather, small animals whose hair either was the same hue as the dust or was so dusty that the original color did not show through. The goats were browsing the bushes, but they moved so rarely that she could only identify them by shape.

"Where is the herdsman?" Hedia said, suddenly glad that she had brought the toad with her.

"Boest is midway below us on this slope," Paddock said. "He can watch his herd from there."

What Hedia had taken for a somewhat larger heather bush resolved into the figure of a seated man looking away from her, across the valley. He was wearing a goatskin garment. There was nothing on his head but his own shaggy hair.

She started down briskly, kicking grit into the toes of her sandals. She grimaced, but it was much the same as every other aspect of this place.

I chose to come every step of the way that has led me here, Hedia realized. She smiled again. It felt good to have someone to blame.

Boest was a large man, though what must once have been a powerful build was now cadaverous. He looked up when Hedia reached his side, then resumed slowly scanning the valley and his herd.

"Master Boest?" Hedia said, puzzled but determined not to show it. "I am Hedia, wife of Gaius Alphenus Saxa, senator and former consul of Carce."

"Ah," said Boest without looking up again.

"You are Master Boest, are you not?" Hedia said. *It will really be the sauce on the fish if I've come to the wrong place.*

"What?" said the man. "I'm Boest. I've always been Boest."

"Hello, Boest," the toad said. "I came back with her."

This time Boest turned with something approaching animation. "Paddock?" he said. He frowned. "Is that you? You've changed."

"I thought I'd better change," the toad said. "Before Gilise started look-ing for me, you know."

"Ah," Boest said. "I see that."

Paddock made a sound that might have been a cough to clear his throat, then said, "I thought I might stay with you for a while, Boest. Is that all right?"

The big man frowned again. "You can stay, Paddock," he said. "If you think you'll be all right. I didn't want you to go, you know."

"I'll be all right," Paddock said. "For a few days, you know."

"I'm glad to be the instrument of two friends reuniting," Hedia said, her voice quiet but rigidly controlled. "I came here for information, though, which I'm told you can give me, Master Boest. I'm looking for the Spring of True Answers. Can you lead me to it?"

"I know where it is," Boest said. "But you'll have to go yourself if you really want to. There's no reason to leave here, you know."

"I'm looking for my son," Hedia said, keeping hold of her fraying temper. "I'm told the spring will know where he is, so I need to find the spring. I will pay—"

She hadn't any idea how, but she would figure something out.

"—whatever you wish to lead me to the spring."

Boest smiled at her. "I used to worry about things like that," he said. "I used to worry about so many things. Not now, though. Not since Gilise took my soul."

"Who is Gilise?" Hedia said. Interest began to crowd frustration out of her mind. There could be something to do beyond standing here and listen-ing to flaccid nonsense.

"Gilise is an air spirit," Paddock said. "Gilise visited us when we lived in the valley over the next ridge, Boest and I."

"Gilise is a lovely boy," Boest said, staring at the hills across the valley. His lips quirked into a suspicion of a smile, the first expression Hedia had seen on the big man's face. "I loved him, you know."

"There's water in that valley," Paddock said. "Gilise is still there, but he sent Boest away. I came with him because I couldn't stay with Gilise. And I kept going, because a toad cannot live long in this place, either."

"Streams flow through the layers of rock from the mountains," Boest said calmly. "But not to this valley. The one I used to live in and the one you and Paddock came from, Hedia, but not here where Boest sent me to live after he took my soul."

"But why don't you go back to where the water is?" Hedia said. "And take your soul back?"

"It doesn't matter," said Boest with the same almost smile. "I used to worry about so many things, but not now."

He looked up at Hedia and said, "He bent over me when I was resting, and he put his mouth on my mouth. And I smiled, and he sucked my breath out, I thought, and blew it into a phial and stoppered it."

"Only it wasn't Boest's breath," said Paddock. "It was his soul."

"It was my soul," Boest agreed without emotion.

He paused, then almost smiled again. "Gilise said he loved me, but he was probably lying. I loved him, though that doesn't matter anymore. Nothing matters."

"I see," said Hedia. She did see. It had just been a matter of waiting until the facts came out. "I think I will visit Master Gilise. Are you coming with me, Paddock?"

"You don't need me," the toad said. "I will stay here awhile with my friend Boest."

"As you please," said Hedia. She squatted. Paddock hopped out of the sling before she placed her hand to help him.

Hedia started across the valley, wondering if she should have asked for something to drink. She would probably do better on Gilise's side of the ridge, and she didn't suppose Boest had much liquid to spare.

Twenty feet down the slope, Hedia looked back. Boest was slowly scanning the valley, as he had been when she first saw him.

The toad was seated in Boest's lap.

ALPHENA SAT BESIDE CORYLUS, facing backward ahead of the cart's single axle. Pandareus and Pulto were on the rear bench, skewing their legs sideways so that their knees didn't touch those of the front passengers.

Although the mail coach forced them so close together, Alphena found she had to raise her voice considerably to be heard over the *thrumm* of the iron tires on the stone pavers. It was like being out in a storm. You only noticed the occasional thunderclaps, but when you tried to speak the pounding of the rain blurred your words.

Corylus twisted to look toward the larger wagon in front in which half the escort rode. Noticing his movement, the driver leaned back and shouted in Sicilian Greek, "We'll be stopping in two miles to change the team. The estate's not far beyond, but if we wait till we're coming back we may not get so good a choice of mules!"

"We're stopping at the changing station!" Corylus said, relaying the information to the men in back. Pulto raised a finger in silent acknowledgment; Pandareus nodded. The teacher was reading a papyrus scroll, though Alphena couldn't imagine how he could with the ride's vibration. The cart's leather top was folded back, so at least Pandareus had plenty of light.

Alphena looked at the youth beside her. Corylus had been born on the Rhine; his height and red/blond hair came from his Celtic mother. His father could not marry as a serving soldier, but he had acknowledged the son as legitimate and would have married the woman when he was discharged. She—Coryla—had died in childbirth, and Cispius had not married at all. Anna, now the wife of Corylus' servant Marcus Pulto, had been the boy's nurse.

Corylus saw even less of his mother than I did of mine, Alphena thought. *Though not much less.*

The Emperor Augustus had made it a point of policy that citizens should have children. His edicts were widely ignored within the nobility, and not even Augustus expected noble mothers to *raise* the children themselves.

Marcia, Saxa's first wife, had borne two children and had died of fever a week after the second. Her sister—also Marcia; women did not have names of their own, only the feminine form of their father's family—was married to Saxa for a few years, but Varus and Alphena saw almost as little of her before the divorce as they did afterward.

Saxa had been kindly enough, but he was no more interested in his children than he was in the crops being planted on his Lucanian estates . . . or, for that matter, in the fact that he *had* estates in Lucania. Hedia, Saxa's third wife, was the first person to really act as a parent to Varus and Alphena.

Alphena smiled faintly. Hedia had come as a real surprise to Saxa's tomboy daughter.

"Corylus?" she said, confident that the noise of the ride would keep their discussion confidential. "What do you think we should do?"

Corylus' eyes narrowed as he returned her gaze. "I think we should go to the estate of Curtianus Major near Aricia . . . ," he said carefully. "And retrieve if possible the amulet which the former owner Herennius may have hidden there seventy years ago. As we planned yesterday."

"Yes," said Alphena. She didn't snap at the answer the way she might have done six months before. "But what should we do *then?* How will the amulet help us find Mother and Varus?"

The driver shouted to his pair of mules, and the coach swayed. Both Alphena and Corylus turned to look forward. There had been some sort of obstacle on the road ahead, but the escorts in the leading wagon had cleared the way. They were clambering back aboard as their vehicle rolled on.

Alphena's own driver clucked his team forward. A cartload of cheap pottery coming into Carce had tipped when a wheel came off, spilling the cargo across the width of the roadway. The escorts had cut the reins of the single ox and manhandled the cart into the ditch. The ox was cropping grass from the shoulder. Earthenware crunched under the wheels of Alphena's mail coach.

The angry carter picked up a large potsherd as if to shy it after the escorts. He dropped it again quickly when he noticed that a similar wagon brought up the rear.

Pulto laughed as their coach rolled on. "That boyo better be well away from the road before the guys behind come up with him," he said. "They're jealous about not having anything to do. They might make something outa him picking up a rock."

"They'll get to lead on the way back," Corylus said, raising his voice as the roar of the wheels increased.

Alphena suddenly thought about her escort as people. They had simply *been* for most of her life, like maids and gardeners and soldiers . . . but soldiers were on the frontier, so she thought about them even less than she did about her servants.

Until she met Publius Corylus. He hadn't formally been a soldier, but he had been raised with them and by them, and he had crossed the Danube with the Scout company of his father's squadron. Had crossed it frequently, from the stories that Pulto's wife told and Florina had relayed to her mistress.

Corylus must have been thinking about Alphena's question while she thought about him. He said, "I don't have enough information to say anything useful. If we find the ear, when we find it, we'll see what it does."

He met her eyes, smiled, and shrugged. He had an engaging smile. "If the amulet doesn't do anything," he said, "or maybe even if it does, we might be able to trade it to Sentius to get Her Ladyship and Gaius back."

Corylus shrugged again. "But who knows?" he said. "I don't think that any

gang of Sentius' could've snatched Her Ladyship away from her escort anyway. Maybe after we learn more I'll change my mind."

But how are we going to learn more? Alphena thought. But Corylus had
already answered that, by saying that he didn't know.

"There has to be a better answer than that!" Alphena said.

"Sometimes there isn't," Corylus said, though he couldn't have known that
she was responding to the words in her own mind rather than to what he
had actually said. "You learn that on the frontier. Sometimes there's nothing
but hoping that your buddies find your body and you get a proper funeral."

His face hardened and his laughter clicked like rocks rattling together.

"And sometimes your buddies are there with you," he said. "I helped bury
a whole platoon once after their barge tipped over in the Danube and they
got swept under ice."

I've seen hundreds of people die in the arena, Alphena thought. *Maybe thousands. But they weren't people to me, any more than my servants were people.
Corylus cared about those soldiers.*

"Publius Corylus . . . ," Alphena said. *The world changed when you thought
about what people were doing, instead of what they were doing for you or to you.*
"Are you going to go to Lusitania for my father?"

Corylus laced his fingers backward, then watched them as he stretched
his arms out in front of him. He wasn't so much looking away from her as
looking toward a neutral point while he gathered his thoughts. He lowered
his arms and smiled at Alphena again.

"I'm not sure," he said, letting the smile widen. "For the same reason. I
don't know enough yet to judge. It may be that Sentius is behind both problems, the rumors about Lusitania and whatever happened to Hedia and
Gaius. Ah—"

"Calling them Hedia and Gaius is fine," Alphena said. She felt suddenly
warm; she looked away. "You and I don't have to stand on ceremony anymore."

"I don't guess we do," said Corylus, looking away. After a moment he said,
"This shouldn't be my job. I'm like my dad. He's about as good a tactician as
you're going to meet, but he never commanded anything bigger than a squadron of cavalry. He'd have been a terrible army commander. I'm not saying
that Carce hasn't had other bad generals, but Dad would have known how
bad he was."

"You're not your father," Alphena said, watching Corylus in profile.

He turned and met her eyes, smiling again. "No," he said, "but I'd be even worse. I don't have Dad's experience, and I've got the same focus on what I can *see* right in front of me."

Corylus shook his head ruefully, though he didn't lose his grin. "If somebody figures out where our friends are, I'll plan the rescue about as well as anybody else could. Maybe even as well as Dad—I spent more time with the Scouts than he did. But as soon as we've got them loose, I'll ask Varus and your mother to take over the planning."

"But you're *smart*," Alphena said, trying to get her mind around what Corylus was telling her. "I've seen you in class. And I've seen you fight."

"Yeah, you have," Corylus said, his grin lopsided now. "And I'd rather have you on my left side than lots of veterans. Pulto—"

Corylus lowered his voice slightly, though there was no chance that the men facing them would overhear the discussion over the rumble of coach wheels.

"—has enough guts for a legion, but he'd freeze if a demon came at him. That's true of most soldiers, most *people*. But—"

Corylus moved his hands in frustration, as if trying to grasp a beam of sunlight.

"—I don't think the way a general has to. Your mother, now, she'd be Hell's own general. I wouldn't exactly feel comfortable serving under her, but I'd know that if she sent me out to be killed there'd be a bloody good reason for it. Even though she wouldn't think twice before she did it."

"I thought my father was a fool," Alphena said. She was speaking almost to herself. She met Corylus' eyes and said more clearly, "I grew up believing he was a fool, and when he married Hedia I wondered if he'd gone mad. But I see now that he was right about H-he . . . about *Mother*. And I think maybe he was less of a fool before than I thought he was too."

Corylus nodded agreement. His eyes were far away for the moment, and a slow grin spread across his face. Alphena felt herself blush.

"I wish Hedia was here to tell us what to do," he said quietly. "And I wish even more that Gaius Varus was here. Because he's got the kind of mind that you need to *appoint* generals. . . ."

The driver shouted to his team; the coach began to slow again. Alphena gripped the frame of the bench so that she wouldn't rock forward too badly when they stopped.

Corylus doesn't use the word because it would mean an unpleasant death for Corylus and Varus both if anyone heard him and reported that he'd said my brother would be a good emperor. But that's what he means.

That was something more for Alphena to think about. There was so much to consider about people, if you just thought of them as people.

CORYLUS HOPPED DOWN AND OFFERED Alphena a hand. She took it instead of slapping him away, as she might have done not so very long ago.

He hid his smile. Many wonderful things had happened in the months since his friend Varus had given a public reading and loosed demons from the Underworld. In some ways the change in Alphena's attitude was the most remarkable of all, as well as being more positive than most of the others.

The coach and escorting wagons had drawn up in the yard of bare dirt in front of the buildings. The main structure had been built as a manor house, but it couldn't have functioned as one in decades, probably not since Herennius was proscribed. It wasn't run-down, exactly, but the repairs had been functional rather than decorative.

As built, the facade had mimicked that of a temple, though it had pilasters instead of columns and the triangular pediment over the doorway was painted instead of being carven stone. The building was now a factory and warehouse for the estate's olive oil production.

The plaster that had flaked away from the pediment over the years had been replaced to waterproof the core of wattle and daub, but there had been no attempt to keep up the decoration. In the corners, fragments of the original showed the feet of reclining figures—white for a woman, reddish for a man. They were probably Venus and Mars, but that didn't matter.

Nothing at all mattered to Herennius, executed seventy years ago. He had died either because he was an enemy of one of the Triumvirs or because he was wealthy and the Triumvirs needed money for their war against the murderers of Julius Caesar.

He'd be dead now anyway, Corylus thought. Perhaps that was all you could really say about any human being: once he was alive, and now he is dead.

Corylus had spotted half a dozen members of the estate staff as the convoy of vehicles drove into the yard; there were at least that many youngsters playing in the yard. More people appeared, most of them heads peering out of windows on both levels of the main building, but moments later a man bustled out the front door. He wore a clean tunic over the undertunic that was probably his sole garb when he wasn't receiving visitors.

He was a big fellow, probably in his early forties. His arms were knotted with muscle, and his hands were calloused.

His eyes scanned the new arrivals and focused on Corylus. Pulto had helped Pandareus out the back. Both had come to join Corylus, but they didn't look as though they might be in charge.

"Gentlemen!" the fellow said. "I am Gaius Julius Andromedus, the manager here. How may I help you?"

Corylus opened his mouth to reply. Before he got the words out, Alphena stepped in front of him and said, "Andromedus, I am Lady Alphena, daughter and representative of my father, Alphenus Saxa, the former consul."

She snapped her fingers and held her hand out. "Master Corylus?" she said.

Corylus, startled, put the document he was holding into her hand. She had not bothered to look back at him.

"Here is our authority," Alphena said, holding the rolled parchment out toward Andromedus. It was tied with red silk and sealed. Seleucus, Saxa's chief librarian, had supervised the creation. It included a copy of the signet of Gnaeus Curtianus Major, the estate's present owner, who had written Saxa eighteen months before to borrow a set of Corinthian bronze vessels for a formal dinner party.

Despite the rush nature of the job, the forgery was a much more impressive document than anything Curtianus himself would have sent. Saxa's staff had been delighted to show their skill.

Corylus didn't let his amusement reach his lips. Saxa, a pleasant and generous man, *had* lent the bronze vessels, so you might say that Curtianus had already been paid for this brief intrusion on his property.

"The senator directed us to pay particular attention to the well that was in use when Marcus Herennius owned the property," Alphena said. Her tone throughout had been one of cool boredom that she must have learned from her mother.

Andromedus took the document from Alphena, but he didn't bother to open it. He might not have been able to read it anyway—it was written in Latin, not Greek—but it would distress Seleucus to learn that his effort hadn't been appreciated.

"Your Ladyship?" Andromedus said in obvious concern. "The owner here is Curtianus and the steward I report to is Phileas. Or do you mean the fellow before Phileas? I was just a foreman then and I don't recall his name."

I won't tell Seleucus, Corylus thought. *And I'll warn Pandareus not to say anything, either.*

Aloud Corylus said, "I believe that's the well, Your Ladyship." He pointed toward a bramble-covered mound; the leading wagon was parked almost in front of it.

"A well?" said Andromedus, turning to follow Corylus' gesture. "Oh, right, but it's been all filled in, Your Ladyship. We've got a pipe from Lake of the Woods if you need water."

"Candidus?" Alphena said to the understeward whom she had brought along. "That well needs to be reopened. Will you need additional resources?"

"No, Your Ladyship," Candidus said. He bowed to Alphena and began organizing the operation with crisp orders. The members of the escort had been chosen for their skills as well as for brawn. Along with the personnel, the wagons carried pry bars, grabs, ropes, and even a shear legs.

Corylus had never warmed to Candidus, but the understeward had always shown himself to be competent. He had ridden in the second wagon instead of in the coach, as he had believed his dignity justified. He might have argued the matter with Pandareus, but Corylus had suggested that Candidus not do so.

Candidus had known better than to have raised the matter with Pulto. On the frontier Pulto had formed his views of the rights of a slave flunky against those of a freeborn citizen and veteran. He was likely to put his opinion to the understeward with more force than delicacy.

Twenty feet to the other side of the disused well was a massive oak tree. A semicircular wicker bench curved around half the trunk. The master—or now the farm manager—would sit on it while judging disputes among tenants, moving with the shade or sun as the season dictated; the parties and spectators squatted on the ground before him.

It was the ancient way of life in rural Italy. Corylus wished Varus were here to discuss it with him.

He grinned. *I wish Varus were here, period. And Hedia too.*

The farm manager was talking to Alphena, who for the most part maintained a cool silence. It was possible that despite preparation they would need something the estate could provide, so Andromedus' goodwill could be useful.

Pandareus examined a flagstone in front of the door, running his index finger over the surface. From the stone's shape Corylus guessed it might have begun life as a memorial tablet.

Under other circumstances Corylus would have joined his teacher, but there was a more useful witness for him to chat with. He walked to the oak tree and sat on the bench, resting his right palm on the trunk. As he expected, after a few moments his mind entered the green silence of the tree's soul.

Corylus' mother and grandmother had managed a hazel coppice that provided spear and arrow shafts for the army. Most of the local residents were Helvetian: Germans from across the Rhine.

The settlers hated and feared the local women, claiming that they were witches and tree spirits. During the terrible storm the night Corylus was born, the settlers had invaded the coppice and cut down the two full-grown hazel trees that grew above the hundreds that were stunted from repeated clipping.

Corylus' mother and her mother had died that night. The next day, all the settlers had died except for the very few who had managed to flee across the Rhine before the men of Cispius' battalion could catch them.

There might have been an investigation if the massacre hadn't been so thorough, but from what Pulto had said, Cispius was as well liked by his noble superiors as he was by the men he commanded. The basic job of the army on the Rhine was to kill Germans, after all.

Officially, Corylus told people that his mother was a Celtic woman whom his father had met while on active service. In Corylus' heart of hearts, he knew that the Helvetians had been right about his mother's race.

They should have remembered that the Army of Carce didn't need witchcraft to handle barbarian murderers, though.

A figure slowly coalesced from the green translucence: a majestic woman, as tall and broad as a statue of Armed Athena. She reached up and combed the fingers of both hands through her long hair; it was blond with a greenish tinge.

"Greetings, Dryas," Corylus said. "If I'm disturbing you, I'll leave."

The nymph gave a throaty laugh. "Do the women you're disturbing often ask you to leave, young man?" she said. "I'm not exactly a woman, of course, but then, you're not exactly a man."

She touched her shoulders with her hands; her breasts bobbled. "In any case," she said, "your visit is welcome. Why are you here?"

"A magical amulet may have been buried in the well here," Corylus said. "That was long ago, during the Proscriptions."

He saw either the nymph or the courtyard of the estate where his body sat; the images flickered back and forth as his interest changed. For a moment he watched Candidus directing a crew with hatchets and pry bars as they cleared the brush growing on the pile of rubble. Pulto and Lenatus watched with professional interest, but the two veterans didn't intervene in a job that was being competently handled.

"Not so very long ago, dear boy," the nymph said. "But perhaps for you, yes."

The courtyard appeared behind her as though carved in full color on the green ambiance. Unfamiliar servants were bringing objects from the house and dropping them into the well. The facade was in its original glory. The reclining figures were indeed Mars and Venus, each reaching out to touch the other's fingers.

The bench around the oak was stone and the well had a stone curb, but Corylus couldn't see a difference between the trunk of the tree in this image and the one he sat beside. As Dryas had implied, time was relative to the life span of the person making the determination.

"Are you a magician?" the nymph said. Her eyes narrowed. "You're not," she said. "I can see that. I know the amulet you mean. I thought perhaps the soldiers had meant to leave it. If you're not a magician, you're better off without it. And even if you were, I think."

She pursed her lips and said, "It came from the Blight. No magic would protect you against the Blight. Let it be."

The imagery of servants hiding valuables blurred into imagery of the courtyard not long after that. The fat steward who had been giving orders was spread-eagled to the ground. The dirt around his head and shoulders was wet. His torso was bloated, and the leather funnel and bucket that had been used to fill him lay nearby.

Another servant with his arms tied behind his back hung by his wrists from a strappado; the rope lifting him to an oak limb had been slacked. If the fellow hadn't fainted, he would have been able to stand upright.

The ground was wet beneath the woman lying beside the steward also, but in her case it was blood dripping from her groin. Her injuries might not have been torture but simply rape by men who saw an opportunity in the present chaos.

It probably didn't matter to the victim. From the way the blood continued to spread, it might be that nothing would matter to her in a few hours.

Soldiers wearing their sword belts but not armor were clearing the well of the rubble that had been dumped into it. The well curb itself had been levered into the shaft, and the stone bench beside the tree had followed it in broken fragments.

"The amulet is still here?" Corylus said. "I don't want it for myself, but another man does. He may hold friends of ours. He'd release them if we gave him the amulet. The Ear of the Satyr."

The nymph shrugged. "You're a short-lived race," she said. "But if you bring the Blight, you will die with all peoples and all things. But all things will die sometime, so that doesn't matter, either."

The image of the Proscriptions blurred again. The soldiers and some of the servants who hadn't been tortured had finished clearing the well.

An outbuilding—it was probably the estate's kitchen—had been demolished for the timbers that provided a frame over the hole. A roped basket was beginning to bring up items placed in it by a man within the shaft. Corylus saw an enameled gold casket that must be the one Atilius said contained the magical papyrus, now illegible.

"The well was such an obvious place," Corylus whispered. He was speaking to himself rather than to Dryas, though she probably heard him. "I don't know why they bothered."

But Herennius and his servants no doubt expected more time before the troops arrived to execute their orders. Not for any factual reason, but just because it *couldn't* already be over for them. Corylus had seen the same despairing wonder on the faces of mortally wounded men. *This can't be happening!*

But of course it was. It always did.

Everything changed again, but Corylus was observing almost the same scene in the bright white light of the present. Pulto and Lenatus had been leaning over the shaft; now they straightened.

"That's got it!" Pulto called. Corylus heard his voice as if through inches of green water.

The grave-faced nymph faded from Corylus' mind. He got up from the bench and walked over to Pulto. Alphena had now joined the soldiers.

"It's time for me to go down and find the Ear of the Satyr," Corylus said cheerfully.

He hoped that no one could tell that he was thinking about the nymph's

warning. He didn't know what the Blight was, any more than a Scout crossing the Danube knew what the Sarmatians might have waiting on the East
Bank. That's why the Scouts were crossing, after all.

But he knew that if he found anything it would be trouble.

VARUS STEPPED INTO BRIGHT SUNLIGHT and tripped on a tilted paver.
He managed to stay upright by lurching forward, which almost made him
bump Lord Arpat. Fortunately, the nobleman was too intent on the men outside the building to pay any attention to what was going on behind him.

Varus took in his surroundings. They were in a round temple. Eight columns of coarse black stone supported a domed roof twenty feet across; there
were no connecting walls between the pillars.

The floor was paved with slabs of the same black rock as the pillars.
Wooden beams formed the rafters, but the roof itself was of bronze sheets.
Varus had never seen a building constructed in this fashion, but the *design*
was familiar.

"This is a tholos," Varus said, gesturing to the building. Domed temples
were not particularly common, but the Temple of Vesta in the Forum and the
Temple of Aesculapius at the healing god's original shrine in Epidaurus were
merely two of the more familiar examples. "Was it built by Greeks?"

The rest of the Indian delegation had stepped outside. The nearby land
in three directions was being farmed. Varus saw bent figures hoeing in the
knee-high grain. At a little distance, a plow drawn by a pair of scrawny oxen
raised a plume of yellow dust.

"The founder of King Govinda's line built the shrine," Bhiku said. "Tra-
ditionally that was ten thousand years ago, but I believe a better translation
of 'ten thousand' in Greek would be 'a very large number.' It was built a long
time ago, certainly."

He turned and gestured in the fourth direction, toward a mound of vine-
covered trees. The mount was not particularly high, but it spread for a considerable distance. "That, however, is very much older. It is called Dreaming
Hill, but it was a city. It is said to be haunted."

Bhiku grinned sheepishly up at Varus. "I say it is haunted," he said. "I do
not believe all the things that others say they have seen among the ruins,
but what I have seen myself is enough to convince me."

A squad of troops stood outside the temple. They were dressed much the same as Bhiku himself—loose cotton vests and pantaloons, without caps. A few wore straw sandals, but most were barefoot. Their weapons were spears and longbows, both made of bamboo. The spear and arrow points were stone.

Arpat was talking with—mostly at—one of the soldiers. The soldier's responses were short and mumbled; his eyes were fixed on the ground as the noble harangued him. Arpat had sheathed his sword after returning from the Otherworld, but his hand returned to the hilt.

Varus moved with Bhiku to the edge of the building, but he stopped when the sage did. Bhiku cocked his head as he listened to the one-sided discussion.

"Arpat wonders why the escort from Ramsa Lal is not waiting for us here," Bhiku said in low-voiced Greek. "The peasant says that they've sent a messenger to their lord, who is nearby. The main body of the escort is at a distance in case something other than the emissaries came through the portal."

Varus thought about the Otherworld. On their way to the stupa, the party had met a bird that stood ten feet high. Its wings were curly stubs, but its hooked beak was shaped like that of an eagle.

"I wouldn't want to meet the bird we saw with only a bamboo spear," Varus said. "I was glad that it decided to go off in another direction when it saw us."

"I was glad of your presence, Lord Varus," Bhiku said. "But the bird could not have opened the portal as I did, let alone broken the barrier between the Otherworld and our world the way a *very* powerful wizard might."

He cocked an eye at Varus. Varus grimaced in embarrassment and shook his head. "Not me," he muttered. "I *know* nothing of magic. I accept evidence that it exists the way I accept that lightning exists."

Bhiku believes that I am the lightning, he thought. *And he may be right.*

A squadron of brightly dressed horsemen rode toward the shrine. There was a path between fields, but the horsemen spread widely to either side of it, trampling the grain and raising a pall of dust that hid the total numbers of the party. There were twenty or more in the leading rank.

Arpat and his two companions strode to meet the newcomers. Bhiku turned instead toward the jungle-covered ruins in the other direction.

"The ancestor who built this shrine," he said, "was a great wizard, and his descendents were still greater wizards. Govinda is the greatest of all. But . . ."

He looked at Varus and said with a wry smile, "The inhabitants of Dreaming Hill, when it was a city and not a ruin, must have been great wizards also, because *feel* the magic which still emanates from this place. I think the ancestor built his shrine here so that it could tap the power of the ancient city."

"But for all the inhabitants' power," Varus said, finishing Bhiku's thought, "the city *is* in ruins."

He smiled slightly and shrugged. "Perhaps," he went on, "because your King Govinda taps only the residue of the power of Dreaming Hill, he won't fly high enough to fall so far. If there is a fall."

"Sometimes I've seen people walking in the ruins," Bhiku said, as though he hadn't been listening. "Sometimes those I saw were not people."

He shrugged and smiled at Varus. "I used to come here frequently," he said. "Never coming closer than we are now. You can enter Dreaming Hill and often people do, woodcutters chopping brush from the edges of the ruins and sometimes treasure seekers. But they don't always come back."

"Do you wish to see the interior of the ruins?" Varus asked, allowing no emotion to enter the question. It didn't appear to him that Dreaming Hill was connected with Govinda and the threat that the Sibyl had warned of, but he didn't know enough to be sure.

"I haven't come to this place in many years," Bhiku said. "Until you and I returned just now from the Otherworld. I decided that while I was sure that there was a great deal to be learned from Dreaming Hill, it was not a place in which I would find wisdom. I still think that."

"I bow to your analysis," Varus said, as lightly as if he were joking. "What do we do next, then?"

Bhiku nodded in the direction of the path, where the horsemen—several hundred of them as the dust settled—had met Arpat and his fellows. The small party of footmen and the servants from Arpat's delegation were gathered a little distance from the wealthier contingent.

"We'll let our betters go off to Lord Govinda," the sage said with gentle irony. "Then you and I will go to my quarters in Raguram's compound. If asked I will introduce you as a student from a distant country, though I doubt that will be necessary. After you've had a chance to view the situation, you will tell me as much of your intention as you're willing for me to know. Then I will help you achieve your wish with such knowledge and strength as I have."

"You don't know what my intent *is*," Varus said. *I don't really know what my intent is.*

"I believe that you are a man who would do as I would do under that same circumstances," Bhiku said. "Since you know the circumstances and I do not, I defer to your judgment."

Neatly turning my comment about Dreaming Hill on its head, Varus realized. The men smiled at each other.

Instead of leaving as Bhiku had predicted, the body of horsemen walked to the shrine where Varus and the sage remained. All of them were dressed in loose silks and carried curved swords. A number also carried slim lances with streamers dangling below their steel points. Arpat and his companions were mounted now also.

The man in the center wore scarlet with a sash and turban of cloth of gold. His sword hilt and the bridle of his mount sparkled with jewels.

Bhiku whispered to Varus, "That's Ramsa Lal in person!"

"You, servant of my enemy!" Lal said in Greek. "Where is the magician Rupa whom I sent with you at the command of my lord Govinda?"

Bhiku bowed low. "Rupa told us that she had business in Carce and that I should take the delegation back, Your Lordship," he said. "I assumed that the business was yours, but I did not enquire."

"That's right, Your Lordship," Yama said, looking less awkward on horseback than he had been during the trek through the Otherworld. "We had planted the vine as the king directed, so it was no affair of ours what your servant chose to do."

Ramsa Lal considered Varus. Because the floor of the shrine was raised, their eyes were on a level.

"The fellows who traveled with you say that you're a wizard, foreigner," Lal said. "Is that true?"

"Not in the way Master Bhiku here is," Varus said. Lal seemed to be in his mid-thirties. Though he wasn't fat, his puffy face suggested dissipation. "I may have powers, but I don't have control of them the way a true magician would have."

"Never mind that," Lal said, flicking the air with the end of his reins. "You're coming back with me. I have a task for a wizard."

"Your Lordship, the stranger must come with us to our master Govinda!" Arpat said. "This business is under his auspices, and he is your master!"

"I bow to Lord Govinda," Lal growled. "His mission is completed, as you have already said . . . and while I bow to Govinda, your master and mine,

I will have his flunkies dragged by the heels if you use that tone on me again, Arpat!"

Bhiku stepped from the pavement and said, "Your Lordship, I'm afraid that our lord Govinda's officials have misstated the situation. This young man is a noble in his own country and has come here to share his considerable wisdom—"

"Be silent!" Lal said. His Greek was accented but easily understandable. "You are in my territory at the behest of Lord Govinda, but do not test my forbearance further, scum!"

To Varus he continued, "Can you ride, foreigner?"

Horsemanship was a common exercise for noble youths, but Varus had never found exercise interesting until he began joining Corylus in the gymnasium over the past year. Varus walked between libraries all over the city, however, as that was the easiest way to get around in Carce. Neither horses nor vehicles were allowed within the sacred boundaries until after dark.

"Not well," said Varus. "I'd better walk."

"As you please," said Lal. He turned to the man on his left—Arpat rode on his right side—and snapped something in an Indian tongue.

"He has ordered his aide to take a squadron and escort the officials to our lord Govinda's palace," Bhiku said. Varus hadn't needed the whispered translation to understand what was happening.

The aide nodded and raised his arm, then shouted an order. A hundred or so men rode away at a walk, which rose to a jog. The members of Govinda's delegation went with them. The servants walked at the end of the file. Arpat turned twice in the saddle to look back with a troubled expression, but he had apparently taken Ramsa Lal's warning seriously.

The horseman who had taken the place at Lal's left shouted a similar order and the remaining body of men moved off. "If you hold us up," Lal said, "I'll have you lashed to a saddle. Do you understand?"

Varus nodded curtly. As he had told Bhiku, there were many of Lal's sort in Carce. Varus didn't like the Carce version, either.

"With your permission, Lord Varus . . . ," said Bhiku, walking at Varus' side, "I will accompany you. For my own interest, that is. I would willingly help you, but I can't imagine how I could."

"I can't imagine, either," Varus said. Lal was holding his horse to an amble. The sage took shorter, quicker steps than Varus, but neither of them had trouble keeping up. "But I can't imagine how I can help myself, either. I am very glad of your company."

It was really the only thing in this business that did please Varus, but it was a major thing.

CHAPTER V

Hedia had been walking with her head down to avoid stumbling on rocks
sticking out of the dust. There was nothing to see in the sky, and it
had a bronze tinge that made her feel hotter and even more out of place.

The change was as sudden as if she had stepped into a pond. There was
no immediate difference on the ground, but the air felt refreshing and the
sky—she *did* look up—was a saturated blue with a few ragged-edged clouds.

Hedia looked back. She couldn't see the valley where she had left Boest
and Paddock. Three steps farther forward and she was gazing down on to a
spread of varied green, a mixture of meadow and groves. The grazing sheep
had three-colored wool, irregular patches of black, brown, and white.

A small frame house with a shingle roof stood in the shade of an oak. A
spring bubbled into a pond nearby and sent a rivulet toward the creek that
wobbled through the valley

Corylus would know what kind of tree that is. Which was probably true, but
there were better reasons to wish that Corylus were present.

Hedia didn't speed her pace, but she found herself smiling as she approached the house. *Even if I don't learn where Varus is, this is a pleasant place
to spend a few days to plan my next move.*

She smiled more broadly. Perhaps Varus could find *her.* He was the magician, after all.

Hedia heard flute music as she neared the house, but she couldn't tell
where it was coming from. A squirrel on the tree's long horizontal branch
chattered at her, then ran higher up the trunk and chattered again.

A man walked out around the tree; he must have been seated on the other side. Instead of the double flute that Hedia was familiar with from stage presentations and dinner entertainments, he held a set of panpipes.

He was *amazingly* attractive. He smiled at Hedia and said, "Hello. My name is Gilise."

"I'm Hedia," she said, giving Gilise her full smile. "I'm *very* glad to see you. If you'll let me drink your water and take a moment to cool off, I look forward to showing you just how glad I am."

Gilise laughed. "I have wine in the house," he said. "And for the rest . . ." He blew a trill on his pipes that echoed the laughter.

Hedia knelt at the pool and cupped both hands in the water, then splashed her face. She rose and loosened her sash, grinning at the young man.

"Maybe I don't need a need a drink so much as I thought," Hedia said, handing one end of the sash to Gilise. A leather sheath sewn into the other end held her little knife.

"What am I to do with this?" he said. He tossed his pipes to the ground.

"Just hold it, silly," Hedia said, grinning even more broadly.

She raised her arms, touching the fingertips together, and pirouetted on her toes. Around her waist the silk was its natural pastel green. When the sash wound out, the fabric was so gauzy fine that the single layer seemed colorless.

Gilise watched, transfixed. These overlength sashes were twenty feet, end to end. Hedia owned several in various colors so that they would go with whichever dress she chose for a special dinner. She had worn the long sash to Polymartium on a whim, but she did many things on whim. Often, as now, she was glad of it.

The hem of Hedia's tunic swelled out with the motion, drifting over her hips. She slowed and halted to face Gilise again.

"Generally I do that on the serving table after the dishes have been cleared," Hedia said. "A hard surface is better, but I don't mind grass."

She reached up and released the lion-headed pins on both shoulder straps. Her tunic fluttered down. "Do you mind grass?" Hedia said.

Gilise reached for her. His smile had become a rictus.

Hedia raised her lips to his, then twisted away with no more contact than a wisp of gossamer brushing his face in the morning. "Lie down, you lovely man," she said. "I want to do the work the first time. You're such a sweet man."

Gilise was half-unwilling, but Hedia shifted one of her hands from his shoulders to reach under the hem of his short lambskin tunic. After an instant's further hesitation, Gilise thumbed the straps aside and stepped out of the garment. He allowed Hedia to guide him onto his back with her tunic beneath his shoulders.

"So sweet . . . ," she whispered.

Hedia squatted for a moment above him, then lowered herself with a sudden rush. She cried out with delight as she impaled herself on his member.

Anyone watching Hedia's gasps and excited moans would assume that she was completely lost in the moment. Certainly she was having fun—

The thought brought a peal of laughter from Hedia's lips.

—but she had realized when she was quite young that the muscular, passionate men she found interesting could be very dangerous to a woman if things got out of *her* control. Hedia was never quite as abandoned as she seemed to be, and at this moment she was as cold as an Egyptian cobra.

But her partner did not and would not realize that—until she wanted him to.

Gilise began to gasp as he climaxed. Hedia ground herself against him and rotated halfway around. She grasped Gilise's ankles and forced her hips even farther down onto him.

"There!" she cried. "There! There! *There!*"

Gilise shouted also, then sank back.

Hedia rotated another half turn to face him again. "Shall I kiss you, now?" she said.

Gilise murmured. Hedia leaned forward. Instead of bending down to kiss him, she stood and tossed one end of her sash over the branch above them. The weighted end carried it true.

"What?" said Gilise, rising to his elbows.

"Just lie back, darling," Hedia whispered. "This will be something you've never had before."

She gripped the dangling end of the sash with both hands and strode forward, using her full weight and strength. The other end of the sash was noosed around Gilise's right ankle. His leg and torso swung off the ground; his flailing arms only eased Hedia's task.

Hedia tied her end of the sash around the moss-covered plaque at the back of the spring. On it a nymph reclined in low relief on her right elbow and held a horn of plenty in her left hand. Hedia knelt against the stone, letting the cool water dribble over her hands and forearms. She was flushed and breathing hard.

Hedia grinned. For various reasons this time, and all of them good.

She rose, touching the plaque with her fingertips but not putting any weight on her arms. Dragging Gilise into the air had used all the strength she had.

Hedia turned to face Gilise for the first time since . . . Her smile widened. Since well before they had finished their session, though in that final passage she had been more concerned with noosing his right ankle than with recreation.

"Why are you laughing!" Gilise cried. His face was very red. He could reach the ground with his left hand, but he wasn't strong enough to push off so hard that he could grab the branch from which he hung. "Let me go, you bitch! Let me go or it'll be the worse for you!"

"I don't think you're in a position to harm me so long as you're where you are," Hedia said calmly. "And you're not going to be freed until you've done exactly what I tell you to do."

"I'll blast you to atoms!" Gilise said, then cried out. His left arm had crumpled, and his full weight dragged again on his ankle. Soft as the silk was, Hedia knew from experience that it cut when the weave was pulled tight.

She laughed. "I don't think that would get you out of your present predicament, even if you were capable of it," she said.

Gilise was gasping. He twisted to grab his right calf just above the knee and raised his torso. That allowed him to breathe more easily, but he wouldn't be able to hold the posture.

"Boest said that you're an air spirit," Hedia said cheerfully. "Does that mean that you can't suffocate hanging like this? I suppose it does."

"What do you want?" Gilise said. He lowered himself again to put his fingertips on the ground. "Just tell me!"

"Boest says that you stole his soul," Hedia said. "He needs it back in order to help me, so I hope you kept it."

"Will you let me down . . . if I . . . give it to you?" Gilise said, breathing hard between spurted words.

"I will release you," Hedia said, "and allow you your life."

She giggled and added, "Although there was nothing so exceptional about your performance that I'll be interested in seeing you again."

She gripped her tunic between thumb and forefinger and tugged it toward her, careful not to bring herself within the circle in which Gilise's body slowly oscillated. Judging by his wheezing misery, she could probably break free if he managed to grab her, but it was a risk she didn't need to take.

"Swear," Gilise said. "You have to swear that you'll let me go!"

Hedia sniffed. She believed in her own honor; she did not believe in "the immortal gods" or whatever other form religious people chose to use.

"I swear by Mother Matuta that I will let you go if you allow me to return Boest's soul," Hedia said, picking the deity whom she had been most recently worshiping. Matuta was as likely to be real as any other god.

"In the house, then," Gilise said. "The space at the back where the eaves continue to the ground. That's a cupboard, and there are shelves with glass phials. The phial on the end, the *right* end, that's Boest. Tell him to breathe it. Now let me go!"

Hedia shrugged into her long tunic. It was protection for her legs against grass edges. *I wonder if there's a length of rope in the house, since I won't be getting my sash back just now. . . .*

"When I come back . . . ," Hedia said, walking toward the dwelling, "I'll let you go, as I've promised."

At the door she paused and turned around. "That's if you've told the truth," she said. "If you've lied, you'll never see me again."

The hanging man continued to rotate slowly. He didn't rouse the effort to speak.

Hedia smiled. Gilise appeared to have understood her.

"How DEEP IS IT?" Corylus asked as he walked to the reopened well. The bench had jammed partway down the shaft, and the rubble of the coping had piled on top of it instead of dropping to the bottom.

"Twenty-two feet down to the water," Pulto said. "Four or five to the bottom below that."

Lenatus coughed and said, "You know, it's a pretty tight fit down the shaft, kid."

"I'm smaller than you, Publius Corylus," Alphena said. "I could look for the locket instead of you?"

Corylus smiled. "I'll be all right," he said, speaking to all the worried faces around him. Even the men of the escort seemed affected by his friends' concern. He would have expected them to be treating the unusual business simply as entertainment.

"When I used to go across the river with the Scouts . . . ," he said. That was only a few years before; it seemed much longer, a thing that happened to someone completely different from the young scholar learning rhetoric from the great Pandareus of Athens. "Sometimes we'd find Sarmatian temples underground. They had little escape tunnels besides the main entrance. If we found an escape tunnel and not the main entrance, I'd go down it because I was small. The Scouts used to call me their little marmot."

"Did your father know the Scouts were using you that way?" Lenatus said with a deliberately blank expression.

"No," said Corylus. He grimaced, thinking of times past. "I'd go through in the dark and open the main entrance. There was never any trouble, and I went down behind my dagger. But Father would've, well . . . I'm just glad he never learned."

"The Old Man knew," Pulto said. "What kind of a CO do you think he was? We'd stay up until the Scouts came in, but we wouldn't drink. When the platoon was back and *you* were back, then he'd kill a couple jars of wine before I put him to bed."

Corylus looked at Pulto. A bright light had just flared across the past and turned it into a completely different place.

Instead of responding, Corylus said, "Well, the sooner I do this, the sooner I can towel off and get myself around some mulled wine."

"Here you go, boy," Pulto said, handing Corylus his equipment belt. Pulto had unclipped the sword, but the long dagger hung in its scabbard. "Just like the old days, hey?"

Corylus laughed. "Fewer horse skulls, I hope," he said. He fastened the belt so that the scabbard hung between his legs where it wouldn't clank against the stone lining.

To Lenatus and Alphena he explained, "The Sarmatians pray to horses, and they're not real careful to clean the meat off the bone before they hang them up."

"Hey, chieftain?" a member of the escort said; his Greek had a Spanish accent. Corylus had seen him around Saxa's town house, but he didn't know the fellow's name.

"Yes?" Corylus said. Everyone was staring at the fellow. Slaves didn't interject themselves into the conversations of free citizens, but neither Alphena nor the veterans chose to shut the speaker down until they heard what he had to say.

"I was the one who went down and hooked the grab each time," the

Spaniard said, nodding to the tripod and pulley that had been used to pull the stones out of the well. "I figure you know what you're doing, I see your knife, but I want to say: there's something down there. I'm not scared, but I was just going halfway down and I felt it. Just so you know."

"Thank you," Corylus said. He knelt and looked down the well. His body would block most of what light entered the shaft, but he didn't consider taking a lantern. Light wouldn't help him feel for objects with his fingers—or, more likely, toes.

"Chief?" said the Spaniard. "I'm a little guy, I fit down the shaft better'n your buddies there"—Pulto and Lenatus—"would. I'll come after you if you need, you know?"

Corylus turned again to look at the fellow. "Thank you," he repeated. "I *do* know. But I don't expect that kind of problem this time."

He'd taken off his heavy sandals. Now he gripped the rope with both hands and stepped into the shaft; it was easy without the coping. He lowered himself hand over hand, holding the rope lightly between one sole and the other instep as well.

That was just in case. Corylus couldn't imagine what sort of case would require him to hold firmly to the rope with his feet alone, but emergencies were by definition unexpected. He smiled.

The smile faded as he felt the shadows close in.

It wasn't physical darkness that was weighing on him—he could twist his head to look upward and see the bright sky. Something cold and bleak and distant crowded against his consciousness and began to seep in.

Corylus knew what the Spaniard meant, now, but it wasn't a danger somewhere down this well shaft. Walls of ice, cliffs of ice, loomed above him.

Corylus was familiar with ice. There were frozen mornings even in Carce, and the Rhine and northern Danube froze solidly every winter. What he saw now in his mind, however, was beyond reason.

These were *mountains* of ice. They ground closer, crushing rock and rivers and farms beneath their glittering bases. Nothing could stop the ice, and it would not stop.

Corylus continued to lower himself into the well. He forced himself to look up. Three heads peered down from the north side of the rim where their shadows fell away from the shaft rather than blocking light to the man beneath: Pulto and Lenatus and Alphena, worry gleaming from their unnaturally blank faces.

"No problem!" Corylus called, hoping he sounded cheerful. There really wasn't any problem here and now, but some place at some time would vanish beneath certain icy doom.

His feet touched the water. He spread them so that if he slipped he would hit soles first instead of taking his weight on the sides of his feet. He continued to lower himself by hand until the water was up to mid-chest. Only then did his feet touch a thin layer of ooze—and below that rocks and pebbles.

"I'm here!" Corylus said. His plan had been to feel the bottom with his toes, but the rubble filtering down from the blockage was too varied for his feet to discriminate. He took a deep breath and submerged.

For a moment buoyancy tried to rotate his feet off the bottom, but he began dropping stones down the front of his tunic. After the fifth or sixth handful of ballast, he stabilized so that he could begin to feel his way around the edge. The shaft's narrow diameter was an advantage now.

Corylus rose and blew out air before gasping repeated deep breaths. His friends were calling, but he ignored them for now. He folded himself back onto the bottom.

There was a layer of rubble, never more than a foot deep, over a rippling surface of living rock. If necessary Corylus would have a basket lowered so that he could put the rubble in it, but for the moment he simply moved each handful behind him as he worked his way around the bottom.

Corylus picked up a flat disk the size of his palm. Because the water was so cold, he almost dropped it onto the pile of other debris he was clearing. Just before he released it, his fingers felt a straight indentation around the edge. Only then did he realize that he held metal, not stone.

He raised the disk above the water. Where his fingers had rubbed the coating of slime there was smooth iron with only flecks of rust. For a moment Corylus thought he must have found a more recent object, because iron should have corroded more after seventy years at the bottom of a well.

The vision of a bearded, broad-shouldered man flooded Corylus' mind. The figure wore only boots and an apron made from the hide of a dappled cow; the cowhide was speckled in many places where sparks had singed it. He used a smooth boulder as his anvil and held the work piece in bronze tongs as he forged it with a stone hammer.

He was forming the locket that Corylus now held, or at any rate half of it.

The smith chanted as he struck smooth, powerful blows, but Corylus couldn't hear sounds to accompany the vision. In the background a boy with a frightened expression squatted behind a bellows, resting while the piece was on the anvil.

The vision faded. The locket felt warm in Corylus' hands.

"I've found it!" he called. "I'm going to loop the rope so that I can stand in it; then you haul me up. I don't trust my grip, the water's so cold."

Corylus placed the locket on the ballast in his tunic. He didn't have anywhere else to put it that he could be certain of finding it again; the shaft was lined with well-fitted stones, and setting it anywhere underwater simply meant having to search for it again.

He lifted the end of the rope he'd descended by into a bight and closed it by two half hitches. After stepping into the loop, his left foot on top of his right, he called, "Haul!"

The rope rose with jerky suddenness, showing that his friends on the surface were bringing it up hand over hand instead of hauling it over the beam they had laid as a makeshift block. Corylus stepped off at the top, gripping Pulto's shoulder as a brace.

His legs were trembling. Aloud he'd blamed the cold water for his weakness, but at the back of his mind was the question of how much of it was a reaction to the vision of the ice mountains. The ice was neither good nor evil, but it was inexorable and it obliterated everything in its path.

"Where is it?" said Alphena. Pandareus joined her, but the veterans moved back. They—Pulto at least, but probably both men—didn't like magic.

Corylus gripped what he thought was the amulet through his sodden tunic, then loosed his sash and shook the rocks he'd taken for ballast out onto the ground. Though he leaned forward, one of the larger stones landed on his toes; that would hurt when the numbness of the cold water wore off.

He reached down the front of his tunic with his free hand, gripped the amulet, and brought it out. In bright daylight it looked like scrap from behind a blacksmith's forge, but the line that separated top and bottom like the two halves of an iron clamshell was clearly visible. He handed it to Pandareus.

"I think this must be the amulet," Corylus said. "When I picked it up, I saw the man forging it for a moment."

Pandareus looked up from examining the piece. He said, "A priest?"

Corylus shrugged. "I thought he was just a smith," he said, "but the marks on his arms and cheeks could have been tattoos. I thought they were smudges when I saw them."

He pursed his lips and added, "I saw ice too, but it didn't seem to have anything to do with the forge. We need Varus to tell us what the visions mean, I guess."

"I certainly wish Lord Varus were here," Pandareus said drily. "For the sake of his knowledge as well."

"Why do they call it 'the Ear of the Satyr'?" Alphena asked. "It doesn't look like any kind of ear to me."

There was a touch of pique in her tone; Corylus realized that he and his teacher had been ignoring her. Pandareus must have thought the same thing, for he handed the amulet—the lump of iron that they thought was an amulet—to Alphena.

"I don't know," Pandareus said. "There may be an ear of some sort inside the case, but I don't see hinges or a catch."

Frowning, Alphena rubbed the iron with the ball of her thumb, then held it to the sun at an angle. "It's pinned shut," she said. "Riveted."

She looked from Pandareus to Corylus. "We could break it open with a chisel?" she said doubtfully.

"Why would you want to do that, lady?" piped a voice from behind her. Alphena spun around; Corylus stepped to the side to see past her.

A marble bench had been thrown into the well to block it. When the fragments were hauled out, they had been piled near the shaft. An arm support in the form of a reclining dog had just spoken.

"Well, I . . . ," Alphena said, cupping her palms over the amulet. "Shouldn't I?"

"Mamurcus made the covering to protect the Godspeaker's Ear," said the stone dog. "Unless you want to destroy the ear, why would you take it out of the case? You can already talk to us."

"He made it out of iron from the meteor that brought the Blight!" squeaked another voice, barely audible. "Mamurcus was a great wizard, though not so great as the Godspeaker, and even the Godspeaker could not save his world and his people."

Corylus walked to the pile of rubble and shifted the curved slab that had formed the seat of the bench. Beneath it was the other arm support—this one in the form of a hen.

"Thank you!" the carving said, more clearly now.

The men who had come with Alphena and a score of farm personnel were listening with various degrees of interest. Those who were close enough to see that carvings were talking gaped with amazement, but most of the spectators seemed to take it for ventriloquism or other trickery.

"What *should* I do to find my brother and my mother?" Alphena said. "They went to Polymartium and disappeared. Something happened there, and something happened to them!"

"Oh, were they wizards?" said the hen.

"Polymartium is where Bacchus plans to return to the Waking World," said the dog. "Do your relatives worship Bacchus?"

"Gaius Varus has, well . . ." Corylus said. He was stumbling to find the right word, then decided that the hen's choice was good enough. "Varus is a wizard, yes. What does that mean?"

"Well, we don't know . . . ," said the hen.

"We're not wizards like you and your brother, lady," the dog agreed.

"But perhaps your brother is still at Polymartium, preparing for the coming of Bacchus," the hen said. "There is great magic going on there now, and greater still to come."

"Even we could feel that, lady," the dog said.

Alphena turned to Corylus and the teacher with a question in her eyes. Corylus said, "I think we should go to Polymartium." Pandareus nodded.

Alphena said, "Candidus, is there a property of my father's midway between here and Polymartium?"

"No, Your Ladyship," the understeward said after only a moment's consideration. "But there's an estate owned by your father's client Gnaeus Fabrius, who lives on his land at this time of year. He would supply our needs, I'm sure, if you didn't want to return to Carce."

"Give the drivers instructions," Alphena said crisply, heading for the mail coach with quick, short steps. "We'll leave immediately."

Corylus and Pandareus exchanged glances as they strode after the girl. *I thought she was a bad-tempered brat, not so very long ago,* Corylus thought.

And perhaps Alphena had been a brat not so very long ago. The times were bringing out the best in people and certainly the best in the sister of his friend Gaius Varus.

"I FELT VERY RIGHTEOUS in refusing a horse when Lal offered one," Varus said as he trudged along beside Bhiku. "Now I find myself wondering just how far it is to where we're going."

He spoke in a normal voice. Ramsa Lal had ridden forward to check with the officers at the head of the column. Though the guards riding to either side might know enough Greek to eavesdrop on the conversation, they showed no sign of wanting to.

"Another mile, I believe," Bhiku said, "but I don't visit Lal's domain often enough to be sure. I wouldn't be in danger really; no one notices a mendicant sage—or a ragged beggar, to the degree there's a difference. But there's nothing in Lal's library of interest to me, and I didn't pass near the palace to reach Dreaming Hill. When I was going there."

He gestured to the hedged fields bordering the road and said, "The landscape here is much the same as that in Raguram's domain, or indeed anywhere within the majesty of our master Govinda."

The fields to either side were separated from the road and from their neighbors by earthen walls that were overgrown with brush and occasional trees. Stumps of varying size showed where woodcutters had removed trees and woody shrubs, which left brambles in primary ownership.

The result was a very effective barrier, but it had little to recommend it for a sightseer. Occasionally a stile or gate gave Varus a glimpse into the fields themselves. A farmer might have found more of interest in the grain crops than Varus did, but even a farmer would have admitted that the crops were identical.

"How does this differ from your Italy, Lord Varus?" the sage asked.

"The only difference I see," said Varus, "is that horns of your oxen curve up till they almost touch points over the animal's head. The oxen I'm used to have horns that curve forward, so they've usually sawed off and capped for safety's sake."

He grinned wryly. "I'm not *very* familiar with them," he said. "But I see them pulling carts on the road when I travel outside Carce."

He smiled more broadly. "And I don't travel outside Carce very much, either," he said. "I never expected to see India."

I didn't expect to see fire demons rising through the floor of the Temple of Jupiter in Carce until it happened. Of the two, I prefer India.

A bubble of noise expanded, sweeping over the mounted soldiers. Troops cried out, but Varus wasn't sure they were speaking meaningful words.

The sky ahead had become a roiling curtain of cloud—not black, but purple and shot through with pastel highlights. "Is that a storm?" said Varus. "I've never seen a sky like that."

Something flew out of the clouds and curved back; its membranous wings shimmered with reflections from a sun lower in the sky than the one overhead in this world. Just before the creature disappeared—it was a winged snake a hundred feet long, by the look of it—it gave a melodious call like that of a dove, but greatly amplified.

Bhiku put his hand on Varus' wrist to halt him. "Bacchus, our god and the King of Kings, is visiting the Waking World again," he said. "I've never been so close to his progress in the past. Indeed, if he turns in this direction we may become part of that progress."

The troops ahead were milling. A few riders came back along the line of march, looking over their shoulders and making halfhearted attempts to pretend that their horses were running away with them.

"I saw this at Polymartium," Varus said. "The start of it, at any rate. When you and your fellows opened the portal to the Otherworld."

"Ah, that was Ampelos," Bhiku said. "This is the god himself, I believe."

The clouds spread overhead, bringing not darkness but filtered light—now rosy, now a green as pale and pure as the undersides of new leaves. A horse screamed as if it were being disemboweled.

A lane cleared ahead as troopers rode into the fields or were bucked off their mounts. Instead of slaughter, Varus saw that a riderless horse was mounting another horse whose rider was still in the saddle. The Indian was pounding his bare hands on the muzzle of the would-be sire without affecting the grin of lustful delight that drew the horse's lips back from square yellow teeth.

The "dam"—which Varus thought was a gelding—braced his spread hind legs to bear the unaccustomed weight. He didn't appear to be distressed.

An east wind swept lightly over the scene, bringing humid air with the scent of flowers. The hedges to right and left writhed as grapevines sprouted, leafed, and flowered.

Two chariots rode out of the sky, drawn by yoked panthers. Both wore fawn-skin tunics, but Varus recognized the man in the nearer one as the leader of the band that had erupted after the ceremony to Mother Matuta.

The other man was not a man or not wholly a man: he was Bacchus. Varus, who had doubted the existence of gods, fell to one knee in shock and reverence.

Radiance flooded from Bacchus like the cloak of a comet. He wasn't tall—no taller than Varus himself—or obviously muscular, but mere sight of him compelled reverence. The god's hair flowed like flames from beneath a diadem of grapevines, and his eyes were sunstruck sapphires.

The chariots drove across the fields to the right of the road. The dikes separating plots shivered and flattened like piles of grain on a sieve. The great leopards bounded, each in unison with its yokemate, and the gleaming cars raced smoothly over the soft terrain.

Behind the chariots came the god's entourage: the hundreds of Bassoi and Maenads who had been men and women, and the others who were part human or had never been human at all.

A goat-footed satyr and a Maenad rode a tiger as large as a bull. The satyr drank from a wineskin, then spurted a stream of ruby fluid onto the ground. Vines sprang up, twisting as they grew; in the space of a breath they bore grapes the size of hens' eggs.

A centaur rode toward a woman who had been working in the field. She leaped to meet his arms and swung herself onto his withers. Holding the centaur's shoulder with one hand, she used the other to sail away her bonnet and to pluck off her loose cotton garments.

Three of Lal's cavalry charged the throng: one couched his lance while his companions drew their curved swords. Varus thought they were shouting, but he couldn't be sure in the tumult.

A Maenad laughed and hurled her thyrsus at a swordsman. The pinecone head pierced the man's breast like the sharp iron bolt of a ballista. The Indian tumbled over the hindquarters of his mount, the brittle fennel stalk sticking up from the center of his chest.

The bamboo lance of the middle rider leafed out with the suddenness of straw catching fire. The metal head winked as it fell, flung from the tip of the lance by swelling foliage. The rider pulled up, shouting in amazement, then tossed the lance away. Instead of lying on the ground, it rooted and twisted upright. The soil in a line to either side began to bulge as the bamboo sent up runners.

The onetime lancer tried to wheel his horse. It threw him off and galloped after the chariots, its silver-mounted reins dancing. A satyr lifted the rider to a sitting position and squirted wine into his mouth. The rider shook himself, then grabbed the wineskin and drank deeply.

A pair of Maenads lassoed the remaining horseman with loops of vine and pulled him off the back of his mount. They kept their nooses tight so that the man landed on his feet, though his knees immediately buckled.

His curved sword sank to mid-blade in the soft ground. The women embraced the man from either side, kissing and fondling him. The trio danced off together, following the chariots and the runaway horse.

Varus stood slowly. His thigh muscles quivered as though he had been straining to lift a weight. Beside him, Bhiku sat cross-legged with his head bent. The sage lifted his head when Varus moved.

Varus blinked. He viewed his surroundings as if through thick glass, distorted by ripples and a green cast, but he could see for miles with perfect clarity in every direction.

Bacchus and Ampelos drove across a landscape that shivered flat to welcome them. The yellow of ripe grain, the gray of dead wood, and all other shades flared into bright greens in the chariots' wake. Laborers dropped their tools and followed. A woman bathing her infant rose and ran after Bacchus. The child lay on the edge of the pond, giggling with happiness.

"How do you feel?" Bhiku said.

"Well, no different than . . . ," Varus said, but his voice trailed off as he realized that he *did* feel different. He was no longer hot and tired. His legs trembled, but he felt a glow of health, as though he were awakening the day after a good workout with Corylus.

Varus looked down at Bhiku and grinned broadly. "I feel an intense desire," he said, "to understand what we just saw and what we're seeing."

He gestured in the direction Bacchus and his troupe had taken. The last members of the entourage were still running and leaping on the horizon, but Varus' vision was clearing. The richly colored clouds had given way to the smears of fuzzy white that had been in the sky when he first arrived from the Otherworld.

Bhiku nodded agreement. "There are different kinds of lust," he said.

The scattered horsemen were beginning to gather again. Only about half the escort was visible, however, and Varus suspected most of the rest would never return.

Some had fled down the road or into the fields to the left. Those who had ridden to the right or had been carried in that direction by their maddened horses had joined the motley rout that followed Bacchus. A few, like the man struck down by a thyrsus in the first moments of the incursion, were dead.

"You and I were the only people who simply stood," the sage said with a slow smile. "Are you fearless, Lord Varus?"

"I'm afraid of many things," Varus said. "But not particularly of death. And

I certainly wasn't going to run away from an experience which was new and wonderful."

The path toward the horizon—the eastern horizon, Varus saw, now that the normal sun hung in the sky—was a lush green wedge through the varied landscape to either side. Trees heavy with fruit sprouted from what must have been grain fields. Irrigation ditches now meandered. The nearest to the road sparkled with wine rather than the trickle of muddy water Varus had noticed before Bacchus swept across the landscape.

Grapevines covered every tree and outcrop. The broad leaves shaded but could not hide clusters of huge purple-red grapes. Bhiku twisted two from a bunch and handed one to Varus.

They bit into the grapes together. They were swollen with wine, not juice. It spurted out and dribbled down Varus' chin.

"This is the finest wine I've ever drunk," Varus said, holding the half grape out where he could examine it. It looked perfectly normal except for the size. "Some of my father's friends would give half their estates for a dozen jars of this."

He tossed the uneaten portion into the ditch. "It's also by far the strongest wine I've ever tried," he added, "and I don't think this is a good time to drink myself incapable. If there ever could be."

Giggling, Bhiku dropped the remainder of his grape also.

"You two!" a voice from behind Varus said. "You're still here?"

"Yes, Your Lordship," Bhiku said, bowing as Varus turned.

Ramsa Lal was approaching from up the road—on foot, however, and bareheaded instead of wearing a crimson turban. His scabbard hung empty at his side.

"Are you such powerful magicians that you can stand against Bacchus?" Lal said harshly.

Varus straightened and spread his feet slightly as he faced the rajah. "Say rather, Your Lordship, that we are philosophers and saw no need to flee when we were not being attacked."

His tone was coldly sneering, scarcely politic behavior toward a superior. On the other hand, Varus didn't recognize Lal as his superior except in terms of physical force. At the moment, Varus thought he could strangle the rajah with his own sash if necessary. Any kind of babbled nonsense would send the nearby guards running away, certain they were being cursed.

Varus smiled. That expression could have made the situation worse, but in fact it seemed to have frightened Lal, much as the gibberish curses had done to the guards.

"Your pardon, Lord Varus," Lal said, stepping back. "I was upset by what has just happened. Ah—*could* you cause the god to turn away from my domains?"

Varus frowned, remembering the radiant power blazing from the face of Bacchus. "Certainly not," he said. "If chance had sent the god directly toward me instead of at an angle to where I stood, he would have rolled right over me."

"We may not be affected by the god's powers in the same fashion as your soldiers were, Your Lordship," Bhiku said, "but chariot wheels would have crushed us the same as they would anyone else."

"I see, I see," Lal muttered, shaking his head. He added something in his own language, then caught himself and said, "Rupa, my own magician, says she can do nothing, and Govinda, our King of Kings and the greatest wizard who has ever lived—even he cannot stop the incursions."

Lal looked down the track that Bacchus and his entourage had blazed. "If they kept going a mile in that direction . . . ," Lal said morosely. "They will have wiped out two villages. If they went a second mile, it will be three villages."

"Wiped out?" Varus said. "It didn't seem to me that many people died, even among the soldiers who attacked the, ah, progress."

"The peasants may as well be dead for all the tribute they'll be paying!" Lal said. "Half of them will have gone off with the god and the rest will lie around and eat the fruit that grows everywhere. The land doesn't get back to normal for five years after an incursion like this. Grain rots in the fields and the next year's crop won't be planted! How am I to feed my troops and pay *my* tribute to our lord Govinda?"

"Perhaps King Govinda will show forbearance," Varus said. "Since you say he too is powerless against the god."

Lal snorted and stalked away. A trooper approached on foot leading a skittish horse, and Lal mounted. He turned in the saddle and said, "Lord Varus, I'll have one task for you to perform in exchange for my hospitality, but that can wait till we reach my palace and refresh ourselves."

"I don't question that you are a great wizard, my young friend," Bhiku said in a low voice as they followed Ramsa Lal's track. More soldiers had rejoined the escort than Varus had expected, but the column more shambled than capered this last part of the journey. "But I wonder what Rupa could not do that Lal believes you can. She is . . . I cannot judge Rupa's power, any more than a slug can judge the size of an elephant."

"We'll listen to what Lal asks," Varus said. "I didn't ask for his hospitality, though, and I'll have no hesitation over turning my back on it if that seems the better course."

Ramsa Lal might have his own ideas about what the foreign wizard would be permitted to do, but that was a problem for another day. After a meal and a night's rest, ideally.

"Ramsa Lal thinks that Rupa is in his service, the same way as his soldiers serve him," Bhiku mused aloud. "He feeds her and he grants her access to whatever she requests, but this is nothing that she could not get from any rajah. In Govinda's domains, or beyond."

"Why *does* she serve Lal, then?" Varus said. They were on the portion of the road that Bacchus had crossed in his progress. The air had a tingle, and the ditches ran with wine.

"Dreaming Hill is in Lal's territory and I know Rupa visits it daily, far more often than I once did," Bhiku said. "But as for why she *serves* Lal, I'm not sure. I'm not sure that she does."

A gate of brick or red stone loomed ahead of them. "I was feeling thirsty enough to drink more of Bacchus' wine," Varus said. "But I hope something less potent will be on offer shortly."

In the back of his mind, though, he was thinking of the cold, smooth face of Rupa. Varus wasn't worried about the task Lal planned to set him: he would attempt it or he would not.

But Mistress Rupa might not be so easy to shrug off.

ALPHENA TWISTED TO LOOK PAST the driver. The wagon in front was rounding a bend. Since they left Polymartium proper they had been following what seemed to be a track laid out by sheep, but the guide—a town councillor, now riding in the lead vehicle—had said that the ceremonial site was nearby.

"I learned on the frontiers that you can't trust rustics about how far anything is," Corylus said. "Or how long it's going to take to get there. Still, it shouldn't be very much longer."

As their mail coach started into the corner, the driver shouted and hauled the reins back, standing on his seat for purchase. The leading wagon had halted in the middle of the road with a score of soldiers in polished armor around it.

Praetorians!

"Hold up there, you!" said the centurion—his horsehair crest was transverse—who had been shouting at the passengers in the lead wagon. He swaggered toward the mail coach, flanked by two subordinates holding javelins.

"I'll take this, my man," Alphena said to the driver. She swung her legs over the seat, then hopped to the ground using her right hand on the coach frame as a pivot. Her tunic was a little longer than the male garment she had worn until a few months ago, but it still wasn't a demure fashion in which to leave the vehicle.

Alphena wasn't feeling demure. Furthermore, it was important that the soldiers realize that she was a woman and therefore not in their minds a threat.

"He *has* held up, sirrah!" she said, trying to copy the tone her mother used when she was putting underlings in their place. "He had no choice but to do so, since some idiot has stopped my servants' vehicle where it blocks the road. Are you in charge here? I am Lady Alphena, here on a mission for my father, Senator Gaius Alphenus Saxa!"

The centurion didn't flinch—the Praetorian Guard reported to its prefect and beyond him to the Emperor alone—but Alphena's tone and words changed his attitude. He straightened *almost* to attention and lowered his right hand with the knobbly vine-wood swagger stick to his side instead of slapping it threateningly into his other palm.

"I'm sorry, Your Ladyship," the centurion said, "but I'm afraid that this area has been sealed by the order of my prefect. There's been some trouble here."

"There certainly has," said Corylus. "The senator has directed us to find out what has happened to his wife and son. They seem to have disappeared during a religious ceremony two days ago, and Senator Saxa is afraid that they were abducted by foreigners who are plotting against the Emperor."

Corylus' voice had startled Alphena, but she didn't look around. He had dismounted discreetly and was remaining politely behind her. He wasn't the sort of man who could approach tense soldiers in a non-threatening fashion.

The centurion grimaced. The Praetorians had originally been the headquarters' guards of a commander. A company of Germans now acted as the Emperor's bodyguard, but five thousand Praetorians provided backup to the City Watch in case of unrest in Carce. They could be sent immediately to deal with trouble in Italy proper, since there were normally no troops here in the center of the empire.

Furthermore, the Praetorians provided many of the officers for the regular legions. This man was neither stupid nor unsophisticated.

"My father the senator is at our house on the Bay," Alphena lied: Saxa was in Carce, not in Puteoli. The centurion didn't have any reason to doubt her, though. "He immediately went to the Emperor with his concerns. By courier they ordered me and Master Corylus to Polymartium while they determined a broader response."

"You said that your prefect ordered you to close off the area," Corylus said sternly. He had picked up her cue. "Was this before he got the Emperor's orders, or has he simply decided to ignore the Emperor's wishes?"

This time the centurion *did* flinch. For the most part the Emperor spent his time in his palace on the island of Capri, leaving the business of Carce to the Praetorian Prefect. A senator who happened to be in Puteoli across the Bay from Capri *might* have gone to the Emperor in a crisis, though, and the Emperor was a notably suspicious man. The prefect wouldn't want to appear to have overridden the Emperor's decision, and a centurion *certainly* didn't want to be the cause of embarrassment or worse for his superior.

"Hercules!" the centurion muttered. Grimacing, he said, "All right, Your Ladyship."

He stepped back from the coach and turned toward the troops around the lead wagon. He gestured with his swagger stick and bellowed, "Silvaticus! This lot can go through!"

"We have a third vehicle following," Corylus said. "We weren't sure what we were going to run into here. We didn't know you were already on the scene."

"The third wagon too, Silvaticus!" the centurion added. To Corylus he said, "I'd say don't make things worse, but I don't bloody well see how they could be worse. *Every* bloody thing's gone to hell. But it's not dangerous; it's not that kinda trouble."

Corylus handed Alphena into the coach and followed. The driver clucked the mules forward even before Corylus had settled beside her.

"You were brilliant," he said. "The way you handled that. I didn't expect Praetorians, though I guess I should have."

"I was frightened," she said, squeezing her hands together. They had started to tremble as soon as she and Corylus were past the guards. "I could have gotten my father executed. I could have gotten all of us executed!"

"You didn't," said Corylus. "You and I don't know what's going on, but if the Praetorians are here, then the stories the escort came back with are probably true. And if that's so—"

Corylus smiled. He seemed to be enjoying this. That was ridiculous, but Alphena felt a rush of relief anyway.

"—then being executed might be a relief compared to what else may be waiting for us and everybody else besides."

Alphena started to speak but burst out laughing. "Publius," she said, "that's a stupid way to make me feel better, *stupid*. But it works!"

They pulled up beside the lead vehicle. Drago and Rago had gotten down with the nervous-looking guide between them. The Illyrians were former pirates, and a stranger could be excused for wondering if "former" was necessarily the correct adjective.

"This guy, Herminus, says from here on out it's on foot," one or the other cousin said. He turned, so Alphena could see the missing ear: Drago. "Is that all right with you, lady?"

What are you going to do if it isn't *all right with me? Build a carriage road over the gully ahead?* Alphena thought.

Aloud she said, "That will be fine. We'll cross the rope bridge."

"Illyrian tribes have queens sometimes," Corylus said softly. "I think that pair have promoted you. You're not just the mistress."

The guards from the leading wagon crossed the swinging bridge with no trouble: the gulley was only twenty feet across, and the banks—though steep—were nowhere more than ten feet above the small stream at the bottom. Herminus, the councillor who had been their guide, waited at the near end.

He bowed to Alphena and said, "Your Ladyship? May I wait for you here? I had nothing to do with the ceremony, I was in my office going over the tax assessments. I—I really would rather stay on this side of the creek."

"Yes, all right, my good man," Alphena said. She hoped she sounded kindly, but the fellow's obvious fear worried her. "We'll still want you when we go back, so don't go far."

Corylus would have led her over the bridge, but she waved him back. There was nothing difficult about it, even when Corylus' weight behind her changed the way the support ropes moved . . . but at mid-point . . . when she was on the other side of the flowing water—Alphena felt, well, felt *odd*.

"I want to do a handspring," she said, turning her head back toward

Corylus. "I've never managed to do a handspring right in the gymnasium, but I feel that I *could* now."

"Umm," said Corylus as he followed her off the bridge. For a moment she thought that was all he was going to say, but he added, "Herminus must have come here after whatever happened. I guess everybody in the district did, just as they'd go see where some scullery maid slipped when she was feeding the hogs and they ate her."

"It doesn't feel *bad*," Alphena said. She wished she could describe what she *did* feel better, but words were her brother's affair. "But it's funny. I can see Herminus not wanting to come back here."

The area was rocky and wooded. There were paths but no open spaces that Alphena could see. "Were there ever farms here?" she asked.

"You couldn't plow it because of the slopes and all the rocks," Pulto said, looking around. "There's goats, though—"

He pointed the toe of one hobnailed sandal at a pile of round droppings near where they stood.

"—and they keep the undergrowth down."

"There should be people here," Corylus said, eying the three paths that branched in equally unpromising fashions before them. "Maybe we should have brought the guide after all."

Someone giggled beyond the screen of bushes. Corylus said, "No, Pulto!" Raising his cornelwood staff, he stepped between his servant and the sound. "Remember the Praetorians!"

Alphena frowned, then realized that Pulto had started to draw a sword from under his outer tunic. That wouldn't ordinarily have been a problem in the countryside—within the sacred boundaries of Carce it was a crucifixion offense—but in the midst of soldiers sent to put down unrest it could easily be fatal.

A middle-aged man and a heavy woman who might have been younger walked down the right-hand path. They were arm in arm. "Who are you?" the man asked.

"Why are we going this way, dearie?" the woman said to her companion. "We were going to find some more grapes, and they're the other way."

"I'm the Lady Alphena," Alphena said, stepping forward. Corylus had started to speak, but she raised her voice to be heard over him. "I'm looking for my mother, the Lady Hedia. She came here to lead the welcoming ceremony for Mother Matuta."

"*I* led the ceremony," said the man. He bowed with grave formality but would have fallen if the woman hadn't tugged him upright. "Lady Hedia merely led the dance. *I* am Doclianus, the priest of Matuta. Or I was." Doclianus turned around and started in the opposite direction.

"Where is my mother?" Alphena said as she followed the couple. She had let her voice rise.

"Her Ladyship is a fine woman," Doclianus said without looking back at Alphena. "I'm sure she worships Bacchus now. We all worship Bacchus; I do and Sophia does and everybody will."

The woman giggled and hugged herself closer to the priest.

"Sophia," Doclianus said. "That means 'wisdom,' did you know? But Sophia is as stupid as one of her husband's cows, aren't you, Sophia?"

"If you say so, dearie," the woman said cheerfully.

"Where is Lady Hedia now, Master Doclianus?" Corylus said in a calm but very firm tone.

"Don't know," said the priest. "Don't care. Bacchus is my god."

The vegetation here—ordinary trees and bushes as it seemed to Alphena—was overgrown with vines from which dangled clusters of grapes the size of a baby's fist. The trees had set fruit also. The several spiky trees in sight of the trail bore huge purple plums. A branch of one had broken under the weight of the fruit.

"The wood's brittle," Corylus said. He touched—caressed, it seemed to Alphena—the trunk of the plum with his left hand. "Somebody should've thinned them before this happened."

Doclianus and Sophia had each plucked a grape. They were feeding each other.

The path opened on to a rectangular clearing. The ground was flatter than anything Corylus and Alphena had seen since they got out of the coach, though there were outcrops in three directions and a ten-foot drop in the fourth.

Eighty or a hundred Praetorians stood at the top of the open space. They weren't in formation, but they were standing close together as though they were uncomfortable. The centurion in command had thrust his swagger stick under his equipment belt so that he could hold his drawn sword. He looked at Alphena and her companions, but he didn't shout a challenge or send a squad toward them.

There were dozens of civilians present also, in couples and small groups.

They mostly sprawled on the ground. Half of them seemed to be in drunken sleep, but others were eating fruit or in some stage of lovemaking.

Alphena noticed a man wearing an embroidered tunic—dress clothing this far from Carce—in a close embrace with a goat. A male goat. She looked away quickly, feeling her cheeks redden nonetheless

"That must be the altar," Pandareus said, gesturing to the low fieldstone pillar a little to the low side of the middle of the clearing.

"That stone there!" said Corylus. He strode toward a knee-high boulder near where they stood. "I've seen that. The smith I told you about in my vision was using it for his anvil when he forged the locket!"

The stone looked perfectly ordinary to Alphena; she could see a dozen others from where she stood that were more or less identical. She touched her chest over the amulet that she wore on a strap between her inner and outer tunics. It was uncomfortably heavy, but she couldn't think of a better way to keep it with her.

Alphena and Pandareus joined Corylus as he touched the stone with his fingertips. Pulto followed, watching what was happening and particularly what might be happening behind them.

Corylus must have felt his companions' doubt, because he grinned at them and said, "I know it was here, but there's nothing in the rock—"

He patted it.

"—to show anything more than weather. It must've been a long time ago, what I was seeing."

"Hey!" said Pulto. "There against the outcrop. That's Manetho, isn't it? Your steward, Your Ladyship?"

"Yes," said Alphena, striding across the clearing. Corylus was beside her, while Pulto and Pandareus followed as quickly as they could

Fury was at the top of Alphena's mind, but the width of the open space gave her time to realize that she was angry, because shouting threats at Manetho would be *something* and she desperately wanted to do something. She had been feeling helpless—helpless and useless—ever since she heard the first report of her mother's disappearance.

But Manetho wasn't responsible for the problem. Granted that the way the understeward sat slack jawed as his owner's daughter approached was behavior that justified being sent to the mines. Manetho himself would agree about that in normal times.

These weren't normal times, and punishing Manetho wouldn't help bring

Hedia and Varus back. Six months ago, that wouldn't have kept Alphena from screaming at the understeward; she might even have used Pulto's sword on Manetho. The law didn't prevent an owner from killing a slave, though many intellectuals would tut-tut about the girl's behavior and it would pain her kindhearted father.

She reached out and squeezed Corylus' wrist with her left hand. He looked at her in surprise.

"I've learned a great deal from Mother," Alphena said. "And from you and my brother. Thank you."

"Umm," Corylus said, facing front immediately. "It's mutual, I assure you."

He sounded as though he meant it, but what precisely he meant wasn't clear. This wasn't the time to pursue the matter, and Alphena wasn't sure that she ever wanted to pursue it.

The understeward's eyes suddenly focused. He lurched to his feet, using one hand to brace himself against the rock behind him. He was holding a piece of fruit—one of the unusually large local grapes—in his other hand.

For a moment Alphena though Manetho was going to throw the remainder away. Instead he popped it in his mouth, chewed for a moment, and swallowed. Juice ran down his chin.

Various ways to handle what had just happened cascaded through Alphena's mind. Ignoring it was simplest and had no immediate disadvantages.

"Good evening, Manetho," Alphena said briskly. "We're here to find my mother and brother. What happened on the day they disappeared?"

Manetho swayed. "Your Ladyship?" he said.

"Yes," Alphena said. "We know that the god Bacchus appeared. What did you see of Hedia and Varus after that?"

Alphena found it surprisingly easy to keep her temper when she reminded herself that she had a task to perform. *Screaming at a servant won't bring Mother back.*

Manetho blinked. Grapevines had naturally plaited themselves into a rope. It dangled in a swag across the face of the outcrop behind him. He reached for another grape without taking his eyes off his mistress.

Corylus took Manetho's hand, not harshly, and said, "That's all right, old man. You've had a few jars, haven't you? Why don't you walk us to the place where all this happened. The exercise will do you good."

"It's the grapes," Manetho said. "They're the best wine you ever drank."

"Come on, let's walk," Corylus said, moving the understeward away from the rock with one hand still on the right wrist. The other held the staff behind Manetho's back, pressing gently. "Which way, buddy?"

He's probably had a lot of experience handling drunks in military cantonments, Alphena thought. Then she thought, *Mother probably has a lot of experience also, but different experiences.*

Alphena paused to pick a grape and nibble before she followed the four men. Manetho was right: the rich purple skin was as full of wine as a goat-skin bottle. It was strong wine too, stronger than the unmixed Caecuban that Hedia occasionally gave Alphena when it was just the two of them together.

"So that you'll know what your limits are if you stay late at a party, dear child," Hedia had said. *I've got to get her back!*

They were headed toward the bottom of the open space. A path trailed off there, back in the general direction of the road a little south of the path they'd come by. They started down it. Manetho walked more or less normally, but Corylus kept his free arm hovering behind the understeward's back in case he had to grab him suddenly.

"Here," said Manetho, stopping. "Down there, that's where it happened."

They were on an outcrop, looking ten feet down at a clearing smaller that the one where they'd seen the troops stationed. In the middle of the open space was a boulder of some size; a rivulet leaked from the heart of the rock on which they stood and licked one side of the boulder.

"See that tree?" Manetho said, pointing past the boulder to the far end of the clearing.

"The olive?" Corylus said.

"Right. The Indian delegates that had come with one of Senator Sentius' understewards, they'd just planted a vine there. They were praying and it got light like there was a fire, only pink—not orange like a fire."

"The vine that's growing on the tree now?" Alphena said. "It's *huge*. At the base it's thicker than my arm. It's *covering* the tree."

"Yes, Your Ladyship," Manetho said. "But they just planted it. And there was the light, a big disk of light, and Lord Varus walked into it. Except . . ."

The understeward shook his head as though to clear it. "Only before that," he said, "Lord Bacchus and his cortege came out—not through the light, just out of it. There were thousands of them, fauns and tigers and all manner of things. I can't really remember the order it all happened. It isn't very clear, any of it. I may be wrong."

"But you saw my brother go into the light?" Alphena said. "What did my mother do? Did you see her?"

"I was with Her Ladyship," Manetho said. "She called to Lord Varus and she started walking toward him. We were down in the clearing already, but not close. I was with her; I was following Her Ladyship; I was doing my duty; I *swear* I was. Only I can't tell you how I felt; it was like I was floating and the gods were dancing with me, only it was women who'd come with Bacchus. And I danced with them; that's all I remember."

"Did the Lady Hedia follow Gaius into the light, Manetho?" Corylus said.

"I didn't see," said the understeward miserably. He shook his head again. "The way I felt, the way everybody felt—it wasn't just me; it was everybody. You had to float with it, everybody did, only . . ."

He took hold of his emotions and straightened, suddenly becoming the trusted servant of a noble household. "Lady Alphena," he said, "when I last saw your mother, she was walking toward the disk of light. Everyone else, *everyone*, was going mad, but she wasn't. She was moving like a fish against the stream, ignoring the riot and the things who'd come out of the light."

Manetho cleared his throat; his voice had begun to rasp. "I don't know what Lady Hedia did after I saw her last," he said, "but she knew what she was doing and nobody was going to stop her. Whatever it was."

Alphena felt suddenly dizzy. "I understand," she said.

"If Lord Sentius was involved with this . . . ," said Pandareus, "as we thought he might be from the first, after all, then there's the possibility that he will be able to return Lady Hedia and Lord Varus to the Waking World, or at least to show us how to go to them."

Pandareus' measured tones were soothing. *He's talking about the problem, not the darkness that threatens beyond the edges of the little that we really know.*

"Mother went somewhere that isn't here anymore," Alphena said. "We need a magician to get her back and get back my brother. My brother, who's the magician we need."

"I want to go down and see that olive closer up," Corylus said. "The rest of you can wait here."

"We can come with you," Alphena said. Her tone was sharper than she'd intended.

"I'd rather—" Corylus said.

"Corylus, do you talk to trees?" Alphena said, letting the words burst out over his objection. She knew the answer from things she had seen and heard in the past months, but he had never admitted it.

Corylus touched his tongue to his lips. His voice had been harsh a moment before. Mildly he said, "Not exactly. But something like that, yes. I suppose I shouldn't be embarrassed or whatever it is. We've seen stranger things than that."

"So we have," said Pulto. "And by Hercules! I wish we hadn't."

Pulto was looking at the ground rather than at any of his companions. Pandareus waited with his usual attitude of quiet expectancy; Manetho seemed to have slipped back into the drunken reverie from which their arrival had roused him.

"If you want to come, come along," Corylus said. He started toward the side where the slope softened enough to allow them to walk down instead of sliding.

"It's happening again," Manetho said without raising his voice. He pointed to the tree through a filter of rosy haze that hadn't been there a moment before. "Lord Bacchus is coming again. And I'm thankful."

"Back to the bridge and the coach!" Corylus said. "Fast!"

"But shouldn't we wait and—" Alphena said.

"No!" said Corylus, grabbing her wrist. "Pulto, leave Manetho and move!"

Alphena turned and ran with Corylus. She didn't pull her hand away from him until he released her himself.

HEDIA DIDN'T THINK BOEST HAD MOVED since she left him. She had drunk her fill before leaving Gilise's valley, but her nostrils and the back of her throat had begun to dry as soon as she started back down the slope to Boest and Paddock.

It used to be Gilise's valley. Hedia laughed and felt better for it.

"Master Boest!" she called as she started up to where the big man sat. She waved the glass phial in her right hand. "I have something for you."

Boest didn't respond. Well, she hadn't really expected him to.

"Greetings, Lady Hedia," the toad croaked. "You made good time."

Hedia waved again but didn't otherwise reply. The last twenty feet were making her stagger. If she hadn't been determined not to give in to weakness, she would have paused for a few minutes before climbing the final portion. She'd forced herself to breathe through her nose, because breathing through her open mouth would have been not only unladylike but also un-couth.

She smiled again. Each breath was painful and her lungs were burning, but there was so much other pain that she didn't particularly notice it.

The gritty soil on this side of the ridge had gotten between Hedia's feet and the leather of the sandals. She had tightened the straps because there was nothing else to do, but she knew her soles were bleeding by now.

She stood for a moment beside the big man. Paddock hadn't shifted his position, but she realized that one of the toad's eyes was watching her. The thought was briefly disconcerting, but only briefly. Hedia was used to accepting the whims of men she was with; and if Paddock wanted to watch her sidelong, that was less surprising than some of the things she'd grown accustomed to.

"I have your soul, Master Boest," she said, holding out the phial. It was the size of a baby's fist. The glass was faintly greenish. In the interior, sparkles swirled on currents in an unseen fluid. The stopper was fixed in place with a blob of yellow wax.

"Ah," said Boest. His head moved slightly so that his eyes could follow one of his goats on the other side of the valley; otherwise Hedia's figure would have blocked his view.

"Do you believe in the power of prayer, Hedia?" Paddock said.

"What?" said Hedia. "No. I make the usual offerings to the gods, of course, but that's because it's proper to do so. I don't imagine that immortal powers will aid me because I burned a pinch of frankincense or whatever."

"I prayed that you would come to us," the toad said. "And you came."

"Yes," said Hedia. "And it rained three days ago on the twelfth of the month. Did you pray for that also?"

She waved her free hand dismissively. "I've brought what Gilise claimed was Boest's soul," she said, raising the bottle slightly for emphasis. "I don't think he was lying. What do I do now so that I can find the Spring of True Answers?"

"Hold the bottle under Boest's nose," Paddock said. "When he begins to breathe in, pull the top off."

Hedia knelt, feeling the grit through the skirt of her tunic. She had scraped her knees already in the course of misdirecting Gilise.

She held the phial beneath Boest's nose as directed, but he tried to twitch

his head away. "Stop that!" she snapped. She gripped his bearded chin between her left thumb and forefinger. He didn't pull away.

"Now breathe in," Paddock said. "*Breathe*, darling, for us."

Boest's nostrils flared. Hedia flicked the top off the phial with her left
thumb as he took a deep breath.

The sparkling lights from the interior of the phial flowed into the big man's
nose. For a moment Hedia thought she saw them winking and shining in his
eyes as well. Boest blinked.

Hedia had seen men in a variety of moods, sometimes several violently
different moods in a matter of seconds as a realization sank in. What she saw
on Boest's face now made her step away so abruptly that she almost fell backward on the slope.

That passed. Boest got to his feet, cradling the toad in his left hand.
Hedia looked up at Boest.

He's bigger than I thought. He's much bigger.

"Welcome back, heart of my heart," Paddock said.

Boest smiled at him. "You've changed, little one," he said in a deep, melodious tone.

"Not in the important ways," the toad said. "My love hasn't changed."

"Lady Hedia," Boest said, nodding to acknowledge her. "I will guide you
to the Spring of True Answers, as you wish. But first we will return to my
valley to see Gilise."

"I told him I would spare his life if he returned your soul, Master Boest,"
Hedia said.

"I would not kill him," said Boest. It was like listening to a waterfall speak.
"But we have things to discuss, Gilise and I. I very much want to have a discussion with him."

Boest offered Hedia his free hand as they started toward the green valley.
She was glad of the support.

CHAPTER VI

Alphena stumbled almost at once. Corylus had led them into the brush instead of following a path, and an ankle-height lip of rock stood up from the surrounding soil. Even after she tripped, the lip was barely visible over the leaf litter. She didn't sprawl on her face—swordsmanship training had made her nimble—but she wasn't nearly as surefooted as Corylus was.

He was a Scout, Alphena remembered. Or at least he had gone across the Danube with the Scouts. The exercise ground—and the arena itself; the word simply meant "a sand surface"—was smooth. Slaughter on the frontiers took place in any kind of terrain and often enough in woodland.

Pulto thumped along behind. Alphena knew the veteran's knees were bad, so this hike must be agony to him. He wasn't having trouble with the ground, though.

The creek must be nearby to the left. Corylus was following his sense of direction and going straight for the bridge, rather taking the paths.

Horns blew from several directions, one of them directly ahead. Alphena heard shouts and music from behind them. A flute skirled, but its notes were almost lost in a joyous harmony warbling from women's throats.

They burst out onto a tract covered in scrub grass and small bushes. The underlying rock was too close to the surface to support more substantial growth. Sheep-sized outcrops thrust up in several places, but the ground was closer to being flat than most of what they'd seen since they left the coach.

A company of Praetorians was forming on their standard to the right. Though the light was fading, their armor and the steel points of their weapons caught the sky's red glow. The cornicine, wrapped in the tube of his curved horn, blew signals to the other scattered companies of troops.

"They're treating this like a riot!" Corylus said. "They're in a single rank. From what Manetho described, there's too many coming for one rank to stop!"

"Who spread 'em out by companies?" Pulto said. He didn't sound winded, but Alphena thought she heard a touch of pain in his voice. "By Hercules' balls! In woods like this!"

The cornicine blew again as Corylus led his group around the right edge of the armored line. The Praetorians held their javelins ready to throw. Alphena heard non-coms snarling commands to individual soldiers, dressing the line.

They seemed ready for a fight. There was none of the nervous antici-pation that had radiated from the company Alphena had seen earlier. Per-haps those troops had settled also, now that they had a real enemy to fight.

A wild whooping and yelling burst from the woods. Alphena looked over her shoulder. Pulto wore a grim expression and carried his sword openly in his right hand; he too was glancing back. Pandareus—*I forgot him!*—was only a stride behind the veteran. Though old, the teacher was wiry and in good condition. He walked between libraries in Carce and lived in a fourth-floor tenement. His expression was interested rather than concerned.

Pouring from the wood line was the horde that Manetho had described: humans wearing mottled animal skins, mixed with fauns, satyrs, and at least one centaur. They shouted in delight, waving pinecones mounted on fennel stalks—thyrsi, which Alphena had seen in processions to Isis through the streets of Carce.

Leading the mob was a man in a chariot. The pair of leopards that drew it were bigger than any lion that Alphena had seen in the arena.

The charioteer waved a torch that lit the whole scene as brightly as the sun, throwing knife-sharp shadows behind the Praetorians. Alphena threw her hand up to shade her eyes.

"There!" cried the charioteer. "That's the woman Rupa described. Bring her to me!"

He's pointing the torch at me, Alphena realized. For a moment her eyes locked with those of the man in the chariot. A tiny jolt touched her mind, the mental equivalent of a spark jumping from silk to her finger on a dry day. She jerked her head around.

"Run!" said Corylus, but Alphena was sprinting for the woods ahead. She wasn't wearing a sword—her role today was to be Lady Alphena—but she would grab one when they reached the vehicles. There was one in the coach for her and a store of extra weapons in both the wagons.

She didn't think a sword would do much good against this army, but it would make her feel better.

The wind had sprung up from the east, bringing perfumes fuller than those of flowers. She had heard Corylus and her brother talk of Alexander's army marching back from India through fields of frankincense and myrrh. Perhaps that was happening here: the invaders had come from a land of incense, and the breeze carried the crushed memory of their passage.

"Ready spears!" shouted the centurion in command. Despite the uproar, his deep bellow was clearly audible. "Loose!"

From the corner of her eye Alphena saw the Praetorians' right arms swing forward; nearly a hundred javelins flickered out in flat arcs. A satyr leaped into the air, spinning end over end like a circus act before he fell back. A javelin had transfixed his body just below the rib cage; the point and half the shaft stuck out from his back. As he pirouetted, the metal butt spike protruding from his belly winked also.

There were other wounds in the Bacchic flood—a Maenad pinned to the Bassarid behind her in a terrible parody of lovemaking, a faun who continued to play his pipes for long seconds after a javelin had transfixed his skull. Half the spears twisted into vine shoots in the air, though, and struck harmless blows. When they fell to earth, they immediately began to sprout.

A seed of emotion had sprouted in Alphena's soul since she locked eyes with the charioteer. As she breathed the rich electric wind, the feeling inside her swelled like the branches budding in the woods through which they ran, pink and white and the tiny yellow-green flowerets of oaks.

"There's the bridge!" said Corylus. "The running water may help!"

"I'm not going," Alphena said. She wasn't sure whether she spoke the words or they just formed in her mind. "I belong here."

She turned and would have run back to the vine-crowned god in the chariot, but Pulto wrapped his left arm around her. "Careful, girlie," he said.

Corylus grabbed Alphena's wrist as he'd done when they saw the portal begin to form. "Alphena!" he said. "Come on now!"

People, some of them Praetorians who had thrown away their shields and helmets, boiled from the woods. The men and women who had come through the portal waved thyrsi; some of the Praetorians brandished flowering branches that they must have ripped from trees as they danced past.

They know! Alphena thought. She turned—Pulto willingly let her go; he must think she had stumbled—and threw her right arm around Corylus.

"Yes, take me!" she said. She tried to kiss Corylus. The red pulsing flame of lust was devouring her body.

Corylus let go of her wrist and caught her by the neck from behind. He peeled her off him one-handed and pushed her into Pulto.

"Get her out of here!" Corylus shouted. "Now! The spell has her and if we don't stop her I'll be *lucky* to be crucified when it's all over!"

"No, don't leave me!" Alphena said, straining toward Corylus with both hands. Pulto's arm had no more flex than an anchor line does.

Pulto sheathed his sword with a skill that Alphena would have appreciated in other circumstances. Holding her with both arms, he lumbered onto the suspension bridge, causing it to pitch wildly. Pandareus was already across.

Alphena screamed with frustration, but nothing she could do affected the veteran's obedience to his commander's son. When she last saw Corylus, he was on his knees beside one of the suspension hawsers of the bridge. He'd drawn his big army dagger.

RAMSA LAL AND MOST of the remaining troops trotted toward the structure ahead, but a horseman rode back to Varus. He said in bad Greek, "Come along, you. The rajah wants you in his private reception room when you arrive."

"We will be glad to see the rajah when we arrive," Varus said, deciding to be polite. "If you'll bring us a skin of wine, it will speed our steps."

"If I tie your wrists to my saddle horn, it will speed your steps!" the horseman snarled. "Or perhaps I should borrow a lance and prick you on?"

"Did your master the rajah tell you why he wants to meet with this foreign wizard?" Bhiku said. He added something in Indian; Varus suspected that he was translating his own question to make sure that the horseman understood the warning.

"I am too pure to soil my spirit by riding on a lower animal," Varus said, trying to sound lofty through a dry throat. "Therefore I travel at the speed of my legs."

Bhiku's quick jingle of Indian was certainly a translation this time.

The horseman jerked his hand away from the pommel of his sword where it had strayed. "I will find wine," he said. He rode after the remainder of the squadron at the best speed his tired horse could manage.

"I wonder if he'll be back?" Varus said. "Do you suppose he thought I was going to turn him into a toad?"

"I've never seen that done," said Bhiku. He raised an eyebrow.

"You're not going to see me do it, either," Varus said drily. After a moment's thought he added, "And I'm not too spiritual to ride a horse, either. I'm just too awkward to do it without falling off."

The battlemented walls were eight feet high; the square towers on either side of the gateway rose four or five feet higher. The whole structure was built of red sandstone blocks a foot in either dimension.

The double gates were fully open, probably their normal state. The squad of spearmen on guard lounged under a marquee strung from three trees outside the gate; the only sign of anyone in the towers was the end of a long bamboo bow propped against the battlements.

To Varus' surprise, the horseman who had been their escort reappeared leading a pair of servants in bleached white garments. Their clothes were clean and new in contrast to the foot soldiers' garb, and silk sashes held up their loose trousers. They were carrying a brass bottle wrapped in what seemed to be sacking.

The horseman pirouetted in front of Varus and Bhiku, then drew his sword and gestured with it as he shouted to the servants in Indian. "They've brought wine cooled in wet moss," Bhiku explained. "Apparently Hanwant, our escort, wasn't looking forward to the chance of seeing the world through the eyes of a toad."

"There are so few enlightened men nowadays," Varus said, taking the cup a servant offered him. The pale yellow wine made his mouth tingle pleasantly. There was only one cup, so he passed it to Bhiku still half-full.

"You don't need to do that!" the horseman said.

"I choose to share with my colleague . . . ," Varus said, wondering if Hanwant could catch the haughty tone he was using. "As we share the dangers of the powerful magic we work."

The servants were ready to refill the cup. Varus checked with Bhiku by raising his eyebrow, then waved them off. They walked through the gateway together; Hanwant hesitated a moment, then rode past so that he could guide them through the courtyard.

"I was tempted to have another cup of wine," Varus said quietly. "But that had been enough to clear my throat, and I don't want to be muzzy when I talk with our host. I normally drink my wine mixed with two or three times its volume of water."

Bhiku laughed. "I normally drink my water stagnant," he said. "I don't think I've had wine a dozen times in my life. But it certainly made me feel better today."

The outer wall enclosed a grassy park in which horses grazed and trees of shapes unfamiliar to Varus grew. There were outbuildings—stables and sheds, but also a dome of colored marble supported by slender pillars. The massive two-story palace ahead would be the focus of any visitor's attention, however.

The horsemen were dismounting at the arched double-height gateway. Grooms led the horses toward the stables at right angles to the palace facade, while the soldiers themselves went inside.

On the ground floor the palace windows were small, perhaps only arrow slits. Those on the upper floor were larger but were shaped into twin arches separated by a pillar so that only a child or very slender adult could slip through the openings.

"Do you have any idea what Lal wants me to do?" Varus asked quietly. Hanwant was well ahead and anyway seemed completely disinterested in what the magicians might discuss among themselves.

"I do not," said Bhiku. "I have been away for many months, remember, as we traveled to Carce by ship. Only after we reached Polymartium and planted the vine were we able to enter the Otherworld and return home more quickly."

To the right of the palace was a low featureless wall that stretched over a greater width than the building proper. Bhiku noticed his companion frowning toward it and said, "That is the tank which fills in the monsoon season and supplies the palace now during the dry season. I didn't notice reservoirs in Italy, but I wasn't looking."

"We have aqueducts from springs in the hills," said Varus. "The winds don't bring rains to Italy as writers say they do here."

I wonder if I'll still be in India when the monsoons come? I wonder what magic Ramsa Lal wants me to perform?

Varus laughed. He grinned at his companion and said, "I don't believe that I'm a wizard in the sense that Mistress Rupa is or even you are, Bhiku."

Varus was answering a question the sage might have been too polite to ask. "I couldn't have opened a gate to the Otherworld as you did or one from it. But regardless of whether or not I'm really a wizard, I can say with certainty that I'm not a fortune-teller. The only way I can learn the future is by living into it."

Hanwant waited for them impatiently at the courtyard entrance. When they joined him, he drew his sword and turned, bellowing something in Indian.

Occasionally he used the flat of his sword to bat someone out of the way—or to bat someone who was possibly close enough to have gotten in the way.

"He's telling everyone to make way for the great foreign wizard," Bhiku said. He wore a slight smile.

"I notice that he's picking particularly ragged spectators on whom to demonstrate his importance," Varus said. "I've noticed similar things in Carce when my servants are escorting me through a crowd."

The rectangular courtyard was bare earth, more than half-covered by shanties and traders' kiosks. The stonework on the interior was plastered white. There were only a few places where the covering had flaked away from the red interior.

Porticos encircled the inner face of the walls; the pillars on the upper level stood in slender pairs instead of the massive single columns below. The archways throughout were formed in multiple scallops instead of the single smooth arc with which Varus was familiar.

Hanwant was leading them to an exterior staircase at a corner of the courtyard. Two men with drawn swords—they might have been members of Lal's mounted escort—guarded the base of the stairs under a marquee of blue silk with gold tassels.

"This way, honored lord," Hanwant said as they approached the stairs. He spoke to the guards in Indian. Their replies were curt, and the verbal temperature rose abruptly.

Bhiku leaned close to Varus and said, "Hanwant wants to take you in to the rajah. They say they're to admit the foreigner—the rajah didn't tell them you were a wizard—but he said they know nothing about rabble from Nivas' troop, which would be Hanwant. Let alone filthy beggar scum."

Bhiku bowed to Varus, grinning.

"Then I'd best see if I can get us all out of the sun," Varus said. Raising his voice, he said, "Noble Hanwant! Noble Hanwant, step aside if you please!"

Pandareus would be pleased with my tone of authority, Varus thought. Training really did count.

Hanwant *did* step back, looking surprised. In a normal voice, Varus said, "Thank you, Hanwant. Your dedication will be noted."

The guards were watching in puzzlement. To them Varus said, "You may escort me to the rajah."

They looked at each other in hesitation. *Do they even speak Greek?*

"You may guide me, or I will turn you into toads and find my own way,"

Varus said, still calmly. He raised his hands at shoulder height, palms toward the guards. They scrambled in opposite directions. One of them dropped his sword in haste.

"Lead me and my colleague to Lord Ramsa Lal, Hanwant," Varus said, nodding.

I'll be lucky if I don't burst out laughing when we meet the rajah, he thought. And Bhiku seemed to be in the same state.

CORYLUS PLACED HIS LEFT FOOT on one bridge hawser and drew his dagger upward in a sliding stroke with both hands. The dagger jerked free, having severed most of the several cords twisted to make the rope; a few strands remained, but Corylus ignored them to shift to the undamaged hawser.

He rotated the dagger to bring the other edge up. Sawing rope—these appeared to have been woven from rye straw—dulled a blade almost as quickly as trying to cut stone.

Since the light of the charioteer's torch had bathed him, Corylus saw everything with unnatural sharpness. The fibers of the rope were individually clear, as were the beard hairs of the Bassarid a hundred feet away.

The latter shouted, "Io, Bacchus!" between gulps from the wineskin in the crook of his left arm. His right hand held a thyrsus. Corylus was in no mood to mock that as a weapon, having seen a Maenad plunge her similar pinecone through a Praetorian's shield.

Despite the clarity with which he observed his surroundings, Corylus felt that his mind was clouded by a red haze. It brightened and sank back as his heart beat. He was keyed up, blazing with emotion but focused on his task. Nothing mattered but his task.

He was blazing with lust.

Corylus drew up on the dagger. For a moment nothing moved; a straight pull was useless on this hawser, even with a sharp blade wielded by a strong young man. He tipped the point slightly down so that the edge would saw upward, but his nervous jumpiness caused him to tilt too much. He cut through only half the rope's thickness. He replaced the blade to finish the cut.

"Io, Bacchus!" warbled a chorus of voices. Corylus looked up as he finished his cut. A Praetorian carrying a wineskin staggered toward him. His free arm was around a naked Maenad, and a blond-bearded faun hugged him close on the other side.

Behind Corylus, the bridge rattled into the gulley. The stream wasn't a real barrier, but the previous Bacchic incursion had stopped at running water. Corylus could at least hope that this one would also. Pandareus and Alphena would be safe.

"Drink with the god!" the Praetorian said, thrusting his wineskin toward Corylus. The man was in his mid-thirties. Though he had lost his helmet, he wore his sword on his left hip instead of his right like a common soldier: he was a centurion, very possibly the centurion commanding the company that the throng had overrun.

"Not tonight, friend," Corylus said, pressing the man back with his left hand. Corylus already felt drunk from the perfumed atmosphere; the gods alone knew what a draft of this magical wine would do to him.

Corylus sheathed his dagger without looking down at it, then groped for the cornelwood staff he'd dropped to free both hands. He felt no desire to kill anything at this moment. Logically considered, being given wine was only a slight problem compared with what could result if he offered lethal violence to a thousand or so drunken revelers—but logic had nothing to do with what he *felt*.

"Well, put this in your mouth, then!" the Maenad cried, lifting her right breast and pushing the erect nipple toward him. She wasn't young, but she was fit and her eagerness itself was a drug.

Lust overwhelmed Corylus. He stood, shoving the centurion so fiercely that the fellow fell backward. Corylus wasn't conscious of what his arm had done.

The Maenad pressed against him, raising her mouth to his. For an instant Corylus saw and felt not the woman groping him now but rather Alphena: her face and naked body, and the eyes hot with lust.

"No!" he cried, breaking free. He turned to leap the gulley—he could do that in his current state—to find Alphena and give her the violent rogering that he now wanted as much as she had.

"No!" Corylus shouted again, to himself this time. If he'd still had the dagger in his hand, he might have plunged it into his own chest in horror.

Corylus ran along the edge of the creek, toward where the throng had entered the Waking World. Just now he didn't trust himself to rejoin his companions on the other side of the water.

Scores of Bacchic revelers capered and called as they filtered through the broken woods. The light was bad and nobody seemed to pay particular attention to Corylus anyway—he was one more running figure in a landscape filled with assorted figures running. A handsome youth in a fawn skin tried to kiss him as they passed in opposite directions, but that was the sort of thing that might happen any afternoon at a public bath.

The effect that the Maenad's passion had on Corylus was wearing off, though there was a dull ache in his groin. His head was buzzing also, but that had been true since the charioteer's torchlight had fallen on him. He was thinking clearly, but his mind lay beneath a surface of seething emotion.

Corylus dodged behind a vine-covered maple to avoid a centaur who was galloping toward him. As the centaur swept past, hooves hammering the ground, Corylus realized that the creature hadn't been attacking. A woman—worn and not young; probably a farmer's wife—rode the centaur with her arms around his human torso. The centaur had twisted around so that they could kiss passionately as they charged off in whatever direction they happened to be going at the time he turned.

"Hello, Cousin," said the woman at Corylus' side. *A Maenad and I didn't know she was there!* he thought as he turned, not frightened but angry with himself for not having seen her before she spoke.

She was the maple sprite, not a Maenad. She looked like a slender woman and was very beautiful. Her shift of green/scarlet/gray was translucent from an angle, transparent when the light of the rising moon fell on the fabric squarely.

"Hello, Acer," Corylus gasped, leaning forward. He braced his hands on his bent knees. He glanced back to make sure no one was chasing him—there were scores of people in sight, but none of them seemed interested in Publius Corylus—and began to gasp through his open mouth. He was weak and trembling, though he knew from experience on the Danube that his strength would rush back the instant he needed it again.

The sprite ran her fingers lightly through his hair and gave a throaty laugh. She said, "I'm glad you came tonight, Cousin. I'm in the mood for company. When Ampelos visited a few days ago I met a satyr who was a lot of fun, but I think you might be even more fun."

Corylus straightened, though he continued to breathe through his mouth. "I can't do that now, Acer," he said. He had his gasping under control, or almost under control.

The sprite laughed again and reached under his tunic to caress his erect member. "Of course we can do that!" she said.

Corylus moved her hand away. "I mean I have to get back to my friends, dear one," he said. "Who's Ampelos?"

Though Corylus' body was certainly ready—he was a healthy young man;

of course his body was ready—lust no longer lay so heavily on his mind that its weight warped all his thoughts. He seemed to be getting back to normal, or he hoped he was.

"Ampelos is leading the troupe," Acer said. She tried to wriggle her hand past Corylu's again, though she wasn't fighting his strength. "He's usually with Bacchus, but he's come himself this time and before."

Light flared as the chariot bounced toward them through the brush, accompanied by scores of leaping figures. "That one!" cried the charioteer, and pointed with the torch.

He's named Ampelos, not Bacchus, Corylus thought, but that didn't matter at the moment.

He wasn't concerned. He had his breath back. The chariot couldn't jump the gulley, and Corylus was sure he could outdistance any of the throng except possibly the lightly built fauns. The cornelwood staff was an answer to them, needs must.

"Got to leave!" Corylus said, turning as he spoke. He intended to take two strides and then leap the gulley. He jerked to a halt an inch into the air over where he'd started.

The grapevines that hung from the maple tree were wrapped around his torso and left ankle. He hadn't felt their touch until they brought him up short. He reached for his dagger with his left hand, but another vine was about his wrist. His right hand was bound to the staff.

"Acer!" Corylus cried, but there was nothing the tree sprite could do. The throng encircled him. The chariot drew up. Ampelos leaned over the side, holding out the torch.

Acer put her arms about Corylus, ignoring the vines wrapping his limbs and torso. "I think I'll send you to my sister, since you're such a sweet boy," she said, and kissed him on the lips.

Light flashed like the sun from a silver mirror. Corylus gasped.

He was in the arms of a different sprite. The maple tree was free of grapevines, and the sky above the woods was a richer, sharper blue than ever in the Waking World.

Corylus was in the Otherworld. There was no sign of Ampelos and his minions.

HEDIA AND BOEST HAD WALKED DOWN from the top of the ridge in silence until they were within fifty feet of the house and the tree from which Gilise hung suspended with his back to them. There Boest paused, digging his toes into the green turf. He stretched his arms out and back, keeping his right hand cupped so that Paddock didn't have to move.

Hedia stopped a pace farther and looked back. "Would you like me to release him?" she said.

"You've come back?" Gilise called. "You took long enough! Come, let me down!"

He flailed his arms, apparently trying to rotate so that he could look at her. Mostly he jounced up and down, making the branch quiver.

"No, I'll take care of that," Boest said quietly. He set Paddock down on the damp grass and walked with a long, easy stride to the hanging man. The toad hopped after Boest, moving in flat hops that covered ground more quickly than Hedia would have guessed.

"Listen, you bitch!" Gilise shouted. "You gave your oath! Demons will gnaw your bones in the Underworld if you don't free me!"

Hanging hasn't improved his temper, Hedia thought, smiling faintly. Or his senses, since he obviously hadn't heard Boest's reply.

Boest took the sash between the thumb and forefinger of his big right hand. He rotated his grip slightly so that Gilise turned to face him.

"Boest!" Gilise said.

"Hello, Gilise," Boest said. "I've come to take my valley back. Is the handcart still in the shed?"

"Boest, you can't kill me!" Gilise said. His voice was as shrill as the north wind through the tops of frozen fir trees. "The woman swore she'd let me go! I gave you your soul back!"

Hedia joined them. Paddock sat nearby on the grass, looking more alert than she had imagined a toad could look.

"I'm not going to kill you, Gilise," Boest said. "You and I are going to give back all the souls you've stolen, not just mine. Lady Hedia says the bottles are in the lean-to, is that right?"

"Yes, that's where they are!" Gilise said. "We'll take them back, just as you say. But let me go now, darling; this is agony, what she's done to me!"

"I'm going to the shed," Boest said to Hedia. "I'll be back in a moment. But leave him as he is, please."

Hedia nodded. She watched Boest stride toward the outbuilding. She felt uncomfortable with the situation, though she didn't think Boest was the sort of man to lie.

"Lady, you have to let me go now before he comes back!" Gilise said. "He'll kill me, you know he will, and you promised you'd let me go!"

He made a desperate attempt to grab her garment, but shooting his arms out made him rock back on the silken cord. She took a half step backward.

"He'll kill me!"

"You deserve to die," Hedia said.

"Boest will not kill you, Gilise," said Paddock. "He gave his word, and his word is good."

Boest returned from the shed, pushing a handcart. It squeaked abominably: the wooden axle was rubbing the hubs of the two wheels without lubrication.

He stopped a little distance from Gilise, smiled at Hedia, and took a hammer from the bed of the cart. It looked tiny in Boest's hand, but Hedia knew the iron head must weigh more than a pound.

Hedia stepped in front of Boest. "Master Boest," she said. "I gave my word. I will not—"

She caught herself. She couldn't stop Boest from doing anything he pleased. Her little knife was still knotted into the end of the sash, and she didn't think it would be much use anyway against the big man with a hammer.

"Master Boest," Hedia said. "Please, if you feel any obligation to me, do not besmirch my honor in this matter."

"I owe you my soul, Lady Hedia," Boest said with a sad smile. "Gilise and I will carry the souls he stole back to their owners. I need him to guide me, if you doubt *my* honor."

"I don't doubt your honor," Hedia said, stepping out of his way. *I never should have doubted him, but I did.*

"But Lady Hedia?" Boest said without moving from where he stood. "He must stay with me until we have finished."

"I will, Boest," Gilise trilled. "I'll make up for my mistakes. I swear I will!"

Hedia smiled at Boest. "I promised him his life and his freedom," she said. "No more than that."

"Then be ready to loose the cord," Boest said. "I will catch him so that he doesn't fall to the ground."

Hedia walked to the springhead and pulled slightly on the sash to give herself slack. She lifted the loop off the stone stele; she could unknot it at leisure.

Boest held Gilise's free ankle with his left hand, then flipped the hammer in the air and caught it by the head. Gilise was babbling something. Boest broke his shin with a quick tap of the hammer handle, an eighteen-inch hardwood baton.

Gilise screamed. Boest gripped his other ankle and broke that shin also. He cradled Gilise's body to the ground as Hedia released the sash. Gilise had fainted.

"I don't know how long it will take to find all the victims," Boest said. "I may have to break his legs several more times as they heal. I hope by the time we have finished Gilise will understand the pain he has brought to others and he'll change his ways after I let him go."

"You used to love him," Hedia said. The smell of Gilise's fear hung over them, like that of a rotting corpse.

"I still love him," Boest said quietly. He looked at the toad and said, "I'm sorry, little one, but I do."

Paddock made a grunting sound. "I've never asked you to lie to me, dear heart," he said. "I never will ask that."

"Lady Hedia, I'll take you to the Spring of True Answers now," Boest said. "It isn't far away."

He looked down at the toad. "And you, little one?" he said.

"I'll wait here with Gilise," Paddock said. "Just watching. You don't need to hurry back on my account."

I promised Gilise his life, Hedia thought. Then she thought, *A quick death would have been too good for him.*

CHAPTER VII

Alphena and Pandareus had the back garden of Saxa's town house to themselves. It wasn't a place in which she had spent much time in the past.

Behind the high wall was an alley, and in the wall was the gate through which deliveries generally arrived. The plantings had been almost an afterthought, though there was a loggia against either corner of the inner wall to suit the family's possible whim.

Originally there had been two fruit trees: a pear and a peach. Now the pear was gone, shattered by a killing frost in midsummer while Saxa was under the control of the wizard Nemastes and they worked magic here. Publius Corylus had recently sent a pomegranate to replace the pear, but no other work had been done in the garden since the spell had been conjured here.

In practice the loggias had been used to store gardening tools until magic had tainted the garden with a *feeling* that the servants found as unsettling as the fumes of burning sulphur. The doorman at the back gate stood in the alley instead of in the garden, looking out through a grate, and gardeners had moved their tools somewhere else. That way they didn't have to enter the garden except to water the trees. They probably wouldn't have done even that except that Alphena checked and kept them to the task.

I might not have bothered about the peach, she thought. *But we couldn't let the gift of Publius Corylus wither and die.*

Pandareus sat beside her in the northern loggia, looking at the painted frieze beneath the roof. Alphena had brought him here because it was private in a fashion that no place else in a house with over two hundred resident servants could be, but as a foreigner of no status he was properly holding his silence until his noble hostess began the conversation.

Alphena took the Ear of the Satyr out from under her tunic. The iron case felt warm between her palms. Instead of talking about the things that mattered, she said, "Is there something important about those paintings, Master Pandareus?"

The things that mattered were first: that they weren't any closer to finding Hedia and Varus than before they went to Polymartium *and* they'd lost Corylus besides. And second: that Alphena had tried to rape Corylus after the charioteer's light had shone on her.

The second thing was what filled Alphena's mind as fully as passion had the previous evening at Polymartium. She had humiliated herself—and Corylus had then rejected her, which increased her misery.

It was possible that Pandareus hadn't seen what was going on. It was even possible that Pulto had misunderstood; certainly he hadn't said anything to suggest that he *had* understood what Lady Alphena was trying to do.

Of course Pulto hasn't said anything to me. He'll talk to Lenatus and who knows what other army buddies, though! And they'll talk to their girlfriends and everybody in Carce will know that Saxa's daughter is a hot-crotch little tramp!

Everybody including Hedia, when she returned. The embarrassment of having failed her stepmother was the worst thing of all.

"Important, Your Ladyship—no," Pandareus said. "But they're quite interesting. You see here"—he stood and indicated the frieze over the ends of the loggia by pointing in both directions—"you have cupids imitating a battle of Greeks and Amazons. On the front and back"—he rotated ninety degrees—"you have the battle of the centaurs and Lapiths, again being fought by cupids."

"I've seen cupids on friezes before," Alphena said, glad to turn her mind from her own thoughts. "Doing farm labor, working in shops—all the things people do."

"Indeed," Pandareus said. "But these cupids are copying the frieze of the Temple of Apollo at Bassae, which is the most perfect work by Ictinus."

"I've never heard of it," Alphena said. "I've never heard of Ictinus, either."

She was mildly irritated. Pandareus should know her well enough to realize that she didn't care about anything in Greece, which Carce had conquered centuries ago. Now it was a source of teachers, like Pandareus himself, and old statues, which impressed Saxa. If Greece had bred gladiators, she might know something about it.

"Ictinus designed the Parthenon," Pandareus said. "Thirty years later, he designed the temple at Bassae, which refined his earlier design—but in the middle of nowhere. Even for those of us who find more importance in Greece than most citizens of Carce can understand."

He smiled gently.

He does know me, Alphena realized. Aloud she said, "I've heard of the Parthenon. Even I have."

"Everything is connected, Your Ladyship," Pandareus said. "If we could understand the connections, we could understand everything. I try to explain that to my students, but I'm afraid most of them would settle for knowing which Stable will win the next day's chariot race. Your brother and Master Corylus being exceptions, of course."

"*I'd* settle for getting them back," Alphena said. "And Mother."

The silly digression had calmed Alphena more than she would have believed. She could think again instead of just wallowing in pointless misery like a landed fish flopping on the sand.

She looked at Pandareus sharply as her mind went into a different pathway. She said, "Did you . . . ?"

Pandareus grinned and sat beside her again. "A teacher of rhetoric learns quickly that some young men, no matter how sturdy and athletic they may be . . . ," he said, "are terrified of speaking in public. A good teacher also learns to calm them when that happens, because his fees depend on their parents as well as those of his more stolid students."

Alphena hefted the amulet. "Should we approach Lucius Sentius and offer to trade this to him if he returns our, our friends?" she said. "It's interesting to be able to talk to statues, I suppose, but it's useless for getting Corylus, everybody, back."

"Well, how do you expect *us* to help you?" piped a voice from the left. One of the Amazons was glaring at Alphena over her odd crescent-shaped shield. "None of us were at Polymartium, were we? And this Sentius didn't make his plans in *this* loggia, I can tell you that!"

"I take the lady's point," Pandareus said with an approving nod to the frieze. "And I very much doubt that Lucius Sentius holds Corylus. He could hold your mother and brother, though I doubt that. I watched what happened to Corylus while Pulto was helping you to safety, Your Ladyship. He vanished with a female whom I took to be a tree nymph, based on my past experience with Master Corylus."

He coughed and added, "I'm sure that Corylus was in good health at the point when the nymph snatched him out of danger."

"I see," Alphena said. What she really saw in her mind was Corylus and the nymph he owed his safety to. Alphena's flash of anger was as hot as her lust the night before had been.

Alphena looked at the backs of her hands until the emotion cooled. Without raising her eyes, she said, "I went mad, near enough, last night. I saw a lot of soldiers who were acting that way too. It didn't seem to bother Corylus, though. Or you, Master Pandareus?"

"Ah!" said the teacher. "I felt emotional pressure, certainly. But you must remember, Your Ladyship, that my life's study has been toward self-control. I do not doubt that you are capable of similar control, but—"

He paused, pursing him lips.

"You can speak freely!" Alphena said. "Pandareus, please—call me Alphena and I'll call you Pandareus and we'll get Corylus and everyone back if we can!"

"Yes," said Pandareus, speaking calmly. "You have the capacity for control, but nothing in your life to the present has encouraged you to practice that control. I wondered at so many soldiers being affected, but I realized that military discipline is externally applied. There is no necessity for a soldier to control himself, as he's in a structure which controls him in all the fashions that the system believes are important."

Alphena thought about what the teacher had said, then nodded. "Thank you," she said. "I feel better."

She stood up and eyed the frieze. She didn't remember which of the painted figures had spoken, but it probably didn't matter. She said, "And thank you, Mistress Amazon, for showing me what to do."

A horsewoman—horse-cupid?—bobbed her lance toward Alphena.

"What is it that you will do, if I may ask, Alphena?" Pandareus said. He had risen when she did.

"I need to go to Sentius' town house and speak to the statues there," she said. "I'll be able to do that posing as a slave, I believe."

The teacher pursed his lips again. "I don't see how that will be possible," he said.

"It's possible with my father's help," Alphena said. "I think."

She drew a deep breath. This had to be done, but she was sick with fear at the conversation she was about to have.

"So I'll go see my father right now," Alphena said. She opened the door toward the front of the house.

THE SCALLOPED ARCHWAY at the top of the stairs didn't have a door, but a dozen strands of tiny silver bells tinkled pleasingly when Hanwant, calling something in Indian, pushed through the curtain ahead of Varus and Bhiku. Hanwant was probably announcing his arrival with the great magicians.

Their guide had paused midway up the stairs to sheathe his sword. Varus didn't know how Ramsa Lal would react to a soldier approaching him with a bare weapon, but if something similar happened in Carce—or, more likely, on Capri—the Emperor's German Bodyguard would be more likely to react than to discuss the matter.

Bhiku gestured Varus ahead. He swept the strings of bells aside with his forearms and almost collided with Hanwant, who had been stopped by a precious-looking little man—short, round, and bald, in bright silk pantaloons and vest. He was barring the way with an arm-thick silver rod that was a foot longer than he was tall.

Varus skipped to the side to let Bhiku enter. They took in the room.

It was a large hall, lit not only by the high windows on both sides but also by skylights in the ceiling. There were gauze curtains on both sides, but dark velvet drapes hung in swags above the southern windows; they must just have been lifted as the sun sank beneath the wing of the palace across the courtyard.

The only furniture was the high-backed chair against the east wall. Varus' eyes took a moment to adapt to the interior's relative dimness. Only then did he realize that a figure, doubtless Lal himself, was seated on the throne. A dozen servants, some of them guards, stood nearby.

Two teams of men wearing loincloths pushed and pulled levers. Ropes connected the apparatus to lengths of carpet hanging edge on to the ceiling, causing them to swing back and forth. The breeze wasn't cool, but it least the movement kept the hall from being stuffy.

"Stand aside, Hanwant," Varus said, tapping their guide briskly on the shoulder. Hanwant jumped back with a frightened look.

He probably took the "toad" threat seriously, Varus thought. Then, *I wonder if the Sibyl could teach me how to do that. Though she doesn't really teach me magic. It just seems to happen when I'm with her.*

"And as for you, little man . . . ," Varus continued to the short official, "my colleague and I are going to greet Lord Ramsa Lal, who has requested our visit because we are wizards. You are welcome to continue chattering with our guide, but if you stand in our way I will burn the flesh from your bones."

He tried to imagine that he was Hedia saying the words. They didn't seem incongruous that way, which they did when coming from his own mouth.

The official bowed very low, holding his silver rod crossways. "Come with me, honored sirs," he said calmly in Greek as good as Bhiku's. "I will lead you to our gracious lord."

Turning, he waddled across the room ahead of them. He suddenly didn't look absurd. *He may be a pompous little twit, but he doesn't lack courage. . . .*

"The wizards summoned by the power of Lord Ramsa Lal have arrived!" the official said in Greek. The burst of Indian with which he followed was presumably a translation.

Lal was talking with a pair of officials in pantaloons and jackets of spotless linen; they wore yellow silk sashes, but they didn't carry swords. He looked up and spoke in peevish Indian.

"What is the beggar from that tallow-licker Raguram's household doing here?" Bhiku translated with perfect aplomb.

Ramsa Lal had changed clothes since Varus last saw him outside the palace. His green and yellow silks were fresh, and a large carnelian was pinned to the front of his turban. On his left wrist was a light bracelet, and the ring on his right little finger held an amethyst the size of a grape. It looked uncomfortable to wear.

"Lord Ramsa Lal," Varus said, striding forward ahead of the official with the rod. "I am here with my colleague Master Bhiku, whose assistance will be necessary if I am to consider your request."

Lal glowered. "I don't see why," he said. "But no matter. Come closer so that—"

He paused, apparently thinking. "You, wizard," Lal said, rising from the throne. "Come with me to my aviary. We'll discuss there what I require. Your dog stays here, but he can have food and water if you like."

Bhiku bowed. "I thank your gracious lordship," he said.

Two swordsmen and half a dozen unarmed attendants started to follow Lal. "Stay where you are!" Lal shouted. "The wizard and I will speak privately!"

Varus said nothing, but he wondered why the nobleman was suddenly so irritable. *He's afraid of something, but it isn't me.* For the first time, Varus found Lal's business of interest rather than being a minor irritation.

The doorway in the north wall led to steps down into a courtyard framed by solid walls, separate from the much larger court on the other side of the wing. A grating of thin wires formed a dome thirty feet above the landing outside the audience-chamber door.

Scores of brightly colored birds swirled in a feathered windstorm when Lal and Varus stepped out; a servant in the hall closed the door behind them. The birds ranged in size from pigeons to peacocks. Most were new to Varus, and all had gorgeous plumage.

In the center of the courtyard was a gazebo. The sides were wire; the roof of thin shakes was smeared white by bird droppings. Varus smiled faintly, wondering whether the roof had originally been covered with a screen the way the sides were.

Lal entered. There was a single chair in the enclosure. Varus expected the nobleman to take it, but instead he directed Varus to sit while he remained standing. That could have been a trick so that he could look down on the wizard, but Varus again had the impression that Lal was too nervous to sit.

"I told you that I have a task for you, wizard," Lal said. He didn't meet Varus' eyes. "It's a personal matter. My eldest daughter has been stolen away by a demon. You must return her to me. The demon is holding Teji in a walled garden three miles from here. When you have rescued her, you may go on your way however you please."

Varus considered what Ramsa Lal had just told him. He was silent for only a few seconds, but it felt longer as his brain processed the words.

At last he said, "That's a remarkably lucid and succinct statement of what you want, Your Lordship. My rhetoric professor, Master Pandareus, would congratulate you on it."

"Well, that's all there is to say," said Lal. He reached for the door. "I'll send you to the demon's garden with a detachment of troops. As soon as you've released Teji, you can go."

The claws of birds walking on the roof scraped and clicked, and their voices grew in volume as they got used to a stranger's presence. Lovely as the birds were, their mixed calls were as unpleasant as the demands of the beggars clogging the Milvian Bridge.

"I have a few questions before I agree to your commission, Your Lordship,"

Varus said. He crossed his hands in his lap to emphasize in a neutral fashion that he wasn't ready to leave yet.

"Accept!" said Lal. "You haven't been asked; I'm *telling* you what you must do!"

"If you believe that, Your Lordship," Varus said quietly, "then I'm scarcely the person you would want fighting a demon on your behalf."

Varus had trained himself to control his emotions. That helped him to retain a philosophical calm when the nobleman shouted at him.

What helped even more was Varus' deep certainty that, because he was a citizen of Carce, nothing that this oddly dressed foreigner said to him was really important.

This was a most unenlightened attitude. If Pandareus were present, Varus would apologize to him for merely having had the thought. That said, it was quite useful in negotiating with a blusterer like Ramsa Lal.

"What is it you want to know?" Lal said curtly.

A *win for thinking like a churlish Carce nobleman*, Varus thought. He said, "Bhiku tells me that Mistress Rupa, a member of your household, is a wizard. Why do you ask me rather than Rupa to free your daughter, Your Lordship?"

Lal grimaced and turned his eyes away. "Rupa is in Italy now," he said. Still without looking at Varus, he added, "The demon stole Teji away not long before I sent Rupa to Carce in accordance with the request of our lord Govinda, King of Kings. Rupa said she couldn't free Teji, so I'm sending you, whom the gods brought to me."

For a moment, Varus felt as though the Sibyl held his hand and he was a disembodied presence. He and the Sibyl watched Ramsa Lal speaking with Rupa in this same gazebo.

Rupa looked even more smoothly stone hard than she had when Varus saw her at Polymartium with the eyes of his body. She looked at Lal and said, "My powers will not return your daughter to you, Ramsa Lal. You must find another magician to achieve your end."

"Where will I find this magician?" Lal said. His left hand twisted the amethyst ring on his right pinkie. "Where?"

The woman shrugged instead of answering. She turned and opened the gazebo door.

*Rupa looked to her right suddenly: Varus felt her eyes bore into him.
Then the scene faded and he was seated in front of Ramsa Lal.*

Varus stood and nodded to the gazebo door. "I'm by no means sure that I
can do something that Mistress Rupa could not," he said. "My colleague assures me that Rupa is a great wizard, which I do not claim to be. Nonetheless, I will attempt to free your daughter."

Lal let out his breath in relief. "Very good," he said. "I've already ordered
your escort to prepare."

Lal led the way out of the gazebo and up the stairs to the audience hall.
The birds whirled and cackled. Occasional feathers drifted about like leaves
in fall.

Varus didn't like or trust Lal, but he had past experience of demons. Free-
ing a young girl from a demon would be a worthy act, even if her father was
as much of a bully as he thought he could get away with being.

But at the back of Varus' mind he remembered his vision of Lal and Rupa:
Rupa didn't say her powers could *not do what Lal wanted; she said that they*
would *not.*

"My, you *sweet* thing," said the maple sprite who held Corylus. She
hugged him closer. "Wherever did you come from?"

"I'm very sorry to intrude this way, Acer," Corylus said, detaching himself from her as politely as possible. "I think your sister in the Waking World
sent me here because I was being threatened. I couldn't have escaped without her help."

"Oh, from Polymartium," said the sprite, trailing her fingertips down
Corylus' arm as he eased back. "That's how she did it. There's always been
magic around the shrine there. It's a pressure here, you know. And it's gotten
worse lately."

Corylus looked at his surroundings while he considered what to do. The
maple tree stood in a clump of orange-flowered azaleas at the base of a hill.
Grass and yellow ragwort covered the slope, with occasional small junipers
and limestone outcrops. Above was forest where the soil was deep enough to
hold the roots of trees.

Corylus took a deep breath. He had been using his full strength ever since
Ampelos and his band had burst out of the glowing lens. Corylus' muscles

were wobbly from physical strain followed by the emotional shock of being well and truly captured by the vines while Ampelos approached.

Corylus seated his staff firmly in the coarse grass and leaned on it while he tried to calm his mind. He wasn't sure what Ampelos had planned, but death and conversion to Bacchic madness were the most likely choices.

The emotions that had drained Corylus weren't limited to fear and anger. Even worse had been the wild lust that had gripped him—and the similar passion that had possessed Alphena. A senator's virgin daughter was an unthinkable partner for a mere knight, but for a moment it had been touch and go as to whether Corylus would be able to withstand his own desire and the girl's urging.

"I'm beholden to your sister in the Waking World for snatching me clear, Acer," he said. "Now I need to get back there, though. Do you know how I can do that?"

For a moment the sprite pouted. Tree spirits were ordinarily good-hearted, but they were also as willful as children and didn't plan any further ahead than butterflies do.

Finally Acer shrugged and said, "I suppose she could do it because of where she grew, Polymartium. There's no shrine here, though."

She gestured toward the hillside, then grinned and pouted again—this time provocatively. "You don't have to go anywhere," she said. "You can stay here. I'd *really* like you to stay here."

A trumpet sounded in the distance . . . or was it an animal hooting?

"I'm sorry, Cousin," Corylus said, backing away. "I really must get back to my friends. I appreciate your kindness."

"Oh, go away then!" the sprite said. "I hope you never get back and you rot here!"

"I'm sorry, Cousin," Corylus repeated. He turned and started up the hill.

You couldn't get angry at a tree sprite, any more than you could get angry at a kitten who bit you or a cloud that rained on you when you hoped to stay dry. None of them had enough depth to be really malicious.

"Cousin?" Acer called when he was twenty feet away.

Corylus hesitated for a heartbeat, then looked over his shoulder. "Yes, Acer?" he said.

"There're nut trees up there," she said. "You'll want something to eat, won't you?"

Corylus hesitated for another heartbeat, then bounded down the slope and embraced her. "Thank you, dear cousin," he said, and kissed her hard. "Now I really have to be on."

The maple sprite didn't try to hold him as he'd feared that she would, but when he glanced back from the top of the hill she was still watching. Corylus felt a great deal better than he would have done if he'd simply continued to walk on.

It doesn't hurt to be nice to kittens and lonely tree spirits.

HEDIA PAUSED WHEN SHE SAW the water bubbling out of the colorful layers of rock. She looked at Boest.

"I've been here before," she said. "The stream here"—she gestured—"said that you could guide me to the Spring of True Answers."

"Ah," said Boest. "Yes, that's where we are, Lady Hedia."

"But I was there already," Hedia said. "I didn't need a guide!"

Boest smiled. He didn't answer.

Varus would tell me that strictly speaking, I didn't ask a question, she realized. Corylus and Master Pandareus would be too polite to say that, but it's what they would think—and what Boest thought.

Hedia giggled. "For a woman who never took any interest in the details of language," she said aloud, "I've certainly managed to meet a lot of pedantic men."

She paused thoughtfully, then added, "The odd thing is, I find that I *like* pedantic men."

"I think you like most men, Hedia," Boest said with a slow smile. "I think you are a good person."

"I think . . . ," said Hedia, turning to face the spring, "that many people would disagree with you. About my being a good person, that is. Not about me liking men."

She stared at the bubbling rock face and pursed her lips. She wasn't sure how to frame her question to the spring. Listening to grammatical pedants hadn't made her more learned, but she did know how careful she had to be.

"I'm sorry that you had to go to so much effort, Hedia," Boest said. "I *am* a water spirit, you see, though what happened to you wasn't at my doing."

He sounded sincere; but then, he always did. Even when he was a soulless shell of a man.

"The spring has a sense of humor, I gather," Hedia said. "Well, I wasn't put to much trouble, really. A dry walk to your valley, but I don't mind paying for information. And I certainly don't mind—"

She stretched voluptuously, savoring the memory.

"—the exercise I got with Gilise. Not at all."

Boest laughed. Hedia thought she heard sadness underlying the humor, but the humor was nonetheless real.

Aloud Hedia said, "What do I ask, Boest? To find my son by the—"

She had started to say *the shortest way.* Instead she said, "The best way."

"Just ask," said Boest, smiling gently. "I'm sorry that the spring tricked you, but it isn't malicious."

Hedia stepped close and rose up on tiptoes so that she could kiss the big man's lips. "Thank you," she said. "And I'm glad to have been able to help you."

That was the proper thing to say, so she would have said it in any case. She was a little surprised to realize that she meant it.

The rock formed into lips through which the fountain flowed. Its laughter gurgled.

"I told you that I knew many things, Hedia," the water's deep voice said. "I knew that you were the one for whom I had long waited. Ask your question."

"Spring," Hedia said in a clear voice. "How may I best reach my son, Varus?"

"Follow the path you took to reach me the first time," said the spring. "Go into the woods. At every branching of the path, turn to your right. That will be the best way in which to find your son."

Hedia frowned and said, "Won't that take me in a circle?"

The spring didn't speak, but behind her Boest said, "This is the Spring of True Answers, Hedia. Were you hoping for something other than the truth?"

She laughed. "Thank you, Spring," she said. "I will follow your advice."

Turning, she said, "And thank *you,* Master Boest. Perhaps we'll meet again, but I believe each of us has our business to take care of now."

"Yes," said Boest. "Paddock and I have a great deal of travel before us. And Gilise, of course. I wish you the good fortune which you have brought to me . . . and to the world, I think. Things are better because you exist."

Hedia sniffed, but her heart was lighter than it might have been as she started along the path into the woods.

AN ENTOURAGE OF TWENTY or more servants had gathered behind Alphena before she had come half the distance to the entrance hall of Saxa's town house. They had been waiting in the bathhouse and gymnasium and in the corridor between them. Pandareus was somewhere in back, but servants pushed past him to get closer to Lady Alphena.

Her chief personal maid bumped her right elbow. Alphena turned and said with false brightness, "My outside escorts always give me enough room, Florina. Perhaps in the future I'll direct them to escort me inside the house also."

Florina jumped aside, shoving an underfootman into the wall. Turning, she hissed to the servants behind, "Move back, you cretins! You're crowding Her Ladyship!"

Alphena gave a tiny smile of satisfaction. *Last year I would have slapped Florina or even jabbed her with my comb. This works just as well, and it's far more ladylike. Mother will be pleased.*

Alphena thought of Hedia. Suddenly Alphena wasn't worried about the interview she was about to have with her father. It might be unpleasant and embarrassing, but anything was worthwhile if it would help get Hedia back.

Alphena could have entered her father's office from the back where the understeward Charias stood to keep lower-ranking servants away. Instead she pointed to Charias and said, "You! Come around to the side door and clear the entrance hall for me. I need to speak with my father."

Charias was relatively young for his status—he was in his mid-twenties, Alphena believed—but he had been promoted because he was sharp as well as being literate in several languages. He judged the situation, bowed, and stepped immediately to the curtained opening to the entrance hall.

Charias might have to answer to the majordomo for leaving his post, but he had obviously decided that was better than trying to dodge the young mistress' clear, forceful directions. That showed good judgment. Alphena was beginning to fray, and a servant who got in her way might see some of the spoiled brat she had been before Hedia began to remold her into a proper lady.

"Give way for the Lady Alphena!" Charias shouted. His voice was a light tenor, but he put his lungs into the words. He achieved volume, if not majesty. "Clear the entrance hall for Lady Alphena!"

Saxa had just returned from the Senate, accompanied by his usual entourage of "clients," citizens whose number raised the prestige of their patron—Saxa, in this case—in exchange for dinner invitations, gifts at the holidays, and the sort of help that the influence of a powerful senator might provide. A score of them waited in the hall. Lesser citizens and the servants escorting the clients were in the street, while men of the highest rank were in the office with Saxa himself.

Two ushers were in the hall. When Charias shouted, they shifted their batons crossways. That was unnecessary: the clients began shuffling out toward the front door without physical prodding.

I wonder how many of them have heard stories about Lady Alphena also? Alphena thought. *Mother will have her hands full trying to find a suitable husband for me. . . .*

But that was a problem for a later time, and it wasn't a problem that concerned Alphena much anyway.

The office door was of intricate leather openwork on a bronze frame. Agrippinus stood before it. Charias stepped forward, but the majordomo gestured him back and opened the door himself.

"Lady Alphena to see her father, Senator Gaius Alphenus Saxa, former consul and governor of the province of Lusitania," Agrippinus said. He didn't shout, but his deep, sonorous voice filled the hall as well as the small office where Saxa stood with two visitors.

Alphena recognized one of the men as Ulpius Vomer, a senatorial acquaintance of Saxa. The other was a stranger, a craggy knight with North African features. Neither was of real importance, and Alphena would have interrupted if they were anyone below the Emperor himself.

Well, I'd apologize if the Praetorian Prefect was there. The little joke—she imagined the words spoken in Corylus' dry voice—made her grin, probably as much a surprise to her father as it was to her.

Saxa was seated with a reading stand to his side and one of his secretaries behind him to take notes. His visitors stood to either side of the door from the hall. They stepped aside and nodded politely to Alphena.

"Good afternoon, Daughter," Saxa said. "My friends and I were about to go to the baths . . . ?"

"Father, I'm very sorry, but I must speak with you on a family matter," Alphena said, impressed that she sounded firm but not shrill the way she had expected to be. Nodding first to Ulpius, then to the knight, she continued, "Gentlemen, I apologize for my intrusion. I will not be long, I assure you."

She was sure she wouldn't be long. Saxa might agree or more likely would forbid her plan, but it wasn't going to take very long either way.

"Lord Ulpius, Master Severianus," Saxa said, rising to his feet. He had been sitting because of protocol: he was the noble householder. "I too apologize. I'll be with you as soon as I can."

Murmuring understanding, the two men slipped out into the hall that

Alphena had emptied to give them room. Severianus eyed her closely on the way.

I wonder what he thinks I've been doing, she thought. *Probably nothing as odd as the reality.*

"You've learned something about Hedia?" Saxa said before the office door had closed behind Ulpius. Not that the perforated panel provided much privacy anyway.

"No," said Alphena. "But I think I can learn something if I can get into Lucius Sentius' town house without his knowledge. With the help of the servants here I can do that as a slave."

"Daughter?" Saxa said. "That's imposs . . . that is, are you feeling well?"

"No, Father," she said. "I'm very frightened. But I've thought about this. I know, I'm not smart the way Varus is or Mother, but I know how to *do* things. This can work and yes, it's dangerous, but I'm going to do it whether you help or not. I owe it to Mother, and I owe it to you because you'll be lost without Mother and I love you and I'm going to!"

There were members of Saxa's household who would help for Hedia's sake and maybe for Alphena's own. Pulto would help, and he probably knew people. They might all be as frightened as she was, but they'd help anyway because it had to be done.

Alphena wiped her eyes, because they were stinging. *I've started to cry!*

"I see," said Saxa. He swallowed and turned toward a sidewall. It was frescoed with a woman riding over the waves on the back of a bull, but Alphena didn't think her father was really looking at the art.

She suddenly realized that the secretary was still on his stool behind Saxa, hunched over a wax tablet. His hand was poised on his bronze stylus, but he was perfectly motionless. She had forgotten the man was there . . . but it didn't matter now.

"I very much want Hedia and my son back," Saxa said. "I will trust you, Daughter, because my wife has shown that she trusts you. And because I don't have a better idea myself. I don't have any ideas."

He wet his lips and continued, "I only ask that you consult Publius Corylus before you act. I know there's a risk—"

Alphena had a flash of memory, pressing her body against Corylus and demanding that he take her. She flushed, but nobody would notice her complexion here in the office.

"—but I see that we must take risks."

"Father," Alphena said, "Publius Corylus is gone also. Has been taken, we think. Master Pandareus and I and Corylus' man Pulto think that."

Saxa winced. "This is terrible, terrible," he said in a quiet voice.

He straightened. "Agrippinus, come into the office!" he called. "And somebody send for Lenatus as well. I suppose he's in the gymnasium. I want him here also."

The office door snapped open; the majordomo stepped through. Past him before the door closed, Alphena glimpsed Charias disappearing through the side doorway of the entrance hall. Six or more servants were probably running to summon the fencing master.

Ordinarily nothing happened in a town house, so when something did it was a matter of great excitement. In the present case, what was happening might mean that every member of the household was sent to die in the imperial silver mines in Spain.

Most of the servants weren't sophisticated enough to realize that, however. They were just excited to have something to discuss other than the affair a new kitchen maid was having with one of the servants who delivered produce nightly from Saxa's estate north of Carce.

"Would you like Pandareus to be present, Father?" Alphena asked.

"What?" said Saxa in what for him was a sharp tone. "No, no. You'll tell him what you want; you don't need me."

There was a bustle from outside the rear door. A servant started to speak, but Lenatus said in a parade-ground voice, "As requested, *sir!*" and flung the door open himself. He must have just stripped off his breastplate, because his tunic was sweaty at the places where the armor squeezed it to his body.

Lenatus is sophisticated enough to know how badly this could go wrong.

"Agrippinus and Lenatus," Saxa said in his newly firm voice. "Lady Hedia and Lord Varus have disappeared. I suppose you know more about that than I do."

He swallowed. "Lady Alphena has a plan to, to deal with the situation," he said. "I don't know the details; I don't *want* to know the details. I want you to do whatever my daughter requests, no matter what it is. Agrippinus, this applies to my whole staff, in Carce and at any other location they may be. You will see to it that everyone understands."

Lenatus nodded. "I report to Lady Alphena, right," he said. "Can I tell Pulto about this? He's in the gym right now. We were sparring."

"You can tell anyone as necessary to carry out Lady Alphena's directions," Saxa said. "Now—"

"Your Lordship, may I clarify one matter?" said Agrippinus. He didn't wait for permission to continue. "With all respect to the courage of Lady Alphena, she is young and hasn't in the past always displayed what she herself in later years will think of as reasonable caution. Ah, this business could verge into matters which the Emperor would consider treason, with consequences which not even your great authority could avoid, Your Lordship."

Alphena started to speak. She realized she didn't know what to say: everything the majordomo had said was true, but it didn't *matter*.

"Agrippinus, you've been legally free for the past five years," Saxa said. Usually he was full of enthusiasm about the trivial things that to him were important. Today he sounded grave and worthy of the high positions he had held. "I have no doubt that thirty years in my household have left you more than comfortable financially. I don't grudge you that."

He paused, but his expression kept Agrippinus silent whether or not he might otherwise have tried to answer.

"This is a matter touching the safety of my wife and son," Saxa said. "I will take any risk for their sakes. If you are unwilling to share those risks, then leave my house at once."

Agrippinus stood stiffly where he was. "Lord Saxa," he said. "I will carry out these orders as I have carried out all your orders over the decades of my service. I would have failed the duties of the office which you have entrusted to me if I had not given you the benefit of my advice."

He bowed in deeper reverence than Alphena had seen the majordomo offer her father in the past.

Turning to Alphena, Agrippinus said, "I await your orders, Your Lady-ship."

"We'll go to the gymnasium," Alphena said. It wasn't private—no place in a house so full of servants was really private—but it came closer than any-where else did. "We'll want Pulto."

Charias, back in position, got out of the way as Lenatus pushed open the rear door of the office. "Clear the way!" Agrippinus said, asserting his author-ity from behind the fencing master.

"Not you, Master Pandareus!" Alphena called. "You're coming with us to the gymnasium."

The teacher had obeyed Agrippinus with the humility that was as natural to him as learning was. Alphena knew that Pandareus was deservedly proud of his knowledge, but he really didn't care about the trappings of honor.

"You know, Agrippinus . . . ?" Lenatus said from beside the majordomo as they walked through the central garden toward the rear of the town house. The servants scurrying away probably weren't listening, but the fencing master didn't appear to be concerned about that. "You saved your life back there when you said you were in with us."

Agrippinus opened the gymnasium door. "Lord Saxa wouldn't have had me executed for that," he said. "Besides, I was merely concerned that His Lordship understood the situation."

Pulto was alone inside the enclosure. He had taken off his armor, but Alphena noted that the sword and dagger on his equipment belt were real, not weighted wooden practice weapons.

"No, His Lordship isn't that kind of fellow, not at all," Lenatus agreed. "The thing is, buddy, it wouldn't have gotten to His Lordship."

Pandareus entered, the last of their group. Alphena started to close the door, then looked back the way they had come. Charias was in the mass of servants. "Charias, mind the door," she ordered crisply, then shut it.

"It seems to me and Pulto that this isn't just family business," Lenatus said. "From what we've seen, the safety of the Republic depends on Lady Hedia and maybe Varus too. So if I thought you were going to run out and probably try to get ahead of the informers by talking to folks in the prefect's office about what might be treason, well, you'd be a danger to the Republic."

"Me and Lenatus, we got a lot of experience dealing with dangers to the Republic," Pulto said. He grinned.

Instead of crumpling, Agrippinus drew himself up to his full height and said, "Then as a citizen of Carce, gentlemen, I thank you. Now, if you're done posturing, shall we get on to Lady Alphena's plan?"

Lenatus laughed and clapped the majordomo on the shoulder. "You're all right, buddy," he said. "Let's do that, and I've got a jar of wine in the equipment locker to keep our throats lubricated while we do."

This may actually work, Alphena thought. Her eyes were stinging again, this time because of joy.

CHAPTER VIII

Alphena shivered in the pre-dawn air. She was wearing the clothing of a young female slave of no particular skills, suitable for a scullery maid or the like: a single light tunic with no overwrap, and sandals coiled from straw rope.

She carried a bindle with a second tunic wrapped around the few possessions that a girl of her type might own: a yellow linen sash; an almost-empty jar of eye shadow; a pair of earrings twisted from gold-washed iron wire; and an ivory comb from which half the teeth had been broken. Agrippinus himself had gone to the Tiber Market and bought a girl named Popiliana, just imported from Syria. She spoke no Latin and her Greek was doubtful; even her Aramaic was so bad that the majordomo doubted it was the girl's first language.

Alphena wore Popiliana's clothes and carried her possessions. The real servant was dizzyingly happy with a pair of embroidered linen tunics, leather slippers, gold ear studs, and a comb that, though horn, was new and had all its teeth.

The linkman at the head of the procession stopped at a door opening on to the alley. The servant beside him banged on the panel with his baton and called, "Hey, is this Sentius' place?"

A voice from inside said something—probably, "Right," but the speaker's accent blurred the word beyond certainty.

Charias walked forward and called, "New intake of servants for Lucius Sentius. Four males and one female, all classed as unskilled and sold without recourse!"

Alphena had wanted to go to Sentius' house straight from the discussion in the gymnasium. Agrippinus had insisted that they put off the operation for at least a day so that he could make preparations, and the two veterans had supported him.

Alphena had raised her voice. Pulto, Lenatus, and the majordomo had looked at her silently, and after a moment Pandareus had said, "They are correct, Lady Alphena."

Sentius' door swung outward. A portly man stepped into the alley. He wore layered tunics and the gold embroidery on his sash winked in the torch-light. "I'll take care of this," he said to the doorman behind him.

"You're Sebethius?" Charias said. He thrust forward a waxed notebook. "Sign and seal this."

Agrippinus *had* been right—of course. Alphena had known that even when she protested. She had just wanted to *do something now*. The others had insisted on doing something that would work. The realization that Hedia would have coldly agreed with them had silenced Alphena with her mouth still open.

Sebethius signed with Charias' stylus, then pressed the wax with the signet ring he wore on a neck thong. It was probably his master's signet, normally carried by the servant in present charge of the household.

Sebethius handed back the receipt. "Come on through," he said to the "newly purchased servants." To Charias he added, "Do they speak Greek?"

Charias shrugged. "The men do, more or less," he said. "I don't know about the woman, but I suppose you can slap her and point; she'll get the idea quick enough. Remember, it's a no recourse sale."

Agrippinus was too senior to act as the foreman delivering a coffle of slaves, but Charias was behaving even better than Alphena had hoped. She had picked the understeward for the task, but Agrippinus had approved the choice without hesitation.

"Well, come on through, then," Sebethius repeated peevishly.

Drago, in front with his cousin, looked back at Charias. "Get in!" Charias snapped. "You belong to Lord Sentius now. Sebethius here will enroll you and tell you your duties."

The four men wearing ragged tunics and carrying bindles like Alphena's shambled in. She followed, and the door closed behind her.

Alphena didn't know what hold Agrippinus had over Sebethius. It might have been as simple as money, but she had a suspicion that the majordomo had used a threat rather than a bribe. Agrippinus had become head of the household of one of Carce's richest senators because he got things done; he was demonstrating his ability here.

They had entered through the kitchen. Pots were bubbling and a morning staff of ten or a dozen were at work. Additional servants idled, flirted, and cadged food.

"Come along!" Sebethius said. "You'll be fed after you're enrolled."

Alphena walked between the four men, all members of her personal escort. They had volunteered for the duty even though they knew by personal observation just how unpleasant death by crucifixion was.

A cook's assistant reached for Alphena's buttocks. She barely saw the movement in the crowded kitchen before Drago—Rago was ahead of her—grabbed the hand and bent the fingers backward. The victim gave a high-pitched scream as joints popped.

"Hey!" called an older man, probably the cook in charge.

"Keep your staff to their business, Olanus!" Sebethius said. "Come on, you new lot."

The central garden was much like Saxa's, but a pond ran down the middle. There were lanterns at the front and back of the garden, but their light didn't tell Alphena whether there were fish in the water.

"What are you doing, Sebethius?" said the man who stepped from the portico to the right. He was well dressed also, but he was older than Sebethius and his sash was dark red instead of yellow.

"Enrolling an intake of servants, Taunus," Sebethius said. "Not that it's any of your business."

"I didn't know anything about a new purchase," Taunus said. His Latin was excellent, but Alphena thought she recognized a hint of German intonation in his voice.

"Well, Taunus . . . ," Sebethius said. "Perhaps when Lord Sentius returns from the country you can reproach him with his failure to keep you informed, eh?"

Taunus glowered. He was standing in the direct path, so his rival under-steward and the "servants" following were at a halt.

Looking at Drago, Taunus said, "By Mars, what is this lot? They look like they ought to be on crosses along the Appian Way! Whyever did you buy them?"

"I didn't buy them, Taunus," Sebethius said. "I'm obeying my lord's direction to sign them in when they arrive. I don't know who made the purchase on Lord Sentius' behalf, or if he did it himself."

This was clearly dangerous for Sebethius, but he was handling it as well as possible. He sounded angry, not frightened; anger was what anyone would expect from an understeward responding to a rival's badgering. He must hope that Taunus wouldn't dare mention the business to their master, which was probably correct, but how in Venus' name had Agrippinus gotten him to take the risk?

Taunus snorted but stepped aside. The column resumed walking toward the front portion of the house.

Alphena saw Taunus looking at her. She deliberately missed a half step as though she had tripped, then hopped forward. That put her past Taunus without incident.

She didn't doubt that Drago could have dealt with the understeward as easily he had with the scullion, but that would have led to serious problems at once. Drago didn't think—none of the escorts thought—in those terms, and Alphena couldn't have prevented the former pirate from acting without destroying the pretence that she was an illiterate Syrian.

Sebethius led them down a short corridor into an office much like Saxa's. Wax death masks looked down from high shelves, and an iron-strapped chest was bolted to the floor in one corner.

A man was sleeping under the writing desk. Sebethius kicked the sole of his nearer foot and snapped, "Get out, Timon. I have business!"

The wall nearest Alphena was frescoed with a landscape including rural buildings and grazing cows. To the left a herdsman led a goat across an arched bridge.

Timon picked up his sandals but scuttled barefoot into the entrance hall. Sebethius watched the door close after him, then looked at Alphena. "How do we proceed, then?" he said in a low voice.

"Enroll us as you normally would," she whispered back. "Then all of you stand outside the office door. I'll be with you shortly."

I hope I'll be with you shortly, but those words didn't reach her lips.

Sebethius took a ledger from a shelf above the chest and opened it on the writing desk. The escort—the male intake—watched uncertainly. They had been told what would happen, but they weren't men who were comfortable in strange situations—and this was certainly strange.

Alphena reached under her tunic and gripped the iron locket. As she did so, the painted herdsman turned and looked at her.

"I WISH . . . ," SAID VARUS. He was hot and sticky, which on dirt roads meant that he was also muddy from sweat mixed with dust. "That I had realized how hot it is in India and how much walking I'd be doing before I announced that I was too pure to ride a horse."

The fifty cavalrymen had mostly ridden ahead. The dust they stirred up hung over the road as Varus and Bhiku tramped along. A squad remained at the rear in case the pedestrians got the idea of going somewhere other than where Ramsa Lal had directed.

Varus had certainly toyed with that idea, and he suspected that his companion had also.

"You could announce that you had been granted an appearance of the godhead," Bhiku said, "and that the ineffable power had given you the dispensation to ride horses without demeaning yourself."

"Umm," said Varus. "That wouldn't help much unless the godhead also gave me the ability to *ride* a horse. Which my own past efforts haven't done. I certainly wish that your nobles appreciated the advantages of mail coaches."

"Women and nobles less athletic than Lord Ramsa Lal often ride on elephants," Bhiku said. Nothing in his voice or that of Varus suggested that they were joking. "The carriers are much like the saddle bags of a horse, though of course larger."

"I will keep that in mind for the next time this happens," Varus said. "Though of course by then I may have my own demon to carry me. That appears to have worked for Lady Teji."

"I wonder if the demon has the ability to carry two people at a time?" Bhiku said. "If one of them is quite old and shriveled up, at least. Draft animals have loading standards, baggage masters have told me."

Varus smiled. Chatting with—exchanging dry humor with—a friend was a way to ignore what they were about to face. Given that there was no way of knowing what that future would be, it was the best way available.

"I believe we're getting near the garden," Bhiku said, glancing at the fields.

"You've been here before?" said Varus, following the sage's eyes. The fields were laid out in strips. Bushes and the occasional spiky tree grew on the dikes separating them. There was jungle beyond, probably following a watercourse hidden somewhere in its green heart.

"No," said Bhiku, "but"—he gestured—"the fields are empty. I would guess that the workers are afraid of the demon. I hadn't heard that he—do demons have gender?—that the demon ever leaves the garden it built, however."

The commander of the troop of horse rode back from the front of the column with several of his officers. Varus said, "I hoped that Hanwant would be in charge or would at least come along with us. He's . . . not exactly a friend, but by now he's at least something of a retainer."

"I'm sure he's happier remaining in Lal's palace," Bhiku said. "As a philosopher, I will endeavor to be pleased at his good fortune."

The horsemen rode past Varus and Bhiku, then turned and walked their horses alongside. The leader—no one had told Varus his name—looked down and said in harsh Greek, "The path Lord Ramsa Lal had cut to the garden is right up here. We'll wait in the road. Don't think that you can run off into the jungle, because we'll be watching you the whole way."

"What do you mean 'the path Lal had cut?'" said Varus.

"The demon built his lair in that patch of jungle," another officer said. He spoke Greek of a sort, but his Macedonian accent made him very difficult to understand. "The peasants heard something and went to look. They found the garden, but the demon came to the gates and threatened them if they tried to enter."

"*Did* someone enter?" Varus said. They had continued walking; now he could see a hole hacked in the yellow-green wall of bamboo ahead at the edge of the empty fields. The other horsemen waited, still mounted, across the road from the opening.

"I prodded a footman through the gates," the commander said. "The demon has six arms. He pulled the fellow's limbs off and flung the parts at me. I was covered with blood."

The commander grimaced. His hand picked at his silken sleeve as if he were trying to pluck away memories.

Varus looked at the man in disgust. It was a moment before he considered that the demon would presumably do the same to anyone else who entered the garden as Gaius Alphenus Varus intended to do in a moment.

"How many human sacrifices do you think you'll have to make before the demon releases Lady Teji, Lord Varus?" Bhiku asked. He was speaking loudly enough that all four officers could hear.

"I told Lord Ramsa Lal to send fifty men with me for a start," Varus said, also in a carrying voice. "He assures me that he'll willingly sacrifice his entire army if necessary to get his daughter back, though."

Varus looked at the commander, then eyed the bulk of the troop nearby. "Remind me that we'll want to save one of this first batch to send back for more."

"What do you mean?" the commander said. Two of his aides had jerked away; the fourth officer looked at his companions in surprise and asked a question in Indian. "We're here to make sure that you do as you've been ordered and go into the garden."

Bhiku cackled. "Is that what you thought?" he said. He shouted a burst of Indian in the direction of the main body of horsemen. The puzzled-looking aide gaped at him.

"Lord Ramsa Lal ordered you to help us in whatever fashion we required, didn't he?" said Varus. "I suppose we'll have to rob you of your will to get you to walk into the garden, but that's merely a wave of the hand."

He raised his left hand, holding the commander's eyes.

The commander and the aide who didn't speak Greek spurred their horses and raced up the road. Their hooves kicked divots from the hard clay beneath the layer of dust. The other two aides were only heartbeats behind. The common troopers were riding off before their officers reached them.

"*Very* well done, Master Bhiku," Varus said.

"And may I congratulate you, Lord Varus," the sage said, "for the way you responded to my cue?"

He coughed into his cupped hand, then said, "Do you wish to go to Lord Raguram, now? I think we can get out of Lal's territory before any of our former escort reports about what happened here. If they ever do."

Varus grimaced. "Bhiku, this is very foolish," he said, "and I certainly don't mean to involve you, but I am going to enter the garden."

"You don't believe in the demon?" Bhiku said, raising an eyebrow.

Varus laughed grimly. "I found the commander to have been quite believable when he described having body parts flung at him."

Varus grimaced and continued, "The problem from my standpoint is that I also believe that the demon is holding a young girl inside. I'm going to try to get her out."

"Ah," said Bhiku mildly. "Do you have a plan for accomplishing that, Lord Varus?"

"I have excellent rhetorical training," Varus said. He frowned and added, "Do demons have better natures, do you think?"

Bhiku shrugged. "This will be the first demon of my acquaintance," he said. "I'll know better shortly, I presume. Shall we go?"

Varus took the older man's hands. "Friend, this is my decision," he said. "You are not to come with me. I'm being foolish."

Bhiku clicked his tongue against his teeth. "Being torn limb from limb may be exactly the martyrdom I need to achieve a higher stage in my next life," he said. "In any case, it will be a *new* experience. And Teji is, after all, a young girl—however regrettable a person her father may be."

"Yes, all right," said Varus.

The path hacked through the bamboo was narrow, but by brushing the bordering stems the two philosophers were able to walk side by side to the gate in the garden's sheer glassy walls.

So far as Hedia was concerned, the woods were no different from those near Polymartium. She had no idea what the trees were, but she wasn't interested in trees. The only reason she knew that the tree in Saxa's back garden was a peach was because she had seen peaches hanging from the branches.

She saw movement behind a screen of leaves thirty feet ahead of her and decided that a breeze had riffled the branches of a hawthorn in front of a boulder. Then the gray mass shoved forward slightly: it was the head of a turtle far larger than the sea turtles sometimes landed by fishermen in the Bay of Puteoli.

Hedia stutter-stepped in surprise, then resumed walking. She didn't think turtles were dangerous, though being stepped on by one the size of an elephant would be, well, as bad as being stepped on by an elephant.

I should be able to outrun it if it charges me, she thought with a grim smile. If she was wrong, it would be an embarrassing way to die, but it didn't appear that anyone was around to report it back in Carce. Hedia had been in situations that would have been even more embarrassing had they turned out to be fatal.

The turtle withdrew its head. She heard it crashing off into the woods—not a spurt of noise, but an ongoing process.

Hedia took a deep breath. She hadn't been in danger, but it was a reminder that these were not the woods north of Carce, however much they might resemble them. She knew that, of course, but exchanging stares with a giant turtle brought reality to intellectual knowledge.

The path split to the right and sharply left. Hedia looked in the direction she would be going, but before she resumed walking she turned her head to look also to the left.

An arbor arched over the path a few feet from where Hedia stood. Its interlocked branches framed a scene that was not part of this portion of the Otherworld and did not resemble anything familiar to Hedia from the Waking World.

She saw within the arbor a slice of verdant landscape, viewed from slightly above. The sea was one boundary, while walls of ice pressed high on the other three sides. Above the whole was blackness, picked out occasionally by jets of silver.

The land was laid out in fields, and there was a sizable town on the coast. It didn't seem to Hedia that the figures moving between houses and doing farm labor were human.

This is the Anti-Thule of which philosophers speculate, said the gurgling voice of the spring. Hedia looked around quickly, but no one else was visible—not even a puddle. The words must have formed in her own mind.

The image in the arbor expanded. Hedia saw—or seemed to see; the image was probably as unreal as the voice—the town from close above. The inhabitants walked on two legs, but they were lightly furred and their ears were pointed like those of cats. They wore loose clothing, but the pouches in which a few carried infants appeared to be part of their own bodies.

The Tyla inhabited Anti-Thule, the spring said. *They were an ancient race, far older than human beings.*

"Why are you showing me this?" Hedia said. She wished she had a face to speak to, though it didn't really matter.

Watch and learn, the voice said.

It was using the same tone of amused superiority with which the voice had directed her to find Boest. That was irritating; but the business with Boest had worked out well, and meeting Gilise had been particularly worth the walk.

The houses of the Tyla were on stone foundations, but their walls and roofs seemed to be made of fabric. The material was so thin that Hedia could see figures moving within.

She watched without asking more questions that the voice would ignore. *No doubt that was the true answer; the spring's other answers have been.*

The scene in the arbor shifted again to the only completely stone building Hedia had seen on Anti-Thule. It was a round temple—a tholos—like the Temple of Vesta in the Forum of Carce. Instead of walls, a dozen pillars carried its domed roof.

A Tylon with pure white fur stood on the first of the temple's three steps, holding a rectangular soapstone tablet. He spoke or chanted, probably the latter. Though Hedia couldn't hear sounds from the image, forty Tyla wearing albatross-plume headdresses faced the one with the tablet and responded together whenever he paused.

This is the Godspeaker of the Tyla, on the Temple of the Moon, said the spring. *He is conducting the morning ceremony with the Priests of the Moon. Without these rites morning and evening, the ice would cover Anti-Thule.*

Hedia's apparent viewpoint drew back to what it had been when she first glanced toward the arbor: a panorama of the green enclave and the ice cliffs lowering above it. At this scale the Tyla were moving flecks, not figures.

The streaks of light you see in the sky, said the spring, *are meteors: pieces of stone and metal from beyond your world. Some of them come from far away even by the standards of the cosmos.*

Hedia frowned, trying to understand what "beyond your world" meant. "Do you mean they come from India?" she said. She couldn't fathom how that could be, but she had already seen many things she couldn't understand.

India is part of your world, Hedia, said the voice. *These objects are from farther away than even Gaius Varus knows.*

I'm imagining the sneer, Hedia thought, but she wasn't sure that was true.

Most meteors burn up or at least break up when they hit the atmosphere of your world, the voice said. *A very few of them, however, are so large and solid that—*

The streak in Anti-Thule's black sky was so bright that Hedia blinked. It ended where the ice cliffs met the Tyla's green fields. Steam blasted skyward and red sparks also sprayed in all directions from the impact. Where the sparks landed on ice they kicked up additional puffs of steam, but those that struck among the houses started fires.

Ripples spread in circles from the impact, throwing down sheds and other structures in the fields and leaving boundary lines twisted. The soil had settled somewhat by the time the shock waves reached the town, but the Temple of the Moon rocked and some of the houses lifted off their foundations.

—they reach the ground intact, the spring said.

The imagery vanished. The arbor remained, but the path ended in brush not far beyond it.

Hedia swallowed. She said, "What am I to do now, Spring?"

I told you to follow the path, taking each right turn, the voice said. This time its tone was one that Hedia remembered using on men occasionally. Very, very stupid men, or so it had seemed to her at the time.

"Yes," Hedia said. Her voice was calm, but her lips were in a firm line.

She resumed walking. After a few steps she glanced over her shoulder, but the arbor was as empty as she would have expected it to be a few months ago.

It was amazing what a human being could become used to in a few months. What she had become used to, at any rate.

Something flitted across the path just ahead, followed by another of the same things. "Things" because as best Hedia could tell, they were winged horses about the size of sparrows.

They certainly weren't dangerous, nor had the turtle been dangerous. It made Hedia wonder what other creatures lived in this woodland, but she didn't suppose the voice had sent her here to die.

It was a more comfortable trek than that across the dry valley in which she had found Boest. Though she could use another drink by now.

The intersection at the end of this stretch of path appeared identical to the first. Hedia now knew to look down the left-hand branch immediately and saw an arbor, woven like the first from living laurels. Again it framed Anti-Thule.

What would happen if I walked through the arbor? Hedia thought. But the landscape of Anti-Thule hadn't been one she wanted to visit even when she first saw it. This was a later view of the place, and the changes made it horrible.

There was a water-filled crater where Hedia had seen the meteor strike. Wisps of vapor rose from its surface, and the ice cliffs appeared to have retreated instead of glazing over the vestiges of the impact.

A hundred feet of the fields surrounding the crater had become barren except for a smudgy blackness like the ashes of burned wool. When Hedia looked at the black surface closely, she saw that it moved the way a frog's throat pulses as the animal breathes.

That is the Blight, said the voice in Hedia's mind. *It will continue to grow unless it is stopped.*

The Godspeaker of the Tyla stood at the edge of the blackened area, holding out his soapstone tablet. The Priests of the Moon were arrayed to either side of him, facing the Blight also. They chanted in unison.

The water filling the crater was opaque, but something beneath occasionally lifted to the surface. It rippled like thick sludge.

The Tyla attempted to stop the Blight by their magic, said the spring. *Their power slowed the Blight's advance across Anti-Thule.*

The crater sloshed violently. At first Hedia thought it was erupting like pools of hot mud on the margins of Vesuvius. A flat head rose from the water and squirmed onto the blighted margin of the land.

It was a catfish, or its ancestors had been catfish. It wriggled from the crater, pulling itself along on fins. Its body was greater than that of an ox, greater than an elephant's. It had no scales, but much of its skin was blotched and scarred. The barbels fringing its lips waved like tentacles.

The Blight changes what it does not destroy, said the spring.

Hedia watched the monstrous fish writhe forward, leaving a smeared trail on the smutty blackness. Many of the priests retreated; even those who stayed where they were showed signs of nervousness.

The Godspeaker continued to chant, changing his stance slightly to the right so that he faced the oncoming fish. The fish lurched forward. Its stiff front fins raised the broad head ten feet in the air.

The Godspeaker gestured with his tablet. Lightning struck from the clear sky, blasting the fish. The spines stood out on fins from which the skin had been burned away and fluids leaked from the corpse.

"They're stopping it," Hedia said. As she spoke, she knew that she was really praying that her words were true. "They're stopping the Blight!"

She expected the voice to speak. Instead the answer came silently from the image: a deep crescent of the crater rim fell into the water, enlarging it. The blackness on the margin crept forward visibly, expanding the barren area except for a dimple of unblighted ground where the Godspeaker stood.

The Godspeaker lowered the tablet and backed away, shaking with exhaustion. The Blight oozed over the soil he had vacated.

The image faded. A breeze touched the arbor, making the leaves of the laurel shiver.

She turned abruptly and resumed walking. Toward the next branching, toward the next vision. She shivered also.

Hedia wanted to scream questions at the voice, but it would either ignore her or perhaps sneer as it had when she asked why it was showing her Anti-Thule. She wasn't willing to surrender her dignity for nothing, and besides, it didn't matter. She hoped that the visions had no purpose at all. Any information she got that disproved that hope would be bad news.

Hedia grinned. She knew people who tried to plan everything. She had decided when she was very young that she would never be able to foresee all the problems that could arise, so she was better off learning to deal with the unforeseen. Thus far that had worked out well . . . and, indeed, had often proved to be a great deal of fun.

Grunts and crackling brush came from the woods to her left. Hedia glanced toward the noise but couldn't see anything through the leaves. *What I'm hear—*

She looked up. A one-eyed giant and a huge ape were wrestling, each of them at least twenty feet tall. They were almost motionless, gasping with the strain. Occasionally a tree limb cracked when they swayed into it.

The cyclops was watching her over the ape's shoulder.

Hedia walked on, holding her head high. She was afraid, but she would *not* display her fear. She never displayed fear.

Life would often be easier if I weren't afraid, though, she thought. This was one of the times that was true.

She came to the third branching and took a breath. She was half-glad that she would put the struggling monsters out of sight when she turned but half-fearful of what vision she would see this time.

Nobody's making me look, Hedia thought. But she didn't actually know that the spring couldn't force her to see what it wanted to show her, and besides, neither fear nor disgust had prevented her from doing things in the past. The Otherworld wasn't the place to begin showing weakness.

Hedia looked immediately for the vision, hoping that this time there wasn't one. Reality, as often, was less pleasant than what she wished.

The arbor showed her that the crater had devoured half the green enclave. The filthy blackness had continued to advance into what had been cultivated fields; the ice that covered most of Anti-Thule had eased back from the margins also.

A pair of giant fish, bigger, if anything, than the one Hedia saw in the previous vision, had crawled beyond the blighted area. Ordinary Tyla, females as well as males, battled the monsters with spears that glittered like glass.

Occasionally a fish lurched forward. The Tyla scattered, but barbels wrapped around any who might be slow and swept them into the toothless jaws.

The white-furred Godspeaker faced the center of the blighted area with the tablet held before him. Two human males flanked him.

The Godspeaker could not destroy the Blight with only the aid of his priests, said the voice of the spring, its first comment on the scene. *He cast forward in time and brought back two human wizards to help him.*

The man on the Tyla's left was squat and broad shouldered. He wore a tunic of unbleached wool and bound his hair with a cloth fillet. If Hedia had seen him on the streets of Carce, she would have taken him for a countryman visiting the city and paid no more attention. He brandished a short iron rod whose end was crudely forged into the two-faced head of the god Janus.

The other human was dark-skinned and dressed in a loose silk jacket and trousers. He was lightly built and could have passed for one of the Indian noblemen whom Hedia had seen at Polymartium. He gestured with an ivory wand.

All three magicians were chanting. The black arc of the Blight had retreated where it was nearest to them.

"Why did the Godspeaker take humans?" Hedia said. "Why didn't he find Tyla wizards instead?"

A fish in squirming effort flopped half its length beyond the edge of the Blight. Four Tyla ran forward, holding an exceptionally long pike as though it were a battering ram. They buried their weapon deep in the monster's side, then started to run back.

The fish thrashed reflexively. The pike-shaft flailed to one side and back again, knocking the Tyla down. It swept the pair nearer the crater into the blackness. The other two crawled away, one helping the other.

The pair in the Blight got up also, but one immediately fell again. The other staggered almost to the edge of the foulness before sinking to all fours. Feathery blackness crawled up his limbs before covering his torso and head like a filthy blanket. His body sank to the ground. The lumps where the Tyla lay would soon be indistinguishable from the desolation about them.

There are no Tyla in the future, said the spring. *You see the last of them here.*

The scene framed by laurel saplings faded. Hedia took a deep breath, then turned and started down the right-hand path.

She didn't care about the Tyla any more than she cared about the many hundreds of animals—and humans, if it came to that—she had seen slaughtered in the arena, but now she had a notion of why the spring had shown her Anti-Thule.

The spring had said the Tyla were gone, but it had not spoken of the Blight. She chose not to ask it that question.

Hedia was sick with dread.

CORYLUS SAT CROSS-LEGGED IN A GLADE near a rivulet dripping down a series of rocky pools. He had gathered a pile of hickory nuts to his left, just as they had fallen from the tree, and to the right was a much smaller pile of nuts that he had husked.

The dryad Carya had lost interest in what Corylus was doing, but she stood beside her tree and watched nonetheless. He smiled and thought, *She hasn't lost interest in* me.

He used his dagger to slit the husk of the next nut, then wrenched it off in four pieces. He tossed them deeper in the woods and dropped the nut itself on the small pile.

"How long are you going to do that?" Carya asked. She was tall and slender, with red-brown hair and amber eyes. The shift she wore was pale yellow, but light reflecting from the leaves gave the fabric a greenish cast.

"I'll do another five or six now," he said. "Then I'll smash them and set them in water to float the shells off the meat while I husk the rest."

"I get bored, you know," she said. "The other sprites don't like me because I'm prettier than they are. I'm not from around here, you know?"

Carya was pretty and certainly exotic, though from what Corylus had seen, dryads of different species were generally catty about their neighbors anyway. He could see other sprites watching from behind trees nearby, but none called to him while he was sitting at the base of the hickory.

"Well, these are vary tasty nuts," he said as though he hadn't heard any implications in what Carya had said. "I'll have to move on as soon as I've eaten, though, since you don't know how I can get back to the Waking World."

He didn't think Carya had been lying when she said she said she didn't know how he could return; most of the tree spirits he'd met were shallow, easily distracted, and often spiteful, but he couldn't remember one lying to him.

Just in case this was the exception, he was offering Carya a chance to change her story.

"I don't see why," she said pettishly. She turned away.

The nuts *were* very good, but the meat could scarcely have been harder to get to. The husks were simply messy: they stained his hands a yellow that he suspected would have to wear off. That wasn't a real problem. If Corylus hadn't thought of crushing the hard shells and floating them away, he would have starved while he was eating.

A young woman—she looked young, anyway—walked out of the woods. She saw Corylus and said, "He*llo*, there. Where did you come from?"

"She isn't from around here, either," Carya said in a peevish tone. "Why are you dropping by now when I've got a visitor, Aura?"

"*Because* you have a visitor, dear," Aura said. Her blond hair was as pale as sunlight glancing from ashes, and her shift shimmered with no color at all. "I'm Aura, master, and I'm glad to see you. I'm from the far south; I'm a breeze."

Corylus dropped the nut and rose. He dusted his palms together, though that wouldn't do anything about the sticky brown sap from the hickory husks. *It isn't going to look any better as a dry yellow stain, either,* he thought.

"I'm Publius Corylus," he said. "I'm here by accident. I'd like to get back to the Waking World, where I've come from."

He was embarrassed at his appearance because she was a pretty woman. It didn't matter to him what he looked like—or to her, either, he supposed, under these circumstances—but reacting to a strange woman as a potential mate was as natural to a young man as breathing was.

"You have a friend, Aura!" the dryad snapped. "I don't! Not since Faunus wandered off."

"I came here with my lover Zetes," Aura said. Her voice was gentle and liquid. "We left Anti-Thule because of the ice. But Zetes was killed. I'll never love again, but I'm not dead."

She stood hipshot, looking at Corylus.

"Do you know how I can return to the Waking World?" he said. He had grown up in the cantonments around military bases. He'd become a handsome youth, and his father was a senior officer. Soldiers weren't allowed to marry while on active duty, but they formed attachments. There were always widows and the girlfriends of men who were on detached service.

Corylus was used to forward women, so Aura didn't shock him. But he was also aware that detached troops generally came home at some point and that not all widows were that in strict fact.

"I could lead you to the Cave of Zagreus," Aura said. "The dragons who guarded Persephone may still be there. I suppose if you got by them you could reach the Waking World through it."

She chipped out a laugh. "The dragons didn't save Persephone's maidenhead," she said bitterly, "but they may be able to keep you out of the cave."

"Is there another path into the Waking World?" Corylus said. He bent and picked up a handful of fallen leaves, then wiped the dagger blade. The juice from the husks might be corrosive as well as sticky. He didn't want to step away from Aura to clean his steel in the stream, but this would do.

"Are you a magician?" Aura said.

"No, nothing like that," said Corylus. "Ah—my friend Varus is, and I think he's here in the Otherworld. If I could find him, that would be as good as getting back home."

Aura shrugged. "I haven't met your friend," she said. "And I don't know any other way for you to return to the Waking World. What do you want to do?"

"You could stay here with me," said Carya. *I'd forgotten her.* "Just a little while?"

Corylus sheathed his dagger and lifted the cornelwood staff that he had leaned against the hickory's shaggy trunk.

"I'm sorry, Carya," he said. "I have business to attend to."

To Aura he said, "I'm ready to go to the Cave of Zagreus, then. I didn't have much to pack."

As he strode off beside the air spirit, he heard Carya behind them say plaintively, "Just a *little* while."

"MASTER HERDSMAN," ALPHENA SAID in a firm voice. "Tell me what you know about Lucius Sentius' plans for my mother and brother. And Publius Corylus, if you've heard anything of him."

The painted herdsman gave Alphena a startled look but said nothing.

Doesn't the amulet work anymore? Alphena thought. She squeezed the rough iron harder.

"You'd do better to ask the goat himself than ask old Moschus there," said the statue of Priapus in the center of the wall painting. "The goat wouldn't know, either, but he's smarter."

"Hey, Big-Dick!" the herdsman said, turning to face the statue. "There's no call to be insulting just because I take a while to get my thoughts together."

"Right," said the statue, a rustic figure with a huge member. Just as most houses had little shrines to the household gods, most gardens had a guardian statue of Priapus. "I'll keep that in mind, shall I? When the lady leaves, we'll discuss metaphysics, you and I."

He looked back at Alphena. "Not that I can help you, either, lady," he said. "Not that way, at least."

He grinned even more broadly and thrust his member in her direction. Before she could respond—coldly—he continued, "I don't know the people you're talking about, you see. If you give me a little to work with, maybe I can do better."

The cattle on the other side of the painted stream were drifting closer. *Can they speak now?* The goat that followed Moschus had stopped when he did. It was cropping scattered blades of grass.

"Well, my mother, Hedia, is beautiful . . . ," Alphena said, realizing as she spoke that a useful description would be difficult. "Ah, much prettier than I am."

Priapus gave a disgusted, "Pfft!" He continued, "Forget about the woman, lady. There's only been one since I've been here on this wall. The master doesn't have much use for them, you know?"

He leered. "Say—you are a lady, right? You're not dressed that way, but you are?"

"Yes, I am," said Alphena grimly. This had seemed so simple—dangerous getting in, but she hadn't expected trouble getting the information *after* she got to Sentius' office. "What about the one woman, then?"

"Oh, she was foreign," Priapus said. "No kin of yours. Rupa, her name was. Not bad looking, that I'll say, but it's the bloody truth that I haven't met many women I wouldn't give the time to. You're not bad yourself, lady."

He waggled his member toward her again.

"What did Rupa say?" Alphena said, jubilant inside. She had been falling into despair. "She's the one—well, she's involved in this, anyway!"

"Ah?" said Priapus. "Well, she was here with a tall young fellow, *very* nice, with reddish-blond hair."

"That's Corylus!" Alphena said. "Where is he now, do you know?"

"I haven't the faintest," Priapus said. "He didn't say a thing, just followed along behind Rupa. Now *she,* she told the master she was going off to his villa west of Carce. Your Corylus was along with her, so maybe he went there too."

"He must have!" Alphena said. She knew as she heard her own voice that if her brother heard the words he would frown and say that it didn't at all follow that Corylus *had* to be at Sentius' country estate.

Well, I won't say "must" to Pandareus when I see him at the house.

Alphena dropped the amulet back to the length of the neck strap, then winced; it was heavy enough that she should have let it down in a more gentle fashion. "Thank you, Priapus," she said over her shoulder as she stepped out of the office.

Sebethius and her escort were waiting in the corridor; Charias and more toughs would join them in the street outside. "Let's go!" Alphena whispered.

They strode into the garden again with Sebethius leading. A pair of gardeners were planting the roses that waited in a handbarrow with their roots balled. The household was awakening, but none of the ten or so servants visible were paying attention to Alphena and her fellows.

We've done it! she thought.

Taunus stepped in front of them. He must have been waiting behind a pillar of the portico surrounding the garden.

"You done, now?" he said to Sebethius.

"What I'm doing is none of your business, German!" Sebethius said.

"Well, I think it is," Taunus said, shoving the smaller understeward to the side. "You see, I've taken a bit of a fancy to the girl here—"

He tried to push past Drago and a Spaniard named Chalcus. Chalcus reached under his tunic and came out with a knife.

"No!" said Drago.

He and his cousin grabbed Taunus, each by one arm, and slammed him backward into the pillar that had concealed him. Neither Illyrian was particularly big, but the German flew like thistledown in a gale until his head cracked against the marble.

Taunus slipped down in a sitting position, then toppled sideways. There was blood on the pillar where his head had struck it.

"Don't run!" Alphena whispered, but her escort hadn't been about to run. They moved with stately determination to the rear wing. The gardeners stared after them with their mouths open, but no one else appeared to have noticed.

Taunus certainly isn't going to be telling anyone for a while.

"I'm returning this lot as unsuitable, Olanus," Sebethius said to the chief cook as they passed through the kitchen, moving a little faster now. "I'll see if the broker's man is still in the street."

A moment later Alphena was back in the alley, trembling with reaction. Charias was speaking to her, but she simply waved toward the main street beyond. She had no breath now for pointless babble.

Besides, they had to start planning their attack on Sentius' country villa.

CHAPTER IX

The thirty-foot walls of the demon's garden were hammered glass, iridescent where a beam of sunlight filtered through the jungle canopy. Varus touched the surface with his hand. It was cool and as undulatingly smooth as a pond on a still day. No one could climb it.

But of course there was no reason to climb the wall. The gates, complex metal laceworks, were closed but not locked or barred. One could walk right in.

Out of curiosity, Varus tried to follow a strand of the filigree with his eyes. So far as he could tell, the pattern didn't repeat from one side of the valve to the other.

"At first I thought these were made of gold," Bhiku said, eying them. "But it's too bright for gold, isn't it?"

"The metal is orichalc," said Varus. The garden beyond the whorls of fiery metal was richly green, but there was no sign of a demon or the missing girl. "It isn't magical, or at least I don't think it is, but I've only known it to be used by magicians."

"I suppose there's no reason we shouldn't go on in," Varus said. He touched the gate, but he didn't push it open just yet.

"Apart from the chance of being torn limb from limb by a demon, of course," said Bhiku. He smiled and put his hand on the left-hand leaf. They looked at each other, laughed, and swung both halves of the gate open as they walked through.

Facing the gate was an ivy-covered terrace with three levels. Had it been bare stone, it would have been much like the stepped base of a temple. On top of the highest level was a small bungalow woven from glass rods in all the soft shades of the rainbow.

A pair of pigeon-sized birds flew from a fruit tree and deeper into the garden, hooting. Their feathers flashed like polished bronze. There was no other movement.

"I can hear other birds," Bhiku said. "And insects of course. But the roars that drove the peasants away seem to have quieted."

Instead of leading straight to the bungalow, the walk curved around a plant whose leaves thrust up like a cluster of green and yellow sword blades. Varus started along the path with the sage falling in step with him.

At his second step, Varus felt his spirit leave his body and begin to climb the steep hillside of his mind. By now this journey was familiar, though he didn't understand it any better than he had the first time he had made it.

Varus smiled. Neither being a philosopher nor being a wizard meant that he knew everything. The only people who knew everything were those who were too colossally ignorant to understand that they were ignorant.

Or perhaps dead. The dead might know everything.

At the top of the ridge, Varus stepped into sunlight. The old woman in blue was waiting for him in a chair that seemed to have been carved from a single block of volcanic tuff. The armrests of porous stone had been worn smooth.

"Greetings, Sibyl," Varus said. "Have you called me here to tell me how to free the Princess Teji?"

He glanced down the other side of the ridge. Far below, but clear in every detail, he and Bhiku were walking in the garden. A stream meandered through fruit groves, every tree different, and the birds flying among them were as varied.

"Greetings, Lord Varus," said the Sibyl, rising to stand beside him. "I cannot tell you how to free Teji."

She gestured to the garden. "See for yourself."

A slender girl in white silk stepped out of the bungalow. The only color in her garments was that of the bright sash twisted around her waist.

"Why have you come here?" she called down to the visitors. "Go away or you'll be killed!"

Bhiku glanced at the physical Varus, but the body standing beside him said nothing. Varus knew from his friends that when his spirit was absent in these trances he was oblivious of the Waking World.

"My friend and I are here to rescue the Princess Teji from a demon,"

Bhiku said, handling the unexpected situation with the aplomb that Varus had already learned to expect from him. "Are you Teji, mistress?"

"I don't want to be rescued!" Teji said. She was untying her sash. "The demon rescued me. Now go away or you'll be torn to pieces!"

"Princess," said Bhiku, "come back with us, please. When you're home, we can discuss this—"

"I warned you!" the girl screamed as she lifted the sash by its two ends and let it unroll. For an instant Varus saw the image painted on the silk: a bright blue demon with six arms.

The demon stepped off the silk and gave a terrible roar. He was twelve feet tall and his fangs were as long as a tiger's.

"Sibyl!" Varus cried. "How do I stop the demon?"

"How am I to help one so powerful as yourself, Lord Wizard?" the Sibyl said.

The demon crouched to leap down on the two men. Bhiku pressed his palms together before him. He stood as straight as his little body could.

"YOU WILL PLACE YOUR NECK under my yoke!" the Sibyl shouted.

Varus stood in his physical body, looking up. A web of lightning wrapped the demon in crackling brilliance. His roar choked to a startled yelp. Off-balance, he toppled like a boulder.

Varus half-lifted Bhiku and jumped sideways as the quickest means of getting them both out of the way. The demon crashed onto the path, scattering sparkling gravel in all directions. He rolled into a stand of blooming rhododendrons beyond. The lightnings binding the demon continued to sizzle.

The girl was staring down at them with a dumbfounded expression. She held the sash loosely in her hands. The silk was spotlessly white, like her other clothing.

Bhiku bounced to his feet while Varus was still lifting himself onto all fours. "That was very impressive, Lord Varus," the sage said. "Rhetorical training is obviously different in Carce from what it is here."

Varus dusted his hands. The pea-sized gravel of the path appeared to be beads of multi-colored glass rather than crushed stone.

He thought of saying that he had been pleasantly surprised, but then he would be expected to explain the situation. Which he was unable to do.

The demon continued to grunt, but all his straining merely meant that his bundled body rocked among the bushes, sometimes making branches crack. Varus led the way past, giving the demon as wide a berth as the bamboo on the other side of the path allowed.

"The claws on his hands are as long as a tiger's," Bhiku said. "I don't doubt that he was able to rip that poor soldier apart."

"I'll do the same to you when I get free!" the demon said in what Varus could best describe as a rasping wheeze. The crackling bonds weren't strangling the demon, but he obviously wasn't getting as much air as he would have liked.

"Then we'll have to make sure that you don't get free," Varus said. He wasn't so much nonchalant as giddy with relief. He had no idea how long the spell would last—or anything else about it, really. All he knew was that for now he was better off than he had expected to be a minute or two earlier.

Teji had gone back inside. The bungalow didn't have a door. Varus looked in and saw the girl sitting on a couch, wringing the blank sash between her hands.

"Princess?" he said. She did not look up.

He stepped inside. Light coming through the colored glass gave the single room a soft, shadowless feel. Bhiku followed him and spoke softly in Indian.

The girl looked up and said in Greek, "What are you going to do with me?" She was trying to sound angry, but the words came out desperate instead.

"As I told you, Princess" Varus said. "We're here to bring you back to your father. You don't have to worry about the demon. He can't get free."

"My father!" Teji said. "Rupa *saved* me from my father! She brought me here and set Baruch to guard me!"

She looked at Bhiku and snarled out a rapid string of words in Indian. The sage stiffened, looking shocked. He said in Greek, "Repeat what you just said in Greek so that my friend can understand you, Princess."

Teji stood up, still twisting the sash. At her full height, she was considerably shorter than Varus. He had taken her for fourteen years old, but close to her like this he realized she might be younger.

"I saw the way Ramsa Lal looked at me," she said. She was facing Varus, but her face was pale and her eyes were unfocused. "My father! He said to his advisors, 'If I plant a field, do I not have a right to eat the crop?' And they stroked their beards and nodded to him and said, 'Yes, certainly, Your

Lordship.' And I went to Rupa because she was a woman and I begged her to save me and she *did*!"

Teji began to cry. She turned away and flung herself on the couch, still sobbing.

Varus looked at the sage. He said, "Logic would point out that she could be lying."

Bhiku raised an eyebrow. "Then logic would be a fool, would it not?" he said.

Varus grimaced. "That's certainly my opinion," he said. "Though it leaves the problem of what we're to do now."

Bhiku pursed his lips, then said, "Princess Teji? What would you like us to do? Ah. I have no power over my lord the rajah Raguram, but I'm sure that he would give you shelter to spite your father if for no better reason. Though Raguram has shown himself a decent man in the past, within the limitations of the flesh."

"I don't want to go anywhere," the girl said. She sat up on the couch and wiped her eyes with her sleeve. "I just wanted to stay here, but without Baruch to protect me I can't do that. Oh, I'm so unhappy!"

She flung herself back on the couch and resumed crying.

"I can probably free the demon," Varus said, speaking to Bhiku just loudly enough to be heard over the muffled sobs. "Of course, he may tear us limb from limb if I do."

Bhiku shrugged. "Well, we accepted that risk when we entered the garden," he said. "Given that we came to make Princess Teji's situation better, and instead we appear to have made it worse, I think we're bound by justice to take the risk again."

"That's my analysis also," Varus said. He smiled wryly. "Unfortunately."

"It is not unfortunate that you are an honorable man," said Bhiku. Raising his voice slightly, he said, "Princess? My colleague is going to release your guardian."

"We're sorry for our mistake," Varus said as he walked out of the bungalow. To Bhiku he added, "I *am* sorry, but I honestly don't think I made the wrong decision on the information I had."

"I see no way we could have gotten better information," the sage said. "Nevertheless, it's an unfortunate circumstance."

The demon continued to grunt and—to the extent he could—thrash in the rhododendrons. Varus grimaced and said, "Master Bhiku, there's no reason you shouldn't leave the garden before I do this."

"I think the reasons for staying with a courageous colleague are better, however," Bhiku said. "Who knows? Your rhetorical training may rise to this test as well."

Varus managed a laugh, but he couldn't pretend that the irony of the situation amused him very much at the moment.

"You wizards!" Teji called from behind them. "Are you really going to free Baruch?"

"Yes," said Varus. He halted close to the struggling demon. He gave off a musky odor.

Varus put his hands on his hips and stood arms akimbo. He was looking down from the vantage point high above reality. "Baruch!" he said. "Arise as you were before and go forth!"

The bonds of lightning vanished with seven distinct *pops*. The demon shook himself and rose to his feet, doing further damage to the bushes.

"I suppose he put them here in the first place," Bhiku said calmly. "Presumably he can replant if necessary."

"My present concern is that he'll use bonemeal to nourish them," Varus replied in the same tone. Corylus talked about trees and shrubs quite a lot, and Varus had learned to be interested in everything that came before him.

Even fertilizer, apparently, though I hadn't been aware of the fact until now when an opportunity to use the information presented itself.

Baruch turned to face them, flexing his six arms. He was even taller than he had seemed when Varus looked up at him on top of the terrace.

"Do you think you can bind me again before I tear your head off, wizard?" the demon said. He spoke in a quiet voice like the rumbling of a lion's throat.

"I don't know," Varus said. "Under other circumstances I would apologize, but given your behavior at the moment I acted, you didn't give me much choice."

Baruch laughed. "Missy?" he said to the princess. "I am here to serve you. What would you have me do with these men?"

"Give them whatever they want, Baruch," Teji said firmly. "They came here to help me. They're friends!"

The demon smiled, a disquieting expression on a broad mouth with large fangs. "What is it you wish, friend wizards?" he said.

"Merely to leave, I think," Varus said. "Unless . . . ?"

He looked at Bhiku.

The sage smiled and said, "I would take a few oranges with me, if that were permitted. I rarely get an orange to eat."

The demon laughed. "You have my mistress' permission to pick fruit," he said. "As much as you like."

Varus and Bhiku started for the gate. There was a heavily laden orange tree on the path, which was a further excuse to get farther away from the demon. Friendly or not, Baruch was *very* large.

"Young wizard?" the demon called.

Varus turned with an orange in his hand. *Has it been a trick to get me to take fruit?* "Yes, Master Baruch?" he said.

"When you speak your spells," the demon said, "you have the voice of an old woman. Why is that, please?"

"I don't know," Varus said. "I can only tell you that the old woman herself says that she is a figment of my imagination. I'm not sure that I believe her, however."

The demon laughed again. "Go then, friends," he said. "And may all your enemies be as unwary as I was. Though it seems to me that you could crush even the most cautious."

"Thank you, Master Baruch," Varus said. He walked toward the gateway and through them, with a feeling of relief. Behind him, Bhiku pulled the gate leaves closed.

"Well, we seem to be exactly where we were to begin with," Varus said. "Except that I'm trembling and completely exhausted."

"The oranges are good, though," said Bhiku. He had bitten out a piece of the rind and was squeezing the juice into his lips. "Shall we make our way to Raguram's domains, now? He would protect you from Ramsa Lal regardless of justice . . . but it *is* nice to have justice on our side, isn't it?"

Varus laughed. "Yes," he said, "it is. Now, how did you get the rind open? I am the child of privilege, you must remember, and I don't have your advantages in dealing with adversity."

"WAIT A MOMENT, IF YOU WILL," Corylus said as he began stripping ripe—or almost ripe—blackberries from a bush growing beside a small stream.

He needed both hands, so he leaned his staff into the crook of his left elbow. His right hand dropped berries into his cupped palm. "How far is the cave we're going to?"

"A few days, I suppose," Aura said. "It depends on how fast we travel."

She pointed up the stream. "We cross here and follow the path along the side of the cliff. It's a box canyon, but the path goes to the top."

Corylus tossed the berries into his mouth in two half-handsful, then squatted to wet his palms and rub them together. He didn't care about the blackberry stain, but he didn't want his hands sticky if he had to change his grip quickly on his staff.

"I'll need something more substantial before long," he said, "but for now let's get to the top of this cliff. How steep is it?"

"Not steep," said Aura, hopping over the creek. "You won't have to use your hands to help you climb."

The path slowly climbing the cliffside was six feet wide at the beginning but had soon narrowed to four. They were about twenty feet above the valley floor by the time they reached that point.

"I'll lead," Corylus said, and stepped in front of the girl. They could have continued to walk side by side, but there was no reason to.

The slope to their right was almost vertical. On the left the rock—it was pinkish-gray granite with flecks of fool's gold—sloped downward sharply. It wasn't sheer, but only a chamois could walk on it.

"Did somebody make this path?" Corylus said. The surface wasn't glass smooth, but it was smoother than the roads leading out of Carce and into the large part of the world that the Republic ruled.

"I don't think so," Aura said. "But I don't know anything about stone."

The valley below was filled with bamboo. Sometimes he heard the creek trickling over its bed, but there was no birdsong or insect murmurs. Often the passage of large animals—and humans are very large in the natural world— silenced the local residents, but Corylus began to feel disquiet nonetheless.

He stopped, slanting his staff before him. He could see twenty feet up the path ahead.

"Aura, I smell something dead," he said. He didn't look back at her. "Have you come this way before?"

"Yes, Zetes and I came this way long ago, before he died," the sprite said. "I've come alone many times since. The path leads to the top of the cliff. Would you like me to lead?"

"Of course not," Corylus muttered.

He moved forward, lifting his sandals only high enough that the soles didn't brush the surface; he set them down with no more sound than a falling leaf. He had once crept into a Sarmatian encampment to determine which wagon was the chieftain's. This was the same, though Corylus didn't know what the danger here was.

In the bamboo below was the body of a great spotted cat. The flesh had rotted away, but enough of the ragged hide remained over the bones to explain the miasma of old death. Its falling weight had splintered canes, but fronds now grew through the ribs and skin.

The cat had been bigger than any leopard Corylus had seen in the arena, and the fangs in its upturned jaw were six inches long.

Now that he was looking into the gully, Corylus noticed other skeletons and scraps of fur among the bamboo. Many of the bones were broken. The fall could have been responsible for some of the breaks, but some of the bones appeared to have been sheared through.

Corylus looked up. The cliff was bulged outward thirty feet up. The full height of the cliffs across the canyon was seventy or eighty feet higher yet. The rock was as smooth as sandstone ever was: a few cracks, a few knobs or pockets. There were occasional splotches of green where a plant had managed to take root, and Corylus saw a single stunted cedar tree.

He couldn't possibly climb the rock face, though. He didn't know a man who could.

Corylus eased forward, looking in all directions before he took the next cautious step. *All directions but back—*

He turned his head sharply. Aura was a proper six feet behind him, plenty of space for him to move fast if he had to . . . and too far for her to slip a knife into the back of the man in front of her. Her fingers were tented before her, and her expression was calm.

"I will lead if you like," the girl said. Corylus looked forward again.

The bones of a human hand and forearm lay ten feet below the edge of the path. The bones were more or less articulated because, though the sinews had shriveled and cracked, ivy vines had wound around them. On the middle finger was a ring of sunbright orichalc set with a brilliantly blue stone.

"There's something here . . . ," Corylus said softly. *Or are the bodies being flung from the top of the cliff?*

He looked up, then down. Perhaps something was crawling up from the canyon, a huge snake that slid out of the bamboo and crushed its victims' bones?

The corner of his eye caught the movement above: a dog-like head the size of a crocodile's was stabbing down at him on the end of a neck thirty feet long. The jaws were open.

Ambush! But Corylus had been on the wrong side of ambush before. He ducked, holding the staff upright with his left arm while his right hand reached for his dagger.

The open maw slammed down on the end of the staff. The butt was resting on the sandstone trail, and the cornel wood didn't flex or split at the terrific impact.

"Nerthus!" Corylus shouted, not really a prayer to the Batavians' goddess but the reflex of surprise. He brought the dagger around and stabbed its twelve-inch blade through the base of the creature's skull where the spine entered. He jumped back, leaving both his weapons because he had no choice.

Aura had retreated a few steps, but she hadn't fled. Corylus looked up as the enormous neck swung side to side, banging the head against the cliff. It looked more reptilian and less like a dog when he saw it in profile. The staff dropped from the monster's palate; by good luck it fell onto the path where it might be retrieved.

Corylus knelt, trembling and gasping for breath. It had happened so quickly that he shouldn't have expended much energy, but his muscles wobbled like those of an old slave in a chain gang.

He'd driven the dagger in with the strength of desperation. It had sunk through spongy bone and brain tissue almost to the cross guard.

The head continued to wave back and forth, but more slowly now; the monster's neck was drooping. Corylus couldn't see where the animal's body was, but there must be a cave concealed by the bulge in the cliff face directly overhead.

The head and neck stiffened. Corylus heard scraping and clattering, like the start of a landslide; then the whale-great body to which the neck was attached launched itself outward. Its four legs were as broad and flat as paddles, but their black claws scarred the rock when they ticked against it.

The creature started to tumble as it plunged, toward the gully. It disappeared into the tall bamboo, then bounced briefly visible before it vanished for good. A distant crashing went on for some time, but the springy canes closed over track the body had plowed through them.

"Hercules our protector . . . ," Corylus breathed. He wasn't of a religious mind, but a sincere prayer of thanks seemed the right thing to do at this point.

He stood up, feeling better—feeling exhilarated, even. *I'm alive!*

Corylus walked to where his staff lay and examined it. Six inches of one end were smeared with blood and mucus; the other end was scratched from transmitting the shock of the monster's lunge to the sandstone. It remained perfectly functional, though: the tough cornel wood was essentially undamaged.

Corylus wiped the messy end with the leaves of a bamboo cane leaning on to the path. Then, holding the staff in both hands, he walked back to where Aura waited.

HEDIA CAME TO THE END of the fourth leg of the path she had been following through the woods. She wasn't back where she had started, as she would have been if the woods were in the Waking World. In fact, she wasn't in the woods at all.

"Good," she muttered, because the visions of Anti-Thule had disturbed her. Although that might have been because she wasn't allowing herself to think about matters that were really disturbing, like being lost in the Otherworld with no clear way either to find her son or to get home.

Still, while Hedia cared even less about the Tyla than she did for the throngs of Levantine beggars clogging the Milvian Bridge, the Blight—as the voice had called it—was evil. Further, she had seen too much of the world and of this Otherworld to believe that she had been shown the visions for no reason.

Before her was a rolling grassland dotted with groves of trees, mostly in swales. The grass had been burned off within the past few months, but new growth had spurted waist high through the layer of soot.

Not far to Hedia's right, a track of dark green vegetation snaked toward the horizon. At first she thought she was seeing willows with stunted trunks, but after a moment's consideration she realized that the trees grew in the bed of a river.

At least there's water, she thought. *Though I may have to dig down for it.*

She looked up. A pair of birds—hawks or buzzards—wheeled slowly in the cloudless sky. When she lifted her face toward them, one bird and then the other also began to drop toward the ground.

Hedia grimaced. Well, if they thought she was dead she would convince them otherwise quickly enough. She shifted her little knife so that its hilt stuck out of her sash. This wasn't polite society, where people would be shocked to see her openly armed.

The trees in the grove behind Hedia were spiky and rough-barked, nothing like those of the wood through which she had walked a moment ago, and the track through them was low and narrow as though it had been worn by pigs. Well, she hadn't wanted to go back anyway.

There wasn't any obvious better direction for her to go, however. The choices were to slide down the bank of the watercourse—an overhang had collapsed nearby—or to strike off across the grassland to another stand of trees. The nearest grove was less than a mile away. Since the sunken river bent in that direction, she could easily try that option if there was nothing useful to be found in the grove.

As Hedia started toward the grove its side seemed to bulge outward as if a boulder had rolled through it. She paused and squinted to focus.

An elephant had just walked out of the trees. It had walked *over* a tree, though it took a moment for the crackling to reach Hedia. The beast was bigger even at this distance than the many hundreds of elephants she had seen—seen slaughtered—in the arena, and its heavy tusks pointed down.

A second and a third elephant followed the first. One lifted slightly on its hind legs, then lowered itself with a lesser crackling; it had hooked a large branch and broken it off to chew.

Well, that's *not the direction I want to go,* Hedia thought.

A shadow passed overhead. She jumped back, fumbling for her knife. One of the birds settled in front of her. Its feet kicked up spurts of dust and soot.

I'm starting at shadows! That was embarrassing, but the shadow could have meant *anything* in this place.

The second bird landed near the first; it hopped around a quarter turn to face Hedia as its fellow did. From their talons and hooked beaks they were hawks, but beak to tail they weren't as long as her forearm. Their backs and wings were rich chestnut, and their breast feathers were white with thin black ticking.

"Are you planning to steal those deinotheres?" the hawk on the left said. "We saw you looking at them."

"She'd better not," said the hawk on the right. "The herdsman wouldn't like it."

"He might like *her*, though," said Left. They were as similar as a pair of shucked oysters. Both birds cackled.

"I'm not going to steal anything," Hedia said, emphasizing her upper-class accent. Could the birds distinguish Latin accents? Since they spoke cultured Latin, they very well might. "I am the Lady Hedia, and I'm looking for my son, Gaius Alphenus Varus. Have you seen him?"

"Is he dead?" said Right. "We only pay attention to people when they're dead."

The birds cackled again.

"I trust that my son is not dead," Hedia said calmly. She'd met this sort before, though they were mostly women and the poncy boys her first husband had favored. *I wonder if these birds are hens?* "And since you're talking to me, you do pay attention to living people."

"Well, yes," said Left. "But you're going to be dead soon, so it's all the same."

Hedia sheathed her dagger. She was glad she'd snatched it out now, because putting it back with a flourish was a more effective way to show contempt than words would have been.

"Perhaps," she said. "Where does the river—"

She gestured.

"—go, if you will?"

"There's hills to the north," Right said. "A hundred miles or so. South it feeds into a swamp. That's about as far away."

"There isn't much water at this time of year," said Left. "A few pools along the way is all."

"She won't care about water," Right said. It bent its head back and combed its outstretched wing, its beak making little clicking noises as it did so. "The king will get her if she goes down to the river."

"Oh, I hope not," Left said. "The king won't leave anything for us."

"Who is the King?" Hedia said, smiling pleasantly. *If my servants were here, I'd have them wring the neck of one and hold the other until it explained the situation clearly. And then I'd have its neck wrung also.*

"You'd better hope you don't learn!" said Right.

"We hope you don't learn!" said Left.

The birds cackled together.

Hedia squeezed her lips into a grim line. She could see a grove beyond the nearest one, another mile or so distant. She could bear left to skirt the elephants. There was no reason the big beasts should pay any attention to—

A man with one large eye in the middle of his forehead stepped out of the nearer grove. He was taller than the elephants and broad in proportion.

His staff had been roughly shaped from a tree; the branches had been broken away, but much of the bark still remained on the trunk.

The cyclops looked at Hedia, then stepped between two of the elephants and started toward her. The smallest elephant started after him, but one of the larger pair screamed and swatted it back with her trunk.

A calf and its mother, Hedia thought. Which didn't matter, but it kept her from focusing on the speed at which the cyclops strode toward her.

The giant moved with the jerky awkwardness of a jagged boulder bouncing down a hill, but he stood fifteen feet tall and his legs were half his height. Each clumsy step covered more ground than Hedia could have run in the same time.

"Oh, good!" said one of the hawks. "The herdsman leaves as many scraps as a lion does. We'll eat well!"

Running is unladylike, Hedia thought. She turned and trotted to the fallen bank. As with showing her dagger, propriety could be buggered under these circumstances. The dagger would be useless against a giant, but she'd manage to scratch him for all that.

The slope to the streambed hadn't been packed down. Crumbs of dirt got between her sandals and the soles of her feet, but she didn't sink in.

Hedia looked left and right. Willow saplings grew in the dry streambed, but they didn't form a real barrier. The cyclops wouldn't be able to run between them, but he didn't need to: like the elephants of his herd, he could crush his way through without slowing.

Hedia saw a darker patch in the far bank beyond the screen of willows. A cave? *Something's* cave, no doubt, but she would take her chances with a hog rather than wait for the cyclops to catch her.

She ran through the willows, trying not to leave footprints. Her sandals scuffed the dry, sandy soil, but the marks were nothing more than the wind had done at various places on the surface.

The cave opening was tighter than Hedia had thought; she would have to crawl and perhaps to squirm. Still, it was better than what the cyclops had in mind.

Men have generally been friendly with me, she thought—and grinned. The cyclops was certainly male—he wore only a skin cape, so there wasn't any doubt about that—but his member was in scale with the rest of his body. There wouldn't be much difference between being torn apart to be eaten and being torn apart by sex.

Though I've always said that I'll try anything once. . . .

Hedia thought of backing into the hole, but she decided that she would rather meet a possible resident face-to-face. The point of her knife might at least provide enough delay for her to back out again.

She crawled in. Her body didn't fill the tunnel, so she could breathe, but the interior was pitch-dark. When she was some distance in—she couldn't really judge, but perhaps twenty feet—she became certain that she had been curving to the right.

Hedia stopped, panting more with relief than exertion. The cyclops wouldn't have been able to enter the tunnel, but he might have thrust his staff in if he suspected his prey had come down it. She was past the length of his arm on the end of the staff now—she thought—and anyway, the tree trunk couldn't bend.

Her eyes had adapted, but there shouldn't have been any light where she was. Instead there was a soft yellow-green glow, much like the flash of a fire-fly. It was very faint and came from farther down the tunnel.

Dim as the light was, Hedia could see that the cave was much enlarged. She could stand without ducking, and she probably couldn't touch both sides at the same time.

She rose to her feet, feeling uneasy again. The illumination wasn't the right color to be sunlight through holes in the ceiling.

At least I can turn around, she thought. She had been expecting to have to back down the tunnel, which would have been even less pleasant than it had been to enter with her shoulders rubbing the dirt.

The tunnel continued to curve beyond where Hedia stood. *I wonder where it leads?* It could scarcely be worse than to follow the river in either direction if the hawks were to be trusted. The birds had irritating personalities, but they hadn't lied about the one statement she had been able to check: the elephants' herdsman certainly was hostile.

The light from farther down the tunnel brightened. A snake crawled around the bend twenty feet from Hedia. The front part of his body was raised so that his head was on a level with hers. There was no way of telling how far back the creature stretched, but even where his neck joined the triangular skull the snake was thicker than Hedia's torso.

The snake wore a crown of yellow-green light, the source of the illumination. His forked tongue sipped the air twice as his eyes held hers.

"I am the King," he said in a soft voice. She expected the snake to slur his words, but his diction was perfect. "You are very welcome in my realm, human."

He started toward her like a river of hot tar.

Hedia turned and threw herself into the tunnel back the way she had come. Dropping to all fours, she scrabbled down the narrowing passage.

Like a frightened rat, she thought. *And that's just what I am!*

She expected the King's fangs to close on her trailing leg before she reached daylight. The tunnel had narrowed and she wouldn't be able to turn and stab the snake. *But as I go down his throat I'll be cutting a furrow as deep as the blade reaches!*

The blade was only the length of her little finger, of course, but she would do what she could.

Hedia slithered onto the streambed and scrambled around saplings while still in a crouch, rising from all fours only when she had reached the fallen stream bank. The King was behind her, chuckling in a bass voice. *I wonder if he's deliberately playing with me?*

She climbed to the plain. She had forgotten about the cyclops until she looked up and saw him twenty feet away.

He roared with triumph through yellow, ragged teeth. The cape tied around his shoulders was the skin of a shaggy bull of some type. The hide had not been tanned or even cleaned properly, and the stench of rotting flesh shoved her back like a wave.

The sky in the east had turned to dark golden clouds rising from the horizon to far into the heavens. Lightning shot through the roiling mass as it rushed toward Hedia and the cyclops.

"Mine!" said the giant. He raised his club.

Hedia crossed her arms before her. *Perhaps he and the snake will kill each other.* But she was between them, and there was no escape regardless of what happened afterward.

The clouds shattered into bright sunlight and a pair of chariots drawn by leopards. Behind followed an entourage of humans and not-humans of scores of types: beasts and satyrs, centaurs and fauns.

Bacchus had arrived with his followers, and the grassland swelled with vines and fruit trees along the track they had made.

Hedia recognized the man driving the left chariot as the leader of the army that had swept into Polymartium. At the time, she had thought she was seeing Bacchus himself.

Bacchus drove the other chariot. He was more beautiful than the sun, and his slender body was the source of the light that had suffused the clouds in which he and his followers swept across the plain. The cyclops turned to face them.

"Stand aside, brute!" said the human in the left chariot.

"You cannot order me, Ampelos!" said the giant. He lifted his staff again. "No one can order me!"

Bacchus hurled his thyrsus like a spear. The pinecone smashed through the cyclops' chest; his skin cape bulged outward in back.

Hedia dodged to the side so as not to be crushed by the huge corpse as it toppled into the ravine. The fennel stalk quivered in the middle of his chest.

"I greet you, Lord Bacchus!" Hedia said, and threw herself prostrate.

Things were looking up. The young god was a *very* handsome figure.

ALPHENA STOOD BESIDE LENATUS. She would rather have gathered her force in a more private place, but the only space in Saxa's town house large enough to hold thirty-odd large men was the central garden on to which virtually every room in the building opened. Any member of the household could inform the authorities about what the master's daughter was planning.

"All right," said Lenatus, addressing the men sitting or squatting at the back of the garden. It was late afternoon, the hottest part of the day, but that couldn't be helped if they were going to arrive at Sentius' villa during the third night watch: the three hours after midnight. "The first thing is, Lady Alphena is in overall charge, but if *I* tell you to do something, you'd bloody well better hop it. Got that?"

Men nodded, clapped, or—in the case of the two Armenians—bowed with their palms flat on the ground. Every member of the three escort squads had volunteered for the business.

Alphena had suspected that there'd been threats against anybody who wasn't keen on going along with a plan that involved magic and rebellion against the Emperor as well as the normal risks of an armed attack. Lenatus had assured her that all the escorts were enthusiastic; in fact, other members of the household had tried to join also.

"We'll be going through the city by squads," Lenatus said. "Lady Alphena will take her own people."

"Hey, we can handle it all ourselfs!" said Rago. "None of you rest need to come!"

Alphena opened her mouth to speak, but Lenatus snarled, "Shut up, Rago, or you'll get a trip back to Dalmatia in chains! You're not soldiers and I don't expect you to be soldiers, but you *can* hold off acting like bloody trash-talking gladiators while you're under Her Ladyship's command!"

Rago hung his head, but his cousin said, "Sorry, headman. Sorry, lady."

"Right," Lenatus said mildly. "Then in ten minutes by the water clock, Charias goes off with Lord Varus' squad."

There were nods and smiles, but none of the men made a loud demonstration this time.

Lenatus had kept the force in individual squads so that they wouldn't march through Carce looking like a gang of cutthroats off to launch an attack. Alphena smiled at the thought. That was particularly important since they *were* a gang of cutthroats planning an armed attack.

"Now, some of you may think Charias is a pansy and wouldn't know which end of a sword to hold," Lenatus said. "Personally I think you're wrong and that's why I chose him, but the truth is that I don't bloody *care* what any of you think. You'll take his orders like they were my orders, or else I'll crucify you when things settle down. Is *that* understood?"

Charias stepped forward. Alphena hadn't expected that, and she didn't think Lenatus had, either.

"Your Ladyship?" the understeward said. "Master Lenatus? I've spoken with the men I'll be leading. I can vouch for their understanding. We won't do anything that will jeopardize the return of Lord Varus and his mother."

"Right," Lenatus repeated. "I'll take the third squad myself; that's Lady Hedia's crew. We'll meet in the stables outside the Tiburtinum Gate where Pulto is waiting with the wagons and the equipment. Which brings me to another point."

Lenatus paused. Alphena glanced at the man she had thought of as her trainer, a free citizen but of less importance in her father's household than an understeward.

She was seeing a different man now. Lenatus was a veteran legionary, a man who had spent twenty years guarding the frontiers from German raiders—and raiding into Germany whenever somebody in authority decided that it was time to teach the barbarians another lesson.

He's probably killed as many people as he's talking to now, and he's willing to kill a thousand more if I tell him to.

"Now look," said this new Lenatus. "The hardware will be in the wagons.

Everybody'll be issued just what he asked for. You can trust Pulto for that, because I trust Pulto. But nobody leaves here with a blade on him. I search each man before he goes out the back gates, and if I find anything the man stays. Caenus? You hear me?"

"I heard you when you said it before," said the little Greek from Gādēs. His tone was sullen. "Dunno what the big deal is. I always carry a knife—but not today; I heard you."

"Today we're not taking a chance that some centurion of the watch is going to get stroppy and decide to search a gang of thugs even if they're escorting a senator's daughter," Lenatus said. "Look, I'm going to turn my back for a minute. If there's something on the ground when I look around again, that's none of my business. Got it?"

He turned. Alphena turned also. Caenus was one of her personal squad.

"Everyone is listening," she said to the veteran in a low voice. "The whole staff. Anybody could report us to the prefect."

"Right," said Lenatus. "And maybe somebody will. The thing is, if somebody does every slave in the staff will be tortured for evidence because their evidence isn't valid *unless* they were tortured. Which means everybody except the informer has a bloody good reason to put a knife in anybody they think is heading out the door to find the prefect. My guess is that nobody is going to leave the grounds until this is all sorted and we're back."

He grinned at her. "And maybe I'm wrong and there'll be a battalion of Praetorians waiting when we get back," he said. "We'll deal with that when it happens, right?"

Alphena grinned back. "Right," she said.

While they were whispering to each other, Alphena had heard occasional clinks as metal fell against stone. Lenatus said, "Anybody need more time?"

After a pause in silence he faced around again. Alphena turned with him. Several daggers and a full-sized cavalry sword—it must have been bound along the spine of one of the taller men—lay on the pavement.

"Right," said Lenatus. "I think we're ready to start now."

"One moment," Alphena said, surprising herself. She looked out at the men she was about to lead against wizardry and perhaps worse.

"None of you have been promised anything except a chance to die," she said. "I'm promising you now that if we come through this, you'll all get your freedom and passage back to your home countries with enough money to set you up there."

"Hey, I was lucky to get outa Syria alive the first time!" called one of the men. Along with the general laughter came muttered agreement in a number of different accents.

"Well, I just wanted to say that," Alphena said. She felt a little embarrassed. "Lenatus, you may take over."

Minimus, the big Galatian from Hedia's escort, stepped forward. "Ma'am?" he said. "Her Ladyship, she's a great mistress. Everybody makes way for her. We'll get her back for you, and the boy too."

Lenatus was waiting at the door of the garden. Men shuffled past—and were searched, just as he'd promised. Alphena waited to follow.

Would they be so keen if they knew I was hoping to find Publius Corylus at Sentius' villa rather than Mother and Varus? she thought. And then she thought, *And would I be so keen if it weren't Corylus?*

CHAPTER X

Hedia remained prone, but through her eyelashes she watched Bacchus step down from his chariot. His sandals seemed to be made of golden light.

"You may rise, child," Bacchus said in a light tenor voice that warmed and thrilled her.

Hedia stood with a sinuous ease that came from thigh exercises and a great deal of practice. The real trick lay in making it look effortless, which it certainly was *not* when she had just crawled down a tunnel on all fours.

She stared at the god, only arm's length away from her. "You're beautiful . . . ," she said. She wasn't certain that the words had reached her lips, though she knew her mouth was open.

Bacchus laughed. The sound was as liquidly golden as every other aspect of this wonderful creature. He said, "And who are *you*, delightful child?"

"I'm Hedia . . . ," she said, managing not to add, *wife of Senator Gaius Alphenus Saxa*, as she usually would. "I . . . oh, I look terrible!"

Usually when Hedia said something of that sort, it was to provide the man with an opportunity to disagree with her. Now, facing this *gorgeous* creature, she meant it in all truth. Her garments had suffered during her exertions with Gilise, and her quick passages in and out of the snake's burrow had completed their ruin. Not just her clothing: her knees and palms were gritty!

Bacchus laughed again and ran his right hand through Hedia's hair. "You are very beautiful, Hedia," he said. "Your soul is truly exceptional, but your body is lovely also."

"There's a thousand women in our train just as lovely," said the man from the other chariot, Ampelos. Hedia remembered being impressed when she saw Ampelos at Polymartium, but here he was no more than the god's shadow. "That's if you find women interesting in the first place."

"I do, dear boy," said Bacchus, continuing to look at Hedia and stroke her hair. "I find this delightful woman very interesting."

"I'll leave you to her, then," Ampelos said.

Hedia had heard *that* tone often enough from the little friends of her first husband, Calpurnius Latus. She could easily imagine the boy flouncing away with a flick of his hips. She didn't bother to glance after Ampelos, though, because her soul was drowning in the god's eyes.

"Come, child," Bacchus said. "My followers are weaving a bower for us to be carried by a pair of elephants. I think we'll find that more comfortable than riding in my chariot would be, don't you?"

"I would crawl on hands and knees to be with you," Hedia whispered. She rose on her toes, pressing her body against Bacchus as they kissed.

Golden. A flow of warm liquid gold filling me . . .

"I AM YOURS TO TREAT as you wish," Aura said as she watched Corylus approach. "I would appreciate it if you allowed me to fetch one thing from the ravine before you act, though. I won't try to escape."

Corylus frowned. *What does she expect me to do to her?* Then he thought, *What do I plan to do?*

Aloud he said, "Go, then."

Aura slipped over the edge of the trail. She kept her feet on the sandstone slope, but she shifted her grip from one bamboo cane to another to support her weight. She moved deeper into the ravine as she worked back in the direction they had come, but she never disappeared from his sight. The leaves scarcely quivered as she moved through the bamboo.

Corylus breathed deeply while he waited. It had all happened so *fast*. He hadn't been frightened when the monster thrust down at him, but looking back, he saw himself as an image in a mirror—and the mirror shattering into a thousand bits, each one a fragment of the soul of Publius Cispius Corylus.

Why did she try to get me killed?

Aura reached for something Corylus couldn't see from his angle, then straightened holding the orichalc ring he had noticed on the skeletal finger. She slipped it onto her left thumb, then leaned forward again. After a long moment she found what she was looking for and began to climb back to the trail. Her left hand held a belt from which hung a dagger in a scabbard of corroded silver.

"You lost your dagger," Aura said when she regained the trail. She offered the gear to Corylus, still holding it by the belt to make clear that it wasn't a threat. "I brought you the one Zetes carried. He wasn't as quick as you were. I've never seen anyone as quick as you."

Corylus held the tip of the scabbard against his staff and drew the dagger with his right hand. The blade was orichalc. He had seen such weapons before: they were as tough as good steel and took a keener edge.

"I would have gone after yours," Aura said, "but you sank it so deeply into Scylla's skull that I didn't think I could have pulled it out."

Corylus grinned wryly, still looking at the gleaming orichalc blade. "I'm not sure that I could've pulled it out," he said, "unless I got a scare like the one I had when I stuck it in. That was as close as I ever need it to be."

The orichalc blade was slightly leaf shaped and too broad to fit in the scabbard of his legion-issue weapon. Corylus unwrapped the ties that, with a flat hook, attached the silver scabbard to its belt.

He looked up at Aura, standing submissively before him. "Why did you try to get me killed?" he asked in a matter-of-fact tone.

"I didn't," she said, "though I supposed you would be. All those before you had been."

She gestured past him. "There's a glade just down the trail," she said. "Beyond this knuckle of rock where Scylla laired. If we go there, we can sit in a degree of comfort. But whatever you wish."

"All right," Corylus said. He thought of telling Aura to walk in front of him, but that would be pointless except as an insult.

He turned and walked down the trail. He didn't understand her behavior, but he wasn't worried about her stabbing him in the back.

There was a notch twenty feet deep in the sandstone wall, rising from the trail to the cliff top. The ground was covered with ferns and flowering plants, some of them with small white or magenta blooms. The cliff had been carved back into a bench on one side.

"Is this artificial?" Corylus said. He gestured upward. "All of it?"

Aura shrugged. "I don't know," she said. She sat on the bench and looked up at him. "I suppose so."

Corylus thought for a moment, then seated himself also. He had the silver scabbard loose; now he removed the issue one from his own belt.

"You said 'Scylla,'" he said. "She had six heads, didn't she?"

"No," said Aura. "She had only one, but that was enough until you came."

Aura crossed her hands in her lap and looked out toward the other side of the ravine. "Zetes and I came by this path," she said. "We hadn't left Anti-Thule very long before and we were exploring. We were following this trail—"

She gestured back the way they had come.

"—and talking about how happy we were to be here."

She looked at Corylus. "We were always happy," Aura said. "We had each other. And then Scylla struck and took Zetes and threw his corpse into the ravine. Not to eat, just to kill."

Her tone was emotionless, as dead as the stone on which they sat. Corylus swallowed. "But why didn't you warn me? I didn't hurt Zetes; I wouldn't have hurt you. *I'm* not your enemy."

"After Zetes died, I have had no purpose but to kill Scylla," Aura said. "I've led creatures up this trail, wolves and bears and big cats—"

She flushed as she held his eyes and added, "—and men, sometimes men. Knowing that one day one of them would kill Scylla and living for that day. And you have killed her."

Aura's face softened and she lost the tone of challenge. "I have no reason to live now," she said, "except to do your will. When you're done with me, I will die and join my lover in oblivion."

Corylus understood the ruthlessness—the frontiers were a hard school, and he had accompanied the Batavian Scouts. The method still puzzled him. He said, "But why didn't you tell me what was going to happen? I was quick enough, but I might not have been."

"Would you have come with me if you'd known the danger?" Aura said in a harsh voice.

"Of course I . . . ," Corylus said, but he paused. He looked down, then met her eyes again. "If you'd made it a condition of leading me to the Cave of Zagreus, I think I would."

Aura shrugged. "Perhaps you would have," she said. "It doesn't matter now anyway."

Corylus didn't let his first—angry—reaction reach his lips. During the pause, he thought. Grinning, he said, "You know, I don't think I could've re-acted better when that head came down at me if I'd been practicing all year. Maybe you were right about how to handle it."

He stood and buckled on his equipment belt. The new scabbard rode easily over his right hip bone, and the horns of the dagger's pommel didn't prevent him from drawing it quickly.

He looked at Aura. "Do you really know how to get to the Cave of Zagreus?" he said. "Or was that just a trick to get me to come this way?"

"It wasn't a trick," the girl said. "There are other ways we could go, but this path is the shortest."

"Then . . . ," Corylus said, "let's be on our way, shall we?"

He offered Aura his hand. She touched fingertip to fingertip, but she rose with no more effort than a breeze ruffling the ferns.

VARUS HAD BEEN HEARING THE SOUNDS for several minutes, but he wasn't sure they were angry voices and not a flock of birds. He looked at Bhiku and said, "Some of the prettiest of your birds seem to have the most unpleasant calls."

"Indeed," said the sage. "If I were a different sort of philosopher, I would form a long exposition about this, showing that the gods always balance good features with ill."

He smiled, turning his face from a prune into a happy prune. "It wouldn't be true, but by choosing my examples I could convince those of my audience who don't think for themselves," he said. "At any rate, that is what I have observed in watching my colleagues. My wealthier colleagues."

"Carce has similar teachers," Varus said. "Ours dress better and appear to eat better than my friend and teacher, Pandareus of Athens."

Of whom you remind me a good deal, his mind added silently.

"In the particular case," Bhiku said, "what we hear is a village squabble of some sort. The plumage of our villagers is much like my own rather than, say, that of a golden pheasant."

The path wound through brush. The knotted stems reached thirty feet high, though they were never as thick as Varus' wrist. At the tops were sprays of small leaves, bobbling even in air that seemed dead still.

The voices hadn't gotten louder from the time Varus first heard them, but the next bend of the path brought him and Bhiku within ten feet of forty or fifty peasants focused on something in their midst. Some of them carried staffs or sickles made by setting sharp flints in a backing of split cane.

Bhiku shouted in Indian. His voice carried like a flung javelin when he chose to be heard.

The men nearest to him turned, saw two strangers, and scurried back. The fear spread, driving a wedge into the middle of the crowd as spectators moved sideways.

Everyone whom Varus saw was male, with the exception of the naked girl in the middle. She was tied to the stake planted at a fork in the path he and Bhiku had come down. Dry palm fronds and lengths of bamboo were piled knee high around her.

"Stop this at once!" Varus shouted, striding forward. His anger surprised him more than it probably did the peasants. *She's only ten!*

A old man stepped forward wearing a turban of red cotton and a pale yellow vest embroidered in black. Twisted into a rope between his hands was a garment of mottled silk.

"Go, stranger!" he said in shrill Greek as he stumped toward Varus. He poked out both index fingers without letting go of the silk. "Serpent woman! Evil! We caught her and we burn her!"

The girl wasn't as young as Varus had thought at first glance, but she was no more than his own eighteen years. The Indians he had seen since his arrival were lightly built and so looked younger than he expected. Unlike the peasants surrounding her, though, the girl's ribs didn't show from hunger. She looked as supple as a rattan vine.

Bhiku appeared at Varus' side. He addressed the old peasant sharply in Indian. Each time the answer began to singsong into a rant, Bhiku brought the peasant back in a tone of command.

When the peasant stopped talking, seemingly calmer, Bhiku nodded and turned to Varus. "The headman says that a woodcutter saw the girl bathing and recognized her as a serpent demon. He took her garment so that she couldn't change into her snake form and ran back to the village to bring help. The headman determined to burn her so that they can be sure her ghost doesn't return to curse them."

"I see," said Varus, but as a placeholder to show that he was considering the matter. He thought of asking Bhiku's opinion. This was India, and the customs of the country were the business of Indians alone, after all.

Italian peasants are probably just as benighted as this lot, he thought. *I certainly wouldn't be interested in their judgment as to what was proper behavior.*

Bhiku was another matter, but Varus wasn't going to ask his friend to tell him whether something was right or wrong. He faced the headman and tried to compose his face like that of a magistrate delivering judgment in a murder trial.

"It may be executing this girl is proper," Varus said, speaking loudly and slowly to help this peasant understand Greek. "I don't know anything about serpent demons. However—"

He gestured to the pile of kindling and fuel about the girl's feet.

"—cruelty of this sort is not proper. Since you're worried about her haunting you if you execute her, it's best that you avoid the problem by leaving her to go her own way. Release her now!"

"You cannot give us orders, stranger!" the headman said. His mouth threw spittle in his anger. He turned his head and shouted to the villagers in their own language. Several of them bent surreptitiously to pick up stones.

Bhiku rattled off a long spate of Indian, loudly enough to be heard on the fringes of the crowd. It brought a series of gasps and cries. Those who had picked up stones dropped them again. Several men at the back edged away, then turned and ran. Within a few moments all the villagers had joined the rush, some of them leaving tools or articles of clothing behind.

The headman turned and shouted at them in anger, then realized he was alone. He looked over his shoulder, snarled what Varus was sure was a curse, and flung the twisted silk down as he fled after them.

Varus took a deep breath. Until the crisis was over, he hadn't appreciated how dangerous the situation had been. Peasants who were willing to burn a girl alive might not have hesitated to stone to death a pair of unarmed strangers who tried to interfere.

"What did you say to them, Bhiku?" he said. "Did you translate my words?"

Bhiku laughed. He said, "I found your rhetoric persuasive, Lord Varus, but I'm afraid it would have been less effective on our local visitors. Instead I told them that you were a great wizard and would blast them all to atoms if they didn't run back to their village at once."

"I—" Varus said in horror. He caught the words in his throat. He considered the situation instead of simply responding as he wished the situation to have been.

Smiling, he said, "I had no conscious intention of blasting those fellows or doing them any other harm. But then, I didn't consciously intend to bind Lady Teji's demon, either. Thank you for using your initiative, Bhiku."

"It appeared to me that the alternative was that we would be stoned to death," the sage said. "I would have been willing to shade the truth to avoid that, but it appeared to me that what I said was true in essence, even if I might have been wrong about the details. You might have brought fire from Heaven onto them instead, for example."

"Yes," said Varus. He managed a smile, but he felt as though he were talking about some third party, a powerful magician, and probably a figure of his imagination, because in his heart he didn't believe in magic. . . .

"We're forgetting the cause of the excitement," Bhiku said. He walked to the girl, holding a sharpened flint between his thumb and index finger; it had probably fallen out of a sickle or other tool in the recent commotion.

Varus retrieved the girl's garment from the bush to which it had stuck when the headman threw it away. He shook it out into a simple shift and carried it to her. The fabric didn't appear damaged by its hard handling. He still wasn't sure what color it was, though, as it appeared to change depending on the light.

Bhiku had sawed through the twine of bamboo fibers binding the girl to the stake. He spoke to her in Indian.

She shrugged into her garment and turned a brilliant smile on her rescuers. "Thank you," she said in perfect Greek. "There was nothing I could do to preserve myself. You have saved my life, Lord Varus. I will repay you when I can."

Varus nodded, blank faced. He was taken aback that she knew his name.

Bhiku had grinned minusculely. The girl turned her brilliant smile on him and said, "Even so great a wizard as Lord Varus is better for having friends, Master Bhiku. And no friend is too weak to help in *some* fashion."

Bhiku bowed. "You are right to correct me," he said. "I apologize."

The girl smiled again. She pressed her hands together before her, fingers pointed up, and bowed. She vanished.

"My goodness," said the sage. He looked at Varus.

"I have no idea of what just happened, either," Varus said. "I'm as glad to have her as a friend, though."

He cleared his throat. "Are we near Lord Raguram's domains yet?"

"Not as near as I would prefer to be without getting a drink of water," Bhiku said, "but perhaps we'll find a spring on the way. Under other circumstances I would suggest we stop by the well of the village which must be nearby—"

He gestured in the direction in which the villagers had fled.

"—but not, I think, at this time. Let's take the other fork."

"I could always blast them to atoms," said Varus as he and Bhiku proceeded. "But on balance, I think waiting to drink until we reach another source of water will be proper training in Stoic resignation."

They walked on. Both men were chuckling.

ALPHENA AND PANDAREUS SAT with the driver on the bench of the second of the six wagons; Lenatus was in the lead vehicle. They were approaching the gardens behind Sentius' country estate without difficulty, though weren't using lanterns and the waning moon had just risen.

"There's plenty of light for them to see us by too," Alphena said to the teacher beside her. "I'm surprised that we haven't met anyone since we turned off the Salt Road."

"Um," said Pandareus. "I'm not out in the country at night often enough to know what may be normal."

Neither am I, Alphena realized. Aloud she said, "It doesn't matter anyway. I have to do this. If it's a trap, I hope we can fight our way out of it."

She was wearing a sword and dagger, though she had decided against armor. Most of the escorts wore at least a helmet, and some of the former gladiators had shields and heavy back-and-breast armor also.

Perhaps thinking along similar lines, Pandareus said, "The men appear to be excited and pleased about this expedition. Do they not expect resistance?"

"I suspect most of them hope there *will* be a fight," Alphena said. "They're bored. *I* hope we'll get in without trouble and I'll find a statue in the garden which tells me where Corylus is, and that we'll free him just as easily."

Pursing her lips, she added, "I think that's likely."

That isn't really true, she thought.

Pandareus looked into the back of the wagon where six heavily armed escorts hunched. Facing forward again, he said, "I think men like these are usually bored. Their activities are of a sort that brings only ephemeral pleasures."

Before Alphena could decide how to reply, the teacher added, "Lest I seem to be criticizing, I would not want a band of rhetoric teachers accompanying me on an outing like this. Though I'm sure we would have a lively discussion on the way."

Their driver murmured to the pair of mules, and the wagon swayed to a halt. Men were already jumping out of the lead vehicle. The garden was enclosed by a six-foot fence of palings, built to keep out goats rather than for show. No lights were visible through gaps in the fence, either in the garden or at the back of the house beyond.

Alphena dismounted, then helped Pandareus down from the seat. The six wagons were in a close line on the cartway behind the fence, and Lenatus was at her elbow.

"Are you ready to go in?" he said brusquely. He was the veteran soldier speaking to the young officer in command for the first time, not the obsequious servant to Her Ladyship.

"Yes, with my own escort only," Alphena said. "I'd like to do this with as little disturbance as possible, but ten men is enough to hold for a moment if there's trouble."

Lenatus' face went harshly blank in the moonlight. Because he didn't respond instantly, Alphena said, "My father will support whatever I decide, but for his sake I would like this to look as little like armed rebellion as possible afterwards."

"Ah!" said Lenatus. "Right."

"Worst case, we can kill all the witnesses," said Pulto, who had joined them. Both veterans were in full legionary armor, though they weren't wearing their helmet crests.

"What?" said Alphena. "There'll be farm laborers in the wings, probably hundreds of them."

"Yeah, but they won't have much in the way of weapons," explained Lenatus. "And we'll have surprise."

"Besides," said Pulto, "a lot of them'll be women and kids."

"That shouldn't be necessary," Alphena said. She was suddenly aware at a visceral level of what it meant to guard the frontiers of the Republic. "Let's go."

"Pulto, you're in charge back here," Lenatus said as he strode to the gate in the fence. Then, to Drago, "First Squad with me, Second and Third in reserve."

"Let's get these bloody wagons turned around," Pulto ordered behind them. He wasn't shouting, but the sounds of weapons and harness would already have been enough to alert any watchman in the garden.

The gate was sturdier than the fence itself and was closed on the inside. Lenatus drew his dagger and said, "I'll slide this past the gatepost and lift the bar."

Minimus gripped the top of the gate with one hand and twisted, wrenching it off its hinges. He shook the panel to toss the crossbar out of its supports.

Lenatus looked at the big Galatian with no expression.

"It didn't make noise like kicking the gate in'd do," Minimus said.

"Right," Lenatus said in a quiet voice. "But don't get smart again, or you'll get this"—he waggled the dagger, then thrust it back into its scabbard—"up through your belly."

Alphena tried to step through the gate. Lenatus blocked her with his left arm without looking at her and went through himself. She had seen him sheathe the dagger. She hadn't seen him draw the infantry-issue sword now in his right hand.

"All right," Lenatus said, walking forward. Rago and Drago followed him, jostling Alphena without quite shoving her behind them.

The Illyrians were stripped to the waist and barefoot. Their torsos showed more scars than Alphena had imagined. Their tattoos must conceal much of the scarring on their arms. They fanned out to either side of Lenatus, and at last she could enter.

The moonlit garden looked ordinary enough. It was a working garden, providing vegetables for Sentius' town house and the villa's own staff.

The pool running most of the length of the central axis was probably for irrigation rather than being a "water feature" in the sense an architect would have meant it, but it was fed by a fountain in the shape of a faun playing double pipes at the head end, near the rear stoop of the house itself. Alphena trotted toward the statue, holding the iron locket in her left hand.

Her sword was in its scabbard, but she could draw it if it was needed. Not as quickly as Lenatus, but quickly enough.

The stone faun lowered the pipes as Alphena approached him; water continued to spurt from the instrument into the long pool. The statue's features were those of a boy, but the now-living eyes she looked into were ancient.

"Greetings, Faun," she said. "I am the Lady Alphena. I'm looking for a friend, a tall man with red hair named Corylus. Have you seen him?"

Pandareus stood beside her with an expression of bright interest. The men of her escort were grouped around them. Mostly they faced outward, but Lenatus and the two Illyrians glared at the statue as though they wanted to lop its head off.

I suppose they could, or at least could crack it to pieces. Tuff isn't very strong.

"I heard Rupa call somebody 'Corylus' this afternoon," the faun said in a nasal voice. "They were on the porch, though. I couldn't turn around and see them, but I recognized Rupa's voice. She's a wizard, you know?"

"Yes," said Alphena. "Are they still in the house?"

"Beats me," said the faun. "I can't turn around, remember? Well, I couldn't till now, I guess."

He turned his head toward the building. As he did so, a woman in a long white garment stepped out onto the porch. Publius Corylus walked stiffly beside her. With them were—pigmies? Monkeys?—wearing headdresses made of long feathers.

The animals—they wore clothing and walked on two legs, but their faces weren't human—began to chant in chirping voices. Nets of green light sprang from their folded hands and fell over Alphena and her companions.

She felt only a tingle, but the men with her froze. Lenatus had opened his mouth, probably to call Pulto for support, but he stood stiff and silent. The faun was a statue again also, facing the pool into which his pipes trickled water.

"Good evening, Lady Alphena," said the woman. "My name is Rupa, and I believe the amulet you're holding will be better in my care."

Smiling like a cruel goddess, she walked toward Alphena. Corylus wore no expression as he followed the wizard.

IN CARCE HEDIA RAN with a fast crowd, all of whom would have said that she drank as hard as any of them. In fact, though she made a point of being among the first to ask for unmixed wine as the party began warming up, she didn't often refill her cup and she almost never became drunk.

Hedia had found that her male companions were more at ease if they thought she was tipsy. She wanted men to be at ease, and she had no difficulty in being uninhibited without needing alcohol to stimulate her.

She was drunk now, or at any rate she was in a state of exhilaration greater than wine or sex or anything else had brought her before. She had been drunk or exhilarated ever since Bacchus took her hand to lift her into his embrace.

"How long have we been here in this basket?" Hedia asked lazily as her fingertips toyed with the fine golden hair of Bacchus' chest.

She had seen the enclosure woven from grapevines before it was hung between the pair of strange-tusked elephants, so she *knew* it was a basket. The interior was that of the finest bedchamber imaginable for the sort of sports proper to a bedchamber, however. The walls and floor were firm when that was desired, resilient to aid a counterthrust, and sometimes soft when Hedia lay back in exhaustion.

At the moment, the floor was as soft as a cloud. She was both as tired as she had ever been in her life and as soaringly excited as butterflies circling to mate above a field of sunlit flowers.

"Shall we go somewhere else?" said Bacchus, offering her a grape that he had plucked from a bunch growing from the sidewall. It was sweet and fiery and the most delicious thing Hedia had ever in her life eaten—save for the grapes she had eaten from the god's fingers previously.

"I'm happy here," Hedia said. "It doesn't matter; I just wondered."

She was transportingly happy. She was happier than she had thought was humanly possible. Perhaps she wasn't human anymore; perhaps intimacy with the god had made her a god as well. . . .

Bacchus combed his fingers through her hair. The tight ringlets of current Carce fashion had relaxed into soft curls that fell to her shoulders; they sparkled with gold and silver and diamonds when the god touched them.

"We'll visit the Waking World," Bacchus said, rising to his feet. He drew Hedia up with no more than the touch of his fingertip on hers. "King Govinda has sent two of his vassals against a rajah who worships me alone. We will rout the attackers."

The wall opened, and they stepped out onto the ground. In the procession's track, trees and vines spread with luxuriant abandon.

"Greetings, Lord Bacchus!" cried nearby members of the throng. The gold and ivory chariot Bacchus had ridden in when Hedia first met him was following the pair of elephants, though no one rode in the car. The giant leopards ramped in their harness, pawing the air, but their roars were joyous rather than threatening.

Bacchus handed Hedia into the car and followed her. "We go to demonstrate our godhood to unbelieving princes!" he called.

The leopards leaped over the elephants, drawing the car after them as though it were made of gossamer. The whole procession surged forward, across the plain and then into the Waking World without a transition which Hedia noticed.

Ampelos followed them in his similar chariot. Hedia avoided looking directly at him—it would provoke him, and Hedia saw no reason to do that—

but a side-glance showed that the youth was as stony faced as his poor emotional control allowed him to be.

Ampelos obviously had only the power of the god's regard. To enter the Waking World, Ampelos had needed the help of magicians preparing the way: Bacchus had simply willed himself and his entourage from one world to the other.

"Why are you attacking underlings if Govinda is your enemy?" Hedia said. She clung to the god's side for the thrill of the contact, but her feet were as solid in the bounding chariot as they could have been on the bedrock of the Capitolium.

The leopards slowed to a playful lope. Dikes fell and hedges parted for the cats. In the chariot's wake, thorn bushes became olives and fruit trees draped with blooming grapevines. Laborers stared after Bacchus or capered in the train following the god.

"When I conquered India, I planted a grapevine in the palace of Govinda's ancestor," Bacchus said, waving his thyrsus like a standard. "So long as that vine grows, the kings of India accept me as their suzerain. Govinda is testing the length of his chain, but not so directly that I have to hang him with it. And the grape still grows in his palace."

"Was it a cutting from that vine that Govinda's delegation planted at Polymartium?" Hedia said. It was hard to remember her normal life in the Waking World, even the last scene she had witnessed there.

"Where is Polymartium?" asked the god. That was an answer of sorts.

An army was drawn up on the plain before them. In the center were a score of elephants on whose backs rested platforms bearing three or four armed men apiece. Some were archers with bamboo bows and long arrows, but others carried pikes as long as the lances of Sarmatian horsemen. The pikemen were in better clothing and sometimes wore steel caps or body armor.

Large bodies of cavalry flanked the elephants. The riders dressed in colorful garments, probably silk, and carried lances and curved swords like those of the noblemen Hedia had seen in Polymartium. Unlike the delegates, these men generally wore armor, often including steel helmets.

There were thousands of cavalry, but on both wings were many thousands more infantrymen. These men were peasants, not obviously different from the gardners who planted the vine at Polymartium. Many carried tools with stone heads or spears made of bamboo cut to a sharp point, but there were so *many* of them.

Hedia had seen the entire Praetorian Guard paraded in Carce, more than five thousand men under arms. This Indian army was far larger than that, many times larger than that.

"We can't fight so many!" Hedia said. Bacchus swept his thyrsus forward and the chariot bounded ahead.

The throng in the god's train followed crying, "Io Bacchus!" from a thousand throats. Hedia clung to her lover and cheered along with the others.

The wall of elephants before them crumbled as the great beasts rose onto their hind legs and began to dance, spilling their riders and shaking off the platforms. The chariots swept through the line. Centaurs, most of them bearing riders waving thyrsi, were almost as swift. The Indian army disintegrated at contact.

Bacchus drew his chariot in a curve to the left, leaving in its wheel tracks masses of grapevines to snake through the sere grass. "Io Bacchus!" Hedia cried, squeezing a wine-filled grape into her upturned mouth. "Io Bacchus!"

They drove through the Indian army's open camp, teeming with families and servants in numbers even larger than those of the men in arms. Shelters of cane and dry grass bloomed; tendrils of vine burgeoned from the ends of the poles that stretched silken tents.

Hedia plucked grapes from the bunches growing from the chariot's railing and hurled them to the Indians. A vine sprang from each spilled droplet when the ripe fruit burst in the hands of startled camp followers. The grapevines grew, flowered, and fruited as Bacchus rolled on.

People were making love, and not only people: an ox coupled with a centaur, and birds tumbled from the sky to tread one another among the spreading vines. Cries of joy and triumph rang out, musical and clear.

Bacchus wheeled the chariot to a halt on the banks of a creek. From the wan appearance of the fringing reeds it must have been nearly dry in this season, but now it foamed and bubbled with red wine.

A section of bank crumbled. The head of a great crocodile pushed out of its summer lair, called back to life not by rains but by the arrival of the god. The crocodile opened its jaws to the stream; wine tumbled into and past them.

Hedia fell into Bacchus' arms. Her universe was peace and joy and love like nothing she had ever known before.

CHAPTER XI

Raguram's palace was a sprawling collection of low buildings. An old woman carrying a bundle of reeds called cheerfully when she saw Bhiku and Varus approaching. The sage called back and waved.

"That's the third person I've heard greet you," Varus said. "You're popular here."

"Well, I've been gone for four months, you'll recall," Bhiku said. "Nona there had been afraid that I was dead."

Would anyone notice if I disappeared for months? Varus wondered. But of course they would: it would be something for the hundreds of servants at Saxa's town house to discuss. For a few days it would replace love affairs, chariot races, and the unjust behavior or this or that other servant as the main topic of conversation.

But after that, the interest would melt away. The only people who would really care were his immediate family and Publius Corylus. The peasants greeting Bhiku had been genuinely friendly, though none of them appeared to be intimates of his.

The palace compound wasn't surrounded by a wall, but a squad of soldiers waited under a palm-thatched awning near the road. Bhiku called to them. The leader, who wore a brown silk tunic and a curved sword, called back.

"I asked Motara where the prince was," Bhiku said to Varus in Greek. "Lord Raguram was in the stables when Motara came on duty an hour ago. He has an office there, so we'll try it before we go into the main palace."

"The feel of this place is different from that of Ramsa Lal's compound," Varus said as he followed the sage through the bustling community. "Better. Though it's all the same things going on and the same sort of people."

"I liked it," said Bhiku. "That's why I settled here when I decided I had traveled long enough."

Varus and Bhiku had mostly discussed geography during their trek to Raguram's palace. The sage's knowledge didn't come from writings. Rather, over many decades he had hiked from the Island of Taprobane in the far south to the mountains rising to the heavens north of Govinda's kingdom, and recently back here to settle with Prince Raguram.

Bhiku chirped a laugh and added, "Whereupon our lord Govinda decided I should go to Italy because I have some small skill in magic. Well, the gods choose what we humans shall do."

Raguram's stables were similar to those of Ramsa Lal, but they were thatched instead of having a tile roof. There was a barrack for the attendants on one side of the central entrance. On the other side was an office guarded by a pair of swordsmen who straightened when they saw Bhiku.

Instead of barring the sage and his companion, one guard greeted Bhiku and gestured him into the room, then bowed.

"Thank you for your welcome, Gol Singh," Bhiku replied in Greek. "My friend and I need to talk with Lord Raguram."

The man sharpening his sword on a bench inside was too well dressed to be a steward, but only context suggested that he was the prince himself. Bhiku said in Greek, "My lord, I've come with a learned man from Carce who has become my friend during our travels. He is Lord Varus, and he is a powerful magician."

Raguram wiped the oil from his curved blade; he got quickly to his feet and sheathed it. Bowing, he said, "Greetings, my teacher. I have missed your wisdom during these past months."

To Varus' surprise, the prince then bowed to him also. "And greetings, Lord Varus," Raguram said. "A man whom my teacher calls learned is learned indeed."

Varus bowed in response, since that appeared to be the polite custom in this country. "Greetings, Prince Raguram," he said. "I should warn you that your neighbor Ramsa Lal may be looking for me. Ah, with a degree of anger against me."

Raguram laughed. He was well into his forties, older than Ramsa Lal, but he was fit and radiated powerful good health. "I haven't begun worrying what my neighbor may think since you left me, Teacher," he said. "And that's even more true since our Lord of Lords Bacchus made a procession through Lal's northern provinces. There's thirty villages that won't be paying taxes for years, and the half of his troops garrisoning the region are now scattered or drunk on their backs."

Varus frowned, remembering what had happened at Polymartium before he stepped into the Otherworld. "What does Bacchus do?" he asked. "Does he slaughter the people he comes across?"

"There are some deaths," said Bhiku, "but not many."

"Probably not as many as snakebite kills in a year," Raguram said with another laugh, "and only the ones who actually try to fight him and his followers. Mostly they just worship the god—or join him. A lot of the peasants go off in Bacchus' procession. Particularly the women."

"Even the soldiers aren't generally killed," Bhiku said. "But they stop being, well, interested in soldiering. Fruit trees give so abundantly that the branches crack, and the wine is much stronger than that of ordinary grapes. To say nothing of the fermented palm sap that serves for the peasants."

A troop of cavalry approached the stables and dismounted with a great deal of loud banter. Varus used the commotion as an opportunity to think while he framed his next question. As the troopers led their mounts in single file, he said, "Do these incursions by the god harm the land, then? Or are they just, well, entertainment?"

"The soil is more productive," Bhiku said. "Even for grains, though of course it needs to be replanted if you want grain instead of grapes and fruit trees."

"The peasants are happy," said Raguram with a wry smile. "I don't mind that, of course . . . but they're too happy to work. Indeed, they're generally too drunk to work. Bacchus went through two of my villages seven years ago, and my taxes from the region still aren't up to half what they were before that happened."

"Bhiku," Varus said. "Why does Govinda want to spread Bacchus' rule to Italy? Because that's what you and your fellows were doing at Polymartium, wasn't it?"

"Lord Bacchus doesn't need a vine shoot to enter the Waking World," said Raguram.

"Yes," said Bhiku. "The portal which we opened—Rupa opened, really, though I might have been able to do it with the shoot itself as a focus. That portal was to allow Ampelos into Italy—and us to return, of course, but there would have been no need for us to be in Italy had we not planted the vine."

He shrugged and added, "Lord Arpat and his fellows did not—could not, I think—tell me why Govinda wanted that, and I kept my distance from Rupa."

"But what could Govinda gain by spreading disruption to Italy?" Varus said. "His kingdom doesn't compete with the Republic. There's all of Parthia and the Gedrosian Desert keeping us apart."

"King Govinda gains nothing by harming you . . . ," Raguram said thoughtfully. "But he would gain if the god's activities in Italy meant that he spent less time here. Govinda would gain very greatly if the god spent all his time in the Waking World in a place other than here."

Raguram grinned again. "For that matter, the king's vassals, myself included, would gain," he said. "Though I have no ambitions beyond what I have now. King Govinda has more general extensive dreams, or so I have gathered."

"Lord Govinda is a great king and a great magician," Bhiku said. "I believe he thinks he would not have an equal on earth, were it not for the god's processions through his kingdom. And Govinda may be correct in that belief."

Varus remembered what the Sibyl had said before he stepped into the portal that Govinda's delegation had opened. "Peasants may not be harmed by the god's incursions," he said, "and . . ."

He paused and smiled at his companions, in much the same black humor as Lord Raguram had shown a moment earlier.

". . . given that I'm not worried about either of you gentlemen informing on me to the Praetorian Prefect, the well-being of the Emperor and his legions isn't a great concern to me, either. Literature and the transmission of knowledge more generally require organization, however. I do care about them."

Varus cleared his throat. He wondered how much what he was about to say would put him in oppoosition to the men who stood before him. Regardless, he said it anyway: "I will prevent Lord Bacchus from extending his incursions to Italy if I am able to do so."

Raguram shrugged. "I don't see what you can do against King Govinda," he said. "He's made sure that all his vassals know how great a wizard he is. But as you said about your emperor, Govinda isn't *my* concern."

There was a commotion outside. Raguram frowned and looked past his visitors to the open doorway. Varus turned his head also.

A servant, not armed but wearing silk garments heavily embroidered with gold wire, stopped panting just outside the office. He babbled to Raguram, obviously upset.

Raguram's face became as expressionless as a rock. "Master Bhiku," he said in Greek. "Who else in my household knows who your friend is?"

"No one save yourself, Lord Raguram," the sage replied.

"Take him to your dwelling and change his clothing," said Raguram. "At once."

The prince strode out of the office, speaking forcefully to the servant as they both headed for the main building.

"Come," murmured Bhiku. "The chamberlain informs us that King Govinda has arrived. He and his entourage were concealed by a cloud so there was no warning of his approach. Govinda informed the chamberlain that he is looking for a Western magician."

Varus matched his step to that of the sage, the same brisk walk that had carried them from Princess Teji's garden to this palace. The sprawling complex was filled with commotion, but the attention seemed to be directed toward the king's arrival.

"Is this safe?" Varus said. He spoke quietly, though he doubted whether any of the peasants and low-ranking servants running about nearby could speak Greek. "For Prince Raguram, I mean."

"That is a matter for my master himself to decide," Bhiku said, "and no one has accused him of cowardice. Even so, I don't expect a pair of scruffy wise men like ourselves to attract much attention. I will give you a tunic."

He chirped his laughter.

"I will give you my other tunic, and you will not dazzle our visitors with magnificence, I assure you. And a pair of straw sandals in place of that very impressive leather pair of your own. Then we will discuss philosophy until someone gives us further directions."

Bhiku's house was a single room with cane walls and a thatched roof under the shade of a giant fig. The creek nearby was dry, but leakage from the reservoir that supplied the community in the hot season kept the tree flourishing. A low platform raised it above the fig's roots, so the floor was cane rather than dirt.

"I have few amenities to offer," Bhiku said, taking a cotton tunic from a peg beside the door. There was no furniture; a bowl and a water jug, both of earthenware, were the only objects visible. The lower two-thirds of the jug's surface was dark with moisture, showing that someone had refilled it no later than this morning, even though the sage had been gone for months.

"All the better for our purpose," Varus said as he stripped off his wool tunic. Though it was woven very fine, he would still be pleased to exchange it for the worn cotton garment that the sage offered. "Though I'm a little surprised, since you're obviously held in high regard by your, ah, fellows as well as by the prince himself."

"This hut is my choice," Bhiku said. "As it was my choice to settle with Lord Raguram. I would guess that your own choice is more . . . full, if I may put it that way?"

"My normal life is vastly more luxurious," Varus said, amused at the sage's delicacy. Varus handed his tunic and sandals to a boy who appeared—without being summoned, as best Varus could tell—with a pair of worn straw sandals in exchange. "This is much closer to what my personal *choice* would be, though I would want books. Many more books."

Bhiku laughed and sat cross-legged. Varus squatted. The cane floor was resilient and the straw sandals as comfortable as the suede slippers he would have worn indoors in Carce.

He opened his mouth to say as much to Bhiku, but Varus felt his soul leave his body and begin to climb the night black slope to the ridge on which the Sibyl always waited for him.

What will Bhiku think? Varus wondered, remembering the concern his sister and Corylus had felt when he first began to have these spells. And as the thought formed in his mind, Varus realized that Bhiku was scrambling up the rough trail beside him.

"Master Bhiku!" Varus said, embarrassing himself. "That is, I'm very glad to see you, but I've never before seen anyone in these visions. Well, except the Sibyl."

The sage smiled, making his face look like that of a friendly monkey. "You have books, Lord Varus," he said. "I have gained my knowledge by other means. Although—"

He looked back the way they had come. Varus followed Bhiku's gaze, but as usual he saw only a featureless blur.

"—I could not have found my way here without you to guide me."

They reached the top of the ridge and the sunlight of which there had been no hint on the slope below. The old—the ancient—woman waited for them, leaning on a cane of twisted ivory.

"Greetings, Lord Varus," she said. The hood of her blue cape was thrown back. "And greetings to you also, Master Bhiku. I have few visitors in present days."

Varus had been poised to introduce Bhiku to the Sibyl. That was pointless, and Varus realized that he should have known it was pointless before he formed the words.

Smiling wryly at himself, he said instead, "Sibyl, a king named Govinda is looking for me in the Waking World. I am told"—he didn't doubt it, but he was being precise, as Pandareus would expect—"that he is a magician."

"Govinda is indeed a magician, Lord Wizard," the Sibyl said. Her cackling laughter was uncannily similar to Bhiku's. "And there are two magicians searching for you. Govinda's ancestor accompanies him."

She turned to look down the other side of the ridge. Varus walked over beside her, gesturing Bhiku to join them.

They viewed Raguram's palace from above. The open ground between the back of the main building and the masonry reservoir was filled with soldiers wearing helmets and carrying spiked shields. They were on foot, but horses and elephants waited outside the front of the palace. Raguram and his chamberlain faced the visitors, bowing to their leader.

That leader was a young man—no more than thirty—dressed entirely in cloth of gold, including his tight turban. He held a small black mirror in his left hand. The bald old man beside him was stark naked. Both were slender—the old man's ribs were visible, though he didn't look starved—and their similar hawk features suggested relationship.

"That is King Govinda," Bhiku said. "I don't recognize the man with him, though. And why is he naked?"

"The old man is the spirit of Govinda's ancient ancestor," said the Sibyl. "He is confined to the speculum of cannel coal which Govinda holds, but you see him from this vantage point. Those in the Waking World hear only a voice from the speculum."

"The . . . figures following Govinda?" Varus said. He'd started to say *animals,* but the twelve bipeds wore clothing. He had seen baboons and even dogs prancing on their hind legs in vests and pantaloons, but these creatures seemed subtly different. "What are they?"

Govinda's ancestor pointed past the end of the reservoir. The king and his entourage walked in that direction, carrying Raguram with them perforce. Raguram's own retainers were mostly keeping their distance, though the chamberlain stayed with him and the pair of guards from outside his office in the stables stayed close behind.

"Those are Tyla priests," said the Sibyl. "They were magicians. When Anti-Thule was destroyed, Govinda's ancestor escaped. Govinda sent his ancestor back to Anti-Thule to bring the priests here."

"Abducted them?" Varus said.

The Sibyl smiled, though her face was so wrinkled that he was partly guessing at her expression. "Govinda gave them a chance to survive," she said, "and the Tyla are enough like humans that they took the chance they were offered. They are magicians, but they could not hold the ice back without the power of the Godspeaker to support them."

Govinda and his ancestor walked around the reservoir; his train followed like an armored caterpillar. The ancestor pointed toward the fig tree.

Bhiku said, "They are going to my hut."

"They're looking for me," said Varus. "As a matter of courtesy, I will return to meet my visitors."

I only hope that my friends survive these next moments, he thought. In the crisis it didn't occur to him to consider his own situation.

"If you are killed," said the Sibyl, "you will not be able to thwart Govinda's plans for Carce."

Then she shouted, *"Be things such as they were before!"* and Varus was back in his body and wobbling on the balls of his feet.

He stood and walked out of the simple hut. Behind him Bhiku was getting to his feet also, but Varus had attention only for Govinda at this moment. Varus could no longer see the ancestor, but he heard high-pitched words coming from the blackness of the king's mirror-polished disk.

"I am Gaius Alphenus Varus, a nobleman of Carce," he said in a clear voice. "Are you looking for me?"

"You are the wizard from the West," said Govinda in good Greek. He was as tall as Corylus, a physically powerful man.

Suitable for guarding a king were he not one himself, Varus thought. He smiled at the thought.

The smile appeared to anger Govinda. "You will come with me and do my will!" the king said. "Or I will destroy you and destroy all those around you!"

"I will willingly go with you," said Varus.

"Come, then," said Govinda, gesturing Varus to his side.

Master Pandareus would have noted that the explicit acceptance of one of two conditions is the implicit rejection of the second, Varus thought as they walked toward the front of the palace and the mounts that had carried the king and his train. *But it's probably just as well that Govinda's logic teacher was less able.*

HEDIA HAD EXPECTED THE CENTAUR Gryneus to easily win his race against Ophius, a faun; and so he would have done had they run a straight furlong. The course Bacchus had set was a figure eight, however, and the contestants had to make a full circuit of the post in the middle as well. The centaur's speed swung his massive body wide, while Ophius' delicate quickness meant that he scarcely seemed to slow down as he cornered.

"Run!" Hedia shouted, clinging to Bacchus' arm. She wasn't so much cheering for either runner as caught up in the excitement of the race. "Run! Run!"

The spectators, the whole throng of the god's followers, laughed and cheered. There had already been archery and wrestling competitions, and a great deal of rich purple wine added to the jollity.

Ophius was in the lead on the final leg and halfway to the finish line before the centaur rounded the center post for the second time. The dappled Gryneus threw back dirt from all four hooves as he vaulted into a gallop.

"*Run!*" cried Hedia.

The finish line was merely a furrow Bacchus had traced on the ground with his sandal, but it shone like a bar of gold. Faun and centaur crossed it together in a cloud of dust and ran on, slowing gradually.

"Oh, who won, dear heart?" Hedia said, throwing both arms about Bacchus' chest. He was girlishly slim, but the muscles of his torso were as firm as taut bow cords. "Oh, they both won, didn't they? They were magnificent!"

"Then they both won," Bacchus said. He squeezed her, then gently disengaged to free his hands as the contestants shambled back.

Ophius had one hand on the centaur's withers. They both looked as though they were ready to be skinned and ground up for sausage, but they were drinking from wineskins that the spectators offered. By the time they reached Bacchus they stood straight and walked briskly.

Bacchus smiled as he met the contestants and said, "My delightful Hedia says that you both won the race, showing that she is as clever as she is lovely and talented. Gryneus and Ophius, for proving yourselves unbeatable runners, take these trinkets as tokens of the honor in which I hold you."

He held out laurel wreaths; the centaur bowed his head so that the god could place it at the same time that he crowned the faun. The leaves bloomed brighter than gold when Bacchus released them.

Hedia stepped forward and kissed Ophius. The faun's shaggy chest tickled through her sheer garment.

She released him and turned to Gryneus, raising her arms. The centaur laughed and bent forward. Instead of simply receiving the kiss, he lifted Hedia as he straightened again. He held her easily in a long embrace, then lowered her as gently as Bacchus himself would have done.

The spectators cheered even more loudly than they had done for the race itself. Hedia, flushed with delight, returned to the god's side and clung to him.

"My lord Bacchus!" said Ampelos from just behind them. He was flushed also, but his tones were as harsh as a throat so golden could manage.

"Ampelos, my little heart?" Bacchus said, his face showing surprise and perhaps a touch of concern.

"We have dallied here, lord of lords," Ampelos said. "Is it not now time to spread your fame still farther in the Waking World? You have conquered the East; now the Empire of Carce should bow before your omnipotence!"

"Ampelos, dear . . . ," Bacchus said. "This is a pleasant place and there's much here to show our friend Hedia."

"That woman!" the youth said. "You've surrendered your honor to trifle with a woman!"

He's exactly like Latus' little friends, Hedia thought as she disengaged her arm from Bacchus. *Except that he's even prettier.*

Her first husband, Gaius Calpurnius Latus, was sexually adventurous—as adventurous as Hedia, if it came to that—but he preferred boys. They were often charming when they were in a good mood, but she had found them generally more touchy, jealous, and *bitchy* than women of a similar sort.

There were sometimes ways to handle the situation, however.

"Ampelos, dear," Hedia said, moving toward the youth's side. "Wouldn't you like to join us for a little while? I don't know that I've ever seen such a lovely young man as you, and I'd *really* like to get to know you better."

Ampelos stood transfixed. Hedia extended her hand to the boy's shoulder. He jerked away in horror.

"Slut!" he shouted. "Filth! Offal!"

Well, he didn't slap me, Hedia thought. Though she could have worked with a slap; tears of despair sometimes prevailed where a more direct invitation did not. Anyway, it had been worth a try.

"My lord Bacchus!" Ampelos said. "Please, don't let this *woman* corrode your honor. Prove, with me at your side, that you are the great god you are meant to be!"

"Dear One," Bacchus said with a touch of warning in his voice. "I am the lord Bacchus, son of Zeus. I have nothing to prove to anyone."

Ampelos must have heard the warning, because his whole manner changed. "As my lord and god wishes," he said, bowing.

He turned away and remounted the chariot in which he had arrived during the games that Bacchus had called. "With me!" Ampelos shouted. "All those who want to spread our master's name across the Waking World!"

Ampelos and a mixed horde of humans and other followers of the god swept away from the greater throng. They were probably the band of some hundreds that had appeared in Polymartium on the morning of the ceremony. That was so long ago in Hedia's mind. . . .

Bacchus watched his lover drive away with the closest thing to a frown Hedia had seen on the god's face. She touched his shoulder for attention and said softly, "He'll be back soon, my dear lord. You know he gets this way sometimes."

She knew very little about Ampelos personally, but his *sort* . . . Oh, yes, Hedia knew his sort very well.

"We've watched your followers exercise," she said. She felt the shoulder muscles start to loosen though Bacchus didn't look at her. "Isn't it time that you and I got some exercise ourselves? Ampelos may come back and join us, you know?"

Bacchus finally turned and kissed her. "Yes," he said, brightening perceptibly. "We should do that."

HEDIA COULDN'T JUDGE TIME when she was engaged with the god, but it didn't seem long—minutes or possibly an hour—before they were interrupted. A centaur and the Maenad who had returned on his back stood outside the woven bower, their expressions distraught.

"Great lord!" the Maenad cried. "The sun-bright Ampelos has been struck down!"

Bacchus strode from the bower, his face flaming with rage. Without looking back at Hedia, he leaped into his waiting chariot and drove off. The centaur galloped at his side to guide him, and the whole entourage surged to follow.

Hedia stood. *It's like being doused in cold water in the middle of a climax,* she thought, and smiled, because that had happened to her once.

After thinking about it, she pulled her sandals on and walked off at the tail of the throng. She didn't know what was happening, but the cyclops had taught her that she was safer with Bacchus in this portion of the Otherworld than she would be on her own.

CORYLUS PAUSED AS THEY CAME out of broken woodland onto a rolling plain not dissimilar from what he might have seen in the countryside around Carce. There was no path—there hadn't been a path in the woods, either—but when Aura set out through the knee-high grass he followed without hesitation.

I hope she knows where we're going. I certainly don't.

He heard the joyful cries a moment before a leopard came over the rise ahead of them, moving in a slant across their direction. The cat was one of the pair pulling the chariot driven by Ampelos, the man the maple sprite had snatched Corylus away from in Polymartium. The troupe of worshipers walked and danced behind the chariot.

"Wait!" said Corylus. "These aren't friends of mine."

He didn't shout to Aura, but neither was his voice as calmly firm as he wished. He backed two steps so that the large oak on the edge of the woods was close behind him.

Aura turned and joined him without apparent concern. Ampelos had lashed his team on and was bounding downslope ahead of the throng.

"I saw you deal with Scylla," Aura said, her eyes on the chariot.

Ampelos wheeled his leopards and halted the chariot with its right side toward Corylus. At a distance the wheels and chariot frames had looked like gold. Close up they were gold-tinged crystal.

"Did you think you had escaped me?" Ampelos said. He shook the thyrsus in his right hand. It would have looked foolish—a pinecone on a long fennel stalk—if Corylus hadn't seen a similar weapon driven through a Praetorian's armored chest.

I certainly hoped I had, Corylus thought. Aloud he said, "Go your way, Lord Ampelos. I will go mine."

"You will bow to me as the avatar of our lord and god Bacchus!" Ampelos said. "Our lord and god has conquered India. Now I will guide him to sweep over Carce! Bow, vassal!"

"Go bugger yourself, boy!" Corylus said in a low growl.

Ampelos thrust for Corylus' chest. He deflected the blow with his staff as he would have done a Sarmatian lance. The pinecone stabbed deep into the oak behind him.

Ampelos slapped the reins against the necks of his team when the thyrsus missed. The leopards leaped away and swung into an arc. The chariot circled back for another attack.

"Get back!" Corylus said to Aura, though he didn't have leisure to check that she was obeying or even that she understood that he was talking to her. The dryad had shrieked when the thyrsus pierced her tree; he heard her sobbing now.

Corylus moved out onto the plain, both to save the sprite from further injury and because he wanted more space to deal with the charioteer. If the whole throng joined their leader, Corylus hadn't any more chance than a prisoner tarred and hung from a post to light the amphitheatre. If Ampelos thought he could finish the business alone, though, that was another matter.

The mixed throng had halted on top of the hill over which they had come. The slope gave them a good view of the action. They were cheering, "Io Bacchus!" and, "Io Ampelos!"

I hope to disappoint you, Corylus thought. He crouched as Ampelos lashed his chariot forward again. This time he intended to strike over his left side as he passed.

Corylus had fought mounted Sarmatians, and for his purposes a chariot was the same thing. What wasn't the same was that a leopard was a meat eater and very limber, but Corylus had to assume that these had been tamed. Certainly they wouldn't be safe in the midst of Bacchus' drunken followers if they clawed and bit anyone they came close to.

It's a battle. People die in battle sometimes. Maybe this is my time.

Ampelos swung his team to the right. His thyrsus was poised to strike.

The cats were on snaffles because their teeth didn't have the gap where a horse's bit would ride. Corylus sprang forward and caught the bridle of the offside leopard, pulling it hard toward him.

The cat yowled and twisted fluidly, but it didn't try to bite Corylus—the staff was ready to jam down its throat if necessary—or claw him, which he couldn't have prevented. The cat was heavier than he was—closer to the size of a male lion than to a normal leopard—but Corylus' leverage on the bridle allowed him to turn its head and the body after it.

Ampelos had been braced against the chariot's right railing. When the team reversed its curve—the near-side cat followed the lead of its harness mate—the vehicle tilted back and pitched the driver over the low side. Ampelos hit with a thump that Corylus, sprawled on his back, could feel.

The leopard tossed its head and pulled the bridle out of Corylus' hand. The only way he could have held on was to allow himself to be dragged. The cats put their feet under them and sprang forward together. The chariot bounced on its right hub but landed back on its wheels when it next hit the ground. Team and vehicle disappeared around a stand of sumac two furlongs distant.

Ampelos lay sprawled. The thyrsus stood upright, driven at least the length of its head into the turf.

I've never been so tired, Corylus thought, but he knew it wasn't true. He couldn't remember when that had been, though. He couldn't really remember anything beyond the way his lungs burned and every muscle ached. *At least the cat didn't claw me.*

Ampelos was clenching and opening his hands. At last he got his arms under him and started to lift his torso off the ground. Corylus stepped forward and rapped his staff against the back of the youth's head, knocking him facedown into the dirt again.

Corylus knelt and butted his staff onto the ground so that he could lean on it. He glanced toward the throng who had been following Ampelos. The revelers of a moment before were silent and motionless.

Not that I could do anything about it anyway if they decided to finish me, Corylus thought as he hung his head and stared at the ground. *So very tired.*

"I told you so," Aura said from close to his side. "I saw you with Scylla."

"Thank you for your confidence," Corylus muttered. That last sharp blow with the staff had drained what little was left of his strength. *But I couldn't let Ampelos get up, could I?*

"Someone is coming," Aura said. Then, more urgently, "Lord Bacchus is coming!"

Corylus took another deep breath. He gripped the staff with both hands to steady himself and lurched to his feet. Only then did he raise his eyes and turn in the direction of the oncoming chariot.

The frame and wheels of the vehicle glittered in the sunlight, but the driver shone brighter yet. Ampelos was as handsome as any living man Corylus had seen, but he was barely the moon to the sun of the god's radiance.

Corylus had once deflected a Sarmatian arrow shot at him from less than a furlong away, but he knew as he watched the face of the oncoming god that he would not be able to block the thrust of the thyrsus.

Not even if I were in the best shape of my life. Instead of placing himself in a posture of defense, he set the butt of the staff in the ground beside him and stood straight, as though waiting for the Emperor's judgment.

Aura stepped between Corylus and the chariot. She held up the ring she had taken from the skeletal hand where Scylla had laired.

Bacchus drew back on his reins. The leopards braked, spraying dust with the heels of all eight paws. Corylus expected the car to flip over them from the violence of the halt, but it remained as steady as the floor of a temple.

"Bacchus, my lord and god!" Aura called, her voice an unexpected roar that overwhelmed the cheers of the throng on the hilltop. "This man has avenged Zetes, son of your brother Boreas, who was slain from ambush by a monster!"

"And who are you, bold one?" Bacchus said. His thyrsus was lifted to thrust; he didn't put it down, but he dipped the pinecone head slightly.

"I am Aura, lover of Zetes and loved by him," she said. "I regained Zetes' ring, given him by his father, when this hero slew Scylla with no weapons save for what he holds now. I beg you grant him his life on behalf of your nephew whom he avenged."

"He struck down Ampelos," said Bacchus. "I would rather *all* my followers be slain than that I lose this boy who holds my heart."

Ampelos groaned and turned his head slightly, then groaned again.

"Bacchus, my lord and god," Corylus said. "I refused to grant divine honors to a man, because that would dishonor your divine self."

Corylus knelt on one knee and bowed his head. "Lord god," he said, "I am your servant. Do with me as you will."

Since that's what you're going to do anyway, Corylus thought. He kept his face rigid. Army humor was very black, and this would be a *really* bad time to grin.

Bacchus stepped down from the chariot's deck and walked to Corylus. "You may rise," he said.

Corylus obeyed carefully. Aura moved beside him. She slipped the ring onto her thumb, the only digit able to fit the hole of what Zetes had worn on his little finger.

Maenads and others from the vast throng following Bacchus clustered around Ampelos, raising him. One held a wineskin to the youth's lips while another laved his head. The cut in Ampelos' scalp closed as the wine ran through his golden hair.

"What is your purpose here?" Bacchus asked quietly. His voice was like liquid gold.

"My lord," Corylus said, wondering if he should have added *god*, but it was too late now. "Mistress Aura is guiding me to the Cave of Zagreus, from which I hope to return to the Waking World."

Bacchus laughed. To Aura he said, "He is indeed a hero then, little one."

"Yes, my lord and god," the sprite said. "He is."

"Go on your way, then," Bacchus said. "I will not prevent you."

Aura gripped Corylus by the hand and started off briskly at a slight angle to the direction they had followed when they first left the woods. This would take them clear of the huge entourage following Bacchus.

"When we're out of sight," Corylus whispered, "we'll start running for a time."

For as long as I can run, he added silently.

"I AM HERE TO RESCUE Publius Corylus," Alphena said to the woman facing her from the porch. Then as an afterthought she added, "And also my mother and brother."

"I will release your Corylus . . . ," Rupa said, stepping down. Alphena heard the words in Latin, though that might have been the effect of the amulet she gripped in her left hand. "In exchange for what you hold. As for your mother and brother, I have nothing to do with them."

"I am not Publius Corylus," said the figure of Corylus standing behind her. "I am a homunculus formed of straw. The real Corylus is in the Otherworld, traveling to the Cave of Zagreus."

Rupa turned and pointed at the figure with her left hand, fingers splayed. In a tone of cold fury she said, "Begone, then, if you do not wish to serve me!"

A green flash blasted the homunculus to fragments of straw. There had been no sound, but Alphena noticed a faint odor of singed grass.

"It would have been easier for you if my tool had not revealed itself," Rupa said contemptuously. "Be that as it may, you can still save yourself by hand-ing over the amulet."

"You're threatening *me?*" Alphena said in real surprise. She reached for her sword.

"You cannot draw your weapon—" Rupa said.

Alphena brought the sword out with a *sring!* of the blade against the iron lip of the scabbard. Rupa started back.

"Let go of my servants and we'll leave you," Alphena said. She knew that her voice had risen, but it wasn't trembling. She wanted to back away, but Lena-tus and the others were frozen in place and she wasn't going to leave them.

"Your sword cannot touch me," Rupa said. She sounded certain, though she had lost the sneering tone she had used since her appearance. "You can cut my clothes if you choose to, but the steel is nothing to me."

She stepped forward.

One of the two-legged animals—somethings!—with Rupa plucked at the sleeve of her bright white tunic. The creatures wore what seemed to be linen garments hanging from one shoulder. Their legs were vertical beneath their bodies as a human's are, not canted like those of dogs walking on their hind legs.

The creatures' monkey faces and pointed ears were the only features that would keep a human from thinking they were merely small people. Even their fur was so fine as to be overlooked in bad light.

"Lady Priestess!" the creature at Rupa's side said. Alphena heard him speak in Latin, but that must be as much due to the amulet as the stone faun's words were. "You must not touch her! She is protected by the Godspeaker!"

Rupa slapped him away and again moved forward. Alphena expected an-other green flash, this time spraying the garden with blood and scraps of skin.

A lunge would reach her body, but if it skidded off . . . ?

Rupa reached toward the amulet. A crash like lightning and a white flash threw her backward to sprawl in a bed of peonies. Her right sleeve was smol-dering, though the wizard herself appeared to be unharmed.

Alphena didn't understand what had happened, so she said nothing. The air had the sharpness of burned air that made her nose wrinkle. She shot the sword back into its sheath and rubbed her nose with the back the hand she had freed.

I'm not going to let go of the amulet until we're safely out of this, she thought. *And maybe not even then.*

Rupa stood and backed away. "Get out of here, woman!" she said. "There's nothing here for you!"

Alphena licked her dry lips. "Free my servants and we'll leave," she said.

She expected Rupa to speak to the creatures whose magic was holding the escort bound, but they reacted to Alphena's own words alone. They stopped chanting and the mesh of green light vanished.

They're obeying the Godspeaker, Alphena realized. Though she didn't know what that meant.

"By Orcum's balls!" Lenatus said. He looked around in amazement, the tip of his drawn sword twitching in whichever direction his eyes glanced. "What . . . ?"

"Lenatus!" Alphena said. She began to back away. "Get them out of here *now*! Back to the city. I'll come last; I have the amulet, so I've got to."

"Yes, lady," Lenatus said, himself again. He shouted crisp orders that Alphena scarcely heard because she was so focused on Rupa and the creatures with her. They had retreated to the back porch, but they were all watching Alphena.

Pandareus touched Alphena's right elbow, guiding her backward so that she did not have to look around. Gentle pressure eased her around the end of the pool and down the path to the back gate by which they had entered.

Lenatus was waiting there. He laid the gate askew across the posts from which Minimus had wrenched it.

Alphena stood backward in the rear of the final wagon, holding the amulet in both hands until they had reached the main road again. Nothing followed them, but dread of what she had seen and been part of rode with Alphena all the way to her father's town house.

CHAPTER XII

Corylus clung to the trunk of the palm tree with his heels and left arm as he trimmed dead fronds from the bottom of the crest. Phoenix, the tree nymph standing on the ground with Aura, giggled and said, "Ooh! That tickles!"

The sharp orichalc blade made the job easier than it would have been with the working edge of his issue dagger. Corylus could certainly have cut through the stems with the steel, but since he had only one hand, he would have had to chop against the trunk. He would've been careful not to do any real damage, but he would rather have slept on bare dirt than do it.

Of course, Phoenix might have liked it. Women are as different in their tastes as men are.

Grinning at the thought, Corylus sheathed his dagger and called, "I'm going to drop down, so stay clear!"

His feet were twenty feet above the ground, but he'd made longer jumps in the past. The palm's jagged bark provided a better grip for his bare feet than a smoother trunk would have done, but both his soles and the insides of his knees were bleeding from the climb.

The vines that twisted to the crown to dangle their flowers were too slender for him to climb instead of using the trunk itself. The flowers were still closed, though they would probably open when the sun was fully down.

"We're clear," Aura said.

"I could catch you," Phoenix said with another giggle. "I'm stronger than I look, you know."

Corylus pushed himself away and dropped. He would rather have been facing outward in the direction he was likely to roll if he didn't land perfectly, but turning in the air wasn't worth the risk. Though he was as fit as he'd ever been, he was out of practice, and he weighed more than he had on the frontier when he jumped like this regularly.

He hit perfectly and his knees flexed to take the shock. He thought he was going to topple backward, but Aura was suddenly behind him and bracing his shoulders. She was quite strong.

Corylus straightened. His feet, calves, and thighs all ached for different reasons, but he hadn't broken any bones and his scrapes would heal as so many others had done over the years. He turned to the two sprites.

"Now what?" Phoenix said, standing hipshot.

Aura kept her hand on Corylus' right shoulder. She was giving the tree nymph a blank stare.

Corylus sliced another wedge of meat from the fallen coconut that he had opened before he climbed the tree. "Now," he said firmly, "I sleep. I was wrung out from that business with Ampelos, but we couldn't hang around there. Another six hours hiking couldn't be helped, but I'm as tired now I've ever been. Good night, ladies."

"*We* don't sleep," Phoenix said. Corylus knew that if he had been looking at her instead of arranging the fronds into a mattress of sorts he would have seen her pout. That didn't matter.

"Good night," he repeated. He was asleep almost as soon as he closed his eyes.

HE WASN'T SURE when the dreams came, perhaps nearly at once.

Someone gripped him by the shoulder and shook him awake. "No, Corylus," a rasping voice said. "You're still asleep. I have things to show you."

Corylus opened his eyes. A crude iron figure was bending over him: not a man in armor, but a man hammered out of iron.

I don't feel threatened, Corylus realized. *I ought to, but I don't.*

He sat up and saw that the world—well, the Otherworld—had vanished. The palm tree, the two sprites, and the open forest toward which Aura had been leading him were gone, replaced by a gray plain under a sky of paler gray.

The iron figure stepped back. He was bearded, or at least waves that were probably meant for a flowing beard had been forged on to his chin and upper chest. His arms and legs were all a piece with his torso when he was still, only separating when he moved.

"Who are you, sir?" said Corylus as he got up. The figure was no taller than he was, but it projected an enormous solidity.

"I am the other face of Janus," the figure said. "I say 'the other face' because I'm guiding Lady Alphena at present. But come."

He turned and began stumping across the featureless plain. Corylus took two long strides to catch up. There didn't seem any reason to go in one direction or another in this place, but Corylus preferred company to being alone here.

"Where is Lady Alphena, ah, Janus?" he said.

"Not here," said the iron man peevishly. "And that's not what I want to talk about. *This* is what I want to talk about."

He pointed with his whole arm; the fingers were undifferentiated. A circle of the blank sky gleamed like a mirrored ball. It rotated into an image of a city of paper houses on the banks of a river. Figures were going about their business in the streets and plazas.

"Where is this?" Corylus said. "That is, if you please."

"That is central Italy, as you would call it," said Janus. "The Tyla have their own name, of course. In your world the river is the Tiber where it flows through Carce."

When Corylus looked at the figures instead of simply accepting them as the human residents of an unfamiliar landscape, he saw that they were two-legged animals with fox-like faces and tan fur ranging sometimes toward golden. He didn't bother to try to keep his voice calm as he said, "Janus! Is that happening now?"

"There is no 'now' where you and I are, Corylus," said the iron man. "Look around you. If you mean, 'Is this the reality of the Waking World from which you come?' then that depends. Now, come along."

They walked farther across the gray limbo. Corylus glanced over his shoulder, but there was no longer a sign of the shining ball or the world of the Tyla he had seen through the ball.

Janus pointed again. The air darkened, then gleamed and rotated as it had the first time. Corylus felt his gut tighten before he looked, but this scene was one of tranquil pleasure. Men and women sprawled on lush grass or ambled over hills that he recognized as those of Carce. Crops grew though no one seemed to be tending them, and everywhere dangled bunches of ripe grapes.

"It's the Age of Saturn," Corylus said, quirking a smile as he looked at his guide. "The Silver Age of the poets. I prefer this one to the one you showed me first, Janus."

"It is the Age of Bacchus," the iron man said. "It will be the Age of Bacchus for all time, in the place where this is happening. But come, Corylus, for there are other worlds still."

"How many are you going to show me?" Corylus asked, following his guide. It didn't really matter, since Corylus had nothing else to do in this gray waste, but the iron man's peremptory commands were becoming irritating now that the novelty of the situation had worn off.

"One more will be enough, I think," said Janus. He pointed, and as before the air responded with a vision.

Corylus squinted. He thought that something had gone wrong, that the image hadn't cleared yet. He saw only smeared black in the sphere.

"Janus, what is this?" he said. He didn't have his staff or dagger in this dream; he would have felt much better at this moment with the weight of either in his hands.

"This is the Waking World as it will be after the Blight has conquered," said Janus. "This would be the bend of the Tiber, but there are no rivers and no seas and all the world is the same."

"There are no . . . ?" Corylus began. Then he said, "There is no life."

"The Blight is alive," Janus said.

The blackness moved, the way a pool of tar moves on a hot day. *It isn't alive. It can't be alive.*

"It is not life as you know it," Janus said. "It may become all the life there is in the Waking World."

"*May* become!" Corylus said. "Will it or won't it? Is *that*—"

He pointed to the Blight.

"—real, Janus?"

The iron man lowered his arm; the vision became gray, then vanished. Janus made a harsh grating noise that made the hair rise on the back of Corylus' neck.

He's laughing! And that was even worse.

"All the futures you have seen are real," Janus said, pivoting his whole body to face Corylus. "Somewhere, sometime, on some chain of events. As for which one is real in your world, that depends."

If Corylus had been speaking to a man, even a much bigger man, he would have hit him. The thought of hitting this crude mass of iron was absurd.

Corylus laughed and bowed to his guide.

You get a sense of humor on the frontier, especially with a unit like the Batavian Scouts. It isn't everybody's sense of humor.

"What does it depend on, Lord Janus?" Corylus said. "What does the fate of my world depend on?"

"You and your colleagues will determine the branch of reality which your world follows," Janus said. "That is what I came to tell you."

The iron lips twisted into a smile as distorted as every other aspect of the figure. "Now you may awaken."

CORYLUS FELT SOMEONE SHAKING HIM, but when his eyes opened the two sprites were chatting ten feet away. No one else was present.

It was daylight. A pair of tiny monkeys with diaphanous wings flitted through the palm fronds. The flowers hanging from tendrils of vine had closed again.

"He's awake," said Phoenix. The sprites moved to him, Aura slightly in advance of the tree nymph.

"I slept well," Corylus said. He thought that would be a lie—he didn't want to discuss what he had seen—but he found that his limbs felt supple and the aches and scrapes of the previous day's events had been smoothed away. "I want to start immediately for the cave."

"Did you dream?" asked Phoenix.

"Why?" snapped Corylus. Then, realizing how defensive he sounded, he said, "I may have done, yes. But why do you ask?"

The palm sprite shrugged. "I was just curious," she said. "Humans who sleep under the Black Lotus usually do, I've found."

"Ah," said Corylus as he laced his sandals. The soles of his feet were smooth and callused again. "Let's go on then, Aura."

As they set off toward broken woodlands, he glanced over his shoulder. Phoenix waved hopefully, but Corylus was looking at the closed black flowers dangling from the palm crown.

ALPHENA STOOD AT THE BASE of the statue of Marsyas in the Forum, a location Pandareus had suggested. Her escort, which this morning included

Lenatus wearing a cape, encircled her and the teacher, facing outward. There was nothing so unusual about the scene as to draw attention. Though the Forum was as crowded as usual, nobody was paying particular attention to the noble lady and her servants.

"Later in the day, prostitutes gather here," Pandareus said, looking up at the bronze satyr with its right hand raised. "The girls lay their wreaths on the statue's head if they've had a successful night, but the attendants of the Basilica Aemilia—"

He nodded to the two-story building behind them.

"—usually take them away before court sessions open in the morning. I see that they missed one today, though."

A garland of roses lay behind the statue. Alphena suspected that the flowers had been blown before last night; Corylus would probably be able to tell, since his father used huge numbers of flowers in his perfume business.

That's still another reason to wish Corylus were here, she thought. That was the kind of joke he would make, but she found she couldn't smile at it now.

Taking a deep breath, Alphena got to the business that she wanted to discuss with the teacher in private. "Corylus, the straw doll last night I mean, said that the real Corylus was going to the Cave of Zagreus. What does that mean, please?"

Pandareus smiled wryly. "I will try to remember that I'm not lecturing to students," he said, "but rather advising a colleague about how to find our missing associates. Briefly, I don't have any idea where the Cave of Zagreus might be. Zagreus in myth—or what I thought was myth—was the son of Zeus and Persephone and was born in the dragon-guarded cave where his mother was hidden to preserve her chastity. The dragons were unsuccessful in protecting that, obviously."

Pandareus glanced at the statue again. "Followers of the Orphic Cult believe that Zagreus was a prefiguration of Bacchus," he said. "I suppose that's why I thought of coming here for privacy, since Marsyas was the steward of Bacchus."

Pandareus smiled wryly. "I can't help but be a pedant, I fear."

"It was a good location, for whatever reason," Alphena said. Listening to the teacher reminded her of her brother's similar twists of mind through all sorts of literary thickets.

She frowned when she saw what Pandareus was holding. He'd had it the whole morning, but she had been too lost in her own thoughts—her fears—to notice it.

"Master Pandareus," Alphena said. "What is the rod that you have there?"

"Ah!" said the teacher, holding the object out in both hands for Alphena to take. "It was a bed marker in the garden. The others were wooden palings with carved tops, but this was iron and I took it when Rupa and her companions appeared."

He smiled faintly. "I suppose I was thinking of it as a weapon," he said. "When I got a better look at it, I found it more interesting. It seems to be the head of Janus."

The rod was the length of her forearm and hand with the fingers extended. Except for the knob on one end, it was about the thickness of her thumb. The single piece of iron was forged rather than being drawn or turned: the marks of the hammer were visible along its full length. The knob was a double face, chiseled into the metal.

"It was stuck in the ground?" Alphena said. She took the rod. "There's some rust, but not as much as I'd expect of iron left out in the weather."

"I'm not pure iron," said one of the miniature faces. It turned toward Pandareus. "Any more than those bronze coins in your purse are pure copper, Teacher. The wizard Mamurcus made me from a fragment of the same meteor that he used for the locket you're wearing, Lady Alphena."

"This?" said Alphena, pulling the amulet out from beneath her tunics. "The man who made this is named Mamurcus?"

"Well, he was," said Janus. "He's been dead a thousand years, near enough. He made me in Anti-Thule. He took a piece of the meteor back to Italy with him when he fled and forged it into a case for the Godspeaker's ear."

"The Godspeaker was a Tylon!" Pandareus said in obvious delight. "The ears of the Tyla accompanying Rupa were pointed and furry, so of course someone hearing the description would think of satyrs. Even if Mamurcus himself didn't call them that."

He sounds as pleased to have figured that out as he would have been to learn that our friends had all returned to us, Alphena thought. Then she realized that her brother would have been equally thrilled.

"I suppose," said Janus. "Mamurcus knew they weren't satyrs, anyway. I didn't think any Tyla had survived, because the ice started coming down on Anti-Thule as soon as the Godspeaker died. Maybe the Indian wizard came back for them, but they weren't with him when he ran."

Janus shook his little iron head. "That Indian was powerful, let me tell you," he said sadly. "And Mamurcus and me were even better. I was his wand, you see; the Indian had an ivory one. But the Godspeaker was greater yet with the tablet which the Eternals had left under the northern ice, and we all together weren't enough to stop the Blight. After the Godspeaker died, we and the Indian ran. Mamurcus took the ear with him; that was all that was left of the Godspeaker. That locket you've got, that's really powerful if you can handle it."

"It appears to me that Lady Alphena handled it, so to speak, last night," Pandareus said. "Otherwise Rupa would not have let us go."

Janus turned to look at him; the other face was as still as Alphena normally expected a lump of iron to be. "You've got a point there, Teacher," he said. "You wouldn't think it to look at her, would you?"

"I scarcely know what to think, these past few months," said Pandareus. "I have learned not to discount Lady Alphena's resources, however."

Alphena held the amulet firmly in her left hand, though it had seemed to work the same when it was lying between her breasts. She thought in silence, then said, "Janus, do you know how to find Master Corylus?"

I should have said Mother *or* Varus! *I keep thinking about* Corylus!

"Of course," said Janus. "I'm the god of openings. I can open the way to your Corylus, if that's what you want."

The little head nodded toward the south. "My gate is there at the end of the Forum and the doors are open. If you'll take me there and step through the doors, we'll get on with it."

Alphena let out her breath. She was feeling relief for the first time since she had been forced to flee from the Bacchic rout at Polymartium. She had something to do!

"Yes," Alphena said aloud. "We'll do that now."

VARUS EXPECTED TO DISMOUNT in front of Govinda's palace from the platform on the elephant's back, a luxurious room with wicker walls. Instead the great beast paced through the arched gateway and into the hall beyond before stopping.

Varus looked up. The ceiling was forty feet high, supported on pillars of colored marble. Light entered through a clerestory of thin alabaster panels cut into filigrees. Their curves, he suddenly realized, matched the swirling patterns of the tapestries on the walls.

"You may get down, please," said the attendant who had ridden on the platform with Varus and four Tyla, as Govinda called the bipedal creatures. The fellow had been silent except when offering water from a silver flask chilled by wet moss. He wore silk and spoke good Greek, but his eyes had been on Varus throughout the journey.

What did Govinda expect me to do if he'd left me alone? Varus thought. Then, *What does Govinda want me to do?*

Attendants had brought a ladder to the elephant's side. There were scores of servants in the hall, easily visible despite the muted light because their white garments shone against the wall hangings. Varus climbed down carefully because his legs were stiff from having been crossed during the journey.

It was only when he was on the carpeted floor that he really appreciated how big the elephant was. When Varus had climbed a less ornate ladder to mount, he had been too caught up in events to pay much attention to the animal. Now he saw that the animal was bigger than even the gigantic beast he had seen in Puteoli. That one had come down the Nile from the forests to the south of the Libyan desert and was ten feet high at the shoulder.

This elephant and the similar one on that Govinda had ridden were probably two feet taller. Their tusks grew from the lower jaw and curved down, not outward.

Wealthy men in Carce would pay enormous amounts for elephants like this, to display to the public and to kill in the arena. It would demonstrate their wealth, much as Cleopatra had dissolved a pearl in wine and drunk it.

Varus smiled faintly. He wished Pandareus or Corylus were here to talk with. *I could make my observation to the attendant, but he wouldn't understand and he wouldn't care if he did.*

Mind, Hedia and Alphena wouldn't have cared, either. It would still be good to see them back in Carce.

King Govinda and the four Tyla with him had already dismounted from the leading elephant; their mount was being led through the archway at the far end of the hall. Govinda held not the speculum as before but rather a tablet of greenish soapstone. It was about the size of a man's palm, but the slanting break at one end showed that it was a portion of a longer original.

"Come with me, Westerner," the king said. "You have seen my Tyla servants, whom I brought from Anti-Thule. I will show you what else I brought from that place and time, lest you doubt my power."

Varus looked at him and considered. *If he were really so confident of his power, he wouldn't have to brag about it.* Aloud Varus said, "Lead, then."

Govinda turned and walked into the palace courtyard, flanked by the eight Tyla and probably a hundred of the dismounted horsemen who had accompanied him at Raguram's palace. Varus followed without being prodded, as the guards beside and behind him were certainly willing to do.

Perhaps I should change them into toads, Varus thought, smiling. He wondered where Bhiku was.

The palace was a quadrangle. The walls were four stories high in the front through which Varus had come and three stories for the two ends. The final side, the back, was a reservoir much larger that the one standing behind Raguram's complex.

Instead of being open, Govinda's tank was surrounded by a high iron fence with spikes on top and pointing inward, like the wall of saplings that soldiers in the field stacked with the sharp-cut trunks facing the enemy. At both ends were masonry platforms thirty feet above the water. Twenty or more bound prisoners—men, women, and children—stood on each platform, hedged in by the drawn sabers of an equal number of guards.

"I sent a messenger ahead to prepare this demonstration," Govinda said. There was something oily in his voice, like the scum floating on the surface of a swamp. "If you fail to carry out my orders, you will get a closer view yet."

He waved the hand holding the broken tablet. Trumpets blatted from the tower behind them.

The guards jabbed forward the first two prisoners. The woman on the left side had worked a hand loose. She grabbed at the sword blades and so pitched off the platform slinging blood behind her.

Neither prisoner hit the surface. Great blunt heads lifted in sunlit sprays of water, their mouths open. Either could have swallowed the Egyptian obelisk that Augustus had erected in front of his tomb.

The *clop!* of the mouths shutting was like that of a dray of wine casks rolling into a cliff. The mouths opened again as more prisoners fell, kicking with their legs.

"Are those fish?" said Varus. By concentrating on knowledge, he could avoid the horror of what he was watching. He didn't look away: that would imply that this sadistic monster had power over him.

"Their ancestors were fish," Govinda said, watching raptly as a woman tried to throw her infant to the side so that it would be clear of the creature's jaws. She wasn't strong enough to grant her child the clean death of smashing onto the masonry. "My power brought them too from Anti-Thule."

The last of the prisoners flew from the platforms and were devoured. "You see how hopeless you would be if you tried to disobey me!"

We'll see, if and when I do decide to disobey you, Varus thought. Keeping his voice flat, with only a hint of the disgust he felt, he said, "What is it that you want me to do?"

"I want you to fetch something," Govinda said. "I was going to send the beggar-magician who serves Raguram, but my ancestor said that you would be more suitable. Come!"

The palace courtyard was remarkably open compared to the cluttered interior of Ramsa Lal's smaller palace. There were two permanent structures, one to either side of the arch through which Varus had come. On the left was an open-sided pergola over which an ancient grapevine twined. The base of the vine was almost two feet in diameter, thicker than Varus had imagined a grapevine could grow.

To the right was an eight-sided kiosk with walls of translucent alabaster like the clerestory of the hall. These were solid sheets, however.

Govinda led Varus to the door of carved wood. Though it was braced with bronze straps, the door panel itself had been sawn as a single plank.

A boy hung by his hair across the room from the doorway. His eyes were closed, and his face was very pale. The faint pulse in his throat showed that he was alive.

The alabaster walls were creamy white from outside, but from this direction Varus saw separate scenes in each of the six panels. Two were familiar to him: the shrine outside the jungle-covered ruin that Bhiku had called Dreaming Hill, and the hills outside Polymartium where Govinda's delegation had planted the vine shoot. A third panel was covered with black, roiling clouds.

Govinda closed the door behind them. Varus turned to the king and said, "The shoot there—"

He pointed.

"Did it come from the vine just outside?"

"Watch your tone when you speak to me, Westerner," Govinda said.

"I am a citizen of Carce," Varus said. He didn't raise his voice, but he heard in his words the snap of command that Hedia would have given them. "I will grant you the courtesy that I deem you to have earned. Now, is the huge vine in the courtyard the source of the shoot your servants planted in Polymartium?"

Govinda stared at him. The king held the soapstone tablet in one hand and stroked it with the index finger of the other. After a moment, he said, "Lord Bacchus planted that vine when he conquered India. It is a focus for magic generally and for Lord Bacchus."

"This is the messenger you sought," said a rusty voice behind them.

Varus turned. The hanging boy had spoken. His eyes had opened and were focused on Varus.

"Good," said Govinda. He turned to Varus and said, "Now, Westerner, I will set you your task. When you have accomplished it, you and I will never have to see one another again."

"Tell me what you want," Varus said. He didn't bluster and he tried to keep the tension out of his face, but he was well aware that the next moments were likely to be dangerous regardless of what he decided.

HEDIA WAS DANCING. They were all dancing, she thought . . . but she didn't think much or care much. She was tipsy, and she was as happy as she had ever been in her life.

It was a circle dance, the outer round moving sunwise as the inner dancers rotated widdershins. Hedia couldn't remember how often she had linked arms and changed direction as a satyr played the shepherd's pipe in the center of the circle.

Her current partner offered her a wineskin. As she sucked greedily on the wooden teat, he said, "Will you come with me to see the future, Lady Hedia?"

It's Ampelos. He's Ampelos.

"Of course I'll come with you, handsome," Hedia said, allowing the youth to spin her out of the dance with him. The circle shifted, either closing slightly or admitting another pair of revelers.

She didn't know what Ampelos had in mind, but she hoped it was the breakthrough in their relations that she had wanted from the first. It was possible that he had something hostile in mind, but Hedia had honed her judgments of men in a harsh school. Twice she had refused an offer that she would have cheerfully accepted if her instincts hadn't warned her.

She didn't think Ampelos had any dangerous ideas. If she was wrong, well, she would deal with it.

Once, a man decided to take by force what she had not given of her free will. He had found himself screaming and bleeding on the floor a moment after his grip on Hedia's right hand had become carelessly loose.

"My bower, shall we?" the youth said, his fingertips lightly guiding her arm toward an arbor covered with twisting grapevines and their leaves. The sides were open from knee height to the ground, but no one in Carce expected privacy for sex. A wealthy home was full of servants, while poor families were crammed into single rooms.

"Yes, lovely," said Hedia, wriggling her shoulders slightly in preparation for dropping her tunic to where the sash would catch it at her waist.

Ampelos did not have an erection. Well, that too was something she had dealt with before.

They entered the arbor. The skin of a bear with white, silky fur covered the couch in the center. Hedia seated herself near the middle, waiting for her host to tell her how he wanted her disposed.

Ampelos poured wine into a gold-mounted crystal goblet, then stoppered the skin and sat down beside her. Hedia smiled, expecting him to hold out the wine to her or even to kiss the rim before offering it.

Instead he moved his left palm over the cup and said, "Look in the surface, Lady Hedia. I haven't the powers that our lord and god has, but in this place I can scratch some of the patina off the future so that we can look at it."

Hedia dutifully bent forward to peer into the clear scarlet wine. This wasn't what she had expected, but it wasn't harmful. Ampelos was being courteous, and she herself was always courteous when the circumstances allowed.

The wine swirled, though Ampelos held the goblet steady. An image formed in the spirals of bubbles, slowly at first, then suddenly and with startling clarity:

Varus reclined on a couch in an octagonal room.

"That is your son, is it not, Lady Hedia?" said Ampelos.

"It is," said Hedia, her eyes still on the image. "Where is he now?"

On the table beside Varus was a cup that had been carved from ruby or from ruby red glass. It seemed to be empty. A steel pry bar lay across the table also, and a disk that seemed to shimmer as she watched: sometimes dull black but shifting to a hole into infinity.

"This is the sanctum of King Govinda," Ampelos said. "This is what will happen in a day's time or even a few hours from now."

"That's Govinda in the gold suit?" Hedia said. She tried to keep her tone neutral, but she heard the touch of harshness creep in. That didn't disturb her.

The man with the diadem, wearing pantaloons and a puffy tunic made of cloth of gold, was younger than she had expected the wizard-king to be. There didn't seem to be any doubt, though. He held a block of stone carved with letters in a script unfamiliar to Hedia.

Varus might be able to read it, though, or even Corylus. She respected the young men's erudition, though it appeared to her as pointless as trying to determine how far the moon was from the Earth. Which Varus had assured her that very learned scholars were doing . . .

"That is Govinda," Ampelos said. "The tablet he holds is a tool of great magical power, carved before mammals lived on earth, and discovered thousands of thousands of years later by the Tylon wizard who became the Godspeaker."

"What is my son doing?" Hedia said, though it was obvious that Varus was taking the goblet in his hands and raising it to his lips. "It's empty, isn't it? There's nothing in it!"

"Govinda will use the tablet to force your son to drink poison," Ampelos said calmly, "to free his spirit to visit the far past. The poison is clear, but it is not less virulent for that."

Varus set down the goblet and took the black disk and the pry bar, one in either hand. He lay back on the couch and composed himself as if for sleep. His eyes closed.

"It hasn't happened yet?" Hedia said. Her lips were dry. "There's still time to stop it?"

"Govinda leaves the Godspeaker's tablet on the table in his sanctum," Ampelos said. "Where you see the goblet now. If you were to steal the tablet, you could force Govinda to surrender your son and to send you both back to Carce."

The figure of Varus in the wine cup was stiffening. His complexion turned gray. Hedia wasn't sure how much of what she thought she saw was really her imagination painting the tiny image, but it was likely enough anyway.

"How?" Hedia said. She straightened and looked straight at Ampelos. "How do I get to where the thing is? The tablet."

"A grapevine grows beside Govinda's sanctum," the youth said, his tone carelessly flat—as it had been throughout this conversation. "They are both in the courtyard of the king's palace. Our lord and god Bacchus planted it. The vine is the same as the one growing beside his chariot, wherever that may be. If you climb the vine here in the Otherworld, you will come down the vine beside Govinda's sanctum."

Hedia stood. "Take me to the vine," she said.

Ampelos stood also. He poured the wine onto the ground, then tossed the goblet onto the couch. He started across the twilit encampment with Hedia behind him.

CHAPTER XIII

The rolling plain Aura was leading Corylus over was pleasant enough, but the occasional trees drew his attention. Their course had taken them close to a chestnut, a dogwood, and a small grove of walnuts, but apart from greeting the nymphs who chose to show themselves, they had passed on. Aura showed no interest in socializing, and Corylus was willing to focus on reaching the Cave of Zagreus.

I wouldn't have minded chatting with the family of walnuts, though. The nymphs of saplings had waved with a grace attractively at variance with the straitlaced majesty of their mother.

The grass half a furlong in front of Corylus twitched as something raced toward them. "Aura," he said, touching his guide's hand. "Something's coming and I can't see what it—"

A long-legged hare wearing a laurel diadem and a purple tunic burst from the grass twenty feet ahead and stopped, spraying a cloud of light soil in front of him. "Oh my goodness!" he said. "Oh, dear me. I'm sorry, I didn't mean to disturb—"

He disappeared into the high grass again at an angle to his previous course. Corylus thought he heard the word ". . . late . . ." coming from that direction, but he wasn't sure of the word and the speaker may not have been the hare.

"Occasionally," Corylus said, "I forget that I'm in the Otherworld. But then something reminds me."

The ground to their left sloped gently upward; they were following the base of a knoll. Above them were a pair of oaks—a white oak and an ilex—as well as a tall beech. A man hung by his hair from the lowest branch of the white oak; a woman stood near and was jabbing him with a stick.

"Wait," said Corylus.

"That's Calaia," said Aura. She hung back for a moment, then followed when she realized Corylus was walking toward the grove with her or without her. "She's an air spirit. I don't know who the man is."

Calaia turned when she saw Corylus approaching. When she did, he called, "Greetings, mistress. I'm Publius Cispius Corylus!"

He thought of adding a question about what was happening, but that could come later if the nymph didn't volunteer the information.

"I am Calaia," the nymph said. "Aura, take your friend away. I don't need his help."

She held not a club but a switch, an oak twig with a spray of many-pointed leaves on the end. *She's been tickling him, not beating him!*

The man rotated slowly. His arms were bound, and his long chestnut hair was tied around the branch above him.

When he turned enough to see Corylus he called, "You, Corylus! You're human, aren't you? Help me get away from this witch! I wouldn't sleep with her, so she's torturing me!"

"Sister, take him away or I'll have to deal with him myself," Calaia said peevishly to Aura. Looking at Corylus, she went on, "I want him to play with me, sure. What's the harm? He doesn't want to. As soon as he changes his mind, I'll put him back in the Waking World."

"I *can't* sleep with her!" the man said. His face had rotated away from Corylus again, but he was shouting loudly enough to be heard. "My betrothed in India has put a spell on me and I *can't* touch another woman!"

Calaia shrugged. "Then eventually he'll die, I suppose," she said. "I think it would be easier to decide to have sex with me, but it's his choice."

The hanging man was about thirty and muscular, though his legs were relatively thin compared to his mighty arms and shoulders. A pod of leaping dolphins was tattooed on his chest.

A sailor, Corylus thought. *An oarsman.*

"My name's Bion!" the hanging man said as he turned farther. "Please, Corylus! As a fellow human!"

Corylus drew his dagger and stepped forward. The keen orichalc edge could easily cut Bion's hair, and that would free him.

Calaia pointed an index finger. A miniature whirlwind wrapped Corylus' right ankle and tugged him back like an elephant's trunk. Though he fought the pressure, he found his sandal slipping backward.

"Aura!" Calaia said. "I warned you. I'll roll your boy down the hill if you don't take him away."

"Aura, can you help me?" Corylus said, straining against the wind. "I'm not going to leave her to torture this poor bastard!"

Aura stepped between him and the other nymph, holding out the blue ring she wore on her thumb. "Sister, let him go," she said. "This is my lover Zetes' ring. Corylus slew Zetes' slayer and gained me the revenge I've waited for ages to have."

"I have nothing against your boy," Calaia said. "Just keep him out of my business, sister. You have no power over me."

Aura turned to Corylus. "I'm sorry," she said. "She's right. We'd better get along."

"If we're talking about power . . . ," said the tall blond dryad who stepped from the white oak. She grinned broadly and glanced toward Corylus. "Did you want help, Cousin?"

"Very much, Robur," Corylus said. "And you too, Ilex"—for the other dryad had appeared also, slender and dark with very fine features—"if you care to."

"What do you think you're doing?" said Calaia, backing angrily from Robur's advance. "Don't you *dare*!"

Ilex took the switch from the air sprite's hand. "I was going to let it be, even when you broke off a twig," the dryad said. "I thought, 'Well, Calaia can't help being a nasty bitch.' But since you've decided to threaten Cousin Corylus—"

Robur caught a handful of Calaia's blue-blond hair and lifted her, kicking and screaming. Ilex slashed Calaia across the face with the pointed leaves.

"Don't you *dare*!" the air sprite repeated, though Corylus couldn't imagine what she thought the pair of dryads wouldn't dare, given what they were already doing.

"There was a time you might have twisted me about, Calaia," Robur said. She wore a satisfied smile, and there was a smile in her sultry voice as well. "There may be another time when I'm very old. But not now, I think."

"Say, can I join the fun?" said the beech nymph, walking over to join the dryads. She was more slender than the statuesque Robur, but her supple strength was obvious to anyone who watched her move.

Ilex tried to tickle Calaia, but the air sprite grabbed at the switch; her arms weren't pinioned. She tried to kick the dryads, without any result except to sway back and forth in Robur's grip.

Corylus was free of the wind's clutch, but he backed slightly away. He didn't want to go to Bion with a sharp knife in his hand when at any moment one or another of the sprites might come flying at him. The sailor had hung for some time; hanging a little longer wouldn't be fatal.

The beech nymph stepped in quickly and grabbed one, then the other, of Calaia's ankles. Ilex smiled at Robur and said, "Down the hill on three, shall we?" The dryad smiled in agreement.

Calaia was screaming in wordless rage as the nymphs swung her back. Robur hadn't changed her grip from the hair, but Calaia's blind attempts to scratch the dryad's arms were futile.

"One!" said Ilex, She reached in with the switch, then jumped back so that she wasn't in the way.

"Two!" said Ilex, remaining where she crouched. Calaia swung back again. By now she seemed to be crying, though Corylus suspected they were tears of fury.

"Three!"

Calaia sailed off the top of the knoll, tumbling wildly. She hit at the bottom and rolled into a stand of rhododendrons at the bottom of the swale. She scrambled into the brush on all fours and disappeared.

The tree nymphs hugged and laughed in a tight group. "Oh! That was fun!" Ilex wheezed through her laughter.

Corylus stepped around them. He murmured, "Thank you, Cousins," out of courtesy, but he didn't think they paid any attention to him.

"Now, steady," he said to Bion. Aura bent and gripped the sailor by the waist while Corylus reached up with the knife.

The keen blade slipped through the tail of hair as though through sunlight. Bion slumped into Aura's arms. She and Corylus lowered the sailor carefully to the sod.

"Good morning, Master Bion," Corylus said, smiling. "I hope that your life will be less stressful from now on."

GOVINDA LOOKED AT VARUS WITHOUT EXPRESSION. After a moment the king said, "I will show you what I want, Westerner."

Govinda reached into the right side of his tunic and placed the half tablet there. Varus saw a slight bulge on the left side also—the black speculum, he judged.

With his hands freed, Govinda bent and reached under a concealed lip in the parquet floor. The king grunted with effort that Varus understood when a section hinged up: beneath the wood was a layer of gray metal, probably lead.

"Go down," the king said, breathing hard. "There's a ladder. We can't stay long or the air will become stale, but it is the only safe place to show you."

Varus thought for a silent moment. There was no latch on the trapdoor. Govinda could put a weight on top of it or simply stand on the closed lid if he wished, but there was no point in considering possible disasters.

Fire demons could rise from the depths of the Underworld . . . as I have seen them do in the past. He grinned, which seemed to take Govinda aback.

"All right," Varus said, peering through the opening into a vault like the one beneath the Temple of Jupiter Best and Greatest on the Capitoline. Instead of a chest holding treasures similar to the *Sibylline Books*, this was an empty room lined with the same gray metal as the door.

Varus climbed down the bamboo ladder and waited as Govinda followed him. The room was low; Varus didn't have to duck, but Corylus would have, and the king took off his tight turban before closing the lid above him.

For a moment, the room was completely dark. Varus found it difficult to breathe, but that was probably a trick of his mind. An unpleasant trick.

A disk of gray light appeared in the air. Either it brightened or Varus' eyes were adapting to the darkness. It came from the speculum of polished cannel coal, held between Govinda's left thumb and forefinger. Shadows moved in the black surface, then sharpened into buildings.

"This is Anti-Thule," Govinda said. Varus could make out his features faintly in the gray glow. "This is where you will go."

Varus eyed the scene of destruction. The buildings of the Tyla had been mostly paper over frames of withies. All that storms had left of these were broken sticks, sometimes still lashed together. Occasionally he saw tatters of paper clinging to the remnants of a framework.

The Tyla had left their bones also. Rarely were they articulated. Mice or creatures like mice had gnawed them, though there was no evidence that larger scavengers had been at work on the corpses.

"Why aren't we in your room on the surface?" Varus said. "You work magic there, and the panels show distant places."

The king scowled. Varus expected him to snarl that it was none of the Westerner's business—whereupon Varus expected to treat Govinda as a noble of Carce treated uncultured foreigners.

Pulto would call Govinda a wog. Very likely Lenatus would also, though not in the hearing of members of the cultured family that employed him.

"Anti-Thule at the time you will visit it," Govinda said calmly, having mastered his temper, "is a place of great magic. I cannot view it in the chamber above without special precautions, any more than I could stand in the Dardanelles and stop the current. I use this vault because it allows us to view the place safely, as I would use black glass to observe the sun."

He moved his right hand, again holding the broken tablet. The scene in the speculum shifted also, to the ruins of a stone building. It had been circular with a domed roof like the Temple of Vesta in the Forum.

"This was the Temple of the Moon," Govinda said. "The Godspeaker lived here and his power kept Anti-Thule warm. The tablet the Godspeaker brought from beneath the Hyperborean ice made him immortal, or almost immortal. When he was killed—"

"How was he killed?" Varus said.

Govinda looked at him. "I don't know," he said, "and I hope never to learn."

He paused, perhaps to see if Varus would reply. His tone had left Varus with nothing to say beyond, "Go on, then."

"When the Godspeaker was killed," Govinda said, "the tablet that was the source of his power broke. I have half here—"

The king did not gesture with the incised soapstone in his hand, but his meaning was obvious.

"—while the remainder stayed in Anti-Thule."

Now he moved the tablet. The image in the speculum shrank to one of the curved blocks of the temple cornice, now lying on the ground in front of the base. Beneath it was a rectangle of stone, the broken end of a block that would fit against the break in the tablet that Govinda held.

"You will go to Anti-Thule and retrieve this portion of the tablet," Govinda said. "At the moment in the world's age which you see here and to which I will send you, the Tyla are dead—all but those priests whom I preserved as my minions. The ice has not yet covered Anti-Thule, however. When you come back with the half tablet, I will release you."

"Why are you sending me for this, this thing?" Varus said. He turned his eyes away from the speculum. The view of Anti-Thule had been bleak enough before, but in close-up he could see flakes of snow scudding across the ruins. "You didn't know I existed a day or two ago, did you?"

Varus wasn't sure that was true. *He* hadn't known he would be in India until he had stepped out of the Otherworld with Bhiku, but perhaps magic had told Govinda more.

"The messenger must be a wizard, even with my ancestor as guide," Govinda said calmly. "I had planned to send the woman Rupa who serves my vassal Ramsa Lal, but she remained in Italy. I will deal with her later, but for now that left me with only the beggar-sage who serves Raguram. I doubted he had the power to succeed. You appeared providentially, so I chose you, Westerner. If you fail, then I'll send the beggar after all."

"You're a wizard, aren't you?" Varus said, letting a note of challenge color his tone. "Why don't you go yourself rather than send a vicar?"

"I am the only one who can open the portal," Govinda said. "Besides, there is danger, even for so great a wizard as myself. A servant may better take the risk than me."

I am not your servant, Varus thought. But if the choice were between him and Bhiku, then certainly he would go.

"Do you have anything further to show me?" Varus said aloud. "If not, let's get out of this place."

The lead-lined vault threatened him by its presence. So far as he could tell the location gave the king no advantage over him; but Varus was uncomfortable and he preferred to change that if he could.

"All right," said Govinda. The flickering gray light vanished, though Varus' eyes still held afterimages of the bleak destruction. The king's slippers whispered on the floor. There was a squeak and a welcome line of light through the crack; then Govinda banged the lid fully open and started up the ladder.

Varus had an urge to thrust the king aside and climb out of the vault ahead of him. That would be cowardly. *I am a citizen of Carce.* He waited.

"You!" Govinda shouted. "Who are you!"

The king lurched out of the vault with all the speed he could manage, reaching under his tunic for the portion of soapstone tablet that he already had. Varus jumped to the ladder to follow.

"Is that the Temple of Janus?" Alphena said, gesturing ahead as they walked past the front of the Temple of the Divine Julius.

"Well, it would be if it was a temple," said the upturned face of her baton. "Which it isn't, right, Teacher?"

"I would scarcely have the temerity to correct a god," said Pandareus. "Though—"

He grinned.

"—I can imagine circumstances in which I might suggest that my previous understanding must be at fault—and cite my sources. Here, however, I'm in complete agreement with Lord Janus. The structure has no statue, nor is there an altar in front of it. It is an ornamental gateway, not a temple."

"'Lord' Janus, you say," the baton said with a laugh. "I'm the doorkeeper. Do you call your doorkeeper 'lord,' Teacher?"

"You have a romantic notion of the teaching profession if you imagine that my income permits me to own a doorkeeper," Pandareus said. "Or to buy meat for ordinary meals, if it comes to that."

Alphena grimaced. *Pandareus and this little iron head are mocking me.*

But they weren't. They were playing word games, much as Varus and his teacher might have done. By saying "Temple" she had given them a chance to play, but they didn't care about her.

Anyway, she couldn't expect a god to care about her noble birth, and Pandareus hadn't even disagreed with her. *Besides, I need them both.*

The gate, not temple, stood open on both ends. It was a square stone building with an arched doorway on the right side of the wall facing the Forum, and a similar arch and double doors at the other end, ten feet away. Four men, probably public slaves assigned to the structure, sat inside what would be the guardroom on a real gate; they were dicing and drinking straight from a wineskin.

"I'll handle it," Lenatus said—to the escorts, not to Alphena. He sauntered to the nearer archway and said, "You lot. Out!"

Alphena watched in surprise as the slaves got to their feet and left. One turned in the direction of Lenatus, but a comrade grabbed him by the arm and dragged him out the back way with the rest of them.

"I expected an argument, even a fight?" Alphena said. The question was in her tone, not the words.

"I didn't," Lenatus said, returning to her. He was obviously angry about what he was about to do, but he realized there was no point in bringing up the matter again. "I wasn't in the mood for a discussion, and I guess they heard that."

"Well, are you ready, lady?" Janus said. "It's nothing to me—I just spent thirty years standing in a flower bed since Sentius didn't know what I was."

"Could Sentius have used you as Lady Alphena is doing, Janus?" Pandareus said. He had accepted the baton's objection to being addressed as "lord."

"Sentius?" said the baton. "Not him, not in a million years. But that Rupa sure could have if she'd known about me."

"It's as well that she didn't, then," Alphena said. Her mouth seemed dry. Then she said, "Master Lenatus, I don't know what I'll find where I'm going. I'll take your cape, now, if you please."

"Why do you want the cape, Your Ladyship?" Pandareus said.

"She doesn't," said Lenatus curtly as he opened a buckle under the cover of his cape. He reached up with one hand and undid the clasp at his throat while his other hand gripped something hidden by the fabric.

Alphena took the bundle of cape and sword in the crook of her left arm. She would belt on the weapon when Janus had taken her to a place beyond the hundreds of people who might be watching her now.

"All right," she said to the double-faced iron. "I'm ready."

She stepped forward, through the gateway and on into the Otherworld.

"WHERE ARE WE GOING?" Hedia said. She didn't trust Ampelos, but it appeared that they had similar aims.

I wouldn't mind dallying here longer, she thought. *I wouldn't mind dallying a very long time. The danger to Varus is real, though, and family duty comes first.*

"You must be unseen to enter Govinda's sanctum," Ampelos said. "Since you've agreed to save your son's life, I will arrange for you to use the Lamp of Darkness. We will visit the Cabiri, who forged it."

They had reached his chariot. Attendants were already yoking the leopards. The cats twisted when they saw their master and made noises in their throats like angry stones rubbing. Hedia assumed the sound was their equivalent of a happy purr, but she was happier when they fell silent.

Ampelos stepped into the car and took the reins in his hands. Hedia hesitated a moment.

"Well, get in," the youth said curtly. "After you have the lamp, we will go directly to the vine. I want to get this over with as quickly as possible."

Hedia got in and gripped the railing with both hands. It was as well she did. Though the chariot was identical to the one in which she had ridden with Bacchus, she swayed violently when the leopards sprang ahead. When the god himself drove, she hadn't felt the motion.

Hedia smiled, though she decided not to speak aloud. She had thought of putting her arm around Ampelos during the drive, but it was clear that wouldn't be a good idea. She'd hoped that the youth would be more friendly since they had begun acting as allies. She now realized that Ampelos regarded her not with hatred but with disgust.

The chariot bounced through the camp. There were scores of dance rounds, each about a bonfire. The figures capering in opposite circles occasionally combined to make monstrous silhouettes . . . and sometimes the monsters were not tricks of the shadows.

It was my choice to come here, Hedia thought. She smiled. Many of the things she had chosen to do had proved less than great ideas, but she would continue to take chances.

The yoked leopards had a rangy lope different from horses Hedia had seen or mules behind whom she had been driven. They were clear of the camp and racing across a landscape like nothing Hedia had seen in the Otherworld. There was no grass and the low clumps of spiky vegetation were only scattered over the surface of the clay soil.

A creature raised its scaly head from a hole in the ground ahead. The leopards curled their lips back and snarled, the threats syncopating one another.

"You've got no business here!" the reptile shrieked in a perfect Athenian accent. It vanished back into its hole before the cats reached it.

The Moon was bigger than Hedia expected, but dim and sulfurous. Red light flared on the tops of several mountains on the horizon. She wanted to ask how much farther they were going, but that would suggest to Ampelos that she was weak.

He wouldn't answer anyway. That's an even better reason not to ask.

Without warning Ampelos swung the chariot to a halt at what Hedia had taken for a circular pond. It was a pit with no water in it, though the shimmer over the opening continued the illusion even at close range.

Ampelos got down without acknowledging Hedia's presence. "Brothers!" he called, facing the pit. "I have come for the Lamp of Darkness!"

A figure climbed through the opening, followed by his near twin. The screen of light at the opening blurred their figures, but under the sickly moon the Cabiri were even uglier than the distorted versions had been.

"So, you've come back, handsome," said the first. "You're ready to meet our terms?"

From a distance the Cabiri would have appeared to be dwarfs, but either of the pair was as tall as Ampelos; they were actually giants with stumpy legs. They had long faces with shaggy beards and hair; they wore leather aprons, and their arms were as muscular as the forelegs of lions. Wherever their skin was exposed, sparks had scarred it. A stench of burned hair clung to both of them.

"Yes," said Ampelos. "After I've delivered the woman—"

He nodded toward Hedia without ever letting his eyes rest on her.

"—to the vine."

"Now," said the second dwarf. He held an oil lamp of ordinary shape—a flat pitcher with a hole in the middle for filling, a spout where the wick would lie, and a loop handle opposite the spout. It was iron, however, rather than molded earthenware or bronze. "We don't trust you, handsome."

"Why should we?" said the first. "We will turn over the product of our labor, after you pay us for it."

"I will come back and pay you," Ampelos said. "I swear."

"What do you swear by?" said the Cabiri together. Their voices were like rusty iron.

"I swear by my lord and god Bacchus!" Ampelos said. "I will come back and pay my debt to you. I swear it!"

"An earnest," said the dwarf holding the lamp. His hands were broad and long, suggesting paddles when the fingers were closed together. "A kiss to each of us, and then we will wait for your return."

Instead of replying, Ampelos stepped to the first brother and kissed him on the mouth. The dwarf hugged Ampelos closer; his dark, scarred arms encircled the youth like streaks of tar over an ivory statue.

The arms opened. Ampelos stepped away, his face as stiff as that of a badly carved bust. The second dwarf gave the lamp to his brother and kissed the youth in turn. He released Ampelos, chuckling deep in his huge chest.

"Take the lamp, handsome," said the first of the Cabiri, offering it on the shelf of his fingers.

"Give it to her!" Ampelos said, again without looking toward Hedia.

"Our arrangement . . . ," said the other dwarf, "is with you. Take the lamp . . . or complete the bargain and leave it. That's fine too."

"What would we want with a woman?" said the first. They laughed again.

Ampelos accepted the lamp. He turned to Hedia and said, "Here, you'll need it."

Hedia took it by the handle with her left hand alone. She would need one hand for the railing if they were going to travel in the chariot.

"How does it work?" she said. The lamp was heavier than earthenware would be, but it wasn't too heavy to easily hold.

"I'll light it, missy," said one of the Cabiri. He leaned forward and snapped his fingers over the spout. The *crack!* sounded like an oak limb breaking.

Where the flame should be Hedia saw a distortion like that over the mouth of the cave, but that was all. "Is it working?" she said. "Nothing has changed?"

The dwarf who had lit the lamp held his hand out flat again. "Set it here for a moment, missy," he said. "You will see."

"She will not see," said his brother.

Both Cabiri laughed.

Hedia put the lamp on the dwarf's palm, wondering what she was supposed to see. Or not see. When she released the loop, the lamp and the dwarf holding the lamp vanished. All that remained was the shimmer at the spout.

She reached forward very carefully, felt the iron loop, and lifted the lamp again. The dwarf reappeared, smiling broadly. A spark had burned his lower lip; the sore oozed pus.

"Get back in the chariot, woman," Ampelos said, his voice too thin to be a snarl. "You have what you need. We'll finish this."

"See you soon, handsome," said one of the Cabiri to their backs.

As Hedia stepped into the car after Ampelos, the other called, "Don't forget, sweetheart. You swore, you know!"

"Are you aboard?" said Ampelos.

"Yes," said Hedia, her arm gripped tightly to the railing. As the leopards jolted off, she added in a falsely sweet voice, "I hope you three will be very happy together . . . handsome."

The youth hunched and slapped his reins against his team's necks. He didn't speak.

The landscape they bounced over was grassy and spotted with circles of large, vividly colored mushrooms. The fungi were larger than Hedia had seen before. *Our cooks would love them. They'd turn them into a whole village for a banquet centerpiece.*

As the thought formed, the chariot passed close to a stand of mushrooms.

A gathering of mice wearing tunics and caps scattered on two legs into mushrooms, snapping doors closed behind them.

Indeed, they're very like a village already.

On the horizon ahead was a mound of deep green, a striking contrast to the yellowish grass and the brightly polka-dotted fungi. Ampelos drove into it without slowing the chariot.

He didn't explain to Hedia what was happening. *He didn't speak when he could see me, so this shouldn't be a surprise.*

They drove down and into a spiraling aisle between walls of oversized versions of ordinary flowers: foxgloves, hollyhocks, delphiniums, and a score of varieties that Hedia didn't recognize. In the center of the spiral was a circular wooden bench built around a grapevine with the diameter of a large oak tree. Unsupported, it reached up to a hazy blur.

Ampelos drew back on the reins and the leopards cantered to a halt. They were breathing through open mouths, and their tongues lolled. Hedia wondered how fast the chariot had been driving, though distance wasn't always a useful measure in the Otherworld.

"Get out here," said Ampelos. "This is the vine. Climb it until you find yourself in King Govinda's courtyard, then enter his sanctum and take the tablet. The sanctum is only twenty feet away from the vine. No one will be able to see you."

Hedia paused. "How do I get back?" she said.

"The same way you got there!" Ampelos said. He glared at the vine, not the sound of her voice. "Is that so hard?"

"And how will this help Varus?" Hedia said, still in the chariot.

"He won't be fed poison!" Ampelos said. "You'll be able to trade the tablet to Govinda to get the boy back and then you'll both be able to get home. Isn't that what you want?"

"Yes," said Hedia. At last she stepped off the back of the car and walked to the vine.

She looked down at her legs scissoring crisply across a bed of moss as soft as velvet, but the Cabiri had demonstrated that the Lamp of Darkness really did work. She didn't think the dwarfs would have helped Ampelos trick her, at least not without an additional payment.

Hedia grinned. It appeared that Ampelos was already paying with everything he had.

Tendrils sprouted from the vine at frequent intervals. Each one reached upward to where it, like the main stem, vanished hazily in the air. This would probably be a simple enough climb for someone who was used to climbing— no doubt there were such people—but it a was daunting prospect to Hedia, and she had the lamp in her left hand besides.

It wasn't going to get easier if she stood staring at the prospect, though. Besides, Ampelos was watching from the chariot, though he presumably wouldn't know what Hedia was doing so long as she held the lamp.

Hedia stepped onto the circular bench, then put her left foot on the next wrist-thick tendril above it. She grasped a higher tendril with her right hand and raised herself enough to put her right foot on a tendril on that side. Though her left hand was occupied, she managed to brace that elbow on another branching tendril.

The vine's outer surface was smooth, so she wasn't tearing her skin on bark as she had feared. *I won't say this is fun, but it isn't as bad as I thought. And it's almost fun.*

A pair of little eyes glittered at her from over the edge of the tendril she was about to grasp. "Go away!" she said, shouting because she was surprised. A perfectly formed man the length of her middle finger flew off on two pairs of wings like a dragonfly.

Hedia wasn't looking back or looking down. She wondered how she would know when she had reached her goal. *Perhaps Ampelos intends me to climb into thin air and vanish.*

She looked up—that wouldn't give her vertigo or cause her to topple backward—and to her surprise saw just above her the cross timbers of a gazebo over which grapevines wrapped like knots of vipers. Gripping with both arms and her right hand, she dared to look down. The bench seats on the inside of the gazebo were within an inch of her toes.

Hedia tested the wood; it held her weight. She stepped onto the bench, then down to the ground.

Though the grape leaves shaded her, the dusty courtyard beyond was dazzling in sunlight. The air Hedia breathed was hot and dry.

The opening in the gazebo faced a separate building of much the same size but with a tile roof and walls of polished alabaster. A score of soldiers wearing curved swords guarded the closed door. With them were four of the furry dogs-on-two-legs the voice of the spring had called Tyla, when it showed Hedia visions of Anti-Thule.

The guards didn't look especially alert, but neither would Carce's legionaries in heat like this. An awning bleached to a pale cream protected them from the direct sun, but it would do nothing for air that could have come from an open oven.

Hedia stepped out, holding the lamp firmly in front of her. This was the first real test of the lamp's power. She realized that her gut was tense in expectation of shouts and a sudden rush by the guards.

They ignored her. One squat man with a scar across his forehead was facing directly toward Hedia, but his eyes were as unfocused as those of a painting. *I really am invisible.*

Hedia walked briskly toward the hut, the sanctum, as Ampelos had named it. Her sandals kicked up dust, but not appreciably more than the cat's-paws of breeze.

The palace itself was huge. The courtyard made her think of the Forum and the dozens of buildings surrounding it, but this was a single structure.

Hedia paused at arm's length from the troop of guards. There was room for her to step through them at several places, but she would have to be careful.

One of the Tyla was restive, looking about and sniffing the air. Occasionally he chirped querulously, but his fellows ignored him.

Hedia took a deep breath and strode forward. A guard turned to speak to his neighbor as she passed between them, but even then they didn't notice her.

Hedia slid the door handle to the left and heard the bolt withdraw. She opened the door and stepped in, closing the panel behind her as guards gabbled in surprise. She moved to the side so that if they burst in they at least wouldn't trample her, but nothing happened except that the chatter—they sounded like a cage of startled birds—died down after a moment.

Hedia let her breath out. *I wonder if they're telling themselves that they only imagined that the door had opened?* She had seen things herself that she found hard to believe.

She hadn't really registered the hut's interior until she started to relax. The couch on which Ampelos had shown her Varus drinking the poison was empty, but so was the table on which the magical tablet was supposed to be.

The boy hanging by his hair across from the room opened his eyes and stared at Hedia. He had been so still that until that moment he might have been a statue.

Hedia met his stare. The boy did not speak or otherwise react to her presence. She swallowed and decided to ignore him.

Since the tablet wasn't on the table, she had no obvious way to proceed.

She might try to search the palace itself, but there must be a thousand rooms and no reason to believe that the prize was in any of them.

Hedia examined the walls. She had taken their different scenes as paintings on the alabaster. Close up she could see leaves shivering in breezes; the men and women lolling around the vine newly planted at Polymartium were eating the oversized grapes that festooned nearby trees. One of the men was a member of the entourage that had accompanied her to the rites for Mother Matuta.

The images didn't bring Hedia closer to finding the tablet. *Nothing* was helpful.

She turned toward the door, planning to search the palace until some better plan occurred to her. A creak behind her made her look back. A section of floor was lifting on hinges. Govinda's head and torso rose through the opening. He held the inscribed tablet in his left hand.

Govinda shouted a word. Hedia's left hand stung and the lamp flew out of it.

She grabbed the handle and shoved the door open. The guards all faced the doorway; many had drawn their swords. Two Tyla pointed at her.

Without bothering to think about what she was doing, Hedia flung herself into the nearest alabaster panel. Instead of shattering the thin stone, she fell onto a small circular temple set in high grass.

CHAPTER XIV

Hedia's feet landed in a round shrine. The floor was unexpectedly a foot higher than that of the room from which she had leaped to save herself from Govinda, so she stumbled. She was very nearly as supple as a professional dancer, however. She righted herself without falling and sprang out onto the grass rather than grabbing a pillar to halt herself.

She looked in all directions. There were no humans about, and the only animals were birds in the high sky. The sun rippled the plain with its heat; the only shade was the domed shrine and the jungle-covered hill directly in front of her.

The bare shrine was scarcely welcoming, but Hedia found the notion of the jungle even less attractive. She turned to put herself under the dome again while she made her mind up as to what to do. *Maybe being a little higher will help me see something.*

A soldier stepped into the middle of the shrine. He saw Hedia and drew his curved sword. More soldiers followed him.

Hedia ran for the mound of jungle. If Govinda's troops had been keen she couldn't have escaped, but these men seemed uncertain. They were probably afraid.

Hedia was completely certain that she wanted to get away. As for fear, she was too familiar with being afraid to let it affect her behavior.

She wriggled between creeper-festooned trees and scrambled through a curtain of brush. It concealed a pile of tilted blocks that tripped her.

She got to her feet and struggled deeper into the ruins. Leaf litter had decayed to yellow-brown soil dripping from one slanted surface to the next. Some of the blocks had been decorated.

The roots of multi-trunked trees had levered the buildings apart but often held the individual blocks in much the same relationship to one another that they had originally. Occasionally a distorted doorway or a window survived, but generally tree trunks or a wall of earth blocked further passage.

The jungle was so much darker than the grassland that Hedia had come from that she assumed that foliage covered the sky completely. To her surprise she saw many patches of brightness through the leaves when she glanced up. The gloom she felt was more than just a matter of shade after sunlight.

Hedia paused. She thought someone had walked in front of her, a slender man in orange robes; and perhaps he had, but he had walked through a giant tree and the stone blocks around which its roots were wrapped.

The figure vanished. There was other movement nearby, but it was only shimmerings at the corners of her eyes. There was nothing to see when she looked straight toward it.

What are Govinda's men doing? Hedia looked back, but she saw nothing except foliage. She didn't think she'd come far into the jungle, but she might as well try to look through the stone as through the leaves hanging between her and the shrine.

Hedia moved aside the thin canes of a stand of bamboo that she didn't remember going through. Beyond was a heavily overgrown parapet that wasn't familiar, either. *Have I gotten turned around?*

She didn't like the feel of this place. Partly that was because of the things she saw or almost saw among the roots and ruins, but her disquiet was from more than that. There was nothing more tangible, though.

Knowing that she was taking a risk, Hedia crawled onto the parapet and eased her arm through the next layer of undergrowth, then withdrew it and peered down the hole. Whether or not she was going back on the same line by which she had arrived, she was close enough to the edge of the jungle that she could look out at the plain.

The shrine was a little to the left; she had gotten off-line in a matter of twenty feet or less. She could see ten soldiers, though there might be more. Some remained close to the base of the shrine, and none of them had followed Hedia more than halfway to the jungle.

Two Tyla with feather headdresses stood within the shrine. From what the Spring of True Answers had said, the headdresses marked them as Priests of the Moon. They appeared even less willing than the humans to approach the jungle.

She couldn't go back out the way she had come, but this patch of jungle might be narrow enough for her to hike through to the other side. This wasn't a plan for which she could muster any enthusiasm, but she didn't see a better choice.

When she got to the other side, she would consider her next step. At present she couldn't imagine what she would do if faced with another stretch of uninhabited plain.

Hedia struggled over a fern-covered jumble of what had been a balustrade; instead of true rails, the horizontal piece was supported by a sheet of stone into which pilasters had been carved in high relief. For a moment she saw a nude woman spread-eagled on a slab and a group of men in pale robes standing around her. One of the held a stone hand axe high.

The arm that extended from the robe to hold the axe was not human. Neither, in a flash of better light, were the faces of the robed figures. The image dissolved before the axe fell.

Hedia scrambled on, her face set. She had seen hundreds, probably thousands, of people die in the arena, but she was just as glad to have missed the rest of that scene.

A tree had fallen across the direction she was going. The trunk was more than four feet in diameter, but the wood was rotten. Bright yellow shelf fungi stuck out like fins from the bark, and saplings grew upward every few feet along the bole.

Rather than go around—and probably meet some similar obstacle—Hedia gripped a sapling in either hand and pulled herself onto the log. It wasn't graceful, and the garment Bacchus had clothed her in was irretrievably smeared green. It had not stretched or torn, though; what she thought was sheer silk must be some tougher material.

Beyond the tree was a building: a tower with ornate carvings at each of the three levels she could see. The structure rose higher, but vines completely cloaked the upper reaches.

The ground between the tower and the trunk on which Hedia perched was the usual tumble of sandstone blocks and cloaking vegetation. There were also bits of bronze armor, rusted iron that may once have been weapons, and a human skull barely visible through the leaf litter that filled an upturned helmet.

Hedia paused instead of jumping down as she had intended to do. She could see the equipment of several men, and the remains of many times that number might lie concealed in the undergrowth.

She looked around, then sneered coldly at herself: there was nothing to see but trees, vines, and fallen masonry—just as everywhere else in this ruin. Though it couldn't be called a clearing, the area immediately around the structure wasn't as badly overgrown as most of the region, however.

Hedia slid down from the log and walked toward the tower. The many carved projections at least provided the possibility of climbing high enough that she could see beyond the jungle. It wasn't likely, but she didn't see anything better on offer.

Vines draped the tower, but the structure remained intact, unlike the other buildings, which roots had torn apart. Time had crumbled the door in the center of the ground level—Hedia could see holes in the stone jambs to anchor the hinges—but there was a passageway beyond.

On the threshold was a chest of carved stone. A small sarcophagus, she thought at first glance, but the lid was slightly askew and she caught a glitter from the interior. She walked to it, more from curiosity than for any real purpose.

As best Hedia could tell, *nothing* she could do had any real purpose. Ampelos had tricked her into this business in order to get her away from Bacchus.

Hedia smiled grimly. She had been well and truly fooled, but Ampelos might not be so pleased with his success if she managed to survive and find him again.

She gazed into the corner of the chest and saw polished jewels. She pushed the lid farther open with the scrape of stone on stone, thinking that it might be this corner only. The chest was as full of jewels as a transport urn is of grain coming from Africa. There were rubies, sapphires, and at least one emerald the size of her fist. The gems glowed with rich color even in the jungle's gloom.

Movement flickered. Hedia turned, jumping away from the chest. She did not see a *thing*, but a tunnel in the air behind her fractured into planes as jumbled as the blocks of the fallen buildings.

A figure moved toward her from one plane to the next nearer one, the way a ball bounces among the surfaces of the handball courts at the baths. It was tall. The head was human, but the torso was not. The long upper pair of arms ended in fanged pincers, but there were three tentacle-like pairs lower on the body; the legs squirmed like snakes.

Hedia thought to run along the face of the tower and into the jungle, but that would be pointless. She couldn't have outrun a healthy man through this undergrowth and broken masonry, and this creature's legs rippled like water over the obstacles in its planes of existence.

She climbed over the jewel chest—she couldn't vault it, not as weary as she was—and ran into the corridor beyond. The creature was twelve feet high, taller than the stone ceiling. Hedia hoped to come to a branching too narrow for it to follow, even on hands and, well, legs.

The walls *were* narrowing: they brushed Hedia's arms on both sides, and the ceiling lowered also. She dropped into a crawl. The passage darkened beyond its initial gloom as something followed her into the corridor.

"There's no point in running, Lady Hedia!" a musical tenor voice called. It spoke perfect Latin, the words' only distortion coming from the echoing stone. "There is no way out of the tower except to me. I will be more merciful than starvation."

Hedia didn't answer. She had no reason to believe the pursuing monster. Even if she had, she would let her blood out with her little knife before she surrendered to those pincers.

Ahead of her was a ring of light. It was probably very faint, but she could see it the way she could stars on a dark night.

"Hedia, come back!" the voice called. "You think you see escape, but this passage ends in something far worse than death."

The passage continued to narrow; Hedia crawled with increasing difficulty. She reached out with her right arm to cock her shoulders at an angle. She had almost reached the ring of light.

"Hedia, beyond is only limbo and the Eternals," the voice said in liquid tones. "You will curse yourself to life without existence, for eternity. If you pass the barrier of light, you will not be able to die, but you will never live. Come back while you can, or you will regret it forever."

Hedia squirmed through the ring of light. For an instant she felt a spider-web drape her bare shoulder.

Then there was blackness and Eternity.

VARUS FOLLOWED GOVINDA UP the ladder as quickly as he could, even more glad to be out of the vault than he was curious about what was going on in the sanctum. The outside door was now open.

The king was shouting at the guards clustered there. He pointed at the wall panel that showed the shrine where Bhiku had brought Varus and the officials back to the Waking World. In its background was the jungle-covered ruin that Bhiku had called Dreaming Hill.

After a moment's hesitation, the soldiers shuffled into the little building and jumped *through* the panel as though it were empty air instead of the sheet of alabaster that Varus had seen as they approached. A pair of Tyla followed the soldiers.

Govinda bent to pick up a piece of iron—a lamp, apparently—giving Varus an unobstructed view of the panel for the first time. The soldiers had spread out and were walking toward Dreaming Hill. They weren't moving very quickly, and several of the men waved their curved swords in front of them as though they were brushing away spiderwebs.

"What are they doing?" Varus said, nodding toward the backs of the guards. Presumably if he wished, he could step through into the shrine himself. *I didn't particularly like the place when I was there before.*

Govinda was looking at the iron lamp. He said nothing.

"Are your men going into Dreaming Hill?" Varus said. He was irritated at being ignored and kept in the dark, though he supposed he shouldn't be in a hurry to get to the business Govinda planned for him.

"He could not force his men to enter Dreaming Hill," said the boy hanging by his hair. His voice was clear, but it roused no echoes. It sounded as though he and Varus were standing on top of a mountain. "Even Govinda could not force them to do that. But sometimes men do enter the hill, because it hides great treasure."

"A thief entered my sanctum," Govinda said abruptly. He opened a waist-high basket and set the lamp inside. The basket appeared to be empty. "Either my men will catch and deal with her, or she will go into Dreaming Hill and the hill will deal with her. It's no concern of ours either way."

He gestured to the couch beside the small table and said, "Lie there while I prepare for your journey."

Varus seated himself, then reclined on his left elbow as he would have done at dinner in Carce. He wondered vaguely whether he would ever see Carce again. That wasn't really a concern.

He remembered that he had entered the lens at Polymartium in order to prevent King Govinda from bringing the Republic to ruin. Now that he was here, though, Varus was focused on the things he was learning; which he could not have learned in any other fashion.

Govinda reached into the basket and brought out . . . brought out nothing, so far as Varus could see, though his fingers were curved as though there was something in them. He placed "it" on the table and returned to the basket.

Varus stretched out an index finger, moving it to and then into the air where the king had set the invisible object. Air was all Varus found.

"Are you satisfied?" Govinda said in a sardonic tone. "There is nothing until I bring the ideals to life. There is no other wizard of my power!"

"Go on, then," Varus said. In the back of his mind he saw the Sibyl smiling. She was always with him, whoever or whatever she was. Govinda's boasts did nothing to change reality, and the Sibyl's view of reality obviously differed from that of the king.

Govinda took the black speculum from his tunic and set it on the table, then brought out the tablet. He held the tablet in both hands instead of setting it with the speculum. Glaring at Varus, the king began to chant in Indian or at least in an unfamiliar language.

I wish Bhiku were here, Varus thought. *He could tell me what the king is saying.*

But the little sage *would* be here unless Varus were successful in his task; and Govinda's offhand comment that on this journey "the beggar-sage" would probably fail—and therefore die—had sounded truthful. *Besides, it's knowledge.*

The air above the table grew hazy, then abruptly coalesced into a flat ruby cup and a steel bar the length of Varus' extended arm. Govinda stopped chanting and lowered his hands with the tablet. He hunched slightly and seemed for a moment to have shrunk in on himself. Great wizard the king might be, but the incantation he had just performed was more than a conjuring trick.

Govinda put one hand on the hilt of his curved dagger and took several deep breaths before he raised his eyes and said, "Here are your tools, Westerner. You will drink the juice of the upas tree, then take the speculum and the lever into your hands and lie back. The juice will free you to pass the gate into Anti-Thule."

He gestured toward the wall panel filled with swirling blacks and grays like the smoke of a bitumen fire. The others showed images of scenes that appeared real, though only those of the shrine by Dreaming Hill and the altar at Polymartium were familiar to Varus.

"Well, get on with it," Govinda said sharply.

Varus looked at the king. After a moment, Varus smiled. "I daydream, Master Govinda," he said mildly. "I regret if this inconveniences you."

Varus took the cup in his right hand as he would have done at a drinking party and raised it to his lips. The crystal rim was cool as Varus expected, but the clear fluid was icy. Though tasteless, it made his tongue sting.

He emptied the cup and set it down on the table, then took the pry bar in his right hand and the disk of cannel coal in his left. The steel, as usual for metal, felt cooler than the air around it.

To Varus' surprise the black speculum was as warm as though it had been sitting in the bright Indian sunlight. His fingertips flicked away for a moment, but the disk wasn't hot enough to keep him from holding it normally.

His hands and feet were prickling. He supposed they would go numb shortly. He crossed the pry bar over his belly, still holding it, and put the speculum on his chest. He would have smiled at Govinda, but his lips were frozen in a rictus.

Govinda held out the tablet in his left hand and chanted in counterpoint to the hanging boy. Both voices seemed muffled and began to fade. Varus could not turn his head, but from the corners of his eyes he saw shapes begin to clarify in the panel of swirling blackness.

Varus was very cold. *I wonder if my body is shivering?* He could not tell; he could not feel anything. Govinda drew the dagger from his sash.

The last thing Varus saw in the Waking World was Govinda leaning forward and drawing the edge of his dagger across the throat of the boy. Blood gushed as though from a fountain.

PORTIONS OF THE ROCKY SLOPE were very steep. Corylus used his staff frequently to support him, while Bion depended on his impressive arms and grip to pull himself over obstacles that his relatively feeble legs couldn't have managed on their own.

Aura climbed without effort, never even having to dab a hand down. Corylus had thought of the nymph as slight, which in a manner of speaking she was, but she covered ground with the nonchalant ease of a legionary in light marching order.

Corylus reached a broad ledge, or at any rate a twenty-foot-wide shelf where the slope was gentle enough to hold soil and therefore grass. Bion was struggling below; he had grabbed a bush that came out by the roots instead of holding him.

"Let's take a break," Corylus said. He moved sideways till he was above the sailor, then lay flat and stretched down his staff. Bion grabbed the end gratefully and hauled himself up with Corylus anchoring him.

The sailor flopped onto his back and gave a great sigh. "Give me a rope," he said with his eyes closed, "and I'll climb all day. If I liked rocks, I'd have stayed a goatherd like my old man."

"What are your plans, Bion?" Corylus said. "We're glad to have your company—"

He was, at any rate; Aura probably didn't care.

"—but when we reach the Cave of Zagreus, I hope to return to Carce in the Waking World. Do you want to come with me?"

"I don't know where Carce is," said Bion. He didn't move from where he lay, but he had stiffened. "I want to go back to India, to my wife. I didn't want to leave in the first place, but Nearchos didn't give me a choice. Well, he gave me the choice of helmsman on the *Bird* or pulling an oar on one of the crappy barges the Indians use on the river. We brought some along as lighters."

Bion rolled onto his elbow and opened his eyes. "It was just bad luck," he said. "I'd gotten permission to stay back with my wife. Arrios, the port helmsman, could handle my job at the starboard oar, and he could train up a bosun's mate for his place. But then the day before the supply fleet started downriver Arrios caught a fever and died," *blip!*—

Bion snapped his fingers.

"—and Nearchos came looking for me. The *Bird of the Hydaspes* was one of the ninety-four big ships, and he was going to have a trained helmsman on her. That was all there was to say about it."

Corylus was looking back down the slope they were climbing. It seemed farther than he remembered to the green plains they had left that morning. He thought he saw a herd of goats ridden by dwarfs gamboling on the lower slopes. When a pair faced off on an outcrop long enough for Corylus to get a good look, however, he saw that they were unicorns as big as horses and the riders were apes who looked like men in fur garments.

"Well, I'd married a local woman, a princess I guess," Bion said. "I loved her right enough, and I didn't think anything of it when she said that if we married it'd be us for the rest of our lives. I guess people mostly don't think about that, right? And I'm a sailor. . . . But you see, she really did mean it. And she was a wizard. I'd known that, but I hadn't known how much of a wizard she was. She couldn't stop Nearchos and the king above him, but she bound her soul and mine together the night before the fleet raised anchor."

"I only know of one Nearchos," Corylus said. He didn't believe what he was thinking, but the thought wouldn't go away. "He was the admiral of the fleet Alexander sent to Babylon while he marched his army back from India through the Gedrosian Desert."

"Right, that's Nearchos," Bion said, nodding. "You've heard of him in Carce? That'd please him to learn. He's a vain bastard, but I guess he had to be to take the job on. I heard there's two thousand—that's *thousand*—ships all told."

He laughed. "Not that I can count that high," he said. "It's a lot, anyhow; that much I can see. Well, I could see before Calaia grabbed me."

"She's a sea breeze," said Aura. "I've never met a nice one yet."

"Well, *I'm* glad to be shut of her; that I'll tell you," the sailor said. "We were out to sea; that's a true fact—"

He looked at Corylus. "But say, friend—the king wasn't marching through the desert; there's no food to speak of there. He's coming back along the shore and we'll meet him every night with the supplies. That's what we're doing, you know? We're the supply fleet. Only the winds had been against us the whole two weeks before I was taken, so we had to stand out to sea."

"The winds never did change," Corylus said. "They never do in summer. Nowadays captains use the seasonal winds to go to India and come back when they change, but nobody knew about them in Alexander's day."

Corylus wished Pandareus and Varus were here to hear the helmsman . . . but he wished even more that Bion had stayed back in India as he wanted and none of this had happened. He seemed a decent fellow; not so different from Publius Cispius and the soldiers Corylus had grown up with on the frontiers.

"What do you mean, 'Alexander's day'"? Bion said, sitting bolt upright. "Look, how long has it been since that bitch took me? Just the night before the day you saved me, right?"

"Three hundred and fifty years," Corylus said quietly. He couldn't remember precisely how long it had been before Alexander's death during the 114th Olympiad that the king had left India, not long, though. "A little longer, I suppose."

"Oh, by Fortune!" Bion said. He leaned his face into his hands, then repeated in a whisper, "By Fortune . . ."

"I suppose Calaia brought you here because you would have died in the Waking World," Aura said, considering the matter as a puzzle rather than a tragedy. "She didn't care if you died, but you wouldn't have been much use as a lover if you were dead, would you?"

"I *couldn't* touch her!" Bion said. "Oh, I was willing enough—it'd been two weeks since we sailed, like I said. Nearchos didn't let any women come on board, but they came with the army onshore, you know? We were going to land every couple days, so that was fine for the ones whose women were coming along. And there was plenty of slaves and freelancers besides, for the fellows who hadn't brought their own."

The failure of the fleet to land had been a near disaster for the army. Alexander had marched inland because the desert, though harsh, was better than the coastal strip where there was no drinkable water and no food at all. When Corylus learned about the event as history, he had never thought to wonder what it had meant to the crews manning the ships.

"It was in the middle of the night," Bion said. He'd taken his hands away from his face, but Corylus wasn't sure that the sailor was actually looking back the way they had come. The unicorns and their riders had disappeared. "I was on watch, but it got very still and the corposants were dancing on the mast and rigging. I called to Hermes—he was the captain—because I thought we might be about to get a storm . . . but everybody was asleep, not just Hermes. Everybody but me."

Bion rubbed his forehead with both hands. His fingers were thick as tent pegs, with pads too callused to show wear from the rocks they had recently been gripping.

"I can't believe it's been so long," he muttered. "And for what? It was just a quick tumble for her, but for me . . ."

"Breezes are usually whimsical," Aura said. "It's easier that way."

Her eyes glazed, focusing on the past. "It would be much easier for me," she said in an afterthought.

"There was a little whiffle of wind," Bion said. "It'd been dead still or I maybe wouldn't have noticed it. And there she was standing beside me, Calaia was. She ran her fingers over my shoulders and told me how strong I was, and she riffled my hair."

"You were in the stern?" Corylus said, trying to imagine the scene. He didn't know how big the *Bird of the Hydaspes* had been, but he supposed it was at least three or four hundred tons like the ships from North Africa that brought grain to Carce. A good-sized vessel, certainly.

"Right, standing by the crossbar of the steering oar," said Bion. "I was too surprised to do anything, but then she started to touch me—and it didn't do any good because my wife, you know? She'd fixed me so it wouldn't. And Calaia got mad and just *grabbed* me, and we were here."

He rubbed his head again. "What will she think?" he said. "What will my wife think after all these years?"

"I think we'd best get on," said Corylus, getting to his feet.

He didn't give the obvious answer to Bion's question, because that would be cruel: *Your wife, your new bride, doesn't think anything. She's been dead for centuries.*

"ARE YOU SURE—" Alphena said to the iron face when her second step into the short passage brought nothing but echoes. It was a silly question, it just meant she was nervous, and she *hated* being nervous—

The third step took her out of the urine-smelling enclosure and onto the bank of a stream running quickly enough that the pebbled streambed was distorted by the current. There were clumps of reeds in eddies where an outcrop had deflected the flow, but for the most part the water was clear.

"Yes, I'm sure," said Janus. "I told you that I open things, lady. I close them, also, but that's not what you asked for."

No longer was Alphena's guide the baton in her right hand: Janus was a man-sized figure standing beside her with what was probably meant for a sardonic smile. The iron's crude workmanship didn't improve from becoming larger. He had arms and legs, but they were just as coarsely modeled as the head of the original had been.

"Thank you," said Alphena. Hedia had repeatedly told her that courtesy even to social inferiors—and almost anyone was socially inferior to the daughter of Senator Gaius Alphenus Saxa—often reaped benefits. At worst she might be thought of as harmlessly eccentric by her noble acquaintances.

Hedia didn't have to tell her daughter that simple courtesy would not make her appear weak. No one who knew Lady Hedia thought of her as weak.

Alphena dropped the borrowed cape and belted on the sword it had concealed. Lenatus carried an infantry weapon instead of the horseman's longer spatha that Corylus preferred. The shorter blade was both more familiar to Alphena and better suited to her height and short arms.

"Will I need the cape?" she asked her guide.

"We're going a quarter mile up the stream," said Janus, pointing. She had the impression that the figure would have shrugged if he had been able to. "Whatever you wish."

"Let's go," Alphena said, then reached back and snatched up the cape. She strode swiftly forward, forcing herself not to look at Janus. She knew she was dithering, but no one had a right to complain if it didn't slow her down!

A pair of gossamer female figures, suggestions in the air rather than forms, drifted from the rocks ahead. They joined hands and swirled in a dance as light as spider silk in a sunbeam. They each opened a hand to Alphena as she approached, but she hugged herself closer and pretended not to notice them.

"Who were they?" she said in a soft voice to Janus as they passed on.

"Thoughts, perhaps," said Janus. "Not my thoughts."

They were my thoughts, Alphena realized. Then, *I'm nervous because I'm going to see Corylus again.*

She laughed and stood straighter as she walked toward Publius Corylus. *I've faced demons; I've faced monsters. I can face Corylus, and I can face the fact that I love him.*

Aloud Alphena said, "You said Mamurcus made you in Anti-Thule. Is that in Italy, or is it farther away?"

Janus turned his iron face toward her. She noticed that though he appeared to be walking normally, his legs didn't disturb the sedges through which they seemed to move.

"Pandareus is not *your* teacher, is he?" Janus said.

"No, of course not," Alphena said sharply. The question itself was neutral, but she could feel mockery behind it. "I'm a woman; I don't learn rhetoric. Master Pandareus teaches my brother. And Corylus, among others."

"Ah," said Janus. "Well, Pandareus said that I should not discount your resources, Your Ladyship. According to geographers Thule is a place far to the north, near the axis on which the world turns. Anti-Thule is therefore near the southern axis. Only philosophers talk of Anti-Thule in this day, for no one alive has been there."

His caricature of a face smiled. "I am not alive, but I have been to Anti-Thule," he said. "Mamurcus made me there."

"How did you get to Sentius' garden?" Alphena said. A year ago she wouldn't have cared, let alone asked, but now she was thinking about what Pandareus and Varus would want to know, and Corylus would want to know also.

"Sentius is a dabbler, a fool," said her guide. "He gathered all manner of magical paraphernalia and told himself that he was a wizard. Faugh! It was like you claiming to be a savant!"

"Which I do not do," Alphena said deliberately. "Though I know savants, my brother included."

She smiled at Janus and said, "You are a very insolent lump of iron, Master Janus. But one must make allowances for your rustic upbringing, I suppose."

After a moment's delay, Janus burst into laughter like an armload of swords falling down a stone staircase. It was a more musical sound than Alphena would have guessed he would make.

"You are correct, Lady Alphena," Janus said. "And Master Pandareus was correct. But I was saying that Sentius collected objects he was told were magical. Because he was ignorant, he didn't understand what he had. A load of things taken from the collection of Marcus Herennius got stored in a gardeners' shed here at the villa, myself included; and before it was found, an undergardener had used me to mark a row of chickpeas."

He gave a metallic cough. "It was not a prestigious position," he said, "but I like to think that I gave loyal service in it."

"I'm glad you were where Master Pandareus could find you," Alphena said. The statement was true, but she had made it because Hedia was teaching her to say positive things to the people she had to deal with whenever possible.

"I hope we find my mother soon," she blurted, simply because the thought had struck her so forcibly. "Thank you for helping me, L . . . Lord Janus. Even if you don't want me to call you that."

"I believe I had pretty thoroughly explored the nuances of marking chickpeas," her guide said. "I was ready for new challenges."

Alphena giggled. "I think you're really well suited to Pandareus," she said. "I'm sure you were better as a garden marker than he would have been, however."

Janus clanged a laugh again, then said, "I open ways and close them, lady. I don't know anything about causes or results . . . but you were fortunate that Lady Rupa did not notice me when she came to Sentius, because she would have known how to use me."

"What is Rupa doing with Sentius?" Alphena said. "Minimus from Mother's escort said that Rupa made the light that Bacchus came through."

A pair of frogs watched as Alphena and her guide approached. They suddenly shot straight up. They vanished higher into the sky than Alphena's eyes could follow.

"Ampelos, not Bacchus," said Janus tartly. "But you weren't to know, so I shouldn't have mentioned it. I don't have any idea what Rupa intends, but Sentius is no more to her than one of your slaves is to you. She uses his villa and his wealth for her own purposes, whatever those purposes may be."

Alphena remembered the imperious woman she had faced in Sentius' garden. Rupa hadn't made her flinch, but Alphena remembered the fear that had knotted her belly as Rupa reached toward her.

She grinned and added aloud, "I remember the way Rupa fell back when she tried to touch me too."

"The Godspeaker's ear threw her back," Janus said with a note of gloom. "If you hadn't had that, well . . . Mamurcus himself would have had his hands full with Lady Rupa, and Mamurcus was a great wizard."

After another jangle of laughter, Janus said, "Mamurcus made *me*, after all. And he had wit enough to bring what was left of the Godspeaker with him when he fled Anti-Thule after the disaster."

"What about the Tyla?" Alphena said. "They were in Anti-Thule too, weren't they? Did they come here with Mamurcus?"

"He brought only me and the Godspeaker's ear," said Janus. "No, I tell a lie, because he had another bit of the meteor that brought the Blight. He forged it into the case for the ear, what you wear around your neck. Anti-Thule wasn't a place to stand about looking for loot, let me tell you."

His iron lips pursed and he went on, "The Indian wizard may have taken the Tyla magicians with him back to India, but I don't think so. He was trying to free the Godspeaker's tablet from under a stone, the last I saw him. Mamurcus was running to the portal to come home."

"How did Rupa get her Tyla servants, then?" Alphena said. She lifted the borrowed sword to see how it moved in its scabbard. Quite well, she was pleased to find; Lenatus must have kept the lip smooth with beeswax.

"A wizard, a very great wizard, might go back to Anti-Thule after the disaster," her guide said. "The Tyla priests would be glad to return with him, for they couldn't have gotten through the portal by themselves. It would be dangerous—for the wizard, I mean. He—or she—would have to be very powerful. Lady Rupa *is* that powerful."

Alphena paused to look at the bird that was standing on an island in the middle of the stream. It looked like an ordinary kingfisher with a blue back and russet belly, but—

"It's twenty feet tall!" she said.

"Umm," said the figure of Janus. "Thirty at least if it stands normally, I believe. It's squatting now, because I think it's getting ready to dive."

The bird's head turned very slightly. Its eyes were on the sides of its head, so it wouldn't really have had to move to watch Alphena, but it was being cautious.

She was reminded of fights in the arena. Ordinarily when there were multiple gladiators on the sand at the same time, they dueled in pairs. Occasionally, however, a man who had quickly defeated his opponent would help a friend who was being hard-pressed. Fighters always kept an eye out, just in case.

"How deep is the water there?" Alphena asked as she drew her sword. She resumed her course along the bank, but she kept her torso cocked toward the kingfisher and let her peripheral vision keep her on the path.

"It would be over your head, lady," said Janus. "If you like, I can find a ford upstream that will take you to a rock from which you might be able to wade down to this one. But why would you want to?"

"I just want to know what my choices are if the bird—" Alphena said. As she spoke, the kingfisher launched itself into the air and plunged down into the stream. The water sprayed into diamonds in the sunlight. Moments later the bird shot upward to perch again on the islet with a fish crossways in its beak.

A *catfish*, Alphena thought, *a very big one.*

The kingfisher tossed the fish in the air and caught it headfirst in its open beak. In the instants before the fish vanished wriggling down the bird's throat, Alphena saw that it had the head of a man.

"That was Sentius!" Alphena said. "That was the senator who's helping Rupa!"

"So it seems," said her guide. "I would guess that he didn't expect to be used in quite that fashion, though. She needed a gift to pay her way into the Otherworld, and your Sentius was close at hand."

They were past the rock where the kingfisher perched. Alphena glanced over her shoulder and saw the bird watching motionless. Its beak was as thick and cruel as the prow of a warship.

"The bird brought Rupa here?" Alphena said. She wanted to continue watching the kingfisher, but that would be undignified, and she would probably trip or fall into the water besides.

"I doubt it," Janus said. The iron man didn't bother to turn his head as he walked, but Alphena already knew that the figure she saw wasn't really a material being. "Someone, something, did, anyhow. Rupa would have had a much easier time of it if she had used me the way you did."

He grinned at her. "You find ways to manage things, don't you, lady?" he said. "That's what the teacher meant. You don't look like much, but things work for you."

I haven't been eaten by a kingfisher, anyway, Alphena thought. Other than that, things didn't seem to be working particularly well at the moment.

Aloud she said, "Why does Rupa want to be here anyway? What's she doing, if she isn't helping Sentius?"

Alphena remembered the woman's cold eyes as she reached toward her in the garden. She touched her tunic, pressing the amulet firmly against her chest.

"Rupa intends to bring Bacchus back to the West," said Janus nonchalantly. "A western empire brought her soul mate to her but then took him away despite her magic. She thinks the reign of Bacchus will churn the West to chaos, and that would be so were it not for the Blight. Rupa cares nothing about the Blight, but her actions will open the world to it."

"I won't let her," Alphena said, touching her sword again and jerking her fingers away when she realized what she was doing. "We won't let her."

But how will we stop her?

Aloud Alphena said, "But the Blight would kill her too. Wouldn't it?"

"Rupa doesn't care," said Janus. "The Blight cannot invade the Otherworld, but I'm not sure Rupa will bother returning here after the Blight is loosed. She lives for her revenge, and she will have it."

His calm certainty was more chilling to Alphena than screaming panic would have been. She could not get the vision of the world covered in bubbling black filth out of her mind. It stuck to her thoughts and fouled them.

"I shouldn't care, either . . . ," said the figure of iron. Alphena heard an undertone of sadness in his voice, but she knew she might have invented that because she was herself so desperately sad at the thought. "The Blight won't affect me, after all. But when the Blight covers everything in the Waking World there will be no ways to open and no one to open them."

He looked at Alphena. "I will miss you humans," he said.

"I'll be dead before that happens," Alphena said. In another mood she would have made that a boast. In her present bleakness it was closer to being a prayer.

VARUS WAS VERY COLD as he walked the corridors of a library, a wonderful library. Baskets of scrolls stood shoulder to shoulder on the floors. On marble shelves above the baskets were codices bound in wood, leather, and a variety of other materials.

A line of palm leaves, bound at one edge and written in cuttlefish ink, had no covers at all. Varus glanced at them as he passed. They were in Sanskrit, a language that his waking eyes wouldn't have been able even to identify. *Thou shalt do the deed and abide it, and sit on thy high throne . . .* , he read from a random glimpse as he passed by. He wondered how he he could understand the words.

A old man, bald and bent over, was walking beside Varus. He was naked, wizened, and as brown as an acorn. He seemed vaguely familiar.

How long has he been there? Varus thought. Aloud he said, "I am Gaius Varus. Who are you, sir?"

The old man laughed like crickets chirping. "I have no name," he said. "Not one that anybody remembers. *I* don't remember it."

"I recognize your voice," Varus said. "You're Govinda's ancestor. You live in his speculum. I saw you when you came to Raguram's palace and helped him to find me."

"Govinda holds me in the speculum," said the ancestor, "but I do not live anywhere. Except perhaps now with you as we travel to Anti-Thule on Govinda's business."

Varus looked at the pry bar in his right hand. He had been holding the speculum also, but his left hand was empty.

"That's why I'm cold," he said. "I drank the poison. Am I dead?"

The ancestor laughed. "Not now," he said. "You are alive and I am alive. If we succeed you will return and re-inhabit your body, but I will be a spirit in a disk of cannel coal. If we fail, we will both die utterly, body and spirit together."

Varus did not reply. He considered the situation. He wasn't afraid of dying—oblivion was a cessation of human emotions, fear of course included—but under the present circumstances it would suggest that he had been defeated by Govinda.

I should be enough of a philosopher not to care about that, either, he thought. He smiled. *Perhaps after I have crushed Govinda I will become more enlightened.*

As in a normal library, short pillars at regular intervals supported busts of philosophers. Though they were not labeled, Varus recognized each face at which he happened to glance, even those when—as with ben Adhem, Kropotkin, and scores of others—his conscious self had never heard of the man.

"Even if I die . . . ," he said to the ancestor, "I will have learned a great deal by this experience. I suppose it's worthwhile either way."

The old Indian looked at him with a sneer. "Govinda has chosen a madman to carry out his errand," the ancestor said. "A powerful madman, though."

He cackled and added, "Perhaps more powerful than Govinda realizes. Govinda is sane, so greed for wealth and power blinds him to the risk. He thinks he shields himself by sending you and me back to Anti-Thule instead of going himself, but the Blight is not his only danger."

On both sides of the corridor, the wall above the shelf of ranked codices was painted with scenes of Anti-Thule. When Varus concentrated on the decorations, he saw that the figures moved. The center of the panorama was always the white-furred Tylon wizard, the Godspeaker, but in many he was flanked by a pair of humans. The swarthy man in a cotton tunic must be the ancestor.

"Why were you on Anti-Thule?" Varus said. He had other questions, but that was the basic one.

"The Godspeaker took me," the ancestor said. "He had the power of the tablet which he brought from beneath the northern glaciers. It made him greater than me and greater than Mamurcus, the Etruscan wizard whom he took also. We were to help him against the Blight, but the Blight was stronger even than we three combined."

"Does Govinda think he can defeat the Blight if he has the complete tablet?" Varus asked.

His lips were dry. He had seen images of the spreading foulness. The discussion reminded him that he was going to the place where the Blight was. *I'm not afraid of death, but I'm afraid of dying that way.*

"The Blight was scoured in the catastrophe," the ancestor said, "and Govinda cares for nothing but his own wealth and power anyway. When the tablet was broken, I fled home with half. I was a great king while I lived and my descendents were great kings. Govinda thinks to become the greatest yet, the greatest king of all time, but he cannot do that while Bacchus reigns in India."

"When we bring Govinda the remainder of the tablet . . . ," Varus said, "will he use it to drive Bacchus out of India?"

Varus smiled faintly at his presumption in believing that he would succeed, but he *did* assume that. Anyway, there was no point in assuming he would shortly—and perhaps horribly—die.

The ancestor laughed. "Bacchus is a god," he said. "How can a magician, any magician, stand against a god? But Govinda will open a route to Italy, and Ampelos will lead the god his lover there for the sake of Ampelos' own honor. Or so Govinda and Ampelos think in their pride."

Ahead of the ancestor and Varus the corridor seemed to end in a doorway filled with cold gray light. "Is that Anti-Thule?" Varus said.

"That is Anti-Thule," agreed the ancestor. "That is our destiny."

He laughed. He was still laughing when he and Varus stepped into the windswept ruins of Anti-Thule. The sun was low on the horizon, and the cold was like nothing Varus had ever felt.

HEDIA WAS ADRIFT IN TIME. She had no physical being; there *was* no physical being. There was no duration. There was only a present that encompassed all past and all future.

Many people thought of me as only a body, she thought. *A very supple, willing body.* The humor of the situation would have made her smile if she had had physical presence.

Hedia's whole life was before her in minutest detail. She viewed it as though she were picking up each grain of sand on a beach, examining it, and going on to the next.

There were no surprises. It was because Hedia was self-aware that she had made so few concessions to society and its rules. Someone who saw herself and her world less clearly would have tried harder to fit in . . . and would have failed.

Hedia had made mistakes—thousands of mistakes—over the years. Fewer as she gained knowledge and experience, but—she would have smiled again—much worse ones as time went on also.

Hedia didn't regret even the bad ones, the mistakes that could have killed her. She had learned from each one. *If I hadn't done that, I would have done something worse later. I survived, and another time I might not have been so lucky.*

When she was fourteen, she had found herself alone with a colleague of her father—alone in the sense that the score of others present were slaves who couldn't and wouldn't give evidence against a senator. Most of them had been his slaves besides, though that didn't matter.

Her mistake had been in trying to fight. The senator had beaten her unconscious—and might well have killed her—and then had his way. Hedia had no virtue to lose even at fourteen.

A month later the senator had visited again in response to a note saying that Hedia couldn't forget him and that her body was raging for his touch. She thought he might have too much sense than to believe her, but men are arrogant and the senator was rather more so than most.

Hedia had smiled as she knelt before him and lifted the hem of his tunic. He screamed a moment later as she jumped to her feet. She spat his member onto the mosaic floor and slipped from the room while her outside escort waited grinning in the doorway to deal with any of the senator's servants who might try to follow.

The victim himself wasn't running after anyone.

Fighting the first time had been a mistake, but Hedia had learned from it.

There was other existence in Eternity: Hedia felt glowing, pulsing hunger.

She examined the hunger as she did her life, facet by identical facet. At the core of it she found the tiny savage mind of a spider. She remembered the brush of a web across her shoulders as she plunged from the Waking World into this.

Its life is nothing but hunger, she mused.

"ARE YOU SO VERY DIFFERENT, HEDIA?" said a presence in this limbo. Like the spider, like Hedia, the presence *was* but had no separate being.

Hedia tried to examine the presence as she had the spider's hunger. Instead of separate instants like grains of sand, this was Eternal and all encompassing—drops of water in an ocean, infinitely mixing and changing.

"Who are you?" Hedia said/thought. "What are you?"

"WE ARE ETERNAL," said the presence. "WE ARE CONNECTIONS. WE ARE ALL THE CONNECTIONS BUT ONE, AND WE CHOSE TO REMOVE OURSELVES FROM THE COSMOS BEFORE WE BECAME THAT CONNECTION ALSO AND THE COSMOS ENDED."

There was no duration. All time was one time. Hedia *was* and the spider *was* and the Eternals *were*.

"You were trapped here?" Hedia said. *As I am,* she thought, but thought was all existence in Eternity.

"WE ARE NOT TRAPPED," the Eternals said. "WE HAVE WITHDRAWN OUR-SELVES FROM THE COSMOS SO THAT WE WILL NOT DESTROY THE COSMOS. WE CANNOT LEAVE THIS EXISTENCE AND NO ONE CAN JOIN US HERE."

The laughter was cool and, like everything else in this limbo, all encompassing.

"YOU HAVE JOINED US," the Eternals said, "AND YOU HAVE BROUGHT A SPIDER."

"There must be a way out," said Hedia. She was not afraid—there could be no fear or other emotion here—but she had grown up as a woman in a world of powerful men. She always looked for the way out, the way around. There had *always* been a way out.

"WE CREATED A PLACE WHICH WE COULD NOT LEAVE, HEDIA," the Eternals said. "IF YOUR MIND SEES A CONNECTION THAT WE COULD NOT, YOU WILL BE ABLE TO LEAVE."

The cool laughter filled Hedia's existence. Eternally.

CHAPTER XV

Hedia existed.
None of the details—brightness, a crackle like lightning dancing along a water pipe, the ground pitching—mattered compared to the fact that she had a physical body and she controlled it.

She stood on a flagstone plaza facing scores of Tyla with headdresses, each decorated with a pair of long black feathers. In the center, on the lowest step of a round temple, was the white-furred Godspeaker. He held up in both hands a soapstone tablet. All that was familiar to Hedia from the scenes the Spring of True Answers had showed her.

Flanking the Godspeaker but standing just beyond the temple steps were two humans: an Indian clad in cotton and a squat, powerful man in a wool tunic with his hair bound with a fillet. The latter looked like an Italian countryman, but he had the presence of someone used to being obeyed.

The streets beyond the temple were packed with watching Tyla, some of them carrying their offspring in pouches that were part of their belly fur. Their faces were taut with fear; that was obvious even on features so unhuman.

In the distance, beyond the last of the flimsy houses, the air steamed. A fish the size of a warship lifted itself on its fins and flopped forward. One of its barbels had curled about a Tylon; in the instant Hedia watched, the barbel swung its victim into the flat mouth. In the low sun, the smooth skin of the fish gleamed like pus.

What am I doing here? Why am I anywhere?

Hedia wore the clothing in which she had run into the jungle. No one, neither the Tyla nor even the two other humans, seemed to notice her. They were looking at—

There was a flash so bright that the thunder accompanying it went unheard.

The Eternals hung in the air above the plaza. They were not made of light; rather, they were a complete absence of color or density. They filled the sky or replaced it, and they had no shape or limit.

The Godspeaker threw up his hands and shouted, putting the soapstone tablet between him and the presence. A prismatic cone enveloped him. The tablet dropped and bounced when the hands holding it vanished in drifting dust motes like the rest of the Tylon.

The human wizards dodged away from the destruction. The Tyla priests either fell to their knees or tried to flee, though the packed spectators blocked them.

The rainbow light sprang from the crater, bathing the swelling ulcer. Stones and white-hot iron erupted like balls of lava from Vesuvius to fall as burning hail. Fires burst out all over the community. Tyla screamed even louder.

A blob of iron the size of a fist struck in front of Hedia and splashed over the cobblestones; a tiny fleck touched the back of her wrist like a hot needle. She would have a blister the size of her thumbnail tomorrow—if she was alive, if there was a tomorrow.

Water that had seeped to fill the bowl now flashed into steam, popping and sparkling. It mounted in a mile-high column before spreading like a thunderhead. Snow and swirling ice crystals drifted back to earth.

As suddenly as they had appeared, the Eternals vanished with a crash. It knocked Hedia to the ground. Houses lifted off their foundations and slammed back awry.

Moments later an icy wind struck the community from all directions, tearing apart the dwellings and throwing down those Tyla who were still on their feet. Hedia had planted her hands to lift herself; she flattened till the initial blast spent itself. Shreds of paper houses lifted in circles above the plaza where the winds had met.

The Temple of the Moon toppled forward, breaking apart even before it hit the ground. It had probably been falling since the shock of the Eternals' departure, but its weight had made the process ponderously slow compared to the rush of the wind. It covered the place where the Godspeaker had stood.

The blocks tumbled outward, one of them landing on the soapstone tablet and breaking it in half. The outer portion flipped into the air. Before it could hit the ground again, the Indian wizard caught it. He ran past Hedia in a crouch, the tablet clutched to his chest and his face set in a rictus.

She turned her head and saw a rosy disk like the one that she had entered at Polymartium. She didn't know what was on the other side this time, but it probably wasn't Anti-Thule. That was good enough.

Hedia scuttled half the distance on all fours before she got her feet properly under her. As she dived toward the glow she looked back. The remaining human wizard snatched something from the cobblestones: the pointed ear clipped off when the rush of fire destroyed the rest of the Godspeaker.

Then Hedia was through the portal.

CORYLUS PEERED THROUGH THE SPARSE foliage of a myrtle bush toward the entrance of the cave a hundred feet away. The dragons chained there were curled on the barren ground.

"They're breathing!" said Bion, crouching beside him. The bush wasn't big enough to hide two men, but the dragons seemed as somnolent as the cliff face. "They're not dead!"

And why in the name of Hercules would you think they might *be dead?* Corylus thought. Though clearly the sailor must have extremely sharp eyes to detect the rise and fall of the beasts' chests, if that was what he had done.

Aura stepped out around them without even pretending to try to conceal herself. "Publius Corylus, I promised to bring you to the Cave of Zagreus. Have I carried out my promise?"

Well, I won't know that until I enter the cave, Corylus thought. But that was thinking as a student of logic, and right now he needed to think like a Batavian Scout.

"Yes," he said. "Thank you, Aura. You've done as you promised and . . . well, you can do whatever you please now. I have no claim on you."

"I have nothing to do, nowhere to go," the sprite said. Her expression was calm, her voice lilting but emotionless. "If you permit, I will stay with you until you leave or are killed."

Corylus kept his face still, but there was a moment's hesitation before he said, "Yes, you're welcome to stay with us."

She was just viewing the situation clearly, after all. The way a Scout would, though another Scout might not have blurted his analysis so baldly. *Everybody knows what the risks are, but we don't ordinarily dwell on them aloud.*

Because the dragons were curled Corylus couldn't be sure how long they were, but probably about twenty feet. Their bodies were covered with blue scales, iridescent for the most part but marked with bands of duller gray-blue at intervals.

Their wings, four each, were sheets of ridged transparency like those of dragonflies, sticking out at right angles to their bodies from sockets on their shoulders. The creatures were much larger than any bird Corylus could imagine. Though slender as otters, they must weigh at least a thousand pounds each: as much as cows.

Bion stood, lacing his fingers behind his back and stretching his powerful shoulder muscles. "Well, what do we do now, Captain?" he said.

Corylus looked at the sailor. He didn't snarl, because that would have been just as pointless as the *stupid, pointless* question. *If I knew what to do, I wouldn't be standing here like a dock piling!*

"Aura?" Corylus said, letting amusement wash over his frustration. He spoke quietly, but he didn't whisper. "Do you know why the dragons are sleeping?"

Aura shrugged. "They were awake when Zetes and I saw them before," she said. "They walked to the end of their chains and then walked back. You see how the ground is worn."

Corylus started to ask, "The passage to the Waking World is through the cave?" but he swallowed the words. Aura had said so in the past; he didn't need to hear it again. He was only looking for a way to delay what he knew had to be done.

"All right," he said. "Bion and Aura, I won't need your help further."
There's no help they can give.

"I'm going to go between the dragons and into the cave. If you want to follow after I've gotten through, you're welcome to do so, but wait until I'm clear."

Bion blinked and said, "What if they wake up?"

He may have been a very good helmsman, Corylus thought, *but he must have been a trial to his captains. I've never known a man with such a genius for uncomfortable questions that can't be answered.*

"I'll deal with the situation as it arises," said Corylus, attempting—rather successfully, he thought—a lofty unconcern. He wondered how often his father had given a similar answer to similar questions.

And he came home wealthy and with a knighthood, Corylus thought. And smiled and thought, *But most of the men who'd enlisted with him left their bones on the frontiers.*

Corylus twitched his dagger in its sheath—needlessly; the orichalc didn't bind—and shrugged his shoulders. Holding his staff at the balance in his right hand, he walked toward the cave and its guardians.

The dragons didn't move, though as Corylus approached he thought he heard a burring sound like that from the interior of a beehive. The creatures had six legs, short compared to the size of their bodies but still as long as a man's. Rather than being retracted, the claws on the three-toed feet were drawn upwards to keep them from being worn blunt when they weren't needed to rend prey.

Corylus reached the dragons, holding his breath. He didn't think breathing was going to awaken them if the sound of his sandals didn't, but it was *something* to do.

He smiled and let out his breath softly. He had every right to be frightened; but it wouldn't do any good, so he wouldn't give in to it.

The dragons were curled three feet apart, plenty of room to walk between. To Corylus' surprise, their bodies radiated warmth. Their heads were sharply triangular, more like that of a praying mantis than a snake. The silvery links of the chains attached to the neck collars rang in faint counterpoint to the burring from their torsos.

Corylus walked past the dragons and to the cave mouth. They could still turn and follow him in to the length of their chains, but the pressure that had been squeezing his chest released him.

He heard a jingle and looked over his shoulder, missing a step. The dragons had gotten up and were stretching. One of them turned its head to look at him, but they seemed no more interested than a pair of doves watching from the roof of their cote.

Nobody is coming by that way to rescue me. Corylus allowed the thought to bubble out as laughter. Nothing had changed, after all.

The cave was circular in cross section, like a section of water pipe. There were no chisel gouges or marks from casting forms.

Something hung in the air before Corylus, shimmering without solidity. He paused, frowning, then walked forward. Perhaps it was what he had come to find.

It was a circular mirror, hovering at the height of Corylus' face. He saw himself in it, perfect in reduced detail.

There was a flash. Corylus could not move. He was looking toward the entrance of the cave. The huge figure of Rupa walked toward him.

"I have been waiting for you, Publius Corylus," she said, and reached out. There was no contact, but his viewpoint moved toward the entrance. "Soon your lover will arrive. In return for your release she will give me the God-speaker's ear and I will finally be able to take my vengeance on the West. If she does not—"

Corylus was shifted to look into Rupa's magnified face. *She's holding me in her hand.*

"—then you will spend eternity in this mirror."

VARUS AND THE NAKED OLD MAN stepped into windswept ruins and bitter cold. It was bright though the sun was low on the horizon, but the sky was the pale white of watered milk. The sea was behind them, and in all other directions ice glittered on the horizon.

The ancestor looked about. He didn't seem to feel the cold.

Govinda must have sent us back not too long after the time I fled, he said. *The houses had been thrown down, but the wind hadn't started to pull the sides off the frames.*

Varus heard the ancestor speaking Greek. He had a pronounced Ionic accent quite different from the Athenian dialect spoken by orators, but the "words" rang in Varus' mind rather than coming through his ears anyway. The old man had a material body here in Anti-Thule: his feet crunched on the gravel of the shore.

They stood at the edge of the community in the center of the green enclave that Varus had seen in visions, but the houses were bare sticks to which the paper walls and roofs hung in shreds. The few freestanding monuments had toppled, and stone foundations were gapped and crooked.

"Did the meteor knock everything down when it brought the Blight?" Varus asked.

He shivered despite his tunic and the sandals that kept his soles off the cold ground, but he didn't expect to have another opportunity to learn about Anti-Thule. Varus might not survive more than an eyeblink after he returned to Govinda's palace—the king certainly didn't wish him well—but that was no reason not to gain as much knowledge as he could in the time remaining.

No, said the ancestor. *When the Godspeaker brought me to help him, the houses had been repaired. It was a ball of iron, not a rock, and sparks from it started fires before they cooled. I could still smell the sour smoke, but the houses had been rebuilt.*

The ancestor started into the ruined city, going toward where the Temple of the Moon had stood in the visions beneath Govinda's sanctum. Varus paused, then bent and picked up the object that had caught his eye.

It was a long bone, probably a thigh. If Varus had found it on a street in Carce, he would have guessed it was a goat's. Here it must have been from a Tylon. One end had been gnawed off.

I don't know what happened to the Tyla, the ancestor said; he too had paused and was looking back. *Without the Godspeaker there was nothing to stop the cold. I suppose the cold killed them, that and the crops dying.*

The green fields of Govinda's vision were now gray smears on the ground. Freezing had burst the internal structures of whatever plants the Tyla grew for food, not only killing them but also turning them to jelly. The Tyla themselves could not have been much better able to accept the sudden chill.

Varus tossed the bone down. He had noticed furry shadows skittering among the fallen houses. Anti-Thule had mice or things like mice. They remained to scavenge the bodies of the Tyla who had died of exposure, but the mice would die also. The cold was bitter under the long summer sun; when winter came, the ice would cover all of what now was bare ground.

"What happened to the Godspeaker?" Varus asked as he and the ancestor picked their way through the shattered community. The house frames were jumbled like storm wrack on the shore. "Did the Blight kill him?"

The Godspeaker could not stop the Blight, even with Mamurcus and me beside him, the ancestor said. *He knew of a greater power, though, a power greater than all others on earth in all times, that of the eternal beings who created the tablet. The Godspeaker determined to raise the Eternals against the Blight.*

Though the ancestor did not seem to feel cold, his body had normal physical limitations. He paused, then walked around a tangle of frames so twisted that portions of the paper covering remained attached. Varus thought he saw a Tylon's withered body cocooned inside, but he didn't bother to examine it more closely.

The Tomb of the Eternals is near where I was born, the ancestor said. *It was in an ancient ruin called Dreaming Hill. Even sealed it was a vast reservoir of power, and I used that power to grow great. The Godspeaker opened a passage to the tomb in Dreaming Hill and unsealed it.*

The ancestor and Varus had reached the plaza. Debris had blown onto the stone pavement, but the surface was clear of ruined dwellings. Across from them was the fallen Temple of the Moon.

The Priests of the Moon had little power individually, but there were forty of them, the ancestor said as he and Varus walked toward the temple. *The Italian Mamurcus was a great wizard. He had forged an image of his god of openings from metal of the ball which brought the Blight here. I was greater yet, and the Godspeaker with his tablet was a greater wizard than anyone else of his race or mine could be. Together we succeeded in opening the tomb.*

He stopped and brought his left arm around in a sweeping gesture, indicating the devastation. *We succeeded in doing this. We roused the Eternals from their rest to do the Godspeaker's bidding. The Eternals scoured the Blight away with a flame that pierced the sky. And then the flame washed over the Godspeaker, all but his right ear.*

Varus shivered. It was the cold, or at least most of it was the cold. "What happened to the Eternals?" he said. "Are they still . . . ?"

He looked around. For the Eternals, he supposed, but he didn't know what they would look like if he saw them. Everything seemed the same as it had been when he saw Anti-Thule for the first time, but it was so chaotic that he couldn't be sure.

You needn't be afraid of the Eternals, said the ancestor. His mouth quirked into what was probably a smile. *They returned to their tomb as soon as they had destroyed the one who had awakened them.*

"How did you get to India?" Varus said. He spoke slowly, because his mind was occupied in trying to fathom the destruction around him. The ancestor had referred to the event as "the catastrophe." There was no better description of what had happened to Anti-Thule.

I found the half tablet that was free and went back to my home, the ancestor said. *The passage the Godspeaker had opened remained. I saw Mamurcus taking the Godspeaker's ear.*

"What use is the ear?" Varus said.

The ancestor shrugged. *I don't know,* he said, *but Mamurcus was a great wizard. And the Godspeaker was greater yet, even without the tablet.*

Varus was still shivering. "All right, there's the temple," he said. "Let's get the rest of the tablet and go back."

He strode forward. The ancestor walked at his side, but without the assurance of moments before.

What do you suppose Govinda, my descendent, will do when you return? the ancestor said. *He will kill you, will he not?*

"I don't know," Varus said, considering the pry bar as a weapon for a moment. "He may try. I suppose he will."

Varus looked at the older man and said, "I know that I don't want to remain here. I would certainly freeze if I did."

If I return . . . , the ancestor said, *I will not die, because I died a thousand years ago. I will again become a shadow in a speculum, a slave to my descendent who will live forever through the power of the rejoined tablet.*

"I'm sorry," said Varus. "I'm not going to stay here. I'll take my chances with Govinda."

With the Sibyl's help, Varus wasn't afraid of Govinda. He smiled wryly. *I am a citizen of Carce. I'm not afraid of any benighted barbarian, whatever airs he may give himself.*

Varus was joking . . . but not really. Not at the core.

The temple had been carved from stone so dark that it could pass for black in the lighter grays of its surroundings. Varus remembered bright-colored clothing and the patterned coverings of the houses in the visions of Anti-Thule. These ruins had been bleached monochrome by weather or the catastrophe itself.

The tablet wasn't visible, but one of the blocks of the pediment was a finger's breadth off the ground. He knelt and peered; he could see the rectangular outline of the tablet. It had cracked just back from the edge of the block that had fallen on it.

What if the remainder of the tablet shattered instead of just breaking in half? But that was a problem for another time.

Varus slid the tapered end of the bar under the block and lifted; the stone pavement provided a solid fulcrum. It wasn't nearly as difficult to raise the block as he had feared. He squatted and reached out with his left hand to feel for the tablet.

A serpent squirmed from beneath the piece of pediment and raised its wedge head with a hiss. Its fangs were over an inch long.

"Waugh!" Varus said, jumping away; he sprawled on his back. The pry bar clanged when he let go of it, dropping the block.

What are you doing? said the ancestor, looking from the stone to Varus.

"The snake!" Varus said. He pointed. The snake's head wove back and forth, and the fangs dripped pale amber poison. "Don't you see the snake?"

There's no snake here! said the ancestor. His expression changed, hardened. He grasped the end of the pry bar and lifted the block again, then reached under and snatched out the half tablet.

The snake vanished like a mist at sunrise. For an instant Varus thought he saw the face of the girl whom he and Bhiku had saved from the villagers who wanted to burn her alive as a serpent-demon; then she was gone also, leaving only the memory of her smile.

I have it! the ancestor cried, holding up the tablet. The only damage was the rough edge where the original had been cracked in half. *My descendent cannot draw me back so long as I have this. I can live* here *forever!*

Varus saw the black splotch on the tablet. "Put it down!" he said. He took a step toward the ancestor, then froze. This was much more dangerous than the mirage of a snake that had prevented him from touching the tablet himself.

No, you won't take it! the ancestor said; he clutched the tablet to his naked breast. *I can live forever!*

Varus backed away. The ancestor's face went blank. He gave a high, bubbling scream, an inhuman sound like that of steam escaping from under a pot lid. The black smut was spreading from the surface of the tablet, moving toward his head and legs both the way oil flows in winter.

The pry bar lay where the ancestor had dropped it when he straightened with the tablet. Varus thought of reaching for it as a weapon, but that would take him closer to the ancestor, closer to the Blight.

The old man screamed again. He turned and stumbled into the ruins. He was going in the direction of the pit from which the Blight had come originally.

Varus took a deep breath, then ran back the way he had come. When he reached the shimmering lens of the portal through which he and the ancestor had come to Anti-Thule, Varus looked over his shoulder. The ancestor, now a mass of crawling filth, poised on the edge of the black water, then plunged in.

Varus stepped into the rosy portal and started back to the Waking World. The air in the seeming library was comfortably warm, but he was shivering worse than he had in the frozen winds of Anti-Thule.

ALPHENA AND HER GUIDE CAME around another angle of the canyon. The valley broadened so abruptly that she paused, startled by the expanse.

The slopes to either side were gentler than the cliffs they had been follow-ing, and the stream bubbled visibly over rocks for its whole width instead of carving a channel to either side of a line of islets.

Two serpents on short legs paced before a circular hole in the cliff ahead. They were blue in shadow but as iridescent as old glass where the sun struck them. Both turned their heads when Alphena and her guide appeared, but they continued to make slow circuits at the ends of shimmering leashes.

A man and a woman watched the serpents from a safe distance. The woman's bluish shift was as gauzy as a cloud. She faced around and drew the man's attention to the newcomers.

Neither was armed. Alphena kept her hand away from her sword hilt. She continued to walk at a measured pace. Without looking toward her compan-ion, she said, "Lord Janus, who are those people?"

"I wouldn't know," he said carelessly. If he'd been human he would have shrugged, but Alphena didn't suppose an iron statue could do that. "The fe-male is a breeze nymph, though. Do you count them as people?"

"I suppose," Alphena said. "Definitions are the sort of thing you'd better discuss with my brother and Master Pandareus, though."

She cleared her throat to be sure that she wouldn't choke on the words, then called, "I am Alphena, daughter of Senator Gaius Alphenus Saxa. Where is Publius Corylus, whom I've come to this place to"—she stumbled on the thought for a moment before finishing—"to meet."

She had almost said *to rescue.* With a sudden pang Alphena realized how much she wanted to rescue Corylus, for him to owe his safety to her, to see her as . . .

Well, she hadn't said that. No one would ever know what she was thinking.

Janus' metallic laugh chimed out discordantly.

"I'm Bion and this is Aura!" the man called. He was a sturdy-looking fel-low, but he was clearly uneasy with the situation. "Corylus went into the cave. He hasn't come out yet."

Alphena stopped at arm's length from the couple. It suddenly struck her that until her father became involved with an ancient wizard she had never met strangers without a bevy of servants present. Now it had become com-monplace.

"The dragons were asleep then," the nymph said. Face-to-face, she had the combination of willowy beauty and ageless eyes that even Alphena would have recognized as not truly human. That was another thing that she had learned about in the past months. "They got up as soon as he'd gone between them. I don't think he can come out now."

Alphena drew her sword and walked as much closer as she would get while still remaining beyond the reach of the chained guardians. "Corylus!" she shouted. "Publius Cispius Corylus! This is Alphena!"

There was no response from the cave. The dragons paced toward her, their chains clinking along the ground instead of being stretched out. The animals' bodies quivered with taut muscles.

They're trying to lure me closer, Alphena realized. She had seen gladiators let their shields dip as though they were too tired to hold them up properly, encouraging opponents to rush in for a quick kill.

She eyed the dragons professionally. Their heads were broad and flattened. The fangs in the upper and lower jaws overlapped. Their skins looked as thin as silk, but the metallic sheen made her wonder whether they would resist a sword edge like the iron plates of a segmented cuirass.

There's only one way to tell, Alphena decided with gloomy certainty. *I'll thrust for the nearer one's neck, just behind the triangular skull, and hope that he writhes into the other one so that I have a chance to get the blade clear.*

She poised, her face blank.

Rupa stepped into sight at the mouth of the cave. The disk in her right hand threw back a blaze of reflected sunlight.

"Greetings, Lady Alphena!" Rupa called in her perfect Latin. "When we met before, I tried to take the Godspeaker's ear from you. This time I want you to give the ear to me, in exchange for which I will release—"

She held up the disk, canting it slightly so that the surface didn't catch the sun.

"—your lover, Publius Corylus. If not, he will spend eternity in my speculum."

Alphena barely heard the words. Her gaze was frozen on the tiny form of Corylus within the circuit of the disk.

"Rupa?" called the man Alphena had found standing with the nymph. "Is that really you, my love?"

CORYLUS ALMOST FELL ON HIS FACE. His feet were solidly planted on the ground just as they had been the instant before Rupa trapped him in the mirror, but in the minutes since then he had forgotten how to balance.

Rupa walked out of the cave. She made a gesture with her left hand. The dragons, nervously alert a moment before, flopped onto their backs and writhed, their legs kicking and their tails sweeping arabesques above them.

"Bion, my love, my life," Rupa said. Her voice had the same purring passion as the sounds the lolling dragons were making. "You have returned after so many years. You are still mine."

Bion had been standing with Aura where Corylus had left them. The sailor ran forward and threw his arms around Rupa as though she were an attractive young woman instead of being a powerful Indian magician. She responded as a young woman would to her lover. She *was* still a magician, but at the moment the woman in love was foremost.

While Corylus was in the mirror, Alphena must have joined his former companions. She shot her sword back into its sheath and ran to him. In her left hand was an iron baton with a head forged on to the end.

A dragon's tail whipped in front of Alphena—it was chance, not an attempt to trip her—but she hopped over it with the skill of long practice in the gymnasium. To Corylus' amazement, the girl hugged him as tightly as Rupa did Bion. Corylus stepped back, but Alphena came with him.

"Publius Corylus, I love you and I want you!" Alphena said. "I don't care what rank you are; you're made for me and I want you!"

"Lady Alphena . . . ," he said. He didn't know what to say next. Half of him wanted the girl to be a thousand miles away, but the other half was a young man against whom an attractive woman was rubbing her warm body. "You're enchanted and . . ."

"No, I'm not," Alphena said. She stepped back and looked fiercely up at him. "You think this is Bacchus talking or wine or something else forcing me, but it's not. I've gone awful places with you and I've fought beside you. I love you and I want to, I want *you* to make love to me!"

Corylus swallowed. He didn't retreat, because Alphena was now standing a proper distance away and he didn't want to spur her to grab him again. He opened his mouth to say, Lady Alphena, then closed it again. He took her hands between his fingers and said, "Alphena, we'll talk about this later, when we're . . . well, when we're not here."

He swallowed again and added, "And I'll tell you what I think. When I know what it is."

His body certainly knew what *it* thought. His mind thought several different things at the same time. All the choices were bad for one reason or another.

"All right," Alphena said. "But we *will* talk."

She looked at the baton in her hand with a puzzled expression, then thrust it under her sword belt. "Do you know how we can get back to the Waking World? I think Janus could help if we could bring him back."

What she said made no sense to Corylus. He frowned as he considered how to reply. Before he could, Rupa joined them. Bion followed her closely, but his expression was one of blissful vacancy.

"Publius Corylus," Rupa said, "Bion has told me how you saved him and brought him back to me. We will go off shortly to where the troubles of this world and the Waking World both have no meaning; we will not be separated again."

She looked at Bion; puzzlement had edged into his expression. "I have learned many things while I was searching for you, my love," she said in a voice thickened with warm emotion. "I did not find you, but I have learned how to keep us safe from any power in the Cosmos."

Bion took her left hand in both of his; he did not speak.

"Before I leave, Corylus . . . ," Rupa went on, "what is there that I can provide?"

Corylus pondered the question. His mind was spiky and uneven from the time he had spent trapped in the mirror.

"Mother and Varus," Alphena said before his thought formed. "We came to the Otherworld to find them. And to find Corylus."

"Can you help us to find Lady Hedia and Gaius Varus?" Corylus said. "Mistress Rupa, I—I'm glad that you and Bion are together, but I didn't know I was bringing him to you. If you can help us, we'll be grateful and our friends will be grateful, but I don't want you to misunderstand what happened."

He didn't know what happened. The trek across the Otherworld had been much like a patrol on the east side of the frontier, where none of the events had been planned and you were just happy to survive.

"Your friends are both in the Waking World, in Govinda's kingdom," Rupa said. "I can send you to either through the mirror here, as easily as I used it to trap you, Corylus. They are not together, however. Hedia is at Dreaming Hill while Varus is about to enter Govinda's palace from Anti-Thule."

Corylus looked at Alphena. He wanted to say, *Send us to Hedia!* but he wasn't sure how Alphena would react. Varus was Corylus' friend and a magician who might be able to get them back to the Waking World. Despite those things, thought of Hedia's icy practicality was somehow more reassuring.

"Both your friends face danger," Rupa said, "but there is little you could do to help Gaius Varus. Lady Hedia, however, is menaced by armed men."

"Is she?" said Corylus. He heard the tone of his voice change into something like a lion's cough. He placed both hands on his staff and worked his shoulder muscles.

"Mistress Rupa," Alphena said. "Please send us my mother."

Corylus looked out past the playful dragons and noticed Aura. "Wait!" he said. "I need to . . ."

He strode back to the sprite. He didn't run, just in case the dragons' kittenish behavior included snatching at anything moving quickly in front of them.

"Aura?" he said. "Can we help *you*? For bringing me here, as you promised."

"There is nothing remaining for me in this existence," Aura said. "Thank you, though. May the two of you be as happy in your love as Zetes and I were in ours."

"We're not . . . ," Corylus said. He broke off in confusion over what the next word should be.

"You are happier than either of you would be without the other," Aura said. "For your kindness to me I hope you never have to learn the truth of what I say."

"I . . . ," said Corylus.

Aura smiled. "Go," she said as she turned. Faintly as she walked away, Corylus heard her add, "My heart and hopes go with you."

Corylus returned to the cave. The others were watching him, but the sprite's final sad smile filled his mind.

CHAPTER XVI

Hedia's leap through the portal carried her onto the round shrine that faced Dreaming Hill. Two soldiers sat between a pair of pillars, their feet resting on the stepped base. They were looking out; their bamboo spears leaned against the upper edge of the domed roof.

More soldiers—about a dozen of them—and a pair of Tyla squatted around two small cooking fires, heating pastries on grills of green bamboo. The humans at one fire wore silk and had swords, though they had taken off their equipment belts and hung them on a rack made by lashing two pairs of lances into X patterns and laying a fifth lance across those supports. Their round bucklers of brass-bound wood lay under the rack.

The men at the other fire were peasants, like the two sitting in the shrine. They carried no edged weapons. A leather corselet lay behind one man; he and two others wore leather caps. The Tyla sat with them.

Hedia hesitated. Her only "plan" had been to get away from Govinda. She hadn't even been conscious that the panel through which she had jumped led to Dreaming Hill.

At least I'm on familiar ground. Though I didn't much like it the first time.

Before Hedia could make a choice—there were no good options—a peasant at the fire turned to call something to a colleague seated on the shrine. The peasant saw Hedia and instead shouted a warning.

Hedia leaped from the shrine and ran toward Dreaming Hill, just as she had done the first time she had found herself here. It had been a bad choice then and she knew now just *how* bad it was, but there was nothing better on offer.

She ran past the nobles as they lurched up from the fire. One stretched his arm out to grab her but overbalanced. She jumped over his sprawling body instead of dodging around.

Hedia ran through a screen of ferns but was stopped almost instantly by bamboo. The individual canes were deceptively slender, but a stand of them was as impenetrable as brick. She turned left and struggled past the bamboo, hoping that the ferns concealed her from Govinda's soldiers. She didn't have a choice.

She ducked under a stand of leaves the size of small blankets, shiny green on top but on the bottom matted with fine hairs colored a paler yellow-green. The spray of stems supporting them grew from a common center in a block that was hollow in the middle. Each side of the block was carved with a grinning face; human faces, Hedia thought, or almost human.

A woody vine—wrist thick and looking like a branch—crossed the space between a pile of earth-covered blocks and the trunk of a tree thicker than Hedia was tall. A bird flared his wings and landed. His yellow claws kicked bits of moss-covered bark to the ground below.

Looking down, the bird said, "Where are you going, Lady Hedia?"

"When did that become your business?" Hedia said. She had been running almost from the moment the Eternals' tomb had opened. She had no direction and no hope; only fears drove her from one danger to the next.

Suddenly exhausted, she sat on a mossy projection. Its square outlines suggested quarried stone underneath. No matter: the moss and loam were as soft as a cushion.

She smiled wryly. *As tired as I am, I wouldn't notice bare rock. What would my maids think?*

"Well, you wouldn't believe me if I told you it was out of the goodness of my heart," the bird said. "Still, I thought you might appreciate a guide who has lived in the city from before the Eternals removed themselves. There are dangerous creatures in this ruin."

"I know that," Hedia said. "I met one the first time I was here. I'm going to go around him."

"Ah, the Guardian and its chest of jewels," the bird said, nodding. His short, stiff tail twitched to counterbalance his head. "No, you don't need jewels, do you, Hedia? And the Guardian can't move away from its tower; that's its anchor to our world."

The bird cocked his head, bringing his bright red eye into sharp relief against the line of black running across the generally white feathers of his head and breast. "There are more dangers here than just the Guardian. There are creatures who are of this world and can move in it as easily as I can. There is a snake, for example, whose gape will swallow you whole if your course takes you to him."

Mention of the snake brought back a memory to Hedia. "You're one of the hawks I saw in the Otherworld, when the cyclops chased me!" she said.

"Am I?" the bird said carelessly. "I'm a kite, though I suppose 'hawk' is close enough. There are many of us kites, on the plains outside Dreaming Hill and elsewhere."

There aren't many who talk! Hedia thought, but she kept the words in her mind. Aloud she said, "I want to go through this ruin and out the other side. Can you guide me to do that?"

"Easily," the bird said. He laughed like a cricket chirping. "Easily for me but not so easily for you on the ground, I think. But if you're willing to try, I'll guide you. And I'll keep you away from the serpent."

Hedia stood but had to brace herself on a sapling because she felt faint. *I got up too fast,* she thought. *And—when did I last eat?*

"I'll follow," she said. She thought of asking what was on the other side of the ruins. She didn't; the tangled jungle was enough to worry about for the moment.

The trek was hard at the beginning and there were repeated stretches that were worse. What must once have been a courtyard was now an obstacle course in which a thicket of palms stood on stilt roots that lifted the paving blocks askew. There were other places that were almost as difficult.

Hedia occasionally cursed under her breath, but she never complained loudly enough to be heard at any distance. No one was forcing her to do this. She smiled: *I can sit down at any time and wait until I starve to death. Unless the snake finds me first, I suppose.*

The bird flew short distances and perched where she could see him plainly. His white breast feathers were as good as a waving torch in this waste of green gloom.

For the most part he kept her path on the level by leading her around the larger masses of masonry, but once she had to clamber over a wall still laced together by the roots that had lifted apart the individual blocks. The huge trees to either side were impassable, and beyond them was bamboo.

"You're almost to where you're going, Lady Hedia!" the bird called cheerfully. "Climb over this fallen tree."

Hedia looked at it. The trunk was almost as high as she was; it disappeared into the forest at both ends. Bark had started to slough away, showing the yellowish wood beneath; mosses and ferns were thick on the top, and red and yellow shelf fungi grew out from the sides.

She closed her eyes and leaned against the obstacle. *I'm so tired . . .*

But that didn't matter. Hedia opened her eyes and looked again at the tree with the benefit of a moment's rest. She tested a shelf fungus with her hand, then put her foot on one of the lowest fungi and slowly increased the pressure until it supported her whole weight.

Grinning coldly, Hedia walked up the ladder of fungus steps to the top of the trunk. There were no fungi on the farther side, but the ground below was a carpet of ferns. A piece broken off a corner lay on the loam, but she could avoid it easily.

Hedia swung her legs over to that side, then slid down with her knees flexed. Only then did she look around her.

She was standing in front of the tower into which the snake-legged monster, the Guardian, had pursued her. The chest of jewels with its lid ajar sat in the entrance.

Where did the bird go?

She heard the *swish! swish!* that heralded the monster's approach.

"I didn't expect you back, Hedia!" the Guardian said. "Since you've come, though, I'll savor you all the more."

She could see the creature in the maze of shifting planes between her and the entrance to the tower. At each change it was closer.

Hedia turned, desperately hoping that there was some way to get over the tree trunk from this side. There wasn't, but the bird sat watching, just out of reach.

"Have you no honor!" Hedia said.

The bird laughed. "Of course not," he said. "I'm a carrion eater. But I did keep you away from the great python. He would have swallowed you whole, just like the King of Serpents whom you met in the Otherworld. Whereas my friend the Guardian—"

The bird hopped an arm's length farther back on his long yellow legs. Hedia had been inching closer, but he had noticed and understood.

"—leaves scraps."

"And don't think your daughter's magic will save you, Hedia," the Guardian said. "I am not of this world, and this world's magic cannot affect me."

Hedia turned, loosing her sash. The creature stood on its human legs in front of the entrance to the tower, the only place in this ruin that offered sanctuary, if not escape.

She bent and picked up the corner of rock, then knotted it into her silk sash. "My daughter isn't a magician," she said, "and she's not here anyway. But I am here."

Hedia, wife of Senator Gaius Alphenus Saxa, stepped toward the Guardian. It was twelve feet tall, thick bodied, and armed with pincers that were each the size of her torso.

She swung back her makeshift mace. She would only get one blow, but she intended that the creature should ache while it devoured her body.

CORYLUS STEPPED ASIDE TO GIVE Alphena a chance to look through the lens of air also. It had shown him the backs of a squad of Indian soldiers. At least four were noblemen with curved tulwars. There were also two Tyla magicians, who were certainly more dangerous than the spear-carrying peasants and perhaps more than the swordsmen as well.

"I don't see Mother," Alphena said, frowning.

"She was there," said Rupa, watching impassively beside them. "She can't be far."

"The soldiers don't have her," Corylus said. He drew the orichalc dagger, but he held its blade parallel to his staff so that he could use both hands on the wood. "They're looking at the jungle, but they seem afraid of an attack rather than getting ready to go in themselves."

"Them looking the other way makes it easier," Alphena said, drawing her short sword. "How do we"—she looked at Corylus—"get there so that we can find Mother?"

"Through this," Rupa said, gesturing with one hand at the disk of air. "I will send you when you're ready."

Corylus saw the doubtful look on Alphena's face. Grinning, he said, "I guarantee that it will hold us, just the way a mirror would show our whole images. Anyway, it held me."

"This time you will pass through," Rupa said. "That will be different."

Her face and tone were so deadpan that only after a moment's consideration did Corylus realize that she was joking. He smiled. In different circumstances, he and Varus would have a good time chatting with Rupa; and Master Pandareus would as well.

"I'm ready," Corylus said. "Alphena, I'll go first and you come after."

She nodded and moved aside. Corylus stepped in front of the small disk, his staff poised crossways before him.

As suddenly as Rupa had trapped him before, Corylus was standing in a round shrine. The Indians and their Tyla magicians were on the ground just below, as he had seen their images a moment before.

He jumped down, swinging his staff one-handed at the skull of the nearer Tylon. He heard bone crack as he put the dagger in his left hand under the ribs of a swordsman. The fellow's blue silk shirt was loose enough to have concealed armor, but the point met nothing more resistant than skin before it sliced through kidney.

Corylus had struck so quickly that the victim's gasp was lost in the chatter of the nervous guards while they watched the jungle in front of them. The man dropped the sword he held point down and stumbled forward when Corylus jerked the dagger out. He fell onto the feet of the man beside him.

Corylus grabbed the tulwar as it fell, but he fumbled with its basket hilt. The second Indian had started to turn when the edge of Alphena's sword cracked the big bone of his upper arm.

The pain of Corylus' kidney blow was so shocking that his victim had frozen, but Alphena's man screamed and tried to run. He stumbled over his feet and fell; his shield bonged as it hit the hard ground.

The remaining swordsmen were at least marginally alert when Corylus and Alphena hit them, but the Indians weren't trained in the sort of close-up butchery that the legions of Carce made their specialty. Corylus' man got his buckler up, so Corylus chopped through his left ankle with the sword and slanted the dagger upward into the back of his neck as he toppled.

The dagger caught in the spongy bone at the base of the Indian's skull. Corylus dropped it and spun to do whatever was required with the last swordsman.

Nothing was required. The Indian's hand still gripped the hilt of his tulwar as it bounced on the ground. The man ran screaming in the direction of armed peasants, trying to hold his severed wrist with his remaining hand. He wasn't able to pinch off the artery while running; blood squirted ahead of him.

Alphena pointed her sword in the direction of the peasants like a bloody extension of her arm. "Go!" she shouted. "Or die!"

Where's the second magician?

The peasants fled in shouting panic, most of them dropping their spears on the way. Corylus hadn't expected them to fight, but he wouldn't have been surprised if one had thrown a spear at them before he turned. He had batted a spear aside on the Danube, and that one had been cast by a Sarmatian who wasn't shiveringly afraid.

Alphena slowly lowered her arm and sword, though she continued to watch the direction in which the peasants had gone. Corylus checked the swordsmen. The fellow Corylus had knifed in the kidneys remained alive, but he was as harmless as if he were encased in lava. Kidney wounds seemed to be as painful as blazing rock.

The one with the knife stuck in his skull was dead, and the man with the broken arm was unconscious. That last man was the sort who got an extra spear thrust in the ribs as a Scout passed, just to be sure, but he wasn't shamming. Corylus had heard the bone crack under Alphena's sword edge: a numbing blow until the shock set in, and the shock was generally fatal.

The second Tyla magician crawled on the ground, his arms stretched out toward Alphena. *Did she kill him?*

But the creature was chittering and meeping: therefore alive, therefore dangerous. Corylus stepped over the body of his second swordsman to finish the job. Despite the tulwar's curved blade, the point would be effective with a straight thrust.

"Don't!" Alphena said. "He's telling me about Mother."

The satyr's ear had bounced out from under Alphena's tunic in the fighting, but she now held it in her left hand. The Tylon had lost his feathered headdress. He writhed on his belly, but his eyes never left the rough iron amulet.

"Go, then," Alphena said, this time speaking to the Tylon. "Get as far away from here as you can. You'd do better to dance on a pony in a traveling menagerie than to go back to Govinda, but I don't care so long as I never see you again."

She sounds just like Lady Hedia, Corylus thought.

The Tylon turned—it was like watching a snake move—and scampered briefly on all fours before rising to his hind legs and disappearing into the grass in the direction in which the peasants had gone. *They probably weren't returning to King Govinda's service, either.*

Alphena slipped the amulet back within her tunic. "He won't harm us," she said. "Where's the—oh."

The Tylon Corylus had swatted with the staff lay where he had fallen. The back of the creature's skull was dished in; they had much lighter frames than humans, even slender humans.

"He's not going to harm us, either," Corylus said. "What did yours say about Lady Hedia?"

Corylus gripped the dagger hilt with both hands and put his left foot on the head in which it was stuck, then withdrew the blade. He wiped the orichalc clean on the dead man's shirt. Cotton waste would have been better, but the silk was sufficient.

"She ran past them into the jungle," Alphena said. "She didn't have any weapons. He and the other magician were afraid to be so close to the ruins, but they had to obey Govinda's orders."

Alphena had wiped and sheathed her sword; now she picked up a buckler. The pair of parallel handles on the inner curve were intended to be held in one hand. Fortunately, the Indian soldiers were relatively slight; Alphena's hand could grip the shield adequately.

"He said there are terrible monsters in Dreaming Hill," she said, "and there is magic too great for even the Godspeaker."

"I'm not going to be able to help you much with magic," Corylus said. He twisted a shield from the hand of the man he'd stabbed in the head. He had to step on the fellow's wrist because his muscles had locked when the blade split his brain.

"Perhaps the ear will help," Alphena said, "though I don't suppose so if the Godspeaker wasn't powerful enough when he was alive. But it doesn't matter if that's where Mother is."

"No," said Corylus. "It really doesn't matter."

He started for Dreaming Hill with the buckler advanced and the curved sword slanted upward in his right hand. Alphena was on his left, a half step behind.

VARUS FELT RELAXED SIMPLY because he was in a library. *If I opened one of the scrolls, would I be able to read it?*

"Yes," said the Sibyl. "Do you want to read something? That—"

She gestured to a series of what Varus thought from a distance were shards of pale pottery. When she and Varus reached the shelves he saw the shards were the shoulder blades of pigs, covered with symbols brushed on in tiny, precise rows.

"—is the history of the Hsia dynasty of the Serians. You would be the only citizen of Carce to know that history. But of course, if you stay here long enough to read it, there will be no Carce for you to return to."

"I am a citizen of Carce," Varus said with a dry smile. "Duty first, of course."

Then he said, "I didn't know you were with me, Sibyl. I'm glad you are."

The Sibyl chirped her laugh. She took three steps to every two of his, but she had no difficulty in keeping up.

"Where else would I be, Lord Magician?" she said. "I exist only in your mind."

Varus didn't respond this time. The Sibyl knew things Varus had not consciously known until she spoke, and she sometimes described firsthand things from the past before Gaius Varus was born. Common sense told him the Sibyl's claim to be a construction of his mind could not be true, but the rigorous logic that Master Pandareus had instilled admitted the possibility of matters beyond Varus current knowledge.

The Sibyl laughed again, as though she were listening to his thoughts.

The end of the corridor was before them, a blur of brightness. Varus looked at the Sibyl. She smiled and took his hand; her fingers were dry and strong. They walked through the light together.

Varus opened his eyes and sat up. He was on the couch in Govinda's sanctum. The boy's body still hung by its hair, but his face was as white as a bleached toga. Blood from his severed throat painted his torso and legs, and it pooled on the floor. In this hot climate, the body had begun to rot.

"You're awake already?" Govinda said. The king held the gory dagger in his right hand, the half tablet in his left. His gold tunic was sodden with the boy's blood. "You're all right?"

"Yes," Varus said. The Sibyl no longer stood beside him, but he thought he felt the pressure of her fingertips on his right hand. He rolled off the couch and stood on the side opposite the king.

"But where's the tablet?" Govinda demanded. "Did you come back without the rest of the tablet?"

"The tablet is with your ancestor, in Hell," Varus said. "He loosed the Blight. See for yourself."

Varus gestured toward the panel through which he—his soul?—had stepped to reach Anti-Thule. Instead of showing churning blackness as the alabaster had when Varus first saw it, the ruined Tyla community was as clear as the other scenes within this sanctum. The seepage-filled crater was boiling; the bubbles were foul black.

Govinda glanced over his shoulder at the panel. "You cleared the image," he said. "How did you—"

Instead of finishing the thought, he leaned over the couch to stab Varus.

"*You will be utterly destroyed by fire!*" Varus shouted in the cracking voice of an old woman.

A blue flash slammed Govinda out of the sanctum. The door flew off its hinges, and the alabaster panels to either side crumbled to finely divided dust.

The squad of soldiers guarding the sanctum now sprawled in a semicircle centered on the door. They appeared to be dead. Those in the center had been flung farthest, and their clothes were smoldering.

Govinda had been thrown to the ground, but he got up without hesitation. He held the tablet in both hands. The dagger lay on the ground halfway across the courtyard behind him. He began chanting.

Varus walked forward. *As I would have moved across the Rostrum while delivering an oration,* he realized. He thought with a pang of regret of classes in the Forum and how he had struggled, planning every word and motion. *Life was so much easier then.*

"*My anger sends you headlong to dust!*" he shouted.

This time the shock made Varus stagger, but again it threw Govinda backward in a sprawl. The courtyard had emptied of the people who had been thronging it, save for the scattered dead. Soldiers, courtiers, and the hawkers who had been chaffering with them lay as spills of clothing. Some were seared or even burned, but others had no obvious injuries.

Magic of the sort that was being used was dangerous even at a distance from the intended object. *Magic of the sort that I am using.*

Varus felt as though he were on a high pinnacle, viewing the conflict in cool detachment. He stepped forward, shouting, "My *wrath rains down on you!*"

This time his spell met Govinda's in iridescence. Varus felt a push like a warm breeze, much milder than that of previous blasts.

The king had been thrown almost back to the reservoir. The marble sides of the tank bulged outward, then cracked in two places. Water gushed, then shoved over the wall between the breaks in a slopping flood.

It rushed across the ground, dividing around Govinda in a screen of blue fire with attendant pops and crackles. It continued to spread over the courtyard, shoving a berm of mud before it. Water flashed to steam twenty feet from Varus but flowed by to either side.

Varus walked forward. He was breathing hard.

Something huge and gray—*a wave?*—lurched over the fallen wall of the tank. It was the head of one of the fish from Anti-Thule, grown monstrous in the crater of the Blight. It flopped forward on its pectoral fins like a catfish on a mud bank. A second fish followed the first.

Govinda raised the tablet in both hands and began to chant. The fish writhed past him. Both angled toward Varus.

Varus shouted, *"Let fire flame beneath you and burn you up!"*

Govinda fell back again. The flash buffeted both fish sideways, but they rolled onto their flat bellies and gathered themselves to make the final leap toward Varus.

The scale of everything changed. He and Govinda were tall pillars on a plain in which the king's palace was a shadowy outline.

Separately—in another time or place, but visible here—was Baruch, the blue demon who had guarded the Princess Teji. He towered above the giant fish in his frame of reference.

"My mistress sent me to you, Lord Varus," Baruch said. "She thought—"

Baruch seized each fish with two arms and lifted them overhead, twisting and helpless. He brought them down with a double crash, one crushing a wing of the palace with its head, the other slamming a dent in the packed soil of the courtyard.

"—you might welcome a visit," the demon concluded. Booming laughter, he dropped the fish back into the reservoir. Their slimy bodies trembled, but they were dead. Varus had seen fishermen kill fish of normal size with similar motions on the shore of the Bay of Puteoli.

"I'll leave you to it, then," Baruch said. "Little folk like me have no business getting involved with great magicians."

Baruch laughed again and added, "Not that you need any help, Lord Varus."

The demon was gone. Varus stood in the courtyard of Govinda's palace. The plane in which Baruch stood had vanished when the demon did. The tail of one of the dead fish stuck fifty feet out from the reservoir, quivering with tetanic motion as the nerves continued to die.

The fish were hundreds of feet long. If Teji hadn't sent her demon to help me, I would be in the belly of one of them.

Varus breathed deeply. He was for the first time aware of the smells of powdered stone and burned flesh, as well as an odd effluvium that probably came from the fish, though they hadn't had time to begin to spoil.

Govinda got up slowly from the ground. His lips continued to chant or pray, but he seemed to have shrunk in the past minutes. His eyes were those of a trapped rabbit, desperate with fear; his head darted from side to side, looking for escape.

There was no escape. *No, I don't need help with Govinda.*

As Varus' lips opened to form the words, the king straightened. Instead of shouting another spell as he had been doing, Govinda hurled the half tablet with more than human strength.

At me, Varus thought, but the block of soapstone sailed well over his head. *He's defenseless now.*

"You will be devoured by fire!" Varus said.

A blue flash enveloped Govinda; he shattered like a like a glass figurine on a blacksmith's anvil. Nothing remained: no blood, no smoke, not even a thread of his cloth-of-gold garments.

Varus wobbled on his feet. He thought he might have to drop to one knee to keep from toppling over, but he got control of his body without that. *Not that it would matter.*

Steam hissed. The water remaining in the reservoir had been heated by the bolt that had finally destroyed Govinda, Varus supposed.

That didn't matter, either. Varus turned.

The palace was half in ruins. There was no sign of life, even in the sections that hadn't been damaged in the battle.

Where the separate sanctum had stood within the courtyard, a portal high into the sky opened to Anti-Thule as it had been when Varus left it seeming minutes before. A figure of black slime climbed from the seething crater and stood on the lip. It held half the soapstone tablet in either hand.

As Varus watched, the figure brought the parts together, mating them perfectly.

The figure of Blight began to grow; and as it grew, it laughed thunderously.

CHAPTER XVII

Alphena had seen Corylus fight in the past, but it continued to thrill her. He wasn't more skilled than the gladiators she was used to watching: they had nothing to do all day except practice their swordsmanship, while that was only a small part of a soldier's duties on the frontiers. The style, the *tone*, of Corylus' movement in battle was nothing like the business of the arena.

"You fight as though you don't care if you survive," she said.

Corylus pushed through a line of saplings: each spindly trunk reached waist high, with a pair of oversized leaves on top to catch the sun if one of the giants shading it were to fall. He muttered, "I guard myself."

Stepping over a fallen cornice, he said, "Watch your footing here." Then he added, "I guess it's from being with the Scouts. If we got into in a fight, we were usually outnumbered and in a hurry. You had to take the locals out fast. If that meant you got carved some yourself, well, that was better than if you got captured. The Sarmatian women knew how to make it last if they got hold of you."

She and Corylus had just entered the jungle, but Alphena couldn't see the shrine or even daylight back the way they had come. The Tylon had pointed in this direction, but until she had rushed through the outer curtain of vegetation she hadn't appreciated how dense the interior was. The steep mounds to either side must have been buildings, but only occasional stone edges protruded from the leaf mold and fallen branches to indicate that.

"Are you tracking Mother?" Alphena asked.

"No. I can't track in a jungle," Corylus said. "Figuring how many horses were in a raiding party on a dry plain, sure. But I can ask. Keep an eye out."

"What?" said Alphena, but Corylus had already set his shield upright between the prop roots of an odd-looking tree—a palm, she supposed.

Corylus put his free hand against the smooth bark and said, "Cousin, I need your help."

Nothing happened for a moment. Then a slender man stepped out from behind the trunk. "Well, dearie, I couldn't very well say no to you, could I?"

The newcomer glanced at Alphena and added, "Is she joining the party too?"

He isn't a man, she has breasts, and the tree hadn't been thick enough to hide her anyway! But there's a man's member bulging the thin shift over his groin.

"It's not that kind of party, Pandan," Corylus said easily, retrieving the buckler. "Lady Alphena's mother came running in here a minute or two ago. Where did she go, please?"

"Well, she *went* that way," the hermaphrodite said, pointing to their left. Alphena started that way but paused when she saw that Corylus was still waiting.

"*But*," continued Pandan, smirking at her, "she met a bird there and he led her in a big circle around to the tower. It's right there—"

Pandan pointed again, this time in the direction Alphena and Corylus had been going.

"—but *you* don't want to go there, dearie. My sisters there say that the Guardian has her. It would be a crime to lose you too."

Pandan nodded to Alphena. "Or even that one."

Alphena started in a clumsy run in the direction Pandan had pointed. Her shield was out in front of her to batter a way through the undergrowth, but she couldn't see the ground. She tripped almost immediately on a block carved with a dancing monkey in low relief.

"Cousin, don't go that way!" Pandan called. "You'll meet the Guardian!"

"That's what we're here for!" Corylus shouted as he leaped past Alphena; his shield was at his side, edge on to the undergrowth he was running through.

He's graceful as a chamois on a broken slope, Alphena thought. She rolled to her feet and followed. She hadn't dropped her sword or shield when she fell, and the scrape on her right forearm wouldn't keep her from fighting.

Corylus rounded a tree with wide buttress roots. Alphena thought he was slanting to the right of the proper line, but she was too focused on not losing her footing to pay attention. Roots had lifted the blocks of the pavement into a semblance of a storm-tossed sea.

It was easier to follow than to argue, and there was no time to argue anyway. It was very easy to follow Corylus.

"Mother, we're coming!" she shouted. Corylus cocked his head slightly, perhaps enough that he could see her out of the corner of his eye; his expression was fixed and grim.

"Mother, it's me! We're coming for you!"

She knew she was warning the Guardian, whoever it was, but she wanted to turn its attention away from Hedia. Alphena and Corylus had weapons; Hedia did not, according to the Tylon who had seen her run past.

"Mother—"

And they were there, in a space covered by vines and creepers but free of trees and the brush—saplings, mostly—that had been so dense until now. A pylon, perhaps the tower the hermaphrodite had spoken of, rose to their right.

I must have run right along the side without noticing it!

A monster on two legs, twelve feet high, stood near the end of the cleared space. When it turned to face them, Alphena saw that it had the head of a man with hair like a lion's mane. The uppermost pair of arms were huge pincers, while below there were several sets of tentacles.

Hedia stood beyond the monster.

"So!" said the monster in a cheerful tone. "The first course has brought two more bites with her."

Then in a changed voice it went on, "And *don't* think that your amulet will help you, little wizardess! Your magic can't touch me!"

"Can my sword?" said Alphena, moving in on the monster's right side. The tentacles were coiling and uncoiling. The uppermost pair appeared to be over six feet long.

The monster—the Guardian, but what was it guarding?—shot its upper left tentacle out to the side. *It's feinting—*

She stepped back and the right pincer extended on a jointed arm. The toothed edges clacked together where Alphena's head would have been if she hadn't moved. Corylus lunged, pricking the Guardian' chest where a human's ribs would have been. The monster seemed to have an outer covering like a turtle's shell, but the point of the curved sword slid deep enough to draw a line of purple blood.

The middle tentacle wrapped the blade like honeysuckle around a fence post. Corylus drew back sharply. The end of the tentacle writhed like a broken-backed snake, attached to its base by little more than a tag of skin. The Indian sword was impressively sharp.

"I'll heal!" the Guardian said. "You can't do me real harm with those swords!"

Corylus lunged again. The Guardian whirled and reached out with both pincers.

Corylus jumped back. Instead of lunging, Alphena closed with two quick steps and banged the boss of her shield into the side of the monster's scaly leg. It was like hitting a tree, but she knew how a blow on the thigh felt.

The Guardian's right tentacles gripped the edge of her shield, as expected; she slashed them and stepped back. Purple blood oozed for a few moments, but the creature really did heal quickly. The tentacle that Corylus had cut most of the way through was rejoining, though the end still hung limp.

The Guardian roared, spraying spittle in its fury. Corylus retreated. There was a notch out of the upper edge of his shield; a length of its brass strapping dangled loose from the leather base. His counterstroke had sheared off the tip of the upper blade of the Guardian's right pincer; there was a smaller chip missing where the buckler's edge had acted as a butcher's block for the sword.

The Guardian looked at Corylus, then looked at Alphena as a feint obvious to an eye trained by watching so many gladiators in the arena. When the monster lunged at Corylus with another roar, she darted in again. She tried to stab through where the knee would be in a human, but her point struck low and gouged a hand's breadth deep in the calf muscle.

The Guardian turned toward her, gripping her shield with his tentacles and reaching for her head with its right pincer. It would have crushed her skull while she levered her sword loose if the pincer had been whole; instead the lower blade gave her a buffet under the jaw, but the tip of the upper blade was a bloody stump from which muscle had swollen through where the chitin had been lopped off.

There was a loud *whack*. The Guardian's roar choked into a gasp; its arms jerked out straight from its sides as though each pair were being crucified.

The huge body toppled forward, hitting the ground so hard that it bounced. There was a dent in its back over what would have been the base of the spine in a human. Hedia stood behind the creature, holding the end of the sash that she had tied around a piece of masonry.

Alphena drove in her short sword, slanting upward across the Guardian's torso through what she hoped were the heart and lungs. Corylus hacked deep

into the back of the neck, then laid the sword aside to finish the task of be-
heading with his dagger. The blade was orichalc, Alphena saw in surprise.

She tried to wriggle her sword. Though her wrists were strong, the Guardian's flesh was as dense as cold mud.

Corylus finished his task and got to his feet. The head rolled faceup. It
looked less human on close examination. The Guardian's expression was one
of pop-eyed fury.

"Thank you both," Hedia said. "That was remarkable to watch, the way
the two of you moved together."

"It would have come out a different way if you hadn't stunned him when
you did, Your Ladyship," Corylus said, wiping his dagger with a scrap of his
own tunic. "He was wearing us down. There's been other fighters here; I can
see armor in the greenery."

Alphena was on her knees, working her sword up and down to enlarge
the cut. At present she couldn't withdraw the weapon. She was so tired that
she had forgotten her mother's presence.

"Do you suppose it can grow a new head?" Alphena said. The idea of fighting the creature again was a bleak gray wasteland in her mind.

"That doesn't matter," Hedia said, her tone a little sharper than usual.
"Govinda has your brother in his palace, but alone I couldn't find him. The
three of us may do better."

"I have to get my sword out," Alphena muttered. She had only enough
energy for the immediate task. The future was a blur.

"Leave it," said Corylus. "There's more swords out by the shrine. This
one—"

He waggled the sword he'd taken from a man he'd killed.

"—is the best steel I've ever seen, better than Spanish."

"It's longer than I'm used to," Alphena said. "I'll get this in a moment."

The world began to fall into focus again as she thought about details of
equipment and swordsmanship. Familiar considerations grounded her thoughts
and allowed everything else to return.

"Here, I'll do it," said Corylus. He sheathed his curved blade and knelt,
gripping the hilt of her short sword with both hands.

Alphena rose. She started to wobble. Her mother steadied her with both
hands.

Alphena looked around for the first time since she had plunged into the
jungle. The pillar beside them was made of fine-grained basalt rather than

the reddish sandstone of the surrounding ruins. There was a chest in the doorway on this side; the lid was askew.

Beside them, Corylus braced a boot on the huge carcase. "By Nerthus, you weren't joking when you put this in, were you?" he said. "Lenatus didn't skimp your training."

"Mother!" Alphena said. "Corylus! That chest is full of jewels!"

"He used them to trap people into coming here," Hedia said. "I'm not sure they're real."

"Hercules!" Corylus said as he lurched backward, the sword held safely out before him. "I don't know how you got that in, girl, but you've sure impressed me."

A small hawk was perched on a limb twenty feet in the air; his white breast feathers showed in sharp contrast to the moss and ferns covering the bark. Hedia looked at him and said, "He'll have plenty to eat for a while, won't he? But then he'll have to find his own meals."

Alphena didn't understand what her mother had just said, but it didn't matter. She took her sword by the hilt and walked over to the chest.

The stones were brilliant, even in the gloom of the jungle. Most were polished smooth, but a few had been cut into angles like no jewels she had ever seen before. Alphena took one of the latter, a clear gem save for the fire it reflected, and rubbed it down the chine of her sword. It cut the steel like a plow furrowing damp earth.

She dropped the stone into the chest and sheathed her sword. "They're real," she said, returning to the others. "That one was a diamond, anyway."

Hedia shook the rock out and looped the sash around her waist again. "We should go," she said. "Though—there's a shrine outside here that brought me from the palace, but I'm not sure how we can make it take us back."

"Don't worry," Alphena said, stroking the head of Janus. The rod was still firmly under her sword belt, despite her recent violent exercise. "A friend of mine should be able to help with that."

Indeed I can, Your Ladyship, the little iron god said, though she wasn't sure whether she heard the words through her ears or within her head.

"All right," said Corylus. He picked up his damaged buckler.

"I'll trade this for one of the others the guards dropped," he said as he led the way. "I'd like to hang it in a temple as an offering, though. It served me well."

"It served *us* well," Alphena said as she followed Hedia. *I don't want to lose you, Publius Corylus. I never want to lose you.*

VARUS STOOD BESIDE THE SIBYL, gazing down on the world. He hadn't had the experience of climbing the slope to join her this time. His whole previous life was . . . not blurred, really—it was all there in his memory—but it was distant, as though it had happened to another person.

His physical body stood in the courtyard of Govinda's palace. The central building lay in ruins. Much of the roof was missing, and in some sections all four floors had collapsed. Several fires were burning in the wreckage, and no one appeared to be trying to put them out. The only people Varus saw from this vantage point were fleeing; some were injured.

"What happened?" he asked in surprise.

The Sibyl laughed. "You were there, Lord Varus," she said. "Govinda was a great magician. You shrugged off the bolts he loosed on you, but the power had to go somewhere."

"I didn't notice," Varus said; he smiled wryly. "The only reason I noticed the water tank bursting was that it freed the fish to attack me. I concentrated on Govinda."

"And rightly so," the Sibyl said. "He was a great magician, even facing you."

The fish were still trembling as their nerves died. The head of one lay underwater. Baruch had dropped the second fish on top of the first, so its broad gaping mouth was fully visible. They were catfish, or their ancestors had at one time been catfish.

"But this matters nothing," the Sibyl said. "The Blight will soon sweep the world; a wind is rising in Anti-Thule, and it will carry spores of the Blight to every continent as the meteor carried them across the Cosmos to Anti-Thule."

Varus looked at the foulness: the swelling, spreading corruption. The ice cliffs of Anti-Thule were coated with black; Varus thought the Blight was already melting them, but that might have been his despair.

"What can I do, Sibyl?" he said. "How can I destroy it?"

The black figure raised the reunited tablet high. No trace remained of the features of the Indian magician who had accompanied Varus to Anti-Thule. The Blight was humanoid, but its surfaces flowed like pus from an opened cyst.

The Blight laughed. The world shook.

"You can fight it, Lord Wizard," the Sibyl said. "One can always fight evil, but one cannot always win. The Blight holds the tablet complete now, so it has the entire Cosmos behind it; and you are alone."

Varus shrugged. "Then I'll have to destroy it alone," he said. He turned to face the Blight.

CHAPTER XVIII

Varus was aware of his physical body in the courtyard of Govinda's palace, but his mind—his spirit?—walked toward the Blight on a featureless plain. The black figure advanced toward him, holding the Godspeaker's tablet.

"*Be thou smitten with glittering iron!*" Varus said. All the pathways of the *Sibylline Books* were as clear to him as the stone-paved streets of the Forum.

A meteor screamed from the heavens and smashed into the Blight. The figure flew apart like a soft fruit dropped from a height. The smear of blackness re-formed a little closer to Varus.

I could back away to keep it from reaching me! Varus thought. He laughed aloud and continued walking forward. He might not be able to destroy the foulness, but he would rather die than run from it.

Well, he would probably die regardless and all the world with him, but the principle was a good one. Socrates would have approved.

"*Let fire come through the sea and burn you!*" Varus cried. Lightning ripped, shearing the Blight in half and flinging the smoking portions to either side. They oozed forward and flowed back together. When they touched, they rejoined; the figure rose to its seeming feet before advancing farther.

The battle was fought in isolation from the Waking World. Below, the body of Gaius Varus stood in the courtyard of the ruined palace. The fires were gaining strength, but his own strokes—

"*Be there fierce thunderbolts and volleys of lightning!*" Varus said, and lightning lashed three times, each fiery bolt splitting the Blight again. The fragments advanced, re-forming as they crawled closer.

—did not touch the existing ruins. The Blight was not fighting back.

Why doesn't it attack me the way Govinda did? Varus thought as he sent down another meteor. Again it smashed the Blight into a stain on the unharmed surface. Again the edges of the blot drew in the way a splash of water runs down the sides of a bowl to pool in the center.

Govinda had been afraid, at least after his first exchange with Varus. The Blight had no fear, no emotions whatever. It was like the sun that shines on the Earth, unaffected by the concerns of the humans its light falls upon.

Varus stepped forward. "May heavenly fire fall on you!" he shouted. "May heavenly fire fall on you!"

At each command the lightning fell, and after each bolt the Blight crawled closer. It rose, no longer man shaped but a mound taller and bulkier than a human. It toppled onto Varus.

"May heavenly fire fall on you!" he called.

He could see nothing but a wall of purulent foulness, each bit individual and indescribably filthy. A barrier of crackling blue fire separated him from the Blight.

"May heavenly fire fall on you!" Varus shouted.

He felt as though a weight was being lowered onto his shoulders, a burden that slowly increased. Eventually the weight would crush him flat.

"May heavenly fire fall on you! May heavenly fire fall on you!"

Hedia followed her daughter and Corylus, stepping out through the panel in what had been Govinda's sanctum. The naked boy still hung by his hair, but his blood had flooded out when his throat was cut to the backbone. He was smiling faintly.

Hedia sneezed at the puff of smoke that blew across them.

The little building had been wrecked. The panel that she and the others had used to come from Dreaming Hill and the one on the other side of the dead boy were all that remained. The other four had been shattered into alabaster sand.

The second panel was open to Anti-Thule. A volcano had erupted since Hedia's escape, and the red glow of lava was the only light under the pall of smoke rising from the crater.

Things were moving in the ruddy darkness. She couldn't see them well, and she didn't want to see them better.

"This wasn't the window I jumped through when I was getting away from the king," Hedia said. "I went through that one."

She pointed across the room. That side of the building had been destroyed. The couch in the middle was charred, and the table beside it had overturned.

The head on top of the iron baton that Alphena was sticking under her belt smirked at Hedia. In a squeaky voice it said, "Are you complaining, lady? I could've brought you through the one you left by, but you'd have looked like forcemeat on this side."

Hedia bowed and said, "My pardon, master. I applaud your skill and initiative."

Courtesy was easy, even in the middle of a disaster. This was certainly a disaster for Govinda, which didn't in itself bother Hedia. The huge palace had been scarred. The wing to the right had collapsed, the wall of the reservoir across the courtyard had been thrown down, and through missing window casements she could see fires glinting within the central structure.

The atmosphere was of stench and smoke. Bodies were scattered in the courtyard, many of them soldiers. Some had been killed by fire, but their remaining clothing was sodden and the ground was muddy where it had not been seared to terra-cotta.

"There's Varus!" she said.

In her first glance across the devastated courtyard, Hedia had not noticed that there was a figure still standing. He wore the simple tunic of an Indian peasant—cotton instead of the wool of his Italian counterpart—but he was clearly her son. His arms were folded and his face was as grimly steadfast as that of a general of old Carce.

His forebears *were* generals and leaders. Varus was their worthy offspring.

"Look!" said Alphena. "There, in the sky! It's Varus!"

Hedia looked up, frowning. *In the sky?* She sneezed again—another whiff of smoke—and saw it, saw her son, looming over the world in the same posture as his body standing in the middle of the courtyard.

When Hedia saw the figure in the sky, he was solid—but half the time she *didn't* see him. It was as though chain lightning were rippling across a dark meadow; the man standing on the meadow was visible only during the flashes.

"We've found Varus," said Corylus. "Can we take him home through—"

Corylus looked back at the panel they had stepped from. Hedia turned also and saw a thing that was mouth and great bulging eyes squirming through the other panel, the one that had been open to Anti-Thule. The splayed hind feet suggested the thing had kinship with a frog or perhaps with a tadpole on the verge of becoming a frog, but it had grown to the size of an ox.

Hedia shouted, more surprised than frightened. The creature lunged, opening its mouth wide enough to engulf her. Corylus stabbed through the black palate and withdrew. The move was so swift and graceful that only the blood and matter gleaming halfway down his blade showed that he had driven his sword as deep as the monster's brain.

The three of them retreated into the courtyard proper. Instead of a panel of thin stone, the entrance to Anti-Thule had become a boundary, as at the seashore where land and water mingle: now wet, now dry—but never certain.

The image in the sky darkened slowly. The figure of Varus faded as though smoke were drifting between him and those in the Waking World.

A grub with long jaws crawled from Anti-Thule; it moved on a dozen stumpy legs attached to its thorax and dragged a long abdomen behind. Two similar monsters followed, not far back over the black wasteland. Except for size—except for their great size—they looked like creatures one might find in the mud of a fishpond.

That wasn't something Hedia normally looked at.

She smiled. *I don't have a choice this time.*

"We've got to get out of here!" Corylus said, backing. His shield was before him, and he held the curved sword in his right hand.

"We won't be able to get Gaius Varus away," Hedia said. She had seen her stepson in this state before: his body was in the Waking World, but his spirit was far distant. They would have to carry his body to move it quickly, and even a youth as strong as Corylus couldn't carry Varus for any distance with creatures from Anti-Thule harrying them.

"Right," said Corylus. "We've got to keep them off him. Alphena, take my left."

"Wait," Alphena said; she sheathed her sword and ran out into the courtyard. If Corylus was surprised, he gave no sign of it.

The grub humped forward. Corylus parried one blade of the jaws with his shield and struck hard at the base of the other blade. His sword sank deep into the chitin. A quick twist on the hilt cracked away that half of the jaw.

The grub's head was the only part of the creature with a hard shell. It flailed from side to side. The jaw could no longer pinch, but the remaining blade was an edged club that could kill and possibly dismember a man it hit squarely. Corylus backed farther.

Alphena ran to him carrying a pair of twelve-foot spears that the guards had dropped. She gripped the spears below the balances in her right hand but laid the upper portions over her left forearm so that she could still hold her buckler.

These were proper cavalry lances. The shafts were of heavier canes than the simple peasant weapons, and they had steel blades instead of flint or the bamboo itself cut at a sharp slant.

"Keep clear!" Corylus warned, and stepped back again. He sheathed his sword, then tossed his shield behind him. The grub gathered itself for another lunge.

Corylus took a spear with both hands, then butted it firmly on the ground with the point slanting up toward the grub's head. He hunched over the weapon, holding the shaft in both hands with his right sandal resting on the bronze ferrule that counterweighted the head.

The monster drove forward, ramming several feet of the spear through its mouth and brain. The body humped and then slammed back, shaking the ground.

The grub's head and the soft abdomen thrashed in opposite directions. Corylus kept his grip and the bamboo flexed but did not crack. Even so the monster would have battered him against the ground if Alphena hadn't tossed her shield away and gripped the shaft behind him.

Backing together, Alphena and the youth pulled the spear free. The point and several feet of shaft glistened with white slime, but the weapon was un-damaged.

Alphena let go and stepped to Corylus' side. They stood together, hunched and breathing through their mouths. More grubs were nearing the boundary between the courtyard and Anti-Thule. *The boundary between life and Hell.*

Hedia had caught her breath and had taken the time to consider what *she* might best do next. She could pick up a weapon, perhaps another spear, and join the young people. She would more likely get in the way than help, and for the time being they didn't appear to need help.

She thought of going to Varus, standing in the middle of the courtyard, but that would be as pointless as standing beside the statue of Marsyas in the Forum. The bronze satyr would probably provide better conversation than Varus in a trance.

Beside the outbuilding that Govinda used as his sanctum was the arbor and ancient vine down which Hedia had climbed from the Otherworld. A little old man sat there, so still that he might have been a queerly twisted vine shoot. Hedia walked over to him.

The old man seemed as dissociated as Varus; Hedia wasn't sure that he was going to acknowledge her approach, but his eyes suddenly lit on her. He smiled, spoke, and then switched to Greek and said, "Greetings, mistress. My name is Bhiku."

"I am Hedia, wife of Senator Gaius Saxa," she said. Her voice was raspy, though she no longer noticed the smoke or the nearby-lightning smell that had cut the insides of her nostrils like a saw. "May I ask what you're doing here?"

"Ah," said Bhiku. "The mother of my friend Lord Varus. I followed when King Govinda brought him here, and when Govinda loosed the Blight onto the Earth again I decided to stay. This grapevine—"

He gestured upward without looking away from Hedia.

"—seems as good a companion as any to wait for the end of the world. Though I'm pleased to have you join us, the grape and I."

"You were at Polymartium," Hedia said. She had always been good at remembering men, even men with whom she neither hoped nor expected to have any further contact. "You're a magician."

She glanced at her daughter and Corylus. They appeared to have dispatched the grubs and now were prodding at another frog. The butts of two broken lances lay behind them, so they must have replenished their equipment.

"In a small way," Bhiku agreed with a nod. "Not enough even to enable me to help Lord Varus. But I can watch and marvel at his power."

"You think he'll win?" said Hedia, trying to control her sudden unexpected delight. She glanced at the sky past the grapevine's looping tendrils; she could see Varus only dimly, because the smoke smothered even the blue-white lightning.

"No, Lady Hedia," the old man said quietly. "No human could defeat the Blight when it has the use of the Godspeaker's tablet. But your son has been fighting more strongly than I had believed any human could do. You must be very proud of him."

"Yes, of course!" Hedia snapped. She remembered very clearly her glimpse of Anti-Thule at the instant before the Eternals cleansed it, the terrified inhabitants and the crawling filth that prepared to sweep over them. "But my pride doesn't help defeat the Blight, does it?"

"I'm not really a philosopher, an academic, like your son," Bhiku said, "but I have tried to live as a sage, a sophist. The study of wisdom prepares one for death, even the death of all things."

"I don't think you'll find me trembling when the time comes to die," Hedia said grimly. She stepped onto the bench and gripped the vine with both hands. She looked for a fork in which to plant her foot. "As with Lord Varus, however, I'm not ready to give up yet."

Or ever, though she didn't imagine that determination would make her immortal.

Hedia climbed. The bark was rough on hands already tender from previous exertions, and the forks pinched her feet if she put weight on them carelessly.

She glanced over her shoulder. She was viewing the courtyard from much higher than she had climbed. Bhiku looked upward and shaded his eyes with his hands.

The frog was dead. More grubs, frogs, and something like an octopus were approaching. Alphena and Corylus awaited them.

In the middle distance, a monstrous fish squirmed across the foul wasteland. Hedia couldn't imagine what the young people hoped to accomplish against a creature the size of a ship, but they had proved surprisingly resourceful in the past.

Hedia raised her foot for the next crotch and stepped onto solid ground instead. In front of her, Bacchus lounged on a silken couch. Ampelos lay at the other end of the same couch; their feet were crossed together. The camp of the god's entourage spread around on all sides.

"My dear Hedia!" Bacchus said, standing with a movement as graceful as the curve of a vine shoot.

"How did you get here!" said Ampelos.

Hedia looked at the youth as she took the god's hand. "My dear lord and I have a deep connection, Master Ampelos," she said sweetly.

"Indeed we do," Bacchus said. He laughed like golden bells. "And we're going to have another right now!"

"Yes," said Hedia, feeling her body flow against that of the god. "And then I have a favor to ask you."

She knew males of Bacchus' sort too well to try to change his mind at this moment. And besides, Hedia didn't *want* to change his mind.

First things first. There would always be time to die if she failed.

THE SOOTY CLOUDS WERE SCARCELY less black than the scraps of sky that they didn't cover, and sulfur in the air burned Alphena's throat. The baked dirt of Govinda's courtyard had given way to basalt knobs studding soil of black sand and pebbles. The landscape was completely barren.

A thing that might have been an octopus approached her and Corylus. It gripped projections in the ground and pulled itself along, stretching out one ten-foot tentacle after another. The body, dragging behind like a flaccid sack, kept its slit-pupiled eyes trained on the humans.

"Keep the arms off me," Corylus said. He stepped forward, holding his lance very near the butt.

How can I do that? Alphena thought, but she followed at his left side.

Corylus lowered the lance—it must stretch even his strength to hold the pole from so far behind the balance—and thrust through the creature's left eye. Instantly the tentacle that had been reaching for a rock curved up to grasp the spearman's thigh.

Alphena hacked it with her sword—a curved tulwar, the second she'd used since she had dulled both edges of the sword she'd brought—then pivoted and slashed at another arm rising to grab her. Neither blow severed the arm completely, but the ends beyond her cuts dangled by tags of skin. The first dropped from Corylus' leg, and the other only slapped her own.

She and Corylus stepped back. She had trouble not letting her sword drag across the stony soil. That was partly the unfamiliar length, partly a comment on how tired she was.

"What's happening?" Corylus muttered, looking behind them. "What's happening to the world?"

"I don't know," she said. "I think we're in Anti-Thule. Or it's come to us, I guess."

She was bent forward at the waist—they both were, to help them fill their lungs, though sulfur in the air made every breath torture. On the horizon from which the monsters were advancing was a line of volcanoes spewing fire and foul gases that dimmed the yellow-orange glow of the lava.

Eventually the molten rock would spread to where she and Corylus stood, and behind the lava would be the Blight. She and Corylus could do nothing about either catastrophe. The monsters that had swollen and distorted in the Blight's crater were problems on a human scale.

Alphena giggled at the absurdity of that thought. *Say better, close enough to a human scale thus far.* The giant catfish stumping across the basalt would be another matter, but it wouldn't reach them for some minutes yet.

A grub humped over the still-twitching remains of another of its sort. "I'll take it," Corylus said, standing still. Alphena stepped to the left and waved her sword. Sometimes they shouted also, but the grubs seemed to be deaf.

The creature turned toward her and gathered itself; its legs looked like inverted cones of flesh. Corylus stepped in and stabbed into the skull from where the head attached to the body. The grub relaxed, quivering like a shaken aspic.

She and Corylus retreated slightly. They were gasping; they had been gasping from their exertions for a long time now. They had retreated well out into what had been the courtyard, and the bodies of monsters—many still moving, though dead—lay by the score in a line from the place where Corylus had killed the first frog.

"We're lucky they're stupid," Alphena said.

Corylus responded with a cracked laugh. "I don't think anybody watching what we're doing would say that *we* were smart," he said. "But eventually we'd run out of places to run if we tried running. Or we'd die, and that's the worst that can happen to us here."

Alphena looked into the sky where they had seen the image of her brother. Occasionally she had caught a glimpse of him recently, but for the most part smoke hid him. It was as black as the clouds that the volcanoes belched and as foul as the Blight itself.

"I think . . . ," Alphena said. She paused because she couldn't give facts to support what she thought, what she *felt*.

Varus is the philosopher, not me. I can say what I think.

"I think what's happening to the ground is connected to what's happening in, in the sky," she said. "Happening to my brother."

"I wish I could help him, then," Corylus said. "Because it doesn't look like keeping these beasts away is going to be enough."

A pair of frogs advanced side by side, bumping repeatedly in their desire to swallow the humans waiting for them. Alphena said, "I'll take the left one."

That was obvious, but she and Corylus always spoke their intentions before acting. The frog-things were getting in each other's way. The defenders could have had similar problems, but training was as much learning to coordinate as it was basic swordsmanship.

Varus—his physical body—stood only a few feet back of Alphena and Corylus. He was as still as a heroic statue in the Forum. *If we survive this, perhaps he'll get a statue.*

"Now!" Corylus said. He and Alphena lunged forward together, both crunching the points of their swords through the thin bones of the creatures' skulls. Corylus' victim had opened its mouth, so he reached into the great maw; Alphena's had not, so she stabbed between the bulging eyes.

She and Corylus withdrew in the same practiced motion as they had thrust. Alphena had gotten almost blasé about the frog-things. She knew that attitude was dangerous, but she was too tired to have the edge of alertness that she knew was safer.

It would be safer yet to have a cohort of Praetorians with them. She might as usefully wish for Praetorians as wish that she weren't so exhausted.

The great fish was very close. Corylus sheathed his curved sword. He was still using the same one; he had been right about how good Indian steel was.

"Stay here," he gasped to Alphena. "I've got an idea."

He staggered toward the ruins of the palace. *He's as tired as I am,* Alphena thought. *But you wouldn't know it by the way he strikes.*

She was too tired to wonder what her companion was doing. She breathed deeply, watching the approach of a monster too huge for them to kill.

THE RUINS OF GOVINDA'S PALACE were the same as they had been when Corylus and his companions had arrived here—escaped here, as they thought at the time—from Dreaming Hill. Where the palace had been completely flattened Corylus caught glimpses of peasant dwellings that appeared unchanged also.

The courtyard was no longer packed dirt, nor was the landscape beyond sere grasses growing on friable soil. The ground for as far as Corylus could see had become the heads of basalt columns mixed with black pebbles and grit that had weathered from the rock. It was barren except for the human constructions that sat on it like toys on a stone tabletop.

A low hum was the sonic equivalent of the foul black sky. Corylus less heard than felt it through the soles of his feet. He supposed it might be the sound of lava being pumped to the surface where it spilled out in balls and streams of hellfire.

Powerful blows had struck Govinda's palace. Though the main building had not collapsed completely like one of the wings forming the shorter sides, a section had spilled out into the courtyard.

A six-inch wooden roof beam stuck sideways from the pile of masonry. The free end was ten feet in the air, but where it slanted into the broken brickwork it was barely higher than Corylus' chest. He pulled himself onto it at the low end and then walked up the beam as though he were crossing a stream on a fallen log.

He was wrung out, but that was nothing new. He had been with the Scouts when they were returning after raids; anyone who couldn't keep up would have to be left for the Sarmatians close behind.

Corylus was ready to jump on the end of the beam if necessary, but as he had hoped, his weight was enough to rip it loose. It dropped slowly halfway, then crashed to the ground as he jumped off. Dust lifted from the pile and drifted away.

He grabbed the outer end of the beam, lifted it high enough to take some of the weight on his right hip bone, and worked it sunwise a few steps. The dowels joining the beam to its hidden end post cracked.

He walked toward Alphena, one step after another. His eyes were blurry and the timber's weight was a sharp pain on his hip, hands, and arms, but he walked.

Alphena still leaned forward behind the rampart of squirming corpses. She was too exhausted to spare the effort of watching what her companion was doing.

Corylus hadn't asked her to help because he hadn't thought she had enough strength left. She would have either hurt herself or hurt him when she collapsed completely. Now—well, if he dropped this *accursed* beam he was pretty sure he could keep his feet out of the way.

The fish lifted itself and fell, closer each time. It was moving faster than Corylus could, and it didn't have much farther to go. He plodded on. It was like a forced march with full pack, but he'd done that and he would do this too.

Varus hadn't moved. Whatever his soul might be doing in the heavens, it wasn't affecting his body here. Corylus didn't know what would happen to Varus' soul if the fish swallowed his body down or simply crushed it to a smear on the basalt, but it probably wouldn't be good, and that would be very bad for the world.

Alphena finally glanced around and saw Corylus. She sheathed her sword and trotted to him; it was only a few steps by now. Her eyes were alert and her face muscles no longer had the slackness of utter fatigue; these few moments of rest had allowed her to recover, at least briefly.

They might only have a brief time anyway.

Alphena took the beam from the other side, placing her hands just behind his. Her grip was awkward—she could use only the strength of her arms—but she and Corylus shuffled the short distance to the dead frogs and together lifted the beam high enough to drop on the topmost one. The corpses thrashed at the weight, but he flopped onto the beam to keep it from sliding off until the movements of the dead flesh ceased beyond occasional shudders.

The fish was very close. Its pectoral fins lifted the creature up several feet and thrust it forward. Every time the body flopped down, the dense rock jolted like the deck of a skiff in a storm.

The beam pointed up at a shallow angle, but it was the best they could do. Corylus drew his sword and hacked at the upper end, shaping the broken wood into a better point. It was a crime to treat the tulwar this way, but it was what he had. The fine steel held its edge remarkably well despite being used for a task that should have been done by an axe.

Alphena was chopping with a curved dagger. *At the other end of the beam,* Corylus thought, wondering why but too focused to care.

As the fish loomed above Corylus, he jumped onto the beam to brace it. Alphena had dug a notch in the soil behind the makeshift harpoon. She couldn't chip the basalt, but she had worked a depression between a pair of column heads. It wasn't much, but—

The fish lifted, then rocked down toward Corylus. It was like watching Cleopatra's obelisk in the Campus Martius topple toward him. Despite his weight, the beam skidded backward into the notch—and caught, tilting upward as the fish tried to tear itself away from the pain that was driving up through its throat and into its brain. The monster's own mass was destroying it.

When the beam flexed, it flung Corylus backward onto the ground. He tried to roll to his feet, but the shock had numbed the lower part of his body. He *had* to lift the comatose Varus and run back to save him from the fish skidding forward on inertia.

In the convulsions of death, the fish arched up higher than before. It teetered with its spine curved like a ship's sternpost; then its huge white belly started down.

Alphena grasped Corylus by the shoulders and started dragging him to the side. He shouted. "Not me! Get your brother!"

But it didn't matter, because the death was going to crash onto all three of them and wipe them from existence.

Golden light flooded the bleak landscape. The sky had opened and through it raced Bacchus and his entourage.

A goat-legged satyr caught Alphena around the waist and bounded off with her; her mouth was open with shock. As a centaur ran by, the Maenad on his back caught the motionless Varus with a lasso of flowers and pulled him into her arms.

They're safe, Corylus thought. He smiled, realizing that a moment before he hadn't expected to die with a smile.

A chariot drawn by a pair of huge leopards swung to a halt beside Corylus. "There's no time!" he shouted.

The driver was Bacchus, golden and resplendent. He held up his thyrsus. At its touch the fish froze as though it had become a sculpture firmly locked on to its base. Hedia sprang out of the chariot and lifted Corylus with a lithe twist of her shoulders, then stepped back into the vehicle.

Bacchus laughed. The chariot sprang forward. The body of the catfish crashed down, sending a ripple across the grim landscape.

Corylus flexed his knees and got them under him again. The numbness was wearing off. "How did you pick me up?" he said to Hedia.

They were curving in a broad sweep across the black plain. Behind them the bare rock bloomed and burgeoned with flowers and vines. The clouds were scattering under the weight of warm sunlight.

"I have a good deal of experience moving men who can't walk by themselves," Hedia said. She chuckled and added, "You weren't drunk, so that was a little different."

Corylus stood. The leopards bunched their bodies, then extended so fully that their backs curved concave. They covered the waste in huge bounds. Like the wake of a racing warship, a vee of foliage spread behind the vehicle. Members of the god's train followed to either side, each of them bringing the rock to green life as they passed.

The chariot was tight quarters for three. Corylus was even more loath to press against Hedia than he was to touch the god, but fortunately the vehicle was as solid as the Capitolium, so he didn't sway into his companions. Furthermore, Hedia stayed as close to Bacchus as a grapevine to the olive tree planted to shade it.

"Your Lordship?" Corylus said. Or should he have said *Lord Bacchus*? Well, it was done now. "My friend Varus is, that is, you've saved his body, but his soul is fighting the Blight. Somehow, I mean. Can you . . . ?"

"Of course my lord can!" said Hedia. "But he'll do it in his own way, Corylus dear."

They had reached the outskirts of the Tyla community, now scraps of wood and paper with occasional lumps that had been stone structures before the catastrophe. Bacchus reined his team to a halt and turned his attention briefly to Hedia.

"May all the gods smile on you to honor me," Bacchus said as he kissed her.

Corylus swallowed, wondering what he should do. To his surprise, Hedia broke away from Bacchus. She took Corylus' hand, leading him out of the chariot.

"Good hunting, dear lord!" she called back to Bacchus. "You take my heart with you!"

Bacchus smiled like the sun breaking through clouds. A second chariot pulled up beside the god's. Ampelos, whom Corylus had met twice before, was driving it. The youth's face was set; he didn't look at Hedia and Corylus, nor did he seem to be watching the god.

Corylus looked into the sky where he had glimpsed the magnified figure of Varus when he first reached Govinda's palace. The sulfurous clouds had cleared and the air smelled clean, though the volcanoes continued to belch smoke and fire on the horizon. Corylus could see neither his friend nor the blackness that had thickened about him during the course of the battle.

"Don't worry," said Hedia. "My lord has promised that Varus will be all right."

She was still holding Corylus' hand. She squeezed it and then properly laced her fingers before her.

The satyr carrying Alphena trotted up to them. The girl was riding on his shoulders and held a skin of wine. Hedia and Corylus moved toward them, but the satyr twisted, gripped Alphena under the arms, and lifted her down onto the blossoming ground. The satyr stepped back, winked at Corylus, and joined the flood of his fellow Bacchus worshipers as they followed the chariots.

Alphena was flushed. "You look healthy, Daughter," Hedia said calmly. "Though your wardrobe has suffered since I left you."

"There were three of them at the same time," she mumbled in sudden embarrassment. "We needed something to distract one of them."

Corylus remembered the trio of frogs hunching toward them in a formation as tight—accidentally, no doubt, but quite real—as that of a troop of Sarmatian cavalry. It was early in the fight to protect Varus; Alphena was still using her double-edged legionary weapon. She had thrust through her tunic to get purchase and with her left hand ripped off the fabric upward from her sword belt.

The middle frog had lifted to snatch the cloth out of the air when it fluttered overhead. That had allowed Corylus to stab through its left eye with a backhand that continued the motion that withdrew his tulwar from the right eye of the frog he had first dispatched.

He had forgotten that incident: it had happened and it was over. There had been many incidents since that one, and they were all a blur in his mind.

"Yes, I was able to watch you," Hedia said calmly. "It was very prettily done. I've seen dance troupes who couldn't have moved as gracefully as the two of you did."

"Their lives didn't depend on it," Corylus said, too tired to be respectful. He reached out; Alphena handed him the wineskin without either of them needing to speak. He drank, swirling the liquid around his mouth before swallowing. It was the nectar of the gods, a balm to tissues flayed by the sulfurous air.

The chariots had shrunk to specks with the distance. Corylus could follow them only because they were the apex of the wedge of green spreading across Anti-Thule, richer and brighter than the fields that the Godspeaker had protected from the ice before the Blight came.

"Look," said Alphena. She pointed. "Look at the sky."

When they had first arrived at Govinda's palace, Corylus and Hedia had not seen the semblance of Varus in the sky until Alphena had pointed him out. Now, as she spoke, Corylus saw the giant figure of Bacchus blazing with golden radiance from within. Facing the god was a shape, humanoid but featureless. Its blackness was an absence of color and an absence of life.

A centaur rode up beside Corylus. The Maenad riding on his back was blond and built like a wrestler, though she had a pretty face. Varus lay in her arms like a wooden statue. His arms were folded over his chest instead of holding on to the woman, and his legs stuck out straight as they had been when her rope of flowers had snatched him clear of the monstrous fish.

Corylus helped the Maenad lower Varus to the ground. Varus balanced upright, but Corylus suspected that his friend would topple in a strong breeze rather than adjusting his posture.

"What's wrong with him?" the Maenad said, leaning over to wipe Varus' hair out of his eyes.

"He'll be all right soon," Corylus said. She seemed a nice girl, so he tried to sound reassuring. Besides, it was true if any of them were going to be all right.

The centaur had curly black hair and an olive complexion. He looked back at Varus and let his lip curl. Without speaking he moved off at a walk, which built swiftly to a canter, carrying away the woman on his back.

Corylus put an arm around his friend's shoulders to make sure he stayed upright. There was nothing else they could do for him. Varus felt warm and his arms had the usual firm plasticity of the muscles of a living animal.

In the sky, Bacchus pointed his thyrsus at the Blight. The animate blackness held up the Godspeaker's tablet in response. Flashes and fireballs sizzled from the soapstone. Corylus thought—hoped—that they would glance off the god's gleaming figure. The reality was better yet: the missiles vanished midway, like fog above a hot fire.

Bacchus laughed, a cheerful sound like the chuckle of an adult watching a boy putting on grown-up airs. The god stepped forward, ignoring the Blight's fiery threats. Instead of thrusting, he dipped the pinecone top of his thyrsus and lightly tapped the lump that served the black humanoid for a head.

Bacchus stepped back. Corylus expected a flash or a fire, wondering what the violent destruction of the Blight would mean for Varus' soul. He squeezed his friend's body a little tighter.

A vine shoot poked from the filthy blackness, then another. As suddenly as if it were a green blaze, the humanoid slumped into a mound crawling with vines and flowers. It looked like gourds springing from a manure heap.

The Blight settled away from the spirit of Gaius Varus, leaving him draped in grapevines and surrounded by a profusion of blossoms. He turned his head—

And vanished. There was nothing in the sky but sunlight, and Varus stirred in Corylus' arms.

Anti-Thule was a verdant paradise through which caroled the laughter of the God of Wine and Love.

EPILOGUE

Corylus eased back from Varus, but he kept a hand for a moment on his friend's shoulder to make sure he was steady on his feet. "Feeling all right?" Corylus said.

Varus smiled wanly. "I've never been so tired in my life," he said, "but I couldn't sleep now if I had to. I was battling the ancestor, or anyway he'd *been* Govinda's ancestor, but then he buried me and I couldn't get free. What happened?"

"You fought the Blight until the god Bacchus arrived to destroy it," Corylus said. "Disperse it, perhaps. He ended it, anyway."

Trees and flowers were growing everywhere under a bright sun. It was hard to imagine that this had been a poisoned wasteland only minutes before.

Corylus rubbed his temples. Had it only been minutes? It felt like a dream when he tried to remember what had happened. In his memory the immediate past seemed to have been painted on a sheet of glass that had then shattered. Tiny, vividly colored shards flashed before him in no particular order.

"Bacchus destroyed him?" Varus said, frowning. "Why? Why Bacchus, I mean?"

Corylus glanced at Hedia. She looked radiantly beautiful. Her gauzy clothing had received stains and tears in the ruins of Dreaming Hill where he and Alphena had met her, but those garments had been repaired or replaced since she climbed the ancient vine in Govinda's courtyard.

"I don't know," Corylus said. "I think your mother may know something about that, but you should ask her."

"Ah," Varus said in understanding. He smiled very faintly. They were both embarrassed. "I don't think I'll do that, but I will thank her. It was very . . . unpleasant when I was surrounded by that."

He walked to where Hedia stood, holding against her cheek a rose that she had plucked. She seemed in a reverie.

Corylus looked for Alphena and found her lying on her back on the sod. She had twisted her sword belt around so that the long tulwar lay between her legs where it wasn't in the way, but she hadn't taken it off.

"You need to get up," Corylus said. "We've both got to move or we'll cramp like old folk with arthritis."

"I don't want to move," Alphena said, but she tried to get an elbow under her.

Corylus bent over, offering a hand. She took it and rose with a groan, only half-joking.

"Believe me, I do know how you're feeling," he said. "But it's better to walk it out while we can."

Not only had vegetation sprouted instantly across Anti-Thule; the roots of the flowers and grasses had broken the basalt and grit into rich black soil also. Trees had sprouted also. Corylus saw a pair of poplars not far away. He thought of walking to the trees and chatting with the dryads but after consideration decided that he wouldn't.

Alphena hadn't let go of his hand. "What do we do next?" she said. "Can we get home?"

Corylus shrugged. "I have a line on where we entered Anti-Thule, I think," he said. "We can walk in that direction. I'm not sure what we'll find when we get there, though. I suspect more has changed than just the landscape."

"That changed for the better," said Alphena. She looked at him and said, "You saved my life, Publius Corylus."

"Yeah, I did," Corylus said, continuing to walk. He tried to imagine having this conversation with a Batavian Scout—and chuckled. "About fifty times, I'd guess."

He met her eyes and said, "About as many times as you saved mine, Alphena."

Alphena looked down, but she moved closer and put her arm around his waist. "I'm not going to give you up, Corylus," she said. "No matter what Mother says."

"I'm not worried about what Lady Hedia says," Corylus said. You had to have served on the frontier to understand how black a joke that was: the problem wasn't what Hedia said but rather what she would choose to *do*. That was worth worrying about.

He put his arm around Alphena's waist also. The muscles of her hip rippled smoothly as they continued to walk.

"I'm not going to give you up, either," Corylus said. *Until I die.*

WHEN HEDIA APPROACHED WITH VARUS, Alphena felt Corylus start to remove the hand that lay on her buttock. Before Alphena could react, he put his hand back.

They both stiffened when they saw Hedia walking toward them, though. There was no way to avoid that.

"Now that we've had a little time to recover," Hedia said as calmly as if she were choosing a dress for dinner, "I think we should return to Govinda's palace. Do we all agree?"

"Ah," said Corylus. "Yes, Your Ladyship. I think I could lead us in the direction of where we entered Anti-Thule, if that would be helpful?"

The question in his voice showed that he was just as doubtful as Alphena was. Even if what he said was true—and she accepted that it might be, though *she* had no idea of the path she'd taken on the shoulders of the capering satyr—there hadn't been a portal on this side when Bacchus and his train had carried them to Anti-Thule.

Hedia cocked her head. "Yes," she said, "your army training, I suppose. But I think I'd prefer that my son take us there. Varus?"

Varus looked startled. Corylus took the opportunity to drop his hand and ease slightly away from Alphena. Doing that while Hedia's eyes were on them would just have called attention to what was already obvious.

Alphena let out a sigh of relief. At the moment she was both exhausted and giddy. She didn't assume that Hedia would ignore the situation forever, but not having a scene *now* was a much better result than Alphena had expected.

"Mother," Varus said, "I may have power, but I do *not* have knowledge. I don't know how to do that."

"Brother," Alphena said, speaking as the words formed in her mind. "You've never known how to do any of the things I've watched you do, but you did them anyway. Do it again: take us to Govinda's courtyard."

Varus suddenly laughed. "Not Govinda's anymore," he said. "*That* I'm sure of."

His face hardened, and he looked much older than the brother she had grown up with. *"We shall be as we were before!"* he said.

There was no feeling of motion, but the four of them stood beside the ancient grapevine. The dust from the shattered palace had settled, but the fires burning in the ruins had taken firm hold. Hedia sneezed and Alphena felt her eyes begin to water.

"By Mercury," Varus said in reverent wonder. "I could as easily have brought us home, couldn't I?"

"No," said Hedia. "We needed to stop here."

When Alphena had first come to the palace from Dreaming Hill, she had noticed—and had promptly forgotten—a little old man seated in the gazebo under the ancient grapevine. He was still there, but he bounced to his feet when he saw Varus.

"Bhiku!" said Varus, taking two long steps and embracing the old man. "How did you get here?"

"I walked, Lord Varus," Bhiku said in Greek. "By the time I arrived, the surviving residents were fleeing, so I had no difficulty in coming inside. It seemed as good a place as any, as I told your lady mother."

He bowed to Hedia, looking like a polite monkey.

Hedia lifted an eyebrow in minuscule agreement. She said, "Ah, there it is," and walked to the gazebo.

Alphena glanced to see what her mother was talking about. The cape that she had taken from Lenatus lay on a stone box in the gazebo. Then she recognized the box itself.

Hedia slid the lid aside. The jewels that the demon had used to lure victims were even more dazzling in full sunlight than they had been in the jungle-shaded ruins.

Corylus had looked in the same direction, but he ignored the jewels. "This vine is dying," he said. "It's a thousand years old, but now it's dying!"

"My lord Bacchus has decided to leave India," Hedia said. "He decided that Anti-Thule was a suitable place for him to shape a home for his followers. The mundane world can get on about its business without his divine presence."

"Mother?" Varus said. "You convinced him?"

"Ampelos, the god's special friend, helped me convince him," Hedia said calmly. "I had a discussion with Ampelos, and he saw the benefit of Bacchus ruling in a place where no one, myself included, would intrude on his majesty."

Corylus touched the vine with his left fingertips. The broad leaves were withering, and even Alphena could see that a gray glaze had started to spread over the bark.

It meant nothing to her—plants die, and there were many more grapevines—but she understood that Corylus felt otherwise about it. She moved to his side, but at the last moment she didn't touch his arm as she had intended. This distress was a private thing in which she had no right to intrude.

"Very well," Hedia said. "I came for these jewels, which my lord Bacchus left here on his way to conquer Anti-Thule. Publius Corylus, can you carry them back with us? Not the chest, of course, just the contents. I thought that my daughter's cape would make a satisfactory bag for the purpose."

Corylus touched the stone box with his right foot and judged the weight by pushing until it slid slightly. He gave Hedia a slow smile.

"I guess I could manage the chest if I had to," Corylus said with the quiet pride of a strong man: a *man, her* man. "But there's no lack of stone in Carce, so sure, I'll bring the jewels."

"Mother?" Alphena said. "Why? Why did you have us come here to get jewels? Father would buy you anything you wanted, and he's not interested in jewels himself."

She paused and thought of Saxa's collection of curiosities, a hodgepodge of fakes mixed with real wonders. "Unless they're ancient carved gems, I mean."

"Quite true, Daughter," Hedia said. She smiled like a queen, like an empress. "But the Emperor's tastes are more catholic. These will make a fine gift for your father to give the Emperor—after dear Saxa has bought them from the finder, Corylus here, for a sum of . . . several millions, I think."

"Oh," said Alphena. "Oh!"

"Furthermore," Hedia said, "the Emperor should be happy to grant Saxa the small favor of nominating Corylus to a questorship to make him eligible for the Senate. The young man will have the necessary property qualification from the sale of the jewels."

She turned to Corylus. "I believe that will affect your matrimonial prospects, Publius Corylus," she said. "And my daughter's, I daresay."

"Lady Hedia," said Corylus. He was standing very straight, but his voice was choked. "Lady Hedia, thank you."

"It's nothing to do with me, dear boy," she said archly. "They're your jewels, after all."

Corylus turned abruptly. He spread out the cape with a snap and began scooping handfuls of gems into the center of the cloth. Alphena thought she saw a tear on his cheek.

She threw herself into Hedia's arms and began sobbing for joy.

HEDIA FELT QUITE PLEASED WITH HERSELF. She had solved a problem that had concerned her ever since she met Corylus and realized that Alphena already knew him from the exercise ground at the rear of Saxa's town house.

It was as clear as daylight that Alphena would want a physical relationship with the youth. Alphena's stepmother certainly had!

The problem was now solved, and solved in a much more satisfactory fashion than having Corylus murdered. But the problem *was* going to be solved.

Hedia kept her expression one of pleasant blandness. She often showed emotion, but it was always the emotion that she had decided was the proper one under the circumstances.

Turning to her son's little Indian friend, she said, "Master Bhiku, would you care to accompany us to Carce? My husband would be happy to show you a different side of the Republic from that which you saw previously."

"Thank you, Your Ladyship, but I will decline your offer," Bhiku said. His broad smile made him look even more like a monkey than he had already. "I like to travel to new places, but I'm happy to walk. My own world here—"

He gestured. Presumably he meant something more general than the burning ruins about them at present.

"—is new, now that both Govinda and Lord Bacchus are gone."

"Very well," Hedia said; it was nothing to her. "In that case—"

"Your Ladyship?" Bhiku said, interrupting her thought. "I believe Lord Varus is . . ."

Bhiku let his voice trail off, probably because he didn't know how to describe Varus' state any better than Hedia herself did. The boy stood motionless with a slack expression. By now she realized that meant that his mind—spirit? soul?—was somewhere else.

Alphena noticed her brother also. She drew the iron Janus from her sash as she had when she led Hedia and Corylus from Dreaming Hill to the palace.

"I can . . . well, we can, I think," she said.

"Of course I can!" chirped the little figure. "Can you fall off a log, girl? You should be able to open the portal even without me. Your brother could!"

"That will be enough, Master Janus!" Hedia snapped. "My children are both remarkable people, but they have different skills. At the moment Lord Varus is otherwise occupied, so you will please confine yourself to carrying out Lady Alphena's instructions with the deference properly owed to her birth."

That was taking a rather strong line with what was a god of sorts, or anyway a godlet. Nevertheless, Hedia had found that an air of haughty superiority was as useful in some circumstances as tears were in others. Men had a near monopoly on physical force in her world, but a successful woman learned to use the tools at her disposal.

Sex—Hedia's usual first choice—wasn't useful here, but there were other things available.

Janus muttered like a distant cricket, but that was all right. As Corylus lifted the makeshift bag, Hedia turned to him and said, "Master Corylus, I will take your jewels for the time being. Can you carry my son as far as the portal?"

She nodded toward the sheet of alabaster that remained undamaged in Govinda's former sanctum. The panel through which had come the monsters of Anti-Thule had vanished completely. It hadn't left even a dusting of powdered stone like those that lay beneath the frames of the portals that had shattered during Varus' battle with King Govinda.

"Ah, I can, Lady Hedia," Corylus said with a frown, "but Varus can generally walk along if one of us is there to guide him. Whichever you please."

He's treating me like an irritable bitch with a dangerous temper, Hedia thought. She grinned. *Well, I can hardly blame him for that.*

Aloud she said, "I've never noticed that Gaius was particularly mindful of a mother's guidance, but we'll see if this time is different."

She stepped to Varus' side and gently turned him to face the panel. As Corylus said, Varus was easily biddable. He demonstrated no consciousness in the process, though, just a physical response to mild physical pressure.

Hedia started forward with her hand on her son's arm. Varus walked with her.

Alphena strode ahead, holding the iron baton in her right hand. Corylus was close beside, though he didn't have his hand around her waist.

Hedia noted that with silent approval: Corylus wasn't the sort of youth who pushed matters to see how far he could go. That said, he had gotten what he wanted and he hadn't backed off while the outcome was in doubt, as it must have been in doubt until they saw Hedia smile.

Alphena and Corylus waited at the portal for Hedia and Varus to complete their more stately progress. Hedia smiled coolly at them.

She had watched while they battled the demon to rescue her. They were a natural team. After marriage they could each have a thousand other lovers if they wished, though she rather doubted that they would.

Having seen them moving as a single entity against the demon, Lady Hedia had decided that she would not accept a reality that decreed they had to be separated.

VARUS STOOD BESIDE THE SIBYL. He looked down on not only his physical body but also the succession of events that had taken place during the past year, beginning when he first climbed this ridge in his imagination and met the old woman. There was far more than he could see at one time, but he did see it in all details at the time it was happening.

Varus bit his lower lip as he watched the Blight engulf him. "There was nothing I could do," he said. "I fought, but it was like being drowned in a cesspool. Eventually I would have tired, and I would have become part of the filth that was spreading over the world."

"You fought when you knew you could not win," the Sibyl said. "If you had known from the beginning that you could not defeat the Blight, would you have run instead?"

"Of course I fought!" Varus said. He started to add, *What choice did I have?* but those words did not reach his lips.

He watched the Blight throbbing like the intestines of a horse disemboweled in the arena. Varus hadn't seen that while he fought. His world had been foul blackness in all directions. The blue crackling that prevented the Blight from swallowing him would remain only so long as he willed it to remain, and doing that was like carrying the Temple of Jupiter Best and Greatest on his shoulders.

"I did know from the first that I couldn't win," Varus said instead. "But I had to fight. There wasn't anywhere for me to run to, and even if there had been . . . I wouldn't want to remember that I had let that *horror* destroy the Earth."

Varus watched as Bacchus, bathed in golden light, spread the transformed Blight across Anti-Thule like rich compost. Every sort of vegetation was springing up.

"I tried," Varus said to the Sibyl, "but I wasn't strong enough."

"Yes," said the old woman. She pointed at an unfamiliar jungle scene. "Your sister and Master Corylus fought a demon at the Tomb of the Eternals. They weren't strong enough, either."

Hedia, whom Varus hadn't noticed and whom the demon had certainly forgotten, stepped up behind the creature swinging a rock at the end of a silken cord. The demon dropped like a sacrificial bullock struck in the forehead by the underpriest's hammer. Corylus knelt to cut its head off as Alphena drove her sword deep into the broad chest.

"Lady Hedia helped them," the Sibyl said, "as she helped you. But she is a very ordinary matron of Carce, Lord Wizard. She cannot work magic or use a sword."

Varus smiled wryly. "Mother isn't ordinary," he said. "But I take your point."

He looked down at his body, walking on Hedia's arm toward the remaining fragment of Govinda's sanctum. He turned to meet the Sibyl's eyes and said, "Sibyl, why am I here? What is next?"

She smiled, another wrinkle in a face as seamed as a dried apple. "That is up to you, Lord Wizard," the Sibyl said. "This is a fork in the road your future will follow. From here on, the world will be ruled either by logic or by magic. By wisdom or by superstition, as you would have put it not long ago. Which path will the future take?"

Varus stiffened as though she had slapped him. He said, "I can't make that decision!"

"You *will* make that decision, Gaius Varus," the Sibyl said. She did not raise her voice, but Hedia herself could not have put more steely certainty into the words.

Varus rubbed his temples. "Sibyl, why me?" he said.

"Did you not stand alone against all the power of the Cosmos, Lord Wizard?" the Sibyl said.

"Yes, but I couldn't win!" Varus said. "I couldn't even have stood much longer!"

"True," said the Sibyl, smiling again. "The help of the gods was necessary to save you and to save your world. *Our* world, Gaius Varus."

"Then the decision is clear," said Varus. With the words, he felt his spirit fly back to his flesh and his friends as they stepped into a Carce full of magic and wonder.